the EDGE *of* RUIN

ALSO AVAILABLE FROM
MELINDA SNODGRASS AND TITAN BOOKS

The Edge of Reason
The Edge of Dawn (September 2015)

MELINDA SNODGRASS

the EDGE of RUIN

TITAN BOOKS

The Edge of Ruin
Print edition ISBN: 9781783294626
E-book edition ISBN: 9781783294633

Published by Titan Books
A division of Titan Publishing Group Ltd
144 Southwark Street, London SE1 0UP

First Titan edition: November 2014
10 9 8 7 6 5 4 3 2 1

A CIP catalogue record for this title is available from the British Library.

Printed and bound in Great Britain by CPI Group Ltd.

Did you enjoy this book? We love to hear from our readers. Please email us at
readerfeedback@titanemail.com or write to us at
Reader Feedback at the above address.

To receive advance information, news, competitions, and exclusive offers online,
please sign up for the Titan newsletter on our website **www.titanbooks.com**

PRELUDE

Eddie Tanaka dug his elbows into the mud, releasing the sweet and sickening smell of rotting vegetation. He wriggled frantically toward the river. It was monsoon season, and the leaves of the bushes, disturbed by his passage, sent water pattering along the length of his body. Some trickled down his collar and joined the sweat bathing him. His sweat wasn't due entirely to the tropical heat. Most of it was because of gut-trembling, bowel-loosening terror.

What were those things?!

Behind him he heard screams of pain and terror from his colleagues, maddened, triumphant screams from the attackers, and over everything the keening wail of the *things*. Eddie pressed his belly against the muck, reached out for a tree root coiling up from the earth like an exposed rib, and pulled himself forward. Ahead was the soft gurgle and slap of running water. Not much farther now.

He wondered if anyone else had made it out of the lab, and even as he crawled he hated himself for not going back. To look for any other survivors. To help them escape. But the only reason he was alive and outside was because he had been on the catwalk suspended high over the accelerator. There was a narrow access tube used to replenish the hyperpure oil surrounding and shielding the rest of the building from the massive, though brief, release of atomic particles created by their experiments. Experiments that tried to approximate conditions nanoseconds after the Big Bang. Though Eddie was tall, he was also thin, and he had been able to squeeze through the pipe.

The men who attacked the lab offered no mystery. Brandishing knives and machetes, faces obscured behind headcloths, they had extolled their god in voices made shrill by nerves and euphoria. *Allah Akbar, Allah Akbar.* It was what was with them that froze the throat with pure, blind terror.

Things like whirling dervishes constructed of slivered glass. The sound as they spun was a mind-numbing howl. When they swept across a person their passage ripped away clothes and flesh.

Eddie pushed up on his elbows and vomited. He had seen Anne just before he entered the pipe. Clothing and skin flayed off, screaming, still standing, not dead. He retched again and brought up only bile. It wasn't just water and sweat bathing his face now. He tasted tears. Anne had liked him. After they got past him following her into the bathroom that time. They had been discussing the results of that day's experiment, and Eddie just hadn't noticed. *She liked me. She had told me so. And I didn't do anything to help her.*

Tears blinded him and he found the edge of the river without meaning to. Arms flailing, he rolled down the bank and into the water. The current took him. The pockets of his lab coat filled with water, but despite the added drag Eddie waited until the water had carried him perhaps a mile downstream from the lab before kicking off his tennis shoes and shrugging out of the coat. He didn't want the *things* realizing too quickly that someone had survived and escaped.

He had to find a phone. Call the emergency number he'd been given. Tell the man who ran Lumina Enterprises what had happened. Hope he didn't get committed as a madman.

* * *

The low hum from the big jet's engines and the underoxygenated air of the cabin conspired to send her to sleep. Dagmar Reitlingen blinked hard, removed her wire-rim glasses, rubbed her eyes, and pinched the bridge of her nose. Another five hours and they would arrive in Dallas. A three-hour layover, then the two-hour flight to Albuquerque. Add to that the hours she had already spent sitting in the first-class lounge at London's Heathrow airport. The ground crew kept saying there were "phenomena" which were keeping them from departing, but they never said what "phenomena" meant. Dagmar did the calculation and realized she had left her house twenty hours ago. *Only ten more to go*, she thought glumly, *assuming there aren't more "phenomena."*

She had tried to take the Lumina jet, but discovered that Brook was in jail in Baltimore, and the Gulfstream GV was parked in a hangar in Maryland. Since she had a new boss, she didn't feel comfortable just hiring another pilot. It was a quirk of her charming, though secretive, CEO that Lumina Enterprises owned only one plane and employed only one full-time pilot. When she'd crabbed at Kenntnis after one particularly daunting journey back from Singapore, he'd given that rollicking, fixture-shaking laugh, and told her he didn't want his chief officers becoming too distant from the average run of humanity. He'd then added that it wasn't like he made them fly coach. So she only got to travel on the GV when Kenntnis was aboard. She had spent a lot of hours on the private jet, but compared to how many she spent flying it wasn't near enough, and she'd tell him so next time. The thought choked and shifted to a worse thought. Maybe there would never be a next time.

The call had come from George Gold, chief counsel for the company, on Christmas Day, informing Dagmar that certain criteria had been met which set in motion the transfer of control of the company into the hands of—

Dagmar pulled a copy of the *Washington Post* from her briefcase and studied the face of the man who now controlled a vast corporate empire more valuable than Microsoft and far less visible.

Despite the grainy quality of the photo the young man's extraordinary handsomeness came through, although his face was marred by what looked like dark bruises. He was flanked by two older men, one whose severe features showed kinship. It was clear from the relative heights that Richard Oort was not a tall man. His expression was tense and haunted, and he held out a hand as if to ward off the photographer. The headline shouted out BOMB PLOT UNCOVERED. In smaller type was *American evangelist sought to bring about Armageddon in nuclear fire.*

All of Dagmar's instincts screamed out *fraud*, and she said as much to George. The lawyer had disabused her of that notion.

"No, the documents were carefully drawn. Mr. Kenntnis was very specific in his instructions. Oort is to have total control of the company up to and including liquidating all the assets."

As the COO of the company, Dagmar was left shaken and sickened by that bit of news.

"When did this happen?" Dagmar had demanded.

"December second."

"As if Kenntnis knew something might happen."

"I couldn't say."

"Is he dead?"

"I couldn't say."

She had wanted to scream and curse him for the legalistic caution and cold precision. *Tell me if Kenntnis is alive or dead!* But perhaps George didn't know either.

"What do we know about this Oort?"

"He's a policeman. From a well-to-do and respected Rhode Island family. Father's a federal court judge."

So Richard Oort was not a con artist, but he was certainly heedless and indifferent to the welfare of his employees. Why hadn't he obtained Brook's release?

Well, she would find out in a few hours. She hoped that Oort was bright as well as beautiful.

The paper crackled as Dagmar lifted it from her lap and studied that face again. She wondered if this insane action by Kenntnis was due to passion, although she hadn't thought Kenntnis had been inclined that way. But why else would you leave a multibillion-dollar company in the hands of a young cop in a nondescript city in a nondescript state?

The Reverend Mark Grenier stood on the verge at the edge of the westbound I-81 freeway trying to thumb a ride. It wasn't easy to do when your right hand was missing. Overhead the moon struggled among the heavy clouds, occasionally breaking free and touching the ice-clad branches of the trees with silver. There had been an ice storm two nights ago, and the cold was so intense none of it had melted.

He couldn't keep standing still. Grenier began to walk along the shoulder. His thin-soled Italian loafers offered little protection against the cold, and the buttons of his shirt and coat barely closed over his burgeoning paunch, allowing fingers of cold to lick at his skin. He was losing sensation in his feet, and he stumbled on tussocks of winter-brown grass.

He had made bail yesterday and rushed to his Washington apartment, the apartment he'd maintained so he could be close at hand when a president had need of a little midnight counseling. He was desperate for a shower in privacy, the thick lather of verbena soap, the crackle of a starched Egyptian cotton shirt, and the caress of a cashmere sweater to drive away the memory of that polyester prison jumpsuit. But he'd found the locks changed. He rushed to the bank and discovered his accounts had vanished. He had always been a subtle man; he didn't need a skywriter to get the message: He had failed his overlords, and they had jettisoned him.

Resentment burned in his gut. He had given his life to the study and attainment of power, but not just the power of wealth and influence. Through long and arduous study he had become a sorcerer. Magic flowed through his hands and sang in his blood. He had worked hard to open the gates between the dimensions and allow the Old Ones to return, and *they had fucking succeeded*.

Then, because of one tiny miscalculation, because he underestimated the strength of will of Richard Oort, he forever lost his ability to do magic. He remembered that black blade swinging through the air, and the glitter of Richard's pale blue eyes seen over the sword, and then Grenier's hand was gone, the stump pumping a jet of blood into the air. There was a twinge of pain, and the memory of movement from his missing right hand. Grenier laid his remaining hand over the stump. It was as sore as his emotions.

Headlights swept around a broad curve in the road. Grenier stepped onto the edge of the pavement and frantically waved at the car. It was an older model Chevy; two doors, its white paint peeling in leprous gray patches. Grenier had an instant to see the driver's reaction, an upthrust middle finger, before the car swept past. The wind from its passage blew his coat hard against his body, and a blast of exhaust set his eyes to watering. He *hated* pollution. Well, the Old Ones' arrival would eventually put a stop to that. Unless they were thwarted, and that didn't seem likely with Prometheus bound and all hope resting on one slender young man.

He plodded on for another mile or so before another pair of headlights swept across the verge. Light shattered against the ice-encased boles of the leafless trees lining the roadway. It was a big tan RV. To Grenier's surprise it didn't rush past, but instead pulled onto the shoulder.

The passenger-side window lowered. Grenier could barely hear the man's voice over the dull rumble of the RV's diesel engine. "How far you going?"

"As far as you'll take me."

"Hop in."

Grabbing the handhold beside the door with his left hand, Grenier hauled himself onto the running board and into the RV.

He tucked his stump under his coat, a protective if useless gesture. Grenier settled into the passenger seat and studied his rescuer. Early sixties, unusually fit for that age. Grenier noted the almost military haircut, short and tight over the ears, and the way the man canted slightly to the right. Grenier leaned forward slightly and spotted the holstered pistol on the man's left hip. Cop or soldier. He was suddenly acutely aware that he was jumping bail.

He glanced back through the door leading into the body of the RV. A woman sat at the small table. She cradled a long rifle the way another woman might hold a child, or a child might hold a teddy bear. The woman looked to be in her late twenties with brown hair that brushed at her chin, a chin too square for real beauty. Straight, thick eyebrows frowned over brown eyes that welled with tears. Grenier checked, worried that the barrel might soon be facing him.

The man seemed to read Grenier's concern. "It's not loaded," he said in a low voice. "She really freaks if she's not holding it, so I let her." The man put the RV back in gear, and they went bumping off the shoulder and back onto the freeway.

The man held out his hand. "Syd Marten."

Grenier slid his arm from beneath the concealing coat and held up the bandaged stump. Marten jerked back his hand. "Consider your hand duly shaken," Grenier said, stalling for time while he thought what name to offer.

Grenier had been a famous man. Preaching on the Christian cable networks, lending his support to various "culture of life" issues, leading prayer breakfasts at the White House, attacking scientists on the twenty-four-hour news channels, spouting his nonsense with neither challenge nor argument for the national media. He had been written up in *Time* and *Newsweek* as the most powerful voice of America's evangelical movement. Would he be recognized? But while in jail he had grown a beard and mustache, and being assigned by a sympathetic guard to kitchen detail had enabled him to eat constantly as he alternately cursed at and wept for his lost power. He decided to offer a false name.

"Mark Jenkins," Grenier said, using his mother's maiden name.

"Where are you headed?" Marten asked.

"West." It seemed a safe, if vague, response.

"Us, too," Marten said. He gestured at the eastbound side of the freeway with its steady line of cars, their headlights like a chain of diamonds. "If they were smart they'd be hightailing it the other way, too, but their government isn't leveling with them."

"About what?" Grenier probed gently.

Beads of moisture popped out on Marten's forehead, and a trembling shook his body. He wiped away sweat and sucked in a quick, deep breath. "What's happening in Virginia," came the choked reply.

He's been to my compound. He's seen. What a strange coincidence. Grenier wondered if some vestige of his magic was still working. Or perhaps it was one of those flukes of quantum coincidence that scientists struggled to explain. Whatever the reason, Grenier would have to be careful. He thanked the cautious instinct that had led him to give a false name.

"What's happening to our world?" Grenier asked.

"Damned if I know. Whatever it is, it ain't good. I've seen this thing, and I went nuts. Ended up locked up in the booby hatch. Look at her." He gestured back toward the woman. "That's my daughter, Samantha. The girl who had to outjock every jock in the FBI. Prove to me it's okay that she's a girl and not a son . . . like I care, but she just won't accept that."

It was a gift, Grenier thought. He'd always had this ability to engender trust in people and elicit their confidences. His career choices had been obvious, politician or preacher. Preacher had paid better.

"Anyway, she volunteered to go out there. She's in the FBI, just like me. She's a trained sniper, and since she went there all she does is sit and cry. I think this thing, this effect . . . whatever it is, is going to spread. So I loaded up the RV and we left." The man fell silent, but Grenier could tell he was eager to talk more. Grenier inclined his torso forward, softened his expression, begged to receive the confidence. Marten obliged.

"I didn't give notice or anything. The last guy who tried to leave got locked up. Jacobson. They say it's because he refused to go out there, but I can't help but wonder if he got locked up because he's a Jew. Next it'll be the blacks. All the old hates and distrusts are coming to the surface. The world's gone a different kind of nuts."

The same old nuts, Grenier thought, but what he said was, "You seem very sane."

"Yeah, now."

"What did they do for you?"

"Who?"

"The doctors."

"Not a damn thing."

For Grenier a certainty began to grow. It was all too perfect. He was going to do his bit to try to fuck his former masters.

"It wasn't the doctors who fixed me, but this young guy, Richard Oort. I don't remember much about him, but there was this sword."

"With a blade as black as space, shot through with glittering points of light like the swirl of stars, and when it's drawn you feel the bass tones growling and reverberating in your chest like the notes of a massive organ," Grenier said softly as he remembered.

"You know him," Marten said.

"Oh, yes." Grenier softly stroked the bandage over his stump.

"I've got to reach him. Have him help my Sam like he helped me."

"I'd like to find him, too." And Grenier clenched his left fist, and felt his phantom right hand also close. "For a lot of reasons."

The bar wasn't nice enough for Bourbon Street. It was a few blocks and a universe away from the French Quarter, especially the new Disneyfied version of the French Quarter. It was dark and, even in January, hot, and it stank of spilled booze, cigarettes, mold, and infrequently washed bodies.

Doug Andresson couldn't pay for the shot and the beer that stood on the bar in front of him. He'd used what remained of his money on the last round. He watched the head of the beer go sliding down the side of the glass, and for some reason it reminded him of the white foam that would run out of the horses' mouths when his uncle broke the new broncos. Sometimes the fat old bastard would apply the bit so hard that the foam would turn red with blood. He was just as mean of a bastard as his brother, Doug's father.

The memory brought other memories, of a belt laid hard across his back and thighs. It was after his father's beatings that his mother would send him off to Uncle Frank's ranch, separating the father and son. Doug had vowed he'd kill the man. Cancer had done it first.

Doug fumbled in his pants pocket for the can of tobacco. Pulling off the lid, he pinched off a plug and thrust it between lip and gum. The bottom of the can showed silver through the rich mahogany of the tobacco. He was almost out of that, too. He needed money, and he needed it fast. He weighed the pros and cons between a B&E in the Garden District or a mugging on Bourbon Street. Big, fancy houses often had dogs or alarms, and drunks were usually easy. He'd make up his mind after he finished his drink.

It wasn't supposed to have been like this. He was supposed to be on easy street. Grenier had promised him power, respect, and money, but those dickheads couldn't find their asses with both hands, and when the FBI had shown up they'd either dithered or fought. Only Doug had had the brains to head for the property line the minute that big helicopter had come roaring in. All those promises about how he was going to be taken care of, looked after—it was just more crap. He was broke in New Orleans, Grenier was in jail, and eventually the cops would come after him again. They always did.

There was always a level of rage that bubbled all along his

nerve endings, but now a new emotion twined around that life-sustaining feeling—melancholy and loss. He studied the fading bruises on his knuckles, legacies of the blows he'd delivered to the cop's face. Grenier had said Doug was special, but because of that little faggot Doug had never found out if he actually *was* special.

It was time to drink. He spat out the plug. It hit the stained wood of the floor between his feet with a wet splat and formed a starburst pattern. It was kinda pretty. He picked up the whiskey and downed it with one quick swallow. The heat from the alcohol burned the hot place on his gum where the plug had rested, and it felt like he'd swallowed smoke. He chased away the fire with the cold of the beer, draining the mug in five long swallows. He then pushed back from the bar and started for the door.

"Hey!" The bartender's basso shout almost hurt Doug's ears. "You haven't paid for that." The Cajun accent made musical mush of the words

Doug turned slowly back to face the man. The bartender was big, red faced, and fat, with a sweat stain at the neck of his T-shirt. The sandy hairs on his forearms stood up like the bristles on a pig and blurred the anchors and mermaid tattoos that adorned the freckled skin.

"Not going to." He patted his pockets. "No money," Doug said. And then he smiled. His special smile.

The big man's glare faded into nervous confusion, and he lost some of his color. Suddenly he seemed like a flaccid balloon. "Well . . . well, you get out of here, now. Don't want deadbeats. You just go on."

With a jaunty little half wave, half salute, Doug left the bar. Maybe he was special. He had a special kind of crazy that made people afraid. And someday he'd use it again on Richard Oort.

Rhiana Davinovitch nervously touched the earrings running from the tops of her ears down to the lobes. Where once they had been cheap Kmart junk, they were now real diamonds, emeralds, and pearls. She walked over to the hotel window, reveling in the play of muscles and tendons in her legs.

In her father's dimension she wore a different form, and it wasn't a comfortable one. She was glad to be back in the universe that housed Earth. Maybe it was because this world had birthed her. Her mother had been human.

Rhiana looked over to where her father, Madoc, sat watching CNN. Madoc wore his human form, but with the impossibly narrow face, upswept brows, and glittering eyes he still didn't look human, not really.

Rhiana looked back out the window at a sunny California day. Droplets of water from the sprinklers glittered on the leaves on the avocado tree that offered privacy to their cabana at the Beverly Hills Hotel. It seemed weird to be back in California. Her foster parents were only a few miles away, sitting in their tiny 1940s tract house in Van Nuys. Years ago they had driven onto the grounds of the famous hotel just off Sunset Boulevard, and hotel security had reacted to her dad's built-up pickup truck. Her father had blustered, but ultimately they had left without ever crossing the portals of the lobby. Now she was staying here.

There was a knock. Rhiana opened the door. The warm air blew into the over-air-conditioned cabana, carrying the scent of clipped grass and star jasmine and the heavy aftershave of the man at the door. Jack Rendell wasn't what she had expected. Since he had been presented as the replacement for Mark Grenier, she had been expecting another unctuous, older man. Someone to play the role of reverend-as-daddy, but Rendell was young, early thirties at most. He topped six feet, and the tall frame supported an athlete's musculature. His features were regular and handsome in that corn-fed, all-American way that you expected to see in a war movie from the 1940s. But there was an expression deep in his hazel eyes that belied that impression. Something cold and hungry and calculating lived beneath the pleasant exterior.

Rendell was a wildly popular spiritualist with a cable show, the occasional special on network television, and lucrative speaking tours where he put grieving people in touch with the "beloved departed." Unlike many of that ilk, he was not a fraud. Instead he was a major magical talent. Even as introductions were made and handshakes exchanged, Rhiana could feel the power coming off him in waves. It was to be her task to teach him control of his magical ability.

Rendell held her hand an instant too long, stood a fraction too near, and allowed his gaze to drop lasciviously to her bosom. Rhiana longed to be older and sophisticated and know how to handle this. Instead she jerked her hand away and retreated.

Madoc began the meeting. "Grenier is gone. He made bail yesterday, and vanished."

"And this matters how?" Rendell asked. "Isn't he useless now? I don't see any way for him to fuck us up."

The slow pullback of Madoc's lips revealed sharply pointed teeth. Rendell sucked in a quick breath. "I agree, but it would have been so pleasant to punish him for his failures." The tip of his tongue flicked out, and Madoc licked his bottom lip as if tasting that punishment. Madoc returned to the moment. "So, are you ready to approach the Cardinal of Washington, D.C., with your 'visions'?"

"Are you ready to back them up with a miracle?" Rendell countered. Madoc nodded. "I have a question," Rendell added.

"You may ask it," Madoc replied.

"Why aren't you using one of the other heavy hitters from the Religious Right to inoculate the gate? Why come to me and the Catholic Church?"

"Because of the involvement first of the FBI and now the military." Madoc shot Rhiana a sideways glance.

And that was her fault. She had offered Richard's rescuers a piece of information that brought in the cavalry. Despite being his child, despite his seeming forgiveness, she still had a fluttering in the pit of her stomach.

Because he never misses an opportunity to remind me of my

transgression. Which probably makes his "forgiveness" not all that sincere.

"Word has filtered out that there are demons there," Madoc continued "The Catholics are perceived as the go-to guys on demons and exorcisms." He gave a thin smile. "And once the Virginia compound has been rehabilitated it will give us a nice rallying cry for the fundamentalists: that the Papists have taken control of the place where the Lord will arrive for his Second Coming."

Rendell absorbed this, nodded slowly. "Anything else?"

"Yes. When you address your followers I want you to strongly suggest that science and scientists are evil, and that they will block the efforts to bring back the age of magic and miracles. We need the scientific community neutralized and eventually destroyed."

"I don't understand."

"We don't want any dissenting voices," Madoc said smoothly.

And we also don't want anyone looking too closely at how I bound Kenntnis. For while Rhiana had used "magic" to summon the power, it was physics that held the creature trapped. It was possible that physics could offer a means to free him, and Kenntnis/Prometheus/Lucifer unbound would put an end to their conquest of this world.

". . . and we especially need an interdiction of nuclear weapons." Madoc's words penetrated Rhiana's wandering thoughts. "As hostilities increase we want to make certain that the violence is planned, limited, and carefully directed."

Rendell looked up from where he was taking notes on his BlackBerry. "I thought you guys fed on death."

Madoc turned his head slowly and regarded the human. Rhiana saw the black spikes flaring from his human form, anger made manifest. Rendell seemed unaware. "You are mistaken," Madoc said. "Death itself is like eating ash. It's fear, hate, grief, despair, and agony that offer the most nourishment. We would rather have a thousand Rwandas then one Hiroshima."

"Got it," said Rendell. "Oh, I put out the word to my viewers about that guy you wanted to find, and we got—"

Madoc held up a minatory finger. "We are done for now. Let me walk you to your car."

Rhiana frowned at the door that closed behind them. *What was it that he didn't want her to hear?*

She pulled a penny out of her pocket. Set it to spinning and glowing, summoned the power, and sent a tendril undulating among the trees and bushes lining the stone walkway. She took out her cell phone. The spell reached out and touched the BlackBerry in Rendell's pocket, turned it on, and linked it to her cell. Their voices came through clearly.

"He's in New Orleans," Rendell was saying.

"And I've got someone in New Mexico. He's going to kill the paladin, and get the sword for us," Madoc said.

Shock at Madoc's words caused her to drop the phone; the link shattered, and her phone fused into blackened metal and melted plastic. Rhiana had tried not to think of him since their parting in a dell in Virginia, but now Richard Oort's chiseled features filled her mind. She wanted him; to love and to punish, to torment and impress, and now Madoc was going to let him die.

"You promised! You promised!" Rhiana whispered. Her throat was tight and small.

The moment the words were uttered she felt foolish and naive. What were Madoc's promises really worth? Richard was just a human, albeit a unique one, and Madoc and his kind were here to conquer and enslave humans.

Rhiana swept up the destroyed phone and thrust it deep into a pocket. She had to warn Richard. She came up short, picturing how that beautiful face would freeze in aristocratic disdain, how cold those pale blue eyes would become. She had betrayed him. It was foolish to think Richard would ever trust her again. But she had to try. She picked up the hotel phone.

* * *

Dr. Angela Armandariz, Albuquerque's chief medical examiner, walked past body-filled gurneys that lined the hallway. She took this as a clue that there was no more room in the drawers in the actual morgue. She sighed, and gave up any hope of dinner at a reasonable hour. It was a New Mexico tradition to celebrate New Year's Eve with gunfire. This year it seemed that everyone had decided to shoot not into the sky but at each other.

Pallid feet, the big toes adorned by tags, thrust from beneath sheets like displays on a butcher's counter. Her eye was caught by the title on one toe. Dr. Kenneth Wilson. The body on the next gurney was also a "doctor." She counted seven before she reached the double metal doors of the morgue.

Frowning, she lifted a sheet on the last body. Three long gashes stretched from the skull to the groin. The skin and hair on the skull were laid back, revealing bone. The gashes in the groin went deep into the soft tissue. She gently laid the sheet back down, and checked the other six. They all displayed the same horrible mutilations.

She went into the morgue and keyed the intercom to her assistant. "Hey, Jeff, what's with the medical convention in my hall?"

"Not that kind of doctors," Jeff's voice buzzed through the cheap speaker on the intercom. "They were some kind of big brains going up to the Santa Fe Institute. The staties found the van off the side of the road."

"Those wounds didn't look like your average car wreck."

"That's just the start of the weirdness. Diego said the van looked like it'd been clawed open. From the *inside*," he added.

"Uh, thanks, I think."

Angela wrapped her arms around herself, trying to banish the sudden chill that wasn't entirely due to the big coolers and fans in the morgue. She would need to tell Richard about this. She hit PLAY on the cheap boom box, and U2 throbbed through the morgue. Angela slipped the strap of the big rubber apron over her head, snapped on her surgical gloves, and flexed her fingers.

She walked to the stainless steel autopsy table. It held the naked

22

body of a young Hispanic man. Bruises covered his chest and face, as if a mad tattoo artist had lost control of the needle. The head was caved in on one side. To her practiced eye the groove looked like a baseball bat. The waxy skin depressed under the scalpel's blade. She drew it down the length of his chest. A red line, formed by muscle tissue and a bit of sluggish blood, followed the path of the cut. She wondered why she was bothering; cause of death seemed pretty fucking obvious.

She was distracted by the bang and squeak as the double doors were thrust open. "*Put 'em in the hall. There's no room in here*," she called over U2, not bothering to look up.

The music cut off abruptly. Angela whirled, ready to rip someone a new asshole. She relaxed when she saw Lieutenant Damon Weber. His square-jawed face sagged with fatigue, and the dark bags hanging beneath his eyes made him look like a raccoon.

He swiveled his head from side to side, counting the gurneys, but it was a slow and careful movement, as if his neck were made of glass and would snap if he moved too quickly.

"Yes, I am up to my ass in dead people," Angela said.

"At least you don't hear them," Weber said with the briefest of smiles.

"In this wonderful new year I wouldn't put that beyond the realm of possibility. What do you need? And please don't say a report."

Weber shook his head, grimaced. Angela pulled off her gloves and tossed them in the trash. "Here," she said and indicating a wheeled metal stool. The big cop sat down, and she set to work massaging his neck. It felt less like muscles than like metal bands shifting beneath the skin. He groaned and allowed his chin to fall onto his chest.

"I need Richard to come in. How do you think that's going to go over?" The words were muffled, trapped by the tucked chin.

"Like you don't know the answer to that," she said, recalling the discussion at the Lumina offices five days before.

Judge Robert Oort had harangued his son for forty-three

minutes. Angela knew; she had kept time. In this he had been ably and brutally assisted by his daughter and Richard's sister Pamela. Pamela had arrived in Albuquerque the day before, been given a crash course in the World According to the Lumina, been touched by the sword, and had instantly assumed a position of authority.

There were facial similarities between the siblings. They both had high cheekbones, pointed chins, and translucently fair skin, but Pamela's eyes were dark gray rather than pale silver-blue. Richard's held a sweetness and a vulnerability. Pamela's were sharp and judgmental. Pamela was attractive with soft light brown hair. Richard was gorgeous with silver/gilt hair. Angela wondered if that cosmic unfairness had added to Pamela's seemingly constant irritation with her brother. Angela found the young lawyer insufferable, and she said so now.

"Actually, you're a lot alike," Weber said. "Which is probably why she bugs you so much."

"We are not. I would never berate Richard like that." Angela moderated her tone and shook her head. "Not that they aren't right. He probably does need to quit."

"Yeah . . . maybe . . . but not right now. I need him. Ortiz called in last night . . ." His voice trailed away, and Weber scrubbed at his face with a hand.

The rasp of skin on stubble was a reassuringly male sound, and Angela wished she wasn't standing in a morgue, but at her condo fixing breakfast, and hearing that sound as Richard wandered into the kitchen, and . . . She shook off the daydream.

"Yeah, and?"

"It was weird shit. About how he wasn't coming back because he had to go up to Truchas Peak, and wrestle with demons the way his granddad used to."

Fear rippled down Angela's back. Captain Ortiz was a hard-nosed cop with twenty-one years of service. What he lacked in imagination he made up for in tenacity. He would never be fanciful or insane.

"It's because of the gates."

"*No!*" Weber came off the stool with such force that it went squeaking and skittering away across the concrete floor. "Do not say that! This shit cannot have spread this far or this fast. We've gotta have more time, to plan . . . to prepare."

"Prepare for what? To do what?"

"Richard has to tell us that," Weber said.

"Yeah, and you want him to work as a homicide detective, and his dad and sister want him to be Bill Gates, and—"

"And what do you want him to do?" Weber asked.

"I want him to keep me safe." She hugged herself, her fingers dug into her upper arms, and her throat ached with unshed tears. "Because I'm scared, and he's the only person who can do that."

"Poor bastard," Weber said softly.

They stood silently for a few moments. "So what are you going to do?" Angela asked.

"Tell him I need him, and let him decide."

All that remained of her brother's presence in the grand office at the Lumina building was the faint scent of his aftershave. Richard had listened, eyes veiled by his long lashes, two spots of hectic color high on his cheeks, while she and their father had carefully detailed why he had to resign from the Albuquerque Police Department.

"Well," she said with satisfaction. "We won."

"Yes, Richard can be made to see sense." Judge Robert Oort bent and picked up several papers that had gone skittering off the large multicolored granite desk, swept up by the speed of his son's departure.

"So now he can concentrate on saving the world." She laid heavy emphasis on the last three words, only to have her father round on her with fury glittering in his dark blue eyes.

"Don't take that scornful, doubting tone with me. Do you doubt your brother's and my word? And if you do . . . if you think this is all hyperbole and hysteria, perhaps you ought to return to Rhode Island."

"To what?" she asked. "Somebody burned down our house."

"The same somebodies who killed your mother," Robert said quietly. Pain edged the words.

"She committed suicide."

"Richard was right. She had help." Robert slid his glasses back on and picked up another document.

"Maybe if I had experienced some of this instead of just hearing about gates and Old Ones who masquerade as gods, and feed on human misery, I might not think this is some kind of hallucination all of you are sharing."

"You've seen the sword, and felt its effect," the judge said.

That was true, but despite the twisting pain that had seemed to reach down into her very cells when her brother had laid the blade on her shoulder, she couldn't really tell what was supposed to have happened. Supposedly she could no longer do magic. Well, she had never been able to do magic. She said as much to Robert and then added, "It's a specious and circular argument, like saying 'I painted an elephant on my barn to ward off lightning, and, by God, my barn has *never* been struck by lightning.'" She shut the cabinet doors with a bang. "And there is nothing on the news about gates and monsters. Let me see a monster, and then maybe this wouldn't feel so crazy and surreal."

"You have. You've seen Cross," her father said.

"Who lives in a crate behind the building. Not exactly filling me with dread."

"He's the weakest of his kind." Robert shook his head. "Which is rather sad when you consider that he represents the loving, forgiving, and merciful brand of Christianity."

"So, bring on the monsters," she said lightly.

Her father's head jerked up and he stared at her. His jaw worked for a moment. "No. I hope you never have to face them." He paused and stared out the window toward the distant snow-capped peak of a mountain far to the west. "Bad enough that Richard has to. I just hope he's strong enough."

Pamela heard the thread of doubt in her father's voice.

ONE

RICHARD

The 911 operator kept his voice low and steady. "So, where are you now, honey?"

"In the bedroom." A little girl's voice, shaking with terror.

"Are you alone?"

"I've got the baby and Matt."

"Have you locked the door?"

"Daddy hurt Valerie. There's blood everywhere."

I floored it and got my POS used Volvo up to eighty. Now I wished I was driving the Ferrari or the Lamborghini parked underneath the Lumina building. But if I had been driving either of them I wouldn't have had the police radio. I wouldn't have known I was a quarter mile away. I couldn't have responded.

"Julie, have you locked the door?"

"Yes . . . He's got Toby."

I killed the siren and made the turn onto Quincy. Then the screaming started. Even filtered through two phones and the radio the sound was ghastly, agonized. My hands jerked on the steering wheel and I practically drove up over the sidewalk. I got the car back under control and turned into one of the alleys that run behind the houses in this older neighborhood.

From the radio came the sound of panting breaths, each holding a shuddering sob. It took every ounce of control I had not to floor the gas pedal so I could get there faster.

There was a sudden silence. Then Julie's voice whispered, "He's coming."

Lieutenant Damon Weber's voice cut in. "Richard, I'm rounding up SWAT and a negotiator, but it'll be at least twenty minutes before we get there."

"Copy. Damon, we don't have that long."

"You want to go in?"

"I've got to. Have I got any backup?"

"Snyder's coming."

I wanted to curse. In my opinion Dale Snyder was a lazy cop just marking time until he had in his twenty years. We had a strained and antagonistic relationship because he thought I made detective because somebody pulled strings. He wasn't wrong, but personal rivalries became irrelevant when faced with a crisis of this magnitude.

"Tell him I'm going in through the alley and backyard."

"Copy that."

I stopped the car and jumped out. The January sun was warm enough that the garbage cans in their little pens filled the air with that sickeningly sweet scent of rotting food. Nausea gripped my gut. Some of it was the smell. Some of it was fear. It's no fun walking into a domestic situation. It's when most cops get killed.

Opening the trunk, I ripped off my suit coat and donned my vest. The barrel of the shotgun glinted in the sunlight and the wood of the stock felt silky beneath my hand. But I had a hostage situation; I couldn't really use such a weapon. Instead I drew the Starfire.

Okay, so I guess I'm resigning later.

The back wall was a low cinder-block affair only four feet tall. There was a wooden gate so old that the wood had weathered until it looked like frozen smoke. It rested on a concrete path, and I knew it would shriek like a scalded cat if I tried to open it. I braced my free hand on top of the block wall and vaulted over. The winter-dry grass, faded like an old man's hair, crackled beneath my feet.

The yard would have been lovely if it were summer. There were arched trellises supporting the skeletal branches of climbing rosebushes. Water fell with a gentle tinkling down a small stone waterfall and into a fishpond. Gold flashed and flickered beneath the water.

I ran as lightly as I could for the back door, past an incredibly expensive swing, slide, and jungle gym set and a hand-built playhouse designed like a Victorian Painted Lady. The air was deathly still, but suddenly the swings rocked and the chains creaked. I whirled, thinking the father had come through the side yard, but there was nothing there. To my left the manes of five plastic horses on springs, frozen in a wild gallop, formed waves of palomino, chestnut, gray, and black.

The backyard was a child's paradise. It didn't jibe with a man murdering his children. There was a flutter of movement past the window of the playhouse. I drew down on it. Again nothing. My neck hairs felt like they were heading toward the top of my head.

It was like that elusive movement sometimes caught at the border between darkness and headlights, or the shadow you see out of the corner of your eye just before sleep takes you. In the past I would have dismissed it as my eyes playing tricks on me. Now I knew different. Two months ago I had learned there were unseen worlds on the borders of our reality. Dimensions filled with horrific, nightmare creatures. Things that viewed humans as prey. Things that drove us to acts of unspeakable violence. And I sensed they were here with me now.

Unlimbering my cell phone, I hit the speed dial. Damon answered on the first ring.

"This doesn't feel right," I whispered. "There's something here. Something I can't see."

"Then you think this is one of yours . . . ours?"

"I think . . . yes."

30

"Shit, fuck, damn, hell . . ."

I had reached the kitchen door. Now that I was at the house I could faintly hear drumming, rhythmical kicks from inside. The door was pierced by a medium-sized dog door, and I wondered if the dog had also fallen victim to the madman inside.

"Damon, if I have to draw the sword, will you handle Snyder?"

"Yeah, of course. Is he there yet?"

"Not yet," but I'd no sooner finished the final word than Dale Snyder came pushing through the back gate. Just as I had anticipated, the wood shrieked across the concrete walkway. I winced, and Snyder's narrow hatchet face showed a brief flash of contrition, quickly masked.

"What the fuck was that?!" Weber exploded.

"Snyder." I flipped closed the phone and made certain it was set to vibrate rather than ring.

The other detective joined me at the back door. There was no sign from inside the house that the noise outside had been noticed.

"Tried it yet?" Snyder asked in a whisper.

"About to."

It was too much to hope that it would have been unlocked. We pressed our shoulders against the door, but it was sturdy and well hung. It barely quivered. There were windows to the left and right, but wrought-iron bars covered the glass. Seconds, precious seconds, were ticking away. How much longer could that fragile bedroom door withstand the onslaught? I was trying to breathe. Trying to think.

The dog door. I returned the Starfire to its holster and lay down on my back. I'm small, and years of gymnastics had made me flexible. If I could get my shoulders through . . . Snyder held the flap out of my way. I felt the sill of the dog door catch on my back pants pocket. The material ripped loose. Suddenly I was aware of something wet and sticky soaking into my hair. The sweet coppery scent of blood hung in the air, overlaying the spicy scent of cooking tomato sauce, and I choked briefly on bile.

Now that I was inside I realized there was a man's voice muttering in an almost unintelligible monologue, a *basso continuo* beneath the crash of the kicks and the splinter of wood.

"I know what you are. Open you up let the monsters out. Where did you take them?"

I braced my hands against the floor, felt the sluggishly congealing blood well up around my fingers, and sprang to my feet. The cell phone in my pants pocket vibrated, but I ignored it and unlocked the door. Snyder stepped in, and his eyes widened. Mentally I prepared myself and turned. A woman lay in a pool of blood in the middle of the kitchen floor. Wounds like red mouths puckered the material of her white sweater. Her throat was partially cut. A large white Le Creuset pot sat on the stove. The burner was turned on, and there was an occasional wet *plop* as spaghetti sauce roiled in a slow boil.

There was the rending sound of wood tearing, a crash, and Julie's shrill screams. Stealth no longer served any purpose. We ran out of the kitchen, and through a small dining nook which opened into the living room. A young girl lay curled on the hardwood floor, her hands in front of her face. Her palms were slashed and punctured, testament to her desperate attempt to protect herself. Every part of her body bore a wound. Adrenaline sang along my nerves, but it helped dull the horror.

In the short hallway we found the body of a little boy. His throat was cut, and his body also punctured in multiple places. At the end of the hall I saw a man lunge through the door on the left. Even in that brief glance I saw he was soaked in blood. When I reached the door I went left and low, kneeling on one knee, shoulder pressed against the doorjamb to help steady my two-handed grip on the pistol.

"*Police!*"

Snyder was on the other side of the door, drawing down on the tableau in the center of the bedroom. A kneeling man held a little girl pressed against his chest. She was dressed in denim overalls. I found my attention drawn to the daisies embroidered on the yoke. Her brown hair was in pigtails. She was a picture of innocence gripped by a hellish figure. Blood spattered her father's face like macabre measles, and his hands and arms were stained red up to the elbows. The steel of the large kitchen knife was occluded with blood, and its point rested against her breastbone.

Julie's mouth was stretched open in a rictus of terror, but only grunted breaths emerged. In her arms she held a bundle wrapped in a soft white blanket. At first I thought it was a doll, but then the blanket moved, a small waving fist appeared, and I heard a high-pitched mewling. It was an infant.

My mind felt like it was spinning, grasping at plans and feeling them slip away. I frantically scanned the room, trying to locate anything that might be used to break the standoff. A toddler stood on one of the low twin beds screaming at the top of his lungs. A fantastic mural of mountains and castles and unicorns and fairies stretched across every wall. A bookshelf loaded with children's hardcover books stood beneath the one window. The top of the case was covered with dolls and stuffed animals. Their plastic eyes glittered at me as if they were watching me, and damning me for my failure to think. If we took a shot it would most likely tear through the child's body.

Think! Think! Think!

In the father's eyes I suddenly saw madness and determination flare to an even higher level. The muscles and tendons in the man's right hand tensed and flexed on the hilt of the knife. We were so out of time.

I had a split second, and if the gamble failed it would be up to Snyder to take the shot because I would be disarmed. The safety slid beneath my thumb. I didn't bother to holster the pistol. I just dropped the Starfire onto the floor. The heavy *thunk* as it hit the wood had the desired effect. The father's eyes flickered down to the pistol.

At the same time Snyder hissed, "What, are you fucking crazy?"

It had to be one smooth, fast movement. I flowed to my feet, reached back with my left hand, and pulled the hilt of the sword from its holster. Even through the sweat and blood on my hand the gray glass hilt felt cool. My fingers slid between its Escher-like curves; I laid my right hand against the bottom of the hilt and drew it quickly away.

It was as if a cosmic organ had played a chord whose bass tones and overtones extended far beyond the range of human hearing.

"Jesus shit," Snyder yelped.

I knew how it must have appeared to him. As if a night-black blade had emerged from my hand.

"It's real," Snyder breathed.

I wanted to pray, but I knew better. Praying would draw them closer, and they were already here. I could almost hear Kenntnis's rich basso tones as he told me about the sword, *Among its many other attributes, the sword has the ability to restore reason and sanity in certain situations.*

Well, I sure as hell hope this is one of them.

And then the wild light in the father's eyes faded. The knife dropped from his suddenly slack fingers, and the man stared in confusion at his bloodstained hands. But only the touch of the sword could fully reverse the effects of an irrational belief. As I took a step forward the father's eyes widened in surprise, and he turned his head—over toward Snyder and then back to me.

It was instinct more than conscious thought. I threw myself onto the floor in a long dive. I landed on my knees and the heels of my hands, and my chin hit the floor hard enough to set dark spots dancing in front of my eyes. The sword flew out of my hand, and the blade vanished. I was deafened by the crashing report of Snyder's .38. I glanced back. There was a ragged hole gouged into the wood of the door frame. My head had been there only seconds before.

"*Snyder!? What the fuck?!*" Could the madness that had affected the father have somehow been transferred to Snyder? But if that was the case, why hadn't the sword negated the effects on Snyder as well?

The barrel of the .38 was swinging toward me. Snyder's face suddenly seemed very small and distant when compared with the cannon-sized hole at the end of the pistol. Frantically I rolled to the side, but not nearly fast enough. It felt like a fist slammed into my right thigh. For several heartbeats the leg just felt numb; then the pain came crashing down, sharp and hot, as if an electric wire had been thrust through my flesh. I screamed and clutched at the wound. The blood was hot against my skin, my slacks were soaked, but it wasn't the gush of a severed artery. I wasn't dead yet.

But Snyder, walking toward me with a grim expression, was going to change that real quick. His face was tight with concentration and grim determination. This time he wasn't going to miss.

He thinks I'm disarmed. Big mistake, asshole.

Gasping with pain, I coiled into a fetal position, clawed at the cuff of my left pant leg, and pulled it up enough to reach the ankle holster and the tiny Firestar that rested there. I yanked the gun free, swung it up, and double tapped. No real time to aim, but he was only two feet from me. The recoil sent the pistol sliding in my blood-slicked hand. The first round got sucked by Snyder's vest, but it affected his aim, so his third shot buried itself in the floor next to my head. Smoke trailed like ghostly hair, and the biting smell of cordite filled the room. It felt like a percussion band was tuning in my ears.

My second round took Snyder in the cheek. Shattered teeth, bone, blood, and flesh seemed to hang in the air as half his face ripped away. Snyder tipped sideways and fell to the floor. The vibration of his fall shivered through the length of my body. Black spots danced in front of my eyes. More than anything I wanted to rest my head on the floor and slide away into unconsciousness. But there were three children and a madman in the room. I pressed my hand hard against the wound and felt my head whirl from the pain. Whimpering, I dragged myself toward the hilt. Each move pulled a strangled moan from between my tightly clenched teeth. Suddenly the little girl was there, holding the hilt out to me.

I managed to draw the sword. Stretching, I used the point and knocked the knife beyond the father's reach, then crawled another foot forward and laid the blade against the man's knee. He fell back screaming on the floor. His spine arched and his heels drummed as a violent seizure gripped him.

My hands seemed to belong to a stranger. They seemed very far away, and they shook like a person afflicted with Parkinson's. With the last of my strength, I got the blade sheathed and thrust the hilt into the waistband of my trousers. The floor felt very soft as I laid my cheek down. The black spots became a wall of darkness.

TWO

They had walked the dimensions back to the gate in Virginia. Madoc had told her to wait for him in the public rooms of the great stone and log house that had once been both the headquarters for the World Wide Christian Alliance and Mark Grenier's palatial home. She didn't know why she was being left like a piece of luggage to be called for later. Maybe he was up to something. Maybe he was angry. It was hard to read her father. He placed human emotions on his face like a Mardi Gras attendee changing masks.

Eventually she became restless. She hated the white carpet underfoot and the blue velvet upholstered furniture, and what passed for art. There were a few framed studio photographs of Grenier, and some too-bright, too-colorful pictures of Jesus suffering the little children to come to him, doling out the loaves and fishes, praying in Gethsemane. The girl growing up in Van Nuys would have been impressed with the cushy carpet underfoot and the plush velvet beneath her fingertips. But the weeks she had spent living in Kenntnis's penthouse had taught her enough to know that this was kitsch masquerading as elegance.

She pushed open the door leading to Grenier's private quarters. Partway down the hall there was a smear of blood down a panel wall. The FBI had seen that the bodies were removed, but no actual cleanup had occurred. Once the dimensional gate had opened, the humans had retreated. Each day the perimeter of soldiers moved back another mile or so from the compound.

Rhiana wandered into the office. A number of panes in the bay window which cupped the desk were missing. Plywood had been nailed up, but it had been a hurried job, so they were crooked. A hot wind gusted through the gaps. It carried a strange scent. Burnt cinnamon and oil was the only way she could describe it. The edges of Madoc's dimension were pushing deeper into the Virginia valley, and within the confines of that bulge, where one universe extruded into another, living things died. Rhiana assumed the Old Ones would eventually stop the creep. They would have to if they wanted humans to feast on.

The carpet had undulating rents in the fabric. At the extreme edges she could see a pattern of vines. There was a large brown stain on an intact piece of carpet. *Blood.* She wondered if that was where Richard had cut off Grenier's hand. She pictured the scene, Richard slim and quick, a frown of concentration between his brows as he fought, magic against sword.

Would he have used the sword on me if he'd reached me before I bound Kenntnis?

She sat down in the Tempur-Pedic foam chair behind the desk, rested her toes on the floor, and swung back and forth. She noticed a notepad off to the side. In bold print she read:

Drew Sandringham = Richard.

"Richard" had been underscored three times. A green-gray mist spilled out of one of the dulled and grayed mirrors. She swiftly tore off the page and thrust it into her pocket. The mist resolved into Madoc.

"You seem determined to annoy me today," he said without preamble. "I told you to wait in the public rooms."

"I got bored. And what have I done?" Rhiana asked.

"Do you think I can't tell when magic is being done?" Madoc demanded. The edges of his human form frayed. Tendrils of oily green mist leaked from his eyes. Rhiana clasped her hands tightly together and thrust them beneath the desk to hide their trembling. "Don't you *ever* spy on me again. You are told what you need to know. Do you understand me?"

"Yes, Da . . ." Her voice choked on the word. "Sir," she amended.

"Did you warn him?" Madoc asked. Rhiana lifted a shoulder; it was both an answer and a dismissal. "Did you warn him?" Madoc repeated more forcefully.

"Don't you know? I thought you'd know," Rhiana said and added, "Since you're spying on me."

Madoc stared at her. His human features were back in place, and he had the same expression she'd seen on her adopted mother's and father's faces at various points during the past few years. With a sudden insight beyond her eighteen years Rhiana realized that teenagers were baffling and inexplicable whether the parent was human or formless horror. The thought made her giggle.

"This is not a laughing matter."

That was just what they always said. The giggle became a laugh. Then her lungs stopped working, and her tendons seemed to be dissolving. Her arms clasped protectively across her breast, but then a dark red light flowed out of her and into Madoc's gaping maw. He was no longer human.

"Don't, please, stop," Rhiana whimpered, though she couldn't tell if her mouth had actually formed the words.

The sucking pressure stopped. The light snapped back to her, and her body reknit. "Lesson learned?" Madoc asked, and he sounded smug.

With a trembling hand Rhiana swept back her hair. It felt wonderful, warm and smooth against the skin of her palm. Rage took her.

"How could you do that to me? You were *feeding* on *me*! Well, here's a little lesson for you. If I die I'm pretty damn sure that Kenntnis will be freed!"

That wiped the self-satisfied expression off Madoc's face.

"What?"

"I wove my essence, every part of my being, into that spell. So you better keep me safe." Madoc took a step toward her, threat implicit in every line of his once more human body. "And don't think you can make me alter the spell!" Rhiana's throat was tight with tension and fear. It squeezed the words into a harpy's shriek. "If anyone hurts me I'll use my last breath to shred the bonds holding him! So you better treat me right!"

It hadn't been a conscious or even calculated thought. She had drawn her own strength into the binding spell because she had needed a little extra boost of power. But what she'd learned since that day made her glad she had taken the action.

Rhiana had naively believed that the Old Ones all shared the same goals. She hadn't understood that they occupied different multiverses, they were different creatures, they had different goals. *And they were all equally greedy.* Since the gates had opened, Madoc had been involved in a few rather vicious turf wars with other Old Ones. Rhiana had come to realize that she might well be in danger. She just hadn't thought the threat would come from her sire.

"So, when you die we once again lose this world?" Madoc demanded.

"No. Let me live a long and happy life . . . and I mean a *really* happy life, and I'll alter the spell. But only when I'm a lot older. A *whole* lot older." Rhiana waited tensely for his reply.

"Give you whatever you want, is that it?" Madoc asked.

"Yes."

"And does that include the paladin?"

"Yes."

"You don't really want him. You want the fantasy of him," Madoc complained.

"Maybe, but I want the chance to find out for myself," Rhiana answered.

Madoc shook his head. "Once this is known, everyone is going to focus on recasting the spell. Then they'll kill you for your temerity."

It was said matter-of-factly. Rhiana gaped at him. "Wouldn't you try to stop them? Do something to help me? I've done so much for you."

"I, too, am just a servant of the great ones."

Rhiana's surprise and sense of betrayal deepened. "I thought you were, like, really important."

"Sorry. No." It seemed like no matter where she lived she was doomed to the lower class. He seemed to read her emotions. "You're still more important than a human."

"What can I do to . . . to . . ."

"Fix this?" She nodded. "Recover the sword, capture or kill the paladin—I don't care which, and destroy the nascent Lumina. That would help buy you some forgiveness."

"And how fast do I have to do all this?" Rhiana asked. A weight had settled into the pit of her gut, a leaden ball of despair and loss.

"Quicker would be better." He steepled his fingers in front of his mouth. His expression was reflective. "You know, this might actually prove to be helpful. We have the dark paladin and have been trying to figure out what to do with him until we acquire the sword. He can be your responsibility. See to it you keep him happy."

THREE

RICHARD

The smells—disinfectant, overcooked vegetables, bedpans, and the sweet rotten scent of cut flowers too long in water—identified the location. *Hospital.* I had spent way too much time in hospitals. I hated hospitals. I stirred and pain lanced down my leg. Sweat suddenly beaded my forehead and went trickling away into my sideburns with a feeling like ants crawling across my skin.

"Here." A drug dispenser was thrust into my hand. "You'll want this."

The words sang with the lyric cadences of Spain filtered through four hundred years in the mountains of northern New Mexico. I looked over, and Angela bent down and kissed me. Her mouth tasted of coffee and chocolate, two of her favorite vices. The inside of my mouth was like a compost heap. I turned my head away. Angela straightened and gently brushed the hair off my forehead. From the way it was clinging to her fingers I could tell it was sweat matted, and now I was aware of the sheets damp and twisted against my bare backside, the way the skin under my arms stuck to my sides, my own smell. I was suddenly desperate for a shower.

"Pain slows the healing process. Use it." It was an order.

Obediently I depressed the button, and started counting the seconds until the chemical relief arrived. While I waited, I noticed the spill of city lights through the slats and around the edges of the blinds.

"What time is it?"

"Little after ten."

"At night?

"At night."

Slowly the events of the afternoon stuttered into focus. "Snyder?"

Angela shook her head. "Died en route."

I killed someone. Again. But not a perp this time. A fellow officer. *Who tried to kill me.* With this much morphine washing through my system I shouldn't have been able to muster up much more than remote interest, but instead rage seized my throat and cut off my breath. We were policemen, sworn to serve and protect, and that protection extended to our brothers and sisters on the force. *Fuck Snyder, and damn him to hell.* I was suddenly glad I'd killed him.

But that probably wasn't going to be the most politic thing to say when the inevitable board of inquiry was called.

"It was self-defense," I said aloud, testing out my defense, and the best part was that it wasn't a lie.

"What?"

"Nothing. Never mind," And I was on to a new concern. I levered myself up on one elbow and scanned the surface of the small rolling table next to the bed. I cranked around to check the shelf behind the bed. The movement sent agony shooting out of my thigh and into my groin. "The sword!" I groaned. "Where—"

Angela grabbed my hands, trying to steady me. "Damon secured it before the ambulance arrived. Your dad's got it now. It's okay. It's all okay."

The pillows folded up around my ears. I just lay there feeling my heart rate slow.

"Everybody's here. In the waiting room," Angela said. "Damon wanted to watch the local news. See how the whole thing is playing."

"And how bad is it?"

"Well, on the one hand you saved three kids. On the other hand you shot and killed a fellow officer. Are you a hero or a villain?" Her voice took on that breathless singsong of the news whore trying to gin up interest in a story.

"Neither. Both. Confused," I said, trying to match her levity.

"Are you up to talking?" I nodded, and she started for the door.

"Wait." She turned back at my call. I was very careful when I touched the sheet covering my right leg. "How bad?"

"Not very. In and out. You were damn lucky. At such close range the expanding gases bruised the bone in addition to putting a really big hole in your leg. It's going to hurt like hell for a while." A humorous light danced in the velvet brown eyes, and her teeth flashed white against her cocoa-hued skin. "You'll be on crutches for a few weeks. Or if that's too déclassé you can accessorize with a really bitchin' cane and suffer."

She didn't miss the hot rush of blood into my cheeks. I was, in fact, just considering brass versus silver handles. Angela correctly interpreted the blush and laughed.

"It's okay. Your sartorial splendor makes up for the rest of us slobs." This time she made it to the door before turning back. "Oh, one more thing. Your dad is really, really pissed. Just wanted to warn you."

The door fell closed behind her, and even the morphine couldn't calm the sudden flutter deep in my gut that her words elicited. *When he's one hundred and I'm seventy-five he will still have the power to make me feel five,* I thought, and I wondered if every parent had that power or if it was just my tough-as-nails sire. Then the door opened and what seemed like a torrent of people crowded into the room.

Weber grabbed the ugly green armchair and dragged it over to the bed and sat down. Angela stood on the other side of the bed and busied herself untangling the tubes from the IV drips and checking the monitors. They felt more like guards than concerned friends. Next I looked at who they were guarding me from—my family. Which was a heck of thing when you thought about it.

Pamela, who had carried in a bouquet of flowers, stood at the sink filling a vase and arranging the yellow calla lilies with elaborate care. I was terribly aware of my father standing by the window. Occasionally he parted the blinds and looked out. Disapproval was radiating off him, making the small room seem even smaller. Everyone was studiously not looking at each other.

Angela transfered her fidgeting from the tubes to me. Picking up my wrist, she took my pulse. "Must be a pleasant change from most of your clientele," I said. It was a feeble joke, and it was totally swallowed by the tension flaring between all of us.

I coughed, trying to clear the obstruction that seemed to have settled in my throat. I looked to Damon, so I didn't have to look at my angry sister and my expressionless father anymore. "What's going to happen to me?" I asked my boss.

Pamela spoke up. "Well, hopefully you'll get fired. Since you didn't quit like you were supposed to. You told us you were going to quit." It seemed my sister was taking it as a personal affront.

"The call went out. I was close and I was still a police officer," I shot back. In all these years I've never been able to keep from engaging with her.

Damon shook his head. "No, he's not going to get fired. I think he's . . . you're going to come out of this okay. And what does she mean he . . . you were going to quit?" My boss was alternately trying to glare at my sister, smile reassuringly at me, and keep the pronouns straight. He wasn't notably successful, because I ended up on the receiving end of one ferocious glare that wasn't meant for me.

Or at least I didn't think it was meant for me. Maybe Damon really was angry with me. Maybe I should have waited for SWAT. Maybe I should have told him to order Snyder to stay away. Maybe I could have aimed for the leg and not killed Snyder. *No, screw it, he deserved to die.*

Morphine was making me loopy. "He tried to kill me. If he'd

succeeded those kids would have died. I dropped the sword. The father would have gone nuts again. I had to shoot him."

Damon nodded in enthusiastic agreement. "Yes, yes you did, but here's another reason you're going to be fine. You've got one hell of a witness in that little girl. She seemed to want to talk more about how the one policeman tried to kill the other policeman, instead of talking about her father."

"And who can blame her," said Angela. "I get to autopsy these babies." Her glance toward my sister and father was challenging. "At least three of them are alive thanks to Richard." She gave my hand a hard squeeze.

My father's profile didn't alter, but Pamela's back stiffened. Bless Angela for the kindly impulse, but I wished I could have told her that protective justification didn't play well with my family.

"Any idea why Snyder wanted to kill me?" I asked hurriedly.

"Well, putting aside the hating-your-guts part, I convinced Judge Cole to give me a warrant, and I had a little peek at Snyder's bank account. On January third he deposited twenty-five thousand dollars, " Weber said.

"A hit." I tried to wrap my head around the idea. It wasn't easy with the morphine washing through my system, but once I did the rage returned. "Crap, he did this for *money*?"

"Seems likely," Damon said.

"Watch your language," my father said at the same time.

"Now it makes sense what he said. When I drew the sword he said, 'it's real.'"

"Implying he knew about the sword," Angela said. "Which means somebody told him about it. Gee . . . three guess as to who that might have been," Angela added and smiled. If it was meant to be an ironic smile it failed, presenting instead like an angry grimace.

I was hoping everyone would assume Angela's fury related to Rhiana's betrayal of Kenntnis. I knew it had a whole lot more to do with me. I was suddenly so tired of everyone's desires and expectations being focused on me. *Why couldn't Kenntnis have arranged Lumina as an order of warrior monks, or celibate Amazons?*

Damon's hand gripped my shoulder. Wearily I opened my eyes again. Weber smiled down at me. I was momentarily fascinated by the way the light glinted in the graying stubble on his chin. I wondered how he'd look with a beard.

"Hey, we're wearing you out."

"It's okay." I forced a smile and banished the thoughts that would have jeopardized the friendship we'd barely reestablished.

"Look, you rest now. If I bring by a laptop tomorrow, do you think you could write up a report?"

I forced energy into my voice. "You bet."

Suddenly my father stirred. The blinds snapped together with a metallic clink. He walked to the door and I realized that he had barely said a word.

He opened the door and looked back at all of us. "I'd like a few words in private with my son."

I had heard these words too many times in my life not to know what they portended. Bile climbed up the back of my throat. I wanted to beg Angela and Damon to stay. But that wasn't going to happen. The judge brooks no disobedience. Even Weber, a nineteen-year veteran of the police force, was suddenly in motion out the door. But Angela was made of sterner stuff.

"I think Richard has had enough conversation. He needs to rest," Angela said. She folded her arms across her chest, shifted her feet as if she planned on taking root in the linoleum floor, and stared defiantly at my father.

"He can tolerate one more," the judge said, and the level of ice in the words told me that this was a fight even Angela couldn't win despite her reputation as the World's Meanest Chicana. She had met her match in the World's Toughest Man.

"Angela, please, it'll be okay."

At my words she deflated. She leaned down and pressed her lips against mine. Again there was that burst of chocolate and coffee and desperate longing. "I'll be back in the morning. You get some sleep. Don't stress."

Angela walked to the door, then looked back at Pamela, who leaned against the wall, arms folded across her breasts, clearly intending to stay. My sister's face held an odd mix of disapproval, pleasure, and contempt. Angela's eyes narrowed, and I realized she had decided that while she might not be up to my father's weight she was definitely up to Pamela's.

"Either *everyone* or *no one* gets to hang around for the ass kicking," Angela said.

"This is a family matter," Pamela flared back.

My father walked to the door and pulled it open. "All of you, out."

"Papa, I think—" Pamela began.

"Out!" It was the voice that had issued from the bench for sixteen years, and mobsters, drug dealers, and murders had quailed before it.

No wonder I didn't have a chance.

The door closed, and we regarded each other. Two weeks ago he had come to my rescue. After days of beatings and torture I had been at the end of my strength and bravery. He had run into Grenier's office and gathered me in his arms. I had never felt that safe before. Now I was hurt again, but there was none of the warmth and love I had seen in Virginia. Once again I'd disappointed him. A faint shivering invaded my gut, and a tightness filled my chest. This was going to be an ugly one.

"This must stop." Papa removed the hilt from his pocket and laid it on the bed next to my uninjured leg. "*This* is your life now. This and nothing else. Accept that. Because of a fluke of genetics you are the only one who can use this weapon. Had there been a more well ordered manner of selection, I'm sure you would not have been everyone's first choice . . ."

I'd lost track of his words. *But I did well in Virginia. I was clever. What could I have done differently? I didn't break. I took it. I'm not a coward. How could I have done things better, Papa?*

"The madness that infected that father is symptomatic of events occurring across the country and around the globe."

"And because I had the sword I saved those three kids."

"We have far bigger problems than that. It's fallen to you to lead the defense of our world. Instead you're hesitating and regretting and postponing instead of accepting your responsibilities. That has always been your problem, Richard. Always. This weapon"— he gestured at the hilt—"is the only defense we have against these creatures."

"I don't know how to save the world. I knew how to save those kids." I was surprised to discover that the bowel-loosening terror I always felt when he berated me was gone. What I felt was anger.

We were matching stares. I grabbed the control and with a hum raised the top of the bed so I could face him more easily.

"Can you look me in the eye and seriously tell me that I should have done nothing? Just driven on down to headquarters and resigned? Let those children die?"

He didn't even hesitate. "Yes."

I stared at him and wondered who he was. At some point every kid secretly suspects they were adopted. In my case I figured I was a stepchild. I knew I was my mother's child. It was written in my face, and our emotional bond, but I was so different from my older sisters and my father that I figured we couldn't share any genes. It had been a source of grief for me because I so wanted to be his. Now I was grown, and I knew he was my father. And at this moment I didn't want to be his son.

"You don't get the life you wished for, Richard. You get the life you have. Now get on with it." The words were cold, clipped, and precise. "You will resign from the force immediately."

I couldn't look at his face, pinched with anger and disappointment, any longer. I closed my eyes, and suddenly new faces pushed their way forward. Faces of victims as their fear turned to relief at learning of an arrest. The blank surprise and anger that crossed a perp's face at the moment of capture. That sense of enormous satisfaction I'd felt when my testimony had resulted in a guilty verdict, and taken another animal in human skin off the street.

And the face of every criminal I had arrested held a shadow of the faces of the men who had hurt me, disrupted my life, and led me to attempt suicide. That assault had brought McGowan into my life, and with his help I had regained my strength and the will to live, and found my life's work. I had been good at police work, very good.

"Have you anything to say?"

I opened my eyes and looked at him. "I'm going to be on leave anyway because I shot a fellow officer and because I've been hurt. We don't have to deal with this right now." He opened his mouth to continue the argument. I cut him off. "Now, I'd appreciate it if you got me a wheelchair." I picked up the phone and started dialing.

"What nonsense is this?"

"They hired someone to kill me. I don't really want to stay in an unsecured hospital. I'll be safer at Lumina. The limo is big, so I won't hurt my leg . . . too much."

The expression on my father's face was hard to interpret. "You need medical care."

"Angela can look out for me."

"She's a coroner, for God's sake. She cuts up dead people." The words were explosive with fury.

"Yes, and I'm trying to keep from becoming one of her customers."

FOUR

Even at 3:00 A.M. Bourbon Street was rocking. Music poured out of the doors of bars and dives—the sob of a saxophone, the husky voice of a blues singer, the clear blare of a Dixieland clarinet, even the rollicking rhythms of a Celtic band. The moisture-laden air reeked of booze, grease, the pungent scent of seafood, humidity, and humanity.

Neon signs blinked and flared, throwing garish multicolored light across the cheap T-shirts that hung in every store window demanding SHUCK ME, SUCK ME, EAT ME RAW. Signs screamed out ALL NAKED, ALL THE TIME!!! A big-bellied white man, his face beet red and moisture-slick with sweat, shouted at her.

"Come on in, darlin'. You could win a hundred bucks! Mud wrestlin' contest. You'd be a natural." Rhiana froze him with a look.

Dazed people brushed past her, clutching brightly colored plastic cups adorned with umbrellas. No doubt they contained New Orleans's infamous Hurricanes. There was a tingling along her nerve endings, which weren't entirely human. This was a place where the membranes between the dimensions were tissue thin. Were the branes thin because of voodoo, or had belief in magic taken root here because of the lack of separation?

They had stashed the man at the Inn on Bourbon. She reached the hotel and ran gratefully up the steps and into the air-conditioned lobby. Bellmen, all of them African American, cat-footed past her, looking like officers in an operetta with their red uniforms and gold epaulets. The staff behind the front desk were all white. Rhiana wondered if this was how New Orleans had always been, or if it was a small symptom of what was happening with the opening of the gates.

There was a pressure on her chest as if the city were breathing, focusing on her. It forced her to lean against the wall of the elevator. She stepped off the elevator and got her bearings. Down the hallway to the corner room. A room service tray piled with dirty dishes lay on the floor outside. The door was flung open after only a single knock.

The man was of medium height and whip-thin. He wore only a pair of black jeans. There was the white line of an old knife wound across his ribs; his toenails were long and yellowed. The stink of cigarette smoke hung in his clothes and hair, and he needed a shower. Doug Andresson reared back and raked her with a hot look.

"Now that's more what I'm talkin' about. Some *serious* booty." He grabbed Rhiana's wrist and yanked her into the room. "Now get those clothes off, and get your ass in the bed." Whiskey breath gusted into her face.

Rhiana reached out to her power, ready to freeze the breath in his chest, choke him on the offensive words, but she met an implacable wall. *Oh shit, he's a paladin. Magic won't work on him.* She felt a flash of all too human female fear.

Time for a human solution. She swung her purse and hit him in the temple while at the same time she drove the high heel of her shoe into his instep. He howled, clutched at his foot, and hopped. While he was off balance she shoved him hard in the chest. He crashed down on the unmade bed.

"First, I am Madoc's daughter. Second, I'm in charge of you now. Third, I'm going to get you the sword."

As she watched, the furious glare faded from the dark eyes,

and calculation took its place. He wasn't smart, but she bet he was cunning.

"Now get dressed. I'm taking you back to the compound."

"No." He folded his arms behind his head and stared up at her. "I like it here just fine. There's shit to do in New Orleans."

"Oh, really?" She looked ostentatiously around the room. "It's pretty clear from the stink that you haven't let a maid in here in days. I saw the room service tray outside the door. The women are coming here." She forced herself to look at the crusted stains on the sheet. "And you don't look like a music lover."

For the briefest flash she saw Richard's profile, eyes half closed, head thrown back as his hands swept across the keyboard of the piano. She pushed the memory aside.

"I'll keep you supplied with whatever you want, but you need to be where I can find you fast." Rhiana had a sudden inspiration. "And I need to keep you safe. You're very important."

FIVE

RICHARD

The clink of silverware on china had me jerking upright, and the abrupt movement set my thigh to throbbing. The bedside lamp, a tall glass column, switched on, momentarily blinding me. I threw an arm across my eyes, but in that brief moment before spots exploded across my vision I had seen Cross.

"Oh, sorry," the creature muttered. The light was dimmed, and I opened my eyes.

Cross dragged over a chair with one hand while with the other he tried to control the soup bowl. He wasn't notably successful. Soup sloshed across his hand as he failed to keep the bowl balanced. Then the spoon shipped overboard and rang and clattered on the polished slate floor. Cross picked it up, blew across it, sat down, and began slurping. Noodles clung to his lower lip like a walrus's bristles, then were quickly sucked in. Broth dribbled into his beard. Watching the homeless god eat was a stomach-turning experience. I swallowed hard a few times. My stomach sank back down.

I found myself staring at the Old One. In the weeks before Kenntnis's capture our enemies had kept up a constant assault on Cross to keep him splintered. He had been reduced to a fragile stick figure barely able to muster up the strength to "see" magic, which was his primary use to the Lumina. But now that sickly creature was gone. Color shone in his cheeks. His eyes were clear. The envelope in which he wrapped his alien form looked strong and virile. I said as much, and got back Cross's usual tactless response.

"Thanks. You look like shit."

"I got shot. What's your excuse for being so chipper? I thought you'd be almost permanently splintered with all the crap that's going on in the world," I countered.

"Yeah, things are getting rough out there, but when bad shit happens, good people, I mean truly good people, tend to get even better. They're worshiping me *hard,* so I've got a little reserve built up against my asshole brethren. And, don't forget, the chaos feeds me, too."

Well, that was an alarming thought. "Help me up," I ordered. I so didn't want to face what that might portend while flat on my back.

Cross set aside his soup bowl, grabbed me by the forearm, and helped me sit up. He snatched up the pillow and revealed the Starfire and the sword hilt that had been hidden beneath it.

"Little paranoid?" Cross asked. He plumped up the pillow and leaned it against the curving steel and glass headboard. Thrusting his hands beneath my arms, he hoisted me back until I rested against the headboard. He was amazingly strong, and the pressure of his hands both tickled and hurt the muscles and tendons in my armpits. Moving also changed the throb in my thigh to a white-hot line of pain. I clamped my teeth together so hard that my jaw ached, and I still couldn't hold back the strangled moan.

When I could talk again I snapped, "Can you blame me?"

"Nah. Your dad told me what happened. Talk about a co-worker gone bad." Cross paused and cocked his head, considering. The flippant expression faded. "You gotta make sure no one in this building gets similar ideas."

"And just how do I do that?"

"Use the sword."

"Snyder tried to kill me out of greed, not because of all the craziness."

"Yeah, but as our dimensions push deeper into your universe, your reality is going to get really fucked up. People are going to believe crazy, crazy shit, and sometimes the crazy shit's going to start happening. You've gotta at least protect the people around you."

I reset the pillows supporting my injured leg while I chewed on that. "Great, I can just picture how well that's going to go over. Oh, by the way, if you want to keep your job you've got to let me touch you with this *sword*."

"Tell 'em to think of it as your version of a drug test."

I wasn't buying it. I shook my head and then asked, "Will the madness affect your worshipers?"

"Richard, hello." He bopped me on the forehead with the palm of his hand in a send-up of the V8 commercial. "Remember, believing in me is crazy, too." It was said with that patient gentleness you reserve for the old and senile, or the very young.

With an irritable wave of my hand, I brushed off the condescension. "But you appeal to the best of our natures. Even if the underlying belief is irrational, I'll settle for the good result."

"Problem is, once *my* worshipers get organized, and agree to power sharing, *their* worshipers are going to come and kill *my* worshipers, and they've got a lot more warm, crazy bodies than I have."

The silken black duvet cover snagged on a hangnail as I began to pleat it between my fingers. "That's sad."

"Which part? The killing or the fact that charity, love, forgiveness, and mercy are way less fun than righteous vengeance and punishing the infidels and the sinners?"

"Both, and what does that say about us as a species?" I said.

"That you suck, but you sure are tasty." Cross lifted the bowl to his lips and slurped down the last of the soup.

Cross's flippant response hit me wrong. Maybe it was the pain making me testy, but I wasn't finding Cross amusing at—I peered at the Bose clock radio—two seventeen in the A.M. "Kenntnis thought we were worth the trouble. He believed in our ability to grow and change."

"Yeah, but do *you*?" And the creature's brown eyes were suddenly swallowed by his expanding pupils until they were just stone black. I had seen it happen a couple of times, and it still had the nape hairs trying to climb up my scalp. A million years of evolution were screaming at me that this thing was evil, and it would kill me, and I needed to run like a . . . a . . . I tried to not use the profanity, but nothing else would serve. *A motherfucker.*

Papa can't read my mind. He can't know that I'm cursing like a sailor.

But you'll slip and say it out loud sometime.

Stop it! Focus. Answer the question.

What was the question?

Are humans perfectible?

I got control of the cosmic kibitzers in my head, and thought back on the violence I'd witnessed in four years of police work. There was the toddler killed when his angry father had thrust a hose up his rectum and turned on the water as punishment for a full diaper. A woman beaten by her boyfriend until her face was just pulp, knifings at a party, drivers shooting each other because they got cut off in traffic. And beyond my small and petty personal experiences, there was all of history rolling out dark, and violent, and terrifying. There was the destruction of the Cathars. Auschwitz. Pol Pot's killing fields. The body-choked rivers of Rwanda. I lay there unable to muster a single argument for why mankind deserved to survive, and I hated Cross for making me face how evil humans really were. *Maybe we do deserve to be cattle for the Old Ones.*

Then my eye was caught by the Impressionist paintings hanging on the walls to either side of the gigantic bed. Shimmering water, flowers in dreamlike colors, misty landscapes. Twining through my errant thoughts were the haunting strains of *Il mio tesoro intanto* from Mozart's *Don Giovanni*, and then the music modulated in the final movement of Beethoven's Emperor Concerto. I could almost feel the keys of the piano beneath my fingers.

Next I looked at the enormous LED television hanging on the far wall, and I thought about the scientists, inventors, engineers, and machinists who had created that wonder of technology. I remembered thunder shaking the ground and vibrating in my chest that time Papa had taken me to Cape Canaveral to witness a space shot. I had been nine. The ship lifting skyward on a pillar of fire had been blurry because of the tears that filled my eyes. All of these were testaments to mankind's genius.

Is that enough?

Were art and music and technological prowess enough to offset the horror? Well, there was love and sacrifice and generosity that sometimes transcended the hatreds between people.

It wasn't rational, but a certainty that all these things were enough to justify our existence filled me. The tension headache pounding in my temples eased.

"Yes. Yes, I do." Cross must have heard that certainty in my voice, because he straightened in the chair and his eyes became human again. "Now get back out there. Walk on water. Turn water into wine. You may be a fraud, but at least you're *my* fraud, and you're a fraud that appeals to what's best about people. Give them hope. Help them hang on. We need them and we need you."

Cross stood and looked down at me. "You're taking an awful risk. I'm one of the monsters. I just happen to be on your side . . . for now. If I feed and use magic, I get stronger. There's a chance I'll revert to my essential nature, and then you're really fucked."

"And I believe in your ability to grow and change, too." We held a look for a long time. Then Cross nodded and walked from the room.

SIX

In the late afternoon the Round Robin Bar in the Willard Hotel was fairly subdued. The after-work rush of lobbyists, lawmakers, bureaucrats, lawyers, and hookers hadn't yet arrived. Rhiana paused just inside the door and surveyed the room. She knew it was a famous Washington, D.C., watering hole, and this was the place Jack Rendell had suggested after she'd called him and asked to meet, but she'd never been here before. It was pretty, with wide expanses of rich green watered-silk wallpaper bisected with narrow vertical wood panels. It smelled of aftershave and liquor and money.

Jack Rendell leaned on the circular mahogany bar, one foot resting on the brass rail. A wide mouthed martini glass was held negligently between his fingers, and the light through the red glass stem stained his fingers like blood.

There were only a few patrons in the bar, all of them were male, and they all reacted to Rhiana's entrance. The hem of her long black wool coat swung at her knees and brushed at the tops of the stiletto-heeled black boots worn over form-fitting pants. She finished off the ensemble with a cashmere sweater, and a scarf pinned on her shoulder with a large amethyst brooch. There was a rattle like dry leaves in a high wind as *Wall Street Journal*s and *Washington Post*s were hurriedly lowered, and Rendell, sensing the tide of male attention flowing toward a single point, turned. The attention ebbed when it became apparent where Rhiana was heading.

"Hey," Rendell said, saluting her with his glass.

"Hi."

The young bartender hustled their way. His eyes were alight with interest and pleasure as he looked at Rhiana.

"Get you a drink, miss?"

"A Dubonnet on the rocks."

Jack drained his martini and waved the glass at the bartender. "And I'll take another."

"So, how did things go with the archbishop?" Rhiana asked.

"He's conferring with Rome. I expect we'll get some action in a day or two."

"Good."

The bartender deposited the drink in front of her. She took a sip and couldn't control the corners of her mouth.

Jack laughed. "You really are a baby, aren't you? Would you rather have a Coke?"

Rhiana nodded and swallowed past the lump in her throat. She was feeling too depressed and humbled to respond with haughty rage to Jack's familiarity. And she had asked him to meet her. The Coke arrived, and Rhiana gratefully cleared her tongue of the sharp alcohol taste.

"Why did you order it?" Jack asked. "The Dubonnet, I mean? It's not a very common drink anymore."

"My grandmother . . . adopted grandmother. She just loved Jackie Kennedy . . . all the Kennedys really. She talked all the time about how beautiful and sophisticated Jackie was, and how she drank Dubonnet on the rocks."

Jack looked down at her, and some of the sharp calculation faded, replaced by a gentler emotion. "That's kind of sweet. But stick with me, kid, and I'll teach you how to drink." He threw back his head and laughed. "That's a hell of a trade. You teach me magic and I teach you how to booze."

"Shhh. Not so loud," Rhiana said.

Jack looked around the historic old bar. "Why not? All of this . . . this bullshit"—he swept an arm around—"is going to be gone soon."

"Yeah, but we don't want them waking up and panicking."

"Really? I thought the whole point was panic. Well, never mind that. You called me, and I assume it wasn't just for an update, since I've been reporting to your dad."

Rhiana pulled the piece of notepaper from her handbag and laid it on the bar. Jack read the notation and quirked an eyebrow inquiringly at her. "I found this in Grenier's office," Rhiana explained. "Since Grenier thought this Sandringham guy was important, I think we need to find him, and I want you to help me."

"That seems to be all I ever do for you guys. I find people for you," Jack complained. "When do I ever get to be part of the big game?"

"When I do," Rhiana said. "And before that can happen I have to capture Richard." She laid a finger on Richard's name where it was scrawled on the paper.

Her nail resembled a blood-tipped talon. Rhiana stared for a moment at the long acrylic nail. Thought about the optical illusion that had turned Jack's fingers red. Thought about the news coverage of women and children trampled to death during a religious procession in Mexico when word had come that miraculous cures were happening inside the tiny shrine. Thought about the Druidic group that had decided to resurrect human sacrifice as a way to tap the power. The normally unflappable British had been shaken by that event. And these were isolated incidents. More would follow in frequency and intensity. She felt a moment of doubt, but when she weakened the bonds that held her physical body she could feel the power, flame-like, licking at the edges of thought and emotion. It was enthralling, heady, far more intoxicating than the Dubonnet she'd tried.

"Richard is this paladin, right?" Jack asked.

"Yes."

"Do you know anything about . . ." Jack glanced back down at the paper. "Sandringham?"

"I did an internet search. He owns a boutique brokerage firm in New York."

"So if you've already found him you don't need me," Jack said.

"I want you to go with me when I talk to him. There's a connection to Richard. I just don't know what it is."

"Why me?"

"I'm young and a woman, so people don't take me seriously." Rhiana gave a humorless little smile. "At least not yet. But you're a man. You're famous, or at least infamous. People will talk to you."

"Aren't you the Queen of the Night, or the Princess of Air and Fire, or the King of Elfland's Daughter, or some other damn thing? Take one of . . ." He hesitated and nervously licked his lips. "One of *them* with you. The guy will talk, trust me."

Rhiana studied him and couldn't control her amusement. "So, I guess you got a gander at my dad when he's not in his human form."

"And some others." Jack drew a hand across an upper lip suddenly shining with sweat.

Rhiana shook her head. "I don't want the Old Ones knowing what I'm doing until I've finished the job."

"I don't want to piss them off," Jack said.

"If we succeed they'll be very, very happy with me . . . and anyone who helped me."

"What if we don't succeed?"

"I'll take all the blame," Rhiana said.

"Yeah, like I can take that to the bank," Jack said.

"I trust you," Rhiana said simply.

"Why?" Jack asked.

"Because you're smart enough not to totally trust the Old Ones. Because I have something you want, and because you're the only human I know who doesn't hate me."

The words just came tumbling out. Rhiana gasped, lifted a

hand to her mouth. Her stomach clenched down tight, and her mind began whirling, playing the "*I didn't say it. Why did I say that? What if I'd said something else?*" game. She wanted to cry.

He missed the center of the cocktail coaster. The martini glass teetered between cork and wood, then fell. Rhiana watched the tendrils of gin catch the light. Small rainbows raced across the top of the bar.

It was Jack's arms sliding gently around her shoulders that brought her back. "Why not? I like New York. Maybe we can catch a show."

SEVEN

"You must have some protein." Pamela followed her father's voice into the big granite and steel kitchen.

The judge was seated next to Richard in the bay window breakfast nook, and pushing a plate closer to her brother. Richard looked ghastly. His hair was tousled and dark circles hung under his eyes and he had gone beyond white to gray.

"I'll throw up," Richard said and looked up as Pamela entered.

She laid the letter down on the table next to his elbow. "I got this ready for you." She watched as his eyes flicked across the brief and terse lines of text. She knew it by heart.

Dear Sir,
This letter is to inform you of my decision to tender my resignation from the Albuquerque Police Department, effective immediately.
Richard N. Oort

When he looked up at her, she almost took a step back at the bitter fury that twisted his face. "We haven't discussed this. I would prefer to wait until the inquiry is over and I've been cleared."

Their father didn't respond. He just pulled out a pen and held it out to Richard. There was a look of desperate pleading on her brother's face, but he lowered his lashes, veiling his eyes, and his face was suddenly as cold and as expressionless as a statue's. Pamela stiffened; when Richard closed down, there was usually something going on behind the frozen facade. But there was no way he could get out of this. She had made damn sure of that. He took the pen and signed his name.

"It's customary, is it not, to turn in the badge and the gun?" Pamela asked. "Where are they?"

He stared at her, struggled to his feet, and pulled the pistol out of the pocket of his royal blue bathrobe.

"That's just pathetic," she said as she took the gun. The metal was cold and heavy against her palm. "The badge?"

He grabbed up his crutches and swung out of the kitchen. Pamela followed him across the living room, down the hall, and into the master suite. He hobbled into the enormous walk-in closet. His bare heels were a flash of white in the gloom of that vast space. They moved past mahogany shoe racks, sock drawers, cedar-lined sweater drawers, and electric tie holders.

Pamela had always thought Richard had a lot of clothes, but his wardrobe barely made an impression in the closet. In fact, his suits looked like huddled little men overawed by their surroundings. He moved to where a line of sports jackets hung. One was hanging apart, and Pamela suddenly realized the dark stains on the navy blazer were dried blood. It was mesmerizing and horrifying, and she just kept staring at it as Richard dug into the inside breast pocket. He threw a leather wallet toward her, and the badge flashed gold as the top flap fell back. It was petty of him to do that. She wasn't all that coordinated, and he knew it. Sure enough, the wallet grazed her fingers, she grabbed for it with a spastic, jerky motion, and it hit the floor at her feet.

"There. Happy now?" he asked.

She picked it up, glared at him, and then forced her glare a smile. "Ecstatic." She gestured at the coat. "Why are you keeping that thing? It's disgusting."

"Maybe to remember."

"Remember what?"

"What I used to be. What it meant to me. The difference I made."

"Oh, please, don't be so dramatic. It was just a job."

EIGHT

Pamela left with my life tucked away in a cloth tote bag. My father got me settled in a recliner with the rolling computer desk and laptop close to hand, a stack of reports about the various subsidiary companies Lumina owed, and a glass of milk. The hum of the elevator faded away. I gave it a few more minutes just to be on the safe side, then grabbed my crutches and headed back to the bedroom.

Pain raced up and down my thigh each time I planted the crutches and swung through. Gritting my teeth against it, I wished I'd grabbed the cell phone out of the coat pocket. But Pamela would have asked why I needed it, and I wouldn't have had an answer she would have believed. She'd always been suspicious of me. Probably with good reason.

And I'd always disliked her. With good reason. Memories from childhood went stuttering through my head—Pamela humiliating me when I was seven by telling a table full of guests that I sang along whenever I watched *Mary Poppins*. Pamela, pompous at twelve, declaring that she had thrown away my Transformers because they were silly. I had raced to the curb and pushed over the garbage cans, but the truck had already gone by.

It was gross having to touch the coat again. It probably couldn't be salvaged. I just needed to throw it away. But it was my only navy blazer. I cringed on behalf of my credit cards as I considered buying another one. Then the phone was in hand, and I stopped worrying about clothes. What I was about to do would really give me something to worry about. *But only if they found out.* I really should have the courage to just discuss this with my father. My thumb depressed the speed dial button.

He picked up on the second ring. "Weber."

"Hey, it's me."

"Hey, Rhode Island, how you doing?"

"Crappy. It hurts."

"Yeah, but consider the alternative. Hey, we got the shooter in the Mora case," Weber added.

I recalled the facts of the case—Edward Mora, age fifteen, dead on New Year's Eve after a street drag race went bad. His mother had been nearly mad with grief. "Oh, good. Have you told Mrs. Mora?"

"Yeah, and she turned up at booking with an antique cannon of a pistol ready to kill the perp."

"Oh, shoot."

"Fortunately not. I called in a psych team, and they took her off for observation." My phone gave a faint beep.

"Damn, my battery's running down. Let me get to the point. My sister's going to be turning up with a letter of resignation, my gun, and my badge."

"Shit." There was a pause; then he said, "Well, maybe that's for the best . . . considering . . . everything."

"I want you to throw away the letter and bring me back my stuff."

"Your father is going to fucking kill you."

"Only if he finds out, and if he does I can always blame you for intercepting it."

"Gee, thanks, you're a real pal. But why?"

"Because in a weird way being a cop gives me some cred I wouldn't have otherwise. People will be less likely to think I'm a nut."

"What are you planning?"

"I haven't gotten as far as a plan. I'm just thinking right now. But I want my badge, and I especially want my gun. They're going to try again."

"You've got security."

"Would you depend on that alone?"

"Hell, no."

"I rest my case."

There was silence for a long moment. The phone bleeped again. I propped my shoulder against the full-length mirror at the back of the closet. I needed to get off my feet soon.

"Okay, I'll do it. If for no other reason than it will really piss off your sister." We shared a laugh.

"I've got to go."

I hung up, and that's when I noticed the message icon on the screen. I called the voice mail center and waited through the female robot's announcement of "*one call, received on January seventh at 1:55 P.M.*" I had been in the kitchen of the Quincy house. The memory brought back the phantom smell of blood, and a sticky feeling on the back of my head.

"Richard," came Rhiana's voice. She sounded frightened; she was almost whispering.

The sound of her voice sent me swinging wildly between conflicting emotions. Regret that I hadn't handled her better, fury over her betrayal, guilt that my behavior had led to the betrayal, and *way* down deep, the faint coil of attraction and arousal.

"Richard," she said again, as if repeating my name forged a link. "They've got someone to kill you. Someone in Albuquerque. I don't want you dead. Be careful."

Great, why was my luck always so shitty? She couldn't have called the day before?

"*End of message. To delete press seven . . . ,*" came the robotic voice.

I pressed nine and saved the message. And then I entered the number in my address book.

NINE

Pamela had pulled a chair around behind the broad granite desk so she could sit next to her father. They were studying the webs of interlocking contracts between Lumina Enterprises and a surprising variety of subsidiary companies. Pamela's specialty was criminal procedure and constitutional law, so she wasn't all that familiar with contract law—at least as played at this level—but even lacking the background she was impressed. It was almost impossible for someone to use a subsidiary and reach through to Lumina proper.

After a glance at her father's profile Pamela realized her instincts were correct. Her father's expression held grudging respect, and it wasn't easy to earn that. He had been a partner at one of Rhode Island's most prestigious white-shoe law firms, and Pamela had hoped to join him there when she finished law school.

But by the time she was done and had passed the bar, he had been appointed to the federal bench. She opted not to court the inevitable comparison, and so had turned down an offer from the firm. Instead she'd gone to the public defender's office. She liked litigating, and she had earned a fearsome reputation as the PD most DAs wanted to avoid. Her father had been pleased.

She knew that Richard was, supposedly, studying the same information upstairs. Someone would probably have to explain it to him. It still gave her an odd shiver of pleasure that she had been the one to take the accouterments of his life as a policeman down to APD headquarters. She had ignored Weber's coldness; she and her father were right.

The elaborately carved double doors swung open, and Jeannette stepped into the office. The judge looked up and pulled off his glasses inquiringly. Pamela resented the woman's intrusion without buzzing first to see if it was convenient.

"Our company's COO has arrived, sir. Since Mr. Oort . . . Richard, is upstairs I'll—"

"No," her father said. "I want to talk to him first. Give me a minute and then send him in."

"I'm a her, actually," said a woman, who stepped around Jeannette and walked toward the desk. She was dressed in a rather wrinkled rose wool skirt, an eighteenth-century-inspired matching coat, an ivory cashmere sweater with a coral necklace, and high-heeled brown boots. She carried an expensive briefcase in one hand and a newspaper in the other. She paused to glance down at the picture on the front page, then looked up and studied the judge critically.

"No, you are not, in fact, the man who runs this company." She had a German accent, and she sounded snotty. She turned back to Jeannette. Pamela noted that her shoulder-length brown hair had been expertly highlighted. "So, I would like to see my employer now."

Pamela could feel her face going stiff.

"Judge Oort is Richard's father. I'd start with him." There was a pause, and then Jeannette added, "If I were you." Pamela caught the significant look the two women exchanged.

Richard needs to fire this woman. She acts like she runs the company.

"Fine. *Gut.*"

Jeannette withdrew and closed the doors behind her.

Her father stood and extended his hand. "Perhaps I was out of line, but my son is convalescing."

"Convalescing? Why? What has happened?" She looked again at the paper that showed the bruising on Richard's face. "Is it this? Was he hurt more badly than reports indicated?"

Pamela couldn't help but smile at the little throat-clearing her father made, and the way it had the COO's attention instantly focused on him.

"You are?" her father asked.

The woman hurried to the desk and reached across. As they shook hands she said, "Dagmar Reitlingen." Something niggled at the back of Pamela's mind, but when she reached for the elusive memory it went skittering away.

"And I am Robert Oort, and this is my daughter, Pamela."

"Pleased to meet you."

Dagmar next took Pamela's hand. Pamela noticed the woman's short-clipped nails, very out of character with the expensive clothing, and the width across the back of Dagmar's hands. It was the mark of a horsewoman, and Pamela had it, too.

"I would have been here two days ago, but I had the journey from hell," Reitlingen was saying. "We were late leaving Gatwick, and instead of three hours in Dallas it became eight." Her mouth worked as if she were chewing on something. "And *mein Gott*, how absurdly dry it is in this place. Normally, Mr. Kenntnis and I would meet in London. I've only been here once before, just after the building was completed. The heat was shimmering on the pavement, if you can believe it. The sky is still that impossible blue, but at least this time the temperature is bearable."

Pamela felt like she was being pelted by the nonstop words, but her father was faintly smiling. "Is this a long way of asking for a drink?" he asked.

"Why, yes, exactly," Dagmar said and smiled.

"Water or something a little stronger?" the judge asked.

"Oh, don't tempt me. But at this hour of the morning, and as tired as I am, I'd best be cautious. Water, please."

At a look from her father, Pamela moved to the hidden bar and filled a glass with water and ice cubes from the small refrigerator. The polished red metal of the professional espresso machine gave her a distorted view of the COO. She realized the woman was assessing her with sharply calculating eyes, and Pamela realized that just as she had evaluated Dagmar's wardrobe the favor was now being returned. Pamela brought her the water.

The judge settled back into his chair, and indicated the chair on the other side of the desk from him. An offended look, quickly masked, flashed across the older woman's face. *What is she worried about?* Pamela thought.

"Are you here to brief my son, or evaluate if the company is in trouble because of this queer turn of events?" the judge asked, and Pamela felt both stupid and enlightened for not realizing the source of Reitlingen's discomfort sooner.

Once she found out a gaggle of relatives had arrived, she probably thought we were a gang of rapacious hillbillies. Well, she's been set straight now.

"You are very direct," Dagmar answered. "But I think these discussions should best be held with my employer, and not with you . . . no matter how close your relationship. Which brings me back to the convalescing. What does convalescing mean? Exactly. If you please."

"My son was shot yesterday."

"*Mein Gott.* How did this happen?"

"He was responding to a . . . er . . . domestic disturbance call," the judge said.

Pamela watched the color flee from Dagmar's face. "He is *still* working as a policeman."

"No," said Pamela. "He finally listened to Papa. He quit today."

Pamela caught the flicker in Dagmar's brown eyes, and wished she could have trained herself out of pronouncing "Papa" in the French manner. It was such an affectation, and it was so like her mother to have stuck her children with it.

"In my experience that career is either very easy or very hard to leave," Dagmar said.

It was so rude, but Pamela couldn't control herself, "Oh, God, please, not another one! I am so sick of cops."

"Well, let me make you feel better. I was never a policeman. My father, however, he was a policeman, and after watching his life I had no interest in pursuing that career." The older woman paused, and gave a wry smile. "But damn, I wish I could have had the uniform."

"Why?" her father asked.

"My country has always loved a uniform." Dagmar paused, and the smile she gave them was a study in irony. "Often to Germany's detriment. But because I didn't have a uniform it made it harder for me to achieve my goals."

Suddenly it all clicked into place for Pamela. "My God, you're *that* Reitlingen. I thought I recognized the name. You won the gold medal in dressage with the highest overall score ever posted."

"Ah, I was right, you are a horsewoman. I spotted your hands immediately, and your thighs. So many American woman are . . ." She made a gesture that indicated bulges. "How do you call them? Saddlebags, yes? But not ladies who ride."

Her father frowned again. Pamela knew this discussion of horses was not to his taste. "I don't know. When we were taking Pamela to horse shows I saw a good many ladies who would qualify as . . . er . . . large."

"Ah, but they are not *riding*. They were just riding." Pamela saw her father's frown of confusion, but realized she was nodding in agreement and understanding.

Dagmar clapped her hands together with delight. "Yes, you know exactly what I mean. So, do you still ride? I do. Perhaps we can ride together."

"Not anymore. I quit when I started college. I checked out a few universities that offered horsemanship programs, but Papa pointed out that selecting a college based on whether it had a barn was spectacularly foolish." Pamela wondered why in the hell she had added all of that. She slid a glance at her father. He was not looking happy. "He was absolutely right, of course."

"You are very young now, and it is never too late to return to the sport," Dagmar said.

"Why is it that women have this obsession with horses? And apparently none of you outgrow it."

Dagmar gave the judge her shoulder and turned to face Pamela straight on. "Does your brother share your father's disdain?"

"No, he rode, but he decided to focus on gymnastics, and they're not exactly complementary sports."

"I'll take you to Richard," her father said, his tone making it clear that there was to be no more discussion of horses.

TEN

RICHARD

The cards filled the computer screen like signal flags on a mast, but the message they spelled out was *you lose*. I guided the cursor to the red button and depressed the mouse. The cards vanished from the screen. Whoever invented Spider needed to die. Talk about a time sink, and totally addictive. Just mindlessly clicking on the cards, trying to get used to the Mac mouse. It felt weird not to have the right and left buttons.

I should have been doing something useful, but mostly I was fighting nausea brought on by overheated air and Vicodin, and worrying about what I'd done to circumvent my father's will. The fact that it felt like a sauna in the penthouse was another strike against my sister. Pamela hated the cold. She had probably hiked the thermostat sometime during the night. I plucked at my pajama top and pulled it away from my damp skin. My scalp prickled with sweat, and I gave my head a vigorous scratching. God, I wanted a shower, but Angela had said I had to wait a couple of days and then wrap my thigh in plastic wrap or keep my leg out of the water.

Okay, I had to get to work. I virtuously guided the cursor over to the folder titled LUMINA BOOKS. Then, almost like it was a maddened guide on a Ouija board, the cursor circled the file several times, then darted back to the dock at the bottom of the screen. But of course the cursor didn't really have a life of its own;

76

I was just stalling. I set the arrow on the folder and firmly pressed down on the mouse. The subfolders, each one titled with a year, filled the screen. How many years was I expected to go back? I opened one at random and was faced with a P&L statement.

The numbers marched like lines of toy soldiers. It took me back to that six months I had spent working at Drew's brokerage house. Which took me to other memories of Drew. A weight seemed to be pressing down on my chest. Usually when I felt one of the panic attacks coming on, I would go swim laps or run or take a walk.

But all of those coping mechanisms weren't available right now. I needed to find another distraction. I looked up, and the room obliged. The Steinway grand piano was under the large picture window. Through the glass I had a view of the hunched boulders that littered the foothills of the Sandia Mountains. I made a note to tell Jeannette to get my piano out of my old apartment and over to the penthouse. It had been kind of Kenntnis to buy the Steinway, but I preferred the touch on the Bösendorfer. I really ought to practice. I hadn't touched the keyboard in four days. No, longer.

The geometric pattern of the Oriental rug, picked out in rich reds, blues, and creams, offered another distraction. I thought about the women in Turkey and the various "stans" knotting these treasures. Well, for us they were treasures; for their creators they represented a small amount of money and a large amount of drudgery. If we finally achieved a living wage around the world, this art would be lost. But maybe that was a good thing. A machine can't go blind.

I lifted my eyes and looked at the beautiful objets d'art that filled every available surface. There was a tiny Roman marble sculpture of Diana, her features carved in exquisite detail. A Mughal dagger. Egyptian tomb figures. Did the value of the objects keep this room from being a cluttered mess? My uncle's house in Vermont was also filled with collectables, but the only word that came to mind was "tchotchkes".

On the wall to my left stood two tall bookcases crammed with books. They flanked a Caravaggio painting of the Madonna. *Wonder which Old One she'll turn out to be,* I thought. *Or maybe she had been a creation of Kenntnis's? A loving, comforting mother to offset the vengeful, "damn you all to hell" males. Mothers didn't scare you like fathers did.*

It's an uncomfortable moment when you've realized your errant thoughts turned out to have a psychological agenda. I didn't want to dwell on where that thought had come from. I opened up another file. The spreadsheet lay before me, numbers centered precisely between the grid lines. There were lots of them. With big amounts. No, make that *huge* amounts. And I was supposed to juggle, manage, decide how to spend the money represented by those numbers. I closed the file and pushed away the rolling table holding the laptop.

I grabbed up a report from a subsidiary company and started reading. *Nonrefundable fees received at the initiation of collaborative agreements for which we have an ongoing research and development commitment are deferred and recognized ratably over the period of ongoing research. . . .* A pounding settled behind my eyes. It felt like my brain was trying to hammer its way out of my skull. I set that report aside and tried another. *Intangible assets are the singular source of differentiation in a postindustrial economy.*

The pages flapped like a gooney bird attempting takeoff as I threw it back toward the pile, but the slick paper sent it skidding off the other side. It overbalanced the entire dead-tree tower, and all the reports went tumbling to the floor.

Okay, music. I'd play for a while. Maybe sing a little. That would clear my head, and I could come back to the reports refreshed and able to concentrate.

Yeah, right.

ELEVEN

As they rode up in the elevator, Pamela could feel her father's eyes boring into her back. She probably shouldn't have come along, but she was hoping for a chance to talk to Dagmar Reitlingen, and find out what happened to that amazing gray mare she had ridden in the Olympics. Was Mist still alive? Had she been bred? How many foals? Were they competing?

They stepped off the elevator into the foyer. Piano music and Richard's rich tenor met them. The liquid runs reminded Pamela of children laughing, but the gaiety of the music didn't mollify her father. His lips tightened into a thin line.

"Damn the boy," Robert muttered half under his breath.

Pamela and Dagmar had to hurry to keep pace with the judge. Their heels made a discordant syncopation that shattered the purity of the music. Then they were through the archway and into the living room.

Richard sat at the concert grand piano. His crutches leaned against the side of the instrument. His body swayed in time to the music, and a lock of silver/gilt hair flopped against his forehead.

The judge stood between the two women, and Pamela felt her father gather himself. She was startled when Dagmar laid a restraining hand on his arm and held up a finger in a shushing gesture. The older woman then turned back to Richard and watched him intently. Pamela wondered what she was seeing, and really hoped the woman wasn't going to prove to be like every other woman and be swayed by her brother's looks.

As an experiment she tried to look at Richard dispassionately, as an outsider might. Richard's eyes were closed, his concentration was total, and his entire body was immersed in the effort of drawing music from the piano and his body.

Pamela found it disturbing to look at the fading bruises that trickled down from his eye, across his cheek, and along the line of his jaw. For some reason the physical beating made this seem more real and more frightening than the gunshot wound he'd sustained. It wasn't rational, but that's how she felt. *Maybe because cops and guns go together. But cops hit people, too. I see it all the time. Maybe it's weird because it was a cop getting beat up.*

She focused on his hands with their long, slender fingers, and listened to the deep hiss of an indrawn breath followed by the floating ring of his voice, and wondered why she hadn't been granted even a modicum of musical talent.

Richard opened his eyes and, as if sensing the scrutiny, turned his head to look at them. Dagmar drew in a steadying breath.

Maybe outsiders can't be dispassionate, Pamela thought with bitter irony.

Dagmar began applauding. "That was absolutely exquisite. *Im Haine,* 'In the Woods,' poem by Franz von Bruchmann, music by Franz Schubert." Then she leaned in close to Pamela and the judge and added in an undertone, "Well, I'd wondered why Kenntnis gave the company to an unknown. Now I think I understand. I'll just keep reminding myself that I'm a married woman and the mother of two lest I succumb as well." Dagmar's tone was bantering, but the judge took it badly.

In a hissing undertone he said, "I'll thank you not to say such things."

The COO gave him a startled look. "Sorry."

Richard rested a hand on the piano and, wincing, levered

himself to his feet. He nodded to Dagmar. "Thank you, but it wasn't that good. By the way, who are you?"

"I'm Dagmar Reit—" Dagmar began, but the judge ran over her.

"What are you doing wandering about?" he demanded as he walked to Richard, and handed him the crutches with the air of a drill sergeant offering a recruit a rifle. "Angela will flay me alive if you break open that wound."

"I couldn't think anymore," Richard answered. "I thought music might clear my head."

"Well, we've brought you someone who might help," Pamela said as she moved to stand next to the judge. "This is Dagmar Reitlingen, the COO of the company." She indicated Dagmar with a sweep of the hand.

Richard got the crutches tucked under his arms and went swinging toward Dagmar. He stopped, rested on the supports, and held out his hand. "Richard Oort. Pleased to meet you, ma'am." Richard gave Dagmar a sharp look. "And I said something wrong. What did I say wrong?"

Pamela looked from one to the other in confusion. Her father had an expression that she bet was similar to hers.

"Maybe you ought to loan me one of those crutches now that I'm in my dotage," Dagmar said in faltering accents. "Ma'am? When did I become a ma'am?" But then she threw back her head and laughed, and Richard relaxed and also smiled.

It was one of the things Pamela had always hated about her brother. He was always hyperaware of the people around him. Pamela thought it was a way to garner attention, being so sensitive and so attentive to people. A ploy so that people would always talk about how nice he was. *As opposed to you*, came a little voice that partook a bit of her older sister, Amelia, and her mother. Pamela pushed the thought aside.

"Actually, pleased doesn't begin to cover it. I'm ecstatic to meet you. Thrilled. Delirious with joy."

"Don't be so silly," the judge said sharply. Dagmar gave him a startled, disapproving look, and he added with his rather ponderous humor, "You sound like you've swallowed a thesaurus."

Richard ducked his head. "Sorry, but I really am in over my head here, and I desperately need help."

"And I'm happy to do that, but before we get started could I get something to eat? I've been in the air or sitting in airports for the past thirty-one hours, and the food in either place is not of the best," Dagmar said.

"Oh, I'm sorry. That was thoughtless of me," Richard said. "Please, let's go into the kitchen. I don't think the breakfast buffet has been cleared yet."

They all followed Richard as he hobbled through the formal dining room with its cut crystal chandelier like a frozen waterfall over the polished cherrywood table. Dagmar didn't spare a glance at the china and crystal in the buffet, or the magnificent silver centerpiece that featured winged horses and women in diaphanous gowns.

Probably just old hat to her, Pamela thought. When she had first arrived in New Mexico she'd inspected the living quarters very closely on the theory that you could tell a lot about a person by the items he owned, and she was highly suspicious of a man who would leave anything to her brother. Given the rarity of the other objects in the penthouse, Pamela could only assume that the champagne flutes etched with bees and an elaborate *N* had belonged to the Emperor Napoleon. The china was Royal Crown Derby, and it was an antique pattern. She had found other china in a storeroom off the kitchen, not all of it European design. Her best guess, as she held the almost translucent plate with its pale willow pattern, was that it was Chinese and very old. She glanced back at the living room. The sunlight seemed to be haloing the priceless objects on the tables and drawing the colors from the paintings.

Who had he been, this man who had stormed into her brother's life and changed everything?

And not just Richard's life. The unknown Kenntnis had turned Pamela's and her father's lives upside down. Maybe the COO could tell her who he had been, answer her questions and lay her doubts and concerns to rest. She brought her attention back to Dagmar in time to see her father almost tread on the woman's heels because he was walking so close behind her. The way the judge crowded in on her made Pamela think of stalking predators. Dagmar abruptly stopped, and the judge actually bumped into her.

"I won't hurt him. I promise," the woman said. Richard also stopped and looked back inquiringly. Her father and Dagmar measured looks for a long moment; then the judge gave a sharp nod.

No, Pamela corrected herself, *not a predator. A protective parent guarding its young*, and the realization gave her a strange little jolt. The reaction was gone before Pamela could fully grasp the fleeting emotion.

They entered the kitchen, where the sunlight poured in like honey through bay windows surrounding the breakfast nook, and sent searchlight beams down through the skylights, to dance on the lids of the silver chafing dishes lined up on the center island and drew blue fire from the opals embedded in the chocolate brown granite of the countertops. Vases filled with large sunflowers were strategically placed so they would reflect in the brushed chrome surfaces of the appliances and add to the genial air of the big room.

"Oh, good," Richard said. "They haven't cleared breakfast yet. Please help yourself. It's been sitting for more than an hour, so I can't speak to the quality."

"I'm certain it will surpass the McDonald's in DFW," Dagmar replied.

Her father pulled out a chair for Richard and, once he was situated, made sure the crutches were within easy reach. Pamela's attention was split between watching her father fuss and Dagmar pile her plate high with eggs Benedict, bacon, a waffle, fruit, and a wedge of cheese.

"You should have a little something," the judge said. "You didn't eat much at breakfast. Pamela, get him something."

Pamela felt her spine going stiff. Richard shot her a nervous glance. "I'd really rather not. I'm a little nauseated from the Vicodin," Richard said, and this time he split the nervous glance between Pamela and their father.

Dagmar set down the full plate, remarking brightly, "My husband, Peter, is very high-strung and nervy, too. He's also a musician. A violinist. Professional, though." Dagmar returned to the buffet, filled a cup with coffee, and poured in a large dollop of cream. "Although I think you are good enough to have performed professionally," she continued. "Did you ever consider it?"

Now it was her father's turn to go rigid, and for Richard to go red. Dagmar returned to the table, sat down, and gave them all a bright smile. Pamela was surprised when Richard was the first to respond.

"You play the role very well," her brother said. "But I've seen the books, and I sincerely doubt someone as disingenuous and ditzy as you're pretending to be would actually have become the COO of Lumina, so why don't you cut the crap."

Pamela watched her father's brows twitch together in a sharp frown. He hated profanity, and none of the Oort children cursed. Obviously that was something else Richard had learned as a cop.

"*Bitte*?"

"Just ask your questions and stop trying to stir the pot," Richard answered.

"All right," Dagmar said, and her tone was suddenly less jocular. "But let me fortify myself a bit first."

Pamela found that her leg was vibrating with anticipation. To occupy herself she began loading dishes in the dishwasher. Richard sat perfectly still. The judge, seated next to him, was equally composed, and for the first time Pamela saw the resemblance between the two men. Before she had only seen her mother reflected in her brother's features.

"So." Dagmar pushed the now empty plate aside. "Why in the hell *did* Kenntnis put you in charge of Lumina?"

"Well, it's certainly not for my business skills." Richard paused, head cocked slightly to the side. "I suppose to protect it," he said slowly and thoughtfully, almost as if he were answering a question for himself.

"Protect it from whom?"

"Maybe from you," the judge said, suddenly entering the conversation.

"Me? Do I look like an untrustworthy person?" Dagmar said. She sounded more surprised and puzzled than angry.

The judge was not disarmed. In that precise, dry way of his he said, "We haven't had a very good run with CEOs, COOs and CFOs over the past few years—Enron, Global Crossing, Tyco."

"Actually I think it more likely that *you* are a crook," Dagmar replied. "Your son is given control of a fantastically valuable company, and suddenly we have the whole family."

I was right, Pamela thought. *She did think we were carpetbaggers.* Then she noticed how the edges of her father's nostrils went white, and his spine became even stiffer. *And it didn't occur to Papa.* For some reason his lack of acuity bothered her. She quickly pushed aside the thought. Of course it wouldn't occur to him. He was the most honest and just man she knew.

"We are not opportunists or thieves. I resent the implication."

"And I resent your accusation. I'm not the female version of Dennis Kozlowski except with dancing boys."

Pamela saw the woman steal a glance at the indentation at the base of Richard's throat.

Oh, not you, too.

Richard laid the tips of his fingers lightly on the judge's wrist. "Papa. I may not have known Kenntnis long, but I got a good sense of him in that time. He read people very well. If he hired Ms. Reitlingen, then I have confidence in his decision."

"With one glaring exception," the judge said.

Her brother's long golden lashes fluttered down to cover the pale blue eyes; the fair head bowed. For a moment Richard seemed discomfited. Then he looked up. "Are you talking about me or Rhiana?"

"Rhiana, of course," the judge snapped a little too quickly.

"She was a unique circumstance, Papa."

"And who in heaven might Rhiana be?" Dagmar asked.

"Who in hell is the better question," her father said as he pushed back his chair and stood. He moved to the buffet and prepared a plate for Richard. "Well, I've had my say." He looked back at Dagmar. "Just know that Richard has resources beyond you. We will be keeping an eye on things." He returned to the table and set down the plate in front of Richard. "Eat. Pamela, shall we finish what we were working on?"

The order was heard and understood. Pamela followed him out of the kitchen. She looked back once to see Dagmar staring at her father's back. The older woman's expression was not warm.

TWELVE

RICHARD

Ilistened to my father's retreating footsteps, but I waited until I heard the faint whine of the elevator before I turned back to this woman who was now my employee. If it had been hard to give an order to Kenntnis's personal secretary, Jeannette, I couldn't image giving Dagmar Reitlingen an order.

I was startled by her expression when I met her gaze. She looked like she wanted to give me a hug. I felt like I should offer her one instead. "Look, don't worry. I know that might have seemed rude —"

"Seemed?"

"Okay, it *was* rude, but we've all been under a lot of stress. My father really is a remarkable man."

"I'll agree that having all the cards on the table is better than not. And always say something to my face, Mr. Oort. I can tell your father is a . . ." I watched as she paused and seemed to search for a word. "A stern fellow."

"Looking for your English or looking for something less . . . rude?" I gave her a smile, and got one back. One front tooth was slightly crooked, giving her an impish quality. She had a nice face that was framed by light brown hair with blond streaks, and I liked her eyes. They were sort of sherry colored. "I know he's tough, but he never expects more of others than he expects of himself," I added.

I didn't want to face the rather ironic look in her eyes, so I looked out the window. What I had just said brought a cascade of memories. *Huddled at the top of the stairs and gazing down through the bannister rails as Papa put on his overcoat. I could hear the rain thundering at the windows of the house and the wind moaning under the eaves. My mother's soft pleadings. "Please, Robert, you're sick. Call Judge Manley. He'll understand." My father's firm head shake. "No, we have the momentum now. I can win this."*

Later I learned he'd been running a hundred and two fever, but he was fighting against a large developer and the city in defense of a man protecting his pharmacy. He had won, and it had become part of our family's oral history. It meant he expected the same dedication from his kids. I couldn't count how many times I'd delivered papers when I had been sick, or played Little League with a sprained wrist or ankle. You didn't let people down who were counting on you.

I turned back from the window after briefly noting how the rabbit bush and dried, seared ragweed were starting to twitch in a rising wind.

I took a deep breath and said, "Look, you said you liked getting things out front, so I want to be completely honest about the Herculean task you're about to undertake." I gave Dagmar a smile, and I had a feeling it was singularly shit eating and apologetic. "I . . ." I coughed and took a sip of water. It was so hard to say this. "I never balance my checkbook."

Dagmar's voice caught on a laugh. "Well, that *is* shocking."

I held up a hand, but I couldn't help smiling because I was so relieved. "But wait. It gets worse. I've got *five* credit cards, and they're all maxed out."

I steeled myself for the reaction, but all she said was, "Well, those we should probably clear. It wouldn't do for the CEO of Lumina Enterprises to carry such a small amount of debt. When we carry debt, we carry a magnificent amount of it. Mr. Oort . . . Richard, may I call you Richard?"

"I'd prefer it. And it would be great if you didn't . . ." I bit back the rest of the sentence and felt myself blushing.

"What?"

I shook my head. "No, nothing."

Dagmar leaned back in her chair and regarded me. "I think I know what you were going to say, and no, what we discuss will remain between us."

"Thank you."

"As for balancing your checkbook—you're not going to be a bookkeeper. You have a CFO, chief financial officer, for that."

"I do know the differences between CEOs, COOs, and CFOs. I worked for a few months in a brokerage firm." I hated even mentioning it, and I quickly dropped my eyes. This woman saw a little too much for comfort.

"Good, then we're not starting from nowhere. Anyway, you have Mr. Fujasaki and his staff in Tokyo. Your task is to make the large decisions. You set our course, and it's my job as the chief operating officer to see that those decisions are carried out. So, now it's time for your questions."

"Okay. I looked for an annual report so I could get some sense of the company, I mean what it does. But I couldn't find one. So I dipped briefly into the books." Just remembering those lines of numbers made my head hurt. I pressed a hand against my forehead and pushed back my hair. "Wow."

"A lot of money, no?"

"A lot of money, yes."

"And you wouldn't find a report. Lumina Enterprises is that very rare beast, a privately held company. It has controlling interests in companies that are public companies, but the core company is required to report to no one. Our only contact with the wider public is that we pay taxes. As for what we do . . . Mr. Kenntnis's interests were in cutting-edge technology—biotech, high tech, private space ventures, open source code, alternate energy sources. Education—we fund pure science projects such as CERN, endow university science departments. And alleviating poverty, which Kenntnis considered to be the source of many of the world's ills—war, terrorism, overpopulation, pollution. One-third of our annual income is spent on various charitable efforts—building wells in sub-Saharan Africa, Doctors Without Borders, providing medicines to impoverished nations. It takes a lot of money to do good."

I'd known all this for weeks. Cross had given me some of the highlights when I'd first met him and Kenntnis, but it hadn't really registered because it didn't affect me. Now it sure as hell affected me, and I was the guy who couldn't balance his checkbook. I'd sometimes wondered what it would be like to be a Warren Buffet or a Bill Gates with the power to literally change lives. Now I had it. Except to keep doing it, this company had to keep making money, and I was the person in charge.

We were doomed.

I picked up a strawberry and brought it toward my mouth, but the smell was nauseating. I pulled it away and started spinning it by the stem. "Now I'm even more intimidated."

The stem suddenly broke. The strawberry hit the edge of the plate, bounced, and left a smear of red on the etched metal top of the table. I scrubbed away the stain with the tip of my forefinger, contemplated the red-tinged skin, and suddenly saw the blood in the Quincy house again. I jerked my thoughts away, and crashed against the crushing responsibility of Lumina that had been dropped on my shoulders.

"There are real consequences if I screw up." I gave her a sickly smile.

"So, don't screw up." But Dagmar softened it with a smile and then added, "What you told your father about Kenntnis can also be applied to you. He picked you for a reason. He must have had faith in your good sense and your integrity. Listen, you have smart, good people to help you." She scooted her chair in closer to the table and leaned across, taking one of my hands in hers. "Richard, the secret to running a company is both simple and hard to do. You find people smarter than you, and give them their heads to do their work."

"And how do I know if they're good people who I can trust?" It was the million-dollar question.

"You make decisions, and judge from people's reactions to those decisions if you want to keep that person working for you."

Dagmar released my hand, leaned back in her chair, and excavated the center ring of a cinnamon roll, popping the gooey chunk of dough into her mouth. She reminded me of a cat, comfortable, secure, and maybe a little bit complacent. She had me pegged as young and insecure. I wondered if that would change when I pulled out the sword. Or would she just add *nut* to the equation?

"Okay, I'm going to take your advice."

"Excellent."

"Starting with you."

"All right," but she sounded uneasy. I wondered what she was seeing in my face.

"So, it's pretty clear to me that you don't actually know the true purpose of the Lumina."

"I take it you do?"

"Yes."

She leaned back and opened her arms in an expansive gesture. "Enlighten me, please."

The gentle sarcasm was drilling onto a nerve, but I gritted my teeth and plowed on. "The company's just a front."

She laughed. "A front. Well, that's an interesting theory. What was Kenntnis doing that I didn't know about? Something naughty, I hope."

I hated that humoring tone, and how she was turning something deadly serious into a joke. I used the edge of the table to help lever myself to my feet. The laugh stuttered to a stop in the back of her throat as I stared down at her.

"No, something dangerous. Lumina was founded to combat magic, religion, superstition, and ignorance. And Kenntnis dedicated his life to it."

"Magic," Reitlingen said in an amused tone. "Well, it looks like he won that one."

"I'm going to let that go because you don't understand, but you will in a few minutes. One of my . . . associates said that I need to be certain of all my employees. I don't care about their honesty or yours, for that matter. You can all rob me blind, but I have to be sure that none of you will become a conduit for magic, or that you'll be ensorcelled and turned against me."

"All right, this has become silly and annoying—" and her voice had lost its jocularity.

"I am serious," I snapped. "Deadly serious."

I decided it was time for showing and not telling, so I drew the hilt of the sword out of the pocket of my bathrobe. The sunlight was beating on my back and head, and I felt sweat, born out of heat and nerves and annoyance, beginning to trickle down over my ribs with that horrible crawling sensation as if small insects are on your skin.

The chair shrieked across the stained concrete floor as Dagmar thrust it back and jumped to her feet. Fear tightened her features. "You will sit back down, and I am going to call your father," she began in a tone of voice that reminded me of animal trainers.

"Fine. Go ahead. He'll back me up. He's already submitted himself to this. All of my family and friends have. Now I'm asking . . . no, demanding, that you do so as well." I thought I had matched her tone of snapped command, but I wasn't sure.

"What happens if I refuse?" Dagmar asked.

Best to keep it simple. "I'll fire you."

Shock flickered across her face, followed by alarm and then rage. She finally got a smile pasted back into place and said with forced lightness, "Maybe I better find out what you're going to do before I refuse. It might be quite painless, although I'm guessing it's pretty eccentric."

"It's not painless, but I can't predict how much pain you'll feel. The amount of pain seems dependent on how much magic you possess," I said, and wished I hadn't added the last sentence. *Keep it simple. Keep it simple.*

Dagmar stood dithering. I could see her trying to decide if she'd humor me, send for my father, or just call for commitment papers right now. Sometimes a demonstration can save a thousand words. I swept my hand away from the base of the hilt. There was the strange basso *thrum* that shook deep in your chest and laid a pressure against the back of your eyes. Dagmar pressed a hand against her chest and took several gasping breaths.

"You're not having a heart attack," I said gently.

She looked up, and her eyes widened at the sight of the sword I was now holding. I took an instant to contemplate the long black blade filled with distant glittering lights that flowed up and down its length. Whenever I was in the presence of powerful magic, the lights would come out of the blade and form a spinning nimbus of light around the sword and even around me.

"And no, you're not hallucinating. I really am holding a sword." I felt like such an idiot just saying it. For, like, the millionth time I wished that Kenntnis could have recast his weapon into something less silly, archaic, and clichéd. But maybe it was a good thing he hadn't turned it into a gun. Then I would have been saying, *I'm going to shoot you with this gun.* Instead of saying, "I'm going to touch you with the sword." Her eyes widened, and I hurried to add, "Just with the flat side of the blade."

She started backing away. "No, no, I don't think you are."

Suddenly she turned and went running out of the kitchen and through the dining room. So much for my being in command of the situation. I let the blade vanish, stuffed the hilt back in my pocket, grabbed my crutches, and started in gimping pursuit. This was the first time I'd really tried to move fast, and it hurt. I felt the tearing in the stitches and the slow warm trickle of blood down my thigh. Yeah, this was going great.

I nearly caught up to her in the living room. Her high heel had twisted on the edge of the Oriental rug, and she stumbled into an Italian inlaid table. Yelping, she clutched at her knee, looked back at me. I advanced, and she limped frantically through the foyer and began punching the elevator button.

Maybe mad pursuit wasn't the best plan. I stopped under the archway. "Please, wait," I said in the gentlest, sanest tone I could muster. "Obviously I didn't explain things very well. Let me—"

Dagmar's eyes were darting around the foyer. She spotted the door to the stairwell. She ran to it, yanked it open, and vanished down the stairwell. I listened to her footfalls clattering and fading away down the steps. I hoped she didn't break her neck in those high heels. The elevator gave a gentle *ding* and arrived. I hobbled onto it, and dithered between the button for the office and the button for the lobby. I really didn't want my father to know how badly I had screwed this up. I'd try one more time to convince her. I punched the button for the lobby.

THIRTEEN

They were down to a Costco carton of peanut butter and cheese crackers, and had eaten two-thirds of the carton. Grenier's belly felt like an empty sack, and he was past being embarrassed by his stomach's angry rumbles. The trip west had taken much longer than anticipated since they had abandoned the interstate system just inside the borders of Oklahoma because of the crowds of people converging on Oral Roberts University. The plan had been to ride I-44 into Oklahoma City and then transfer to I-40 for the drive to Albuquerque, but the interstate heading into Tulsa was like L.A. on a bad day, and Syd had feared the wild, exalted expressions on the faces of the people.

Grenier couldn't blame him. He'd seen those faces in Serbia and Lebanon, India and Poland, and during government-mandated purges against the religious in China. The Old Ones used religious hatred as fuel for killing because it worked really well, but any kind of fervent, irrational belief that brooked no challenge worked, too. As long as the result was lots of hate, fear, and death, his former masters were indifferent to the source of the conflict.

So to avoid the faithful they had bailed out onto local roads, some no better than farm tracks, and headed south. The vast emptiness of Texas had been a challenge because gasoline was scarce, and the shelves in the groceries of the small towns through which they passed had been very bare. Eventually they quit stopping because of the covetous looks the RV received.

They had driven into the next wave of wild-eyed worshipers around the New Mexico town of Roswell, site of the supposed saucer crash in 1947. A tent city had sprung up in the desert, and everyone was watching the skies. The saucer nuts seemed less prepared than the religious nuts, and they were in a particularly hostile environment. It might be early January and colder than a witch's tit, but it was still the desert. As they drove past the seething crowds, Grenier could hear the low thunder of drums. It seemed some members of the Harmonic Convergence also believed in aliens. A group of young women were whirling in an elaborate dance at the side of the highway. Multicolored scarves, sparkling with sequins, trailed around them, and they sang in eerie high-pitched voices. The only other sounds that penetrated the windows of the RV were the piercing wails of young children and babies. Too young to be true believers, they just knew they were hungry, thirsty, and cold.

Syd had pressed his foot down on the gas. "What the hell is wrong with them?"

Because Grenier was tired and hungry and scared, he forgot himself and answered. "The gates are opening. It makes it harder for people to separate a fervent hope from an actual fact. And it's likely they'll get their wish. Something may come for them." He swallowed hard, remembering the faces and that now he had to fear them. "It just won't be what they expect."

"How to Serve Man shit, huh?" Syd asked, though he had neither expected nor wanted an answer.

They hadn't stopped in Roswell either.

Now they were driving up a long street lined with strip malls and cheap apartment buildings toward the towering gray granite face of the mountain. High up among the tumbled boulders was a seven-story office building. The western side glittered and sparkled, and it wasn't just the windows. Grenier realized the wall between the glass was lined with solar panels.

They left the last of the buildings behind and went winding up a curving driveway toward the building. *Lumina.* He had seen the building many times in photos. This was the first time in person. The one time Grenier had led a crusade in New Mexico, he'd stayed well south of Albuquerque and Kenntnis. Grenier had been a true sorcerer, and it was rumored that Kenntnis could sense magic. In fact it had been Cross, but the humans serving the Old Ones hadn't known that until Rhiana had been placed on the inside, close to Kenntnis.

There were cars in the parking lot, mostly hybrids and small, fuel-efficient vehicles, but it was relatively few cars when compared to the size of the building. As Syd eased them into a couple of parking spaces, Grenier saw the front door of the building burst open. A woman came running out.

She was frantically hopping and hobbling, and he realized she'd broken the heel on one of her boots. She stopped at the bottom of the steps that led up to the building's entrance, unzipped and yanked off her boot. She focused on the still rolling RV and came running toward them, waving her arms over her head.

"Help! Help, please."

Grenier and Syd exchanged glances, and the FBI agent opened his door. The woman jumped onto the first step and hung on to the hand grip, gasping for air.

"Please . . ." pant. "I need . . ." pant, pant. "A ride," pant. "Please." She had a slight German accent.

"Okay, ma'am, just calm down—" Syd began, but the woman interrupted.

"No time. I must get away!"

Syd stood up, the woman retreated back down the step, and Syd jumped down and caught her by the shoulders. "Whoa, whoa, why do you have to get away? What have you done?" His tone was sharp and suspicious.

It must be the nature of cops of every kind, in every place,

Grenier thought as he moved to get out of the RV. His belly gave a monstrous growl, and he belched. The gust of air across the back of his tongue carried the scent and faint taste of his last packet of peanut butter and cheese crackers.

The woman leaned back, trying to pull free. She looked angry. "I haven't done a damn thing. It's my boss . . . former boss. He's quite mad. He's got a sword—"

Syd's expression cleared and he smiled with relief. He squeezed past Grenier, who was exiting the RV. "Honey, Sam, he's here. Come on, you've gotta come out now."

Sam crept to the opening between the cab and the cabin, and peeked around with the air of a timid deer gazing fearfully into an open meadow. Tears welled up in her brown eyes and slowly spilled down her cheeks. "Come on, sweetie. You're going to be okay now," Syd said, ever so gently.

The woman standing barefoot on the cold asphalt was frowning up at the father and daughter. "Pardon me," Grenier said. She hurriedly stepped aside, and he stepped down with a grunt.

Syd had his arm around his daughter's waist now and was gently urging her toward the door of the RV. The German woman's eyes widened when she saw the large rifle that Sam cradled in her arms. The woman slumped and shook her head.

"First swords and now guns. Okay, the insanity seems to be spreading. Would someone please tell me what the hell is going on?"

But Syd ignored the question. Instead he was hurriedly walking Sam toward the building. His head was bent solicitously over hers, and Grenier heard the soothing murmur of endearments and encouragement. "It's okay, honey. We're almost there. You're going to be fine now."

The German stared in bemusement after them. Grenier cleared his throat. She turned to face him. "So, it looks like Richard didn't do a very good job of show-and-tell with the sword."

"Does everybody know about this fucking sword but me?" she burst out.

"A select few, and some of us have a more intimate knowledge than others." Grenier lifted his maimed arm, and smiled as he watched the woman move to the logical conclusion—he had lost his hand to that sword.

"Okay, I am definitely out of here," the woman said and started to walk away.

It suddenly dawned on Grenier that if Richard had wanted to touch this woman with the sword she must have some importance. He grabbed her by the upper arm, digging his fingers deep into her biceps.

"Four months ago I would have done everything in my power to hurry you on your way, but now, well, let's just say that if you give Richard an advantage in the coming battles, then you are going to stay." Grenier dropped his maimed arm over her shoulders and frog-marched her back toward the front doors.

Pamela hung up the phone and looked over at her father. "That was Sydney in the front lobby. Dagmar went running through like the hounds of Hell were after her. It looks like Richard messed things up."

Her father stood up from behind the desk, ripped off his reading glasses, and tossed them down on the piles of papers. "Come along."

When they stepped off the elevator in the lobby, a man's voice was echoing off the black marble and steel panels of the room.

"She went down to Virginia while I was in the hospital."

Richard was there, leaning on his crutches. There was a bloodstain at thigh height on his bathrobe. Her brother's entire focus was on the face of the older man who was pouring out words so quickly that it was hard to distinguish between them.

"By the time I figured out what was wrong with her you were gone." The "her" appeared to be a young woman with chin-length brown hair and wild brown eyes. The man was holding her by the wrist. She bucked and struggled like a hooked fish trying to break the line. Her free hand held a rifle, and that rifle was waving wildly.

"Sir, we need to secure that gun," said Estevan, one of the security guards. Pamela totally agreed.

"I told you it's not loaded," the man snapped. He turned back to Richard. "I really need you to do the thing with the sword. You'll do it, won't you?"

At that moment Dagmar and a fat man entered. He had amazing hazel eyes, and it looked like he'd once had good features, though they were now blurred under a layer of fat. His belly strained at the buttons of an expensive dress shirt. He looked vaguely familiar, but Pamela couldn't place him.

Her brother's reaction left no doubt that he knew the identity of the man. "You!" he said, and the single word was filled with loathing and an undercurrent of fear.

Pamela looked over at her father, but he was also staring at the man with hatred, at least equal to Richard's if not greater.

Richard spun on his good leg, putting himself within reach of the bemused security guard, and yanked Estevan's pistol out of its holster.

A lot of things happened all at once. Dagmar hit the floor. The man with the terrified, rifle-toting woman said, "Huh?" Rifle Girl began to scream. Sydney, the receptionist, joined in. Richard pointed the gun at the fat man.

Estevan said in agonized tones as he shifted nervously from foot to foot, "Sir! Sir! That one *is* loaded, sir!"

"Richard!" She shrieked out her brother's name. "What are you *doing*?"

The fat man was speaking, the words both furious and contemptuous. "Good God, what do you think I could do, here in your own stronghold? Assault you? I'm here to offer you my *help*."

"How dare you come here, sir! Leave at once!" Pamela's father commanded.

Pamela heard the clack of the front door's bar being depressed.

A new voice, a rich contralto, joined the cacophony, "Richard, what are you doing? You've opened your wound."

Angela rushed toward him. Hectic spots of color burned on each cheek, distinguishable despite her rich cocoa-colored skin. She stopped, confused by the sight of the gun, and followed the barrel to the fat man. "Oh shit, Grenier!"

Now Pamela realized who he was. At that point everyone started talking at once and Pamela couldn't untangle a single sentence.

"Shut up!"

It was Richard. His voice carried above the screaming, crying, and talking. *Guess all those singing lessons were good for something,* Pamela thought.

And, amazingly, everyone did.

FOURTEEN

The furnishings and art in the penthouse were stunning and made Grenier's possessions look like cheap Walmart crap in comparison. He'd loved the big stone and timber building on his estate in Virginia. The public rooms had been trailer park chic—blue velvet upholstered furniture and thick white pile carpet with bad modern religious art—but his private quarters had been beautiful. He'd collected eighteenth-century English furniture, silver, and paintings. He'd loved the hunting still-lifes, the way each feather on a dead bird had been so perfectly rendered, but his antiques paled in comparison with the objects in this room. Resentment clawed at the back of his throat. *Of course, I'm just a man, a mortal, and had only a few years to amass my fortune and collection. Kenntnis had had eons.*

He found himself mourning for his lost home and hating them all. Grenier moved away from the center of the room and took up a position against a bookcase. Resting his shoulders against the case, he watched the people swirling, clotting and breaking apart, like balls on a billiard table. Conversations flared and jumped from person to person without any connection or logic. He hoped Lumina wasn't always this disorganized. Perhaps it was his arrival that had thrown them into such total disarray, and perversely the thought made him feel better.

"What is this sword?" the German woman was asking.

Pamela, referring to Sam, said, "Can't somebody shut her up?" Grenier felt like he knew the sister. He'd studied her photo, her education, her cases in the public defender's office in Newport, her boyfriends and lovers, in his effort to understand Richard and find the key to breaking him.

"Who are you?" Judge Oort was demanding of Syd.

"You will help her, right?" Syd was yelling into Richard's left ear while Armandariz said into his right ear, "We need to redress your leg."

Grenier studied the coroner curiously. He had never actually met the woman. *Just nearly killed her when she came between Richard and one of my spells.*

Richard waved Armandariz off. "It can wait. We need to deal with . . ." Richard put a hand in the center of Syd's chest and pushed him back a step to get the former FBI agent out of his personal space. "What's her name?" he asked, nodding at the whimpering Sam.

"Sam," Syd provided.

"Samantha." Pamela Oort seemed to be testing out the name.

"Yeah, but never call her that. She hates it. The whole *Bewitched* thing," Syd babbled as he nervously patted his weeping daughter on the back.

Pamela sniffed and took herself off to sit on the piano bench.

Richard pulled the hilt out of the pocket of his bathrobe, swept his hand away from it, and the blade appeared. There was a flare of intense pain from Grenier's stump as he remembered that blade shearing through his wrist. Rage and tears beat at the back of his throat.

As it was drawn, musical overtones went echoing away into infinity. Sam stopped crying, lifted her head from her father's shoulder, and turned to face Richard. Richard said something to the young agent, but it was so low that Grenier couldn't hear the words. Then Richard touched her lightly on the shoulder with the blade. She cried out, shivered, and would have collapsed to the floor except for her father's supporting arms.

When Sam lifted her head from her father's shoulders, her eyes were clear, her expression calm, if a little bit defensive. The tears were gone. The German woman who'd tried to commandeer a ride dropped into an armchair. She looked shell-shocked.

Grenier was surprised when Richard limped over to confront him. Grenier had pegged the young paladin as a person who avoided confrontation at all cost.

"Why are you here? What do you want?" There was nothing soft in the delivery, and Richard stared defiantly up at him.

"Sanctuary . . . since we're in a medieval frame of mind," Grenier said, with a gesture from the sword in Richard's hand back toward Sam. "My former . . . associates take a dim view of failure."

"What failure?" Richard asked. "You bound Kenntnis." Bitterness lay over the words, but Grenier also heard the deeply buried fear and loss.

"Ah, yes, but I failed to deliver the sword. And in trying to deliver the sword I never got around to killing *you*." The young man before him blanched. It wasn't easy to hear someone so matter-of-factly discussing your death. "So, here I am. Throwing myself on your mercy because you're the only person who can protect me. And if the milk of human kindness doesn't work for you, you can try enlightened self-interest—you might find me useful."

"Tough! Get the fuck out of here, and I hope they *do* kill you," Armandariz said. Anger blazed in her brown eyes.

"Angela." The way Richard said her name demanded silence.

The coroner subsided, and Grenier realized that the young man actually had a commanding presence, but seemed totally unaware of it.

"Taking him in makes a certain degree of sense," the judge said in his dry, precise way from his position on the sofa. "But only if you can trust him. Do you think you can trust him, Richard?"

"Probably not, sir." Richard turned back to Grenier. "Still he has knowledge and information that we need. I think we have to take the risk."

The timid fawn look was back in the blue eyes, as if Richard were already second-guessing his decision. The coroner kept silent, but she still managed to make her feelings known. She threw her hands in the air and stalked away.

Across the room, Sam shook off her father's embrace. "I'm fine. I'm fine now. Really." Her tone and expression radiated embarrassed defiance.

The judge stood. "Richard needs to have that wound dressed again. Many of you have been traveling. We can reconvene after you've all had something to eat."

The plan was met with universal approval. Grenier joined the move toward the arch separating dining room and living room. The judge caught him by the sleeve, holding him back.

"Your Honor, so good to see you again," Grenier said.

The last time they had met, they had been in Grenier's office at his compound and Grenier had been trying to kill the elder Oort with a series of magical spells. But the remark didn't elicit a rise. The judge's control was better than his son's.

"I've had the chance to observe you over the years," Oort said, referring to political events in Washington they had both attended. "My impression was that you were an opportunist. So I expect you can be trusted, at least until someone makes you a better offer. Just be aware that I will never let you accept that new offer."

"A threat? Judge, I thought you were a great liberal defending the rule of law," Grenier answered.

"You shattered those rules when you joined forces with those *things*. And on a very personal level—your people drove my wife to suicide. You imprisoned and tortured my son. I won't allow you to betray us. Have I made myself clear?"

"Very."

FIFTEEN

RICHARD

Lying on your stomach on a bed with your pajama bottoms pulled down to your knees makes you feel either naughty or vulnerable. Unfortunately, vulnerable was winning. My face was pressed into the pillow, and my hands gripped the corners of the pillowcase as Angela probed the wound. I hissed softly, and then her latex-sheathed fingers hit a particularly painful spot. I yelped, and bit the corner of the pillow to avoid any more embarrassing outbursts. The fabric tasted faintly of detergent, and my mouth was already Sahara dry from tension and pain. Chewing on a flannel pillowcase wasn't helping.

Grenier.

I should have kept thinking about the taste of the pillow. Instead my mind went skipping back to Virginia. I could hear the *spark* as Grenier had brushed those stripped electrical wires together. My muscles tightened as if I were once again struggling against the thin cord that had bound me in that straight-backed chair. The cords had cut so deep that blood had trickled along the sides of my hands. Maybe in time I could have used the slick blood to help me worm out of the knots, but I had been distracted by the use the wires had been put to. Just the memory had my scrotum tightening, and my testicles trying to retreat deep into my belly.

And I'm letting him stay.

There was firm pressure as Angela pressed an antiseptic pad onto the hole left by the bullet's exit. What was I doing allowing the man to stay, even temporarily? My brain began a schizophrenic argument.

But he's worked among them. Served the Old Ones. He might be able to help.

But we've already nurtured one traitor. Rhiana had been planted on us. What if Grenier is the same?

But they wouldn't try the same thing twice. They would know that the members of the Lumina would never fall for that again.

Oh really? You're falling for it right now.

Self-doubt and second-guessing is the worst. It felt like a vise had been wrapped around my head and was slowly tightening.

"The sutures have cut into the edges of the skin," Angela said, interrupting my whirling thoughts. Her hand slipped under my knee, and she applied the surgical tape over the dressing. There was the sucking, snapping sound of surgical gloves being stripped off; then a warm palm was laid on my buttocks. "Nice buns. It's been a while since I've seen them."

"Angela!" Thanks to her wandering hands, memories of the last time we'd been in a bedroom together came forcing their way into my thoughts. It had been so damn humiliating . . . a sexual disaster . . .

She bent down, putting her face on a level with mine. "You've got a respite until you recover, but after that . . ." She kissed me.

Her lips were soft and tasted of honey from the lip balm she wore, and I felt like I was drowning. Angela pulled back, looking alarmed. I realized I was gasping for breath.

"Somehow I don't think this is passion," she said. "Anxiety?" I managed a nod. I didn't have enough air to speak. "I'll write a prescription and send Estevan."

The hammering of my heart filled my ears. I couldn't wait for Estevan to drive to Walgreens and come back. I couldn't breathe. I was going to vomit. I caught her wrist and managed to say, "I've got something. Xanax. In a pillbox in the drawer." I indicated the bedside table.

As she pulled out the silver and enamel box, I remembered the day my mother had bought it for me. The family was spending Christmas in Germany, skiing and enjoying the Old World celebrations. We had gone to Rothenburg to shop because the weather was so bad we couldn't ski. Snow was swirling down the narrow, crooked cobblestone streets. Overhead, the upper stories of the medieval houses almost touched.

Many of the buildings had been converted into shops. It was in an antique store that we had seen the eighteenth-century snuffbox. The picture on the lid was of a man's face. He wore a tricorn hat, a powdered wig, and a domino mask. The eyes behind the mask were made from two tiny sapphire chips. There was something in the smile that curved his lips, and the way the gem chips flashed, that I found fascinating. I wondered who he had been. If this had been his snuffbox. When I opened presents on Christmas, this had been wrapped as a birthday present. I had used it as a pill case ever since that fifteenth birthday.

The five-pointed white pills seemed to be rebuking me. Not all that long ago I was priding myself on resisting using the drug. *But that was before Kenntnis was captured and all this got dumped on me.*

I was suddenly afraid that Angela would read my anxiety as rejection. Of course it was, but I didn't want her to know that, so I quickly said, "This isn't about you kissing me."

"I know that, it's about you having to save the world. But my kissing you sure does kick over your neurosis."

She was looking so hurt that I couldn't help it. I closed my fingers tightly around her hand. Her skin was slightly slick from the residue of powder from the glove. "I'm sorry. Thank you for hanging in there with me. I know I'm a lot of trouble, but someday things will settle down and we'll have a chance to really spend time together . . . figure things out." It was an awkward conclusion and elicited the response it deserved.

"Yeah, like that's going to happen anytime soon," Angela said sourly.

SIXTEEN

"In order to understand Richard, you really need to understand his relationship with his father." The speaker was of medium height with graying brown hair and a neatly trimmed Elizabethan-style beard and mustache. He was handsome and very well dressed and had a clipped accent that reminded Rhiana of Richard.

Drew Sandringham sat on one side of the small table in the bar of the Beekman Tower Hotel. Rhiana and Jack sat across from him. Through the wide windows Rhiana had a view across Manhattan. The UN Building caught the light off the East River. Directly across and some ten floors down from their aerie, a woman in a housecoat wandered out the door of her condo and into the tiny rooftop garden. She was a doll-like figure.

"Oh?" Jack said in that encouraging tone that invites more comment.

"Of course it's terrible pop psychology," Sandringham said with a short laugh. "But in this case it is spot-on. Richard has spent his life trying to please Robert and win his approval, without, I might add, any notable success."

The sun appeared to be impaled on the tops of the more distant skyscrapers. Out over the river the clouds were tinged pink, peach, and blue. The light of the setting sun turned concrete and glass into spikes of gold and crystal. It was all breathtakingly beautiful. Rhiana tried to reconcile her old life with the new. The new one had advantages. Money, luxury, power. It also had stress beyond belief. Maybe it was better when she just felt deprived and resentful. At least she could dream. Now she only seemed to have nightmares. Sandringham's voice recalled her to her surroundings.

"Richard tends to form attachments with older men who can fill that father void. I know." He gave them a flash of perfect white teeth, and with a forefinger traced the line of his perfect mustache.

"And you know this how?" Rhiana didn't like the proprietary nature of the man's smile.

"Richard worked for me for a few months after his return from the conservatory in Rome. He had a master's in voice and piano, but he was a little old to start on the competition circuit, and his vocal auditions never yielded any roles. I'm sure some of that was his height. Tenors tend to be short, and female singers tend to be very, very large, and Richard is slight as well as short. I also think some of it was his insecurity. You need one hell of an ego to hold a stage for three-plus hours. Richard has always tried to be overlooked. Hard to do when he's so very handsome." Sandringham paused for a swallow of whiskey.

Rhiana wondered why Sandringham was talking so much. It seemed like an excess of information. Her drink arrived. Rhiana took a cautious sip.

"How do you like that one?" Jack asked.

"It's good." The nutmeg and cream damped down the sharp taste of the brandy. Rhiana had another sip.

They all waited until the waiter left the glass verandah.

"Anyway, Robert asked me to hire Richard as a favor to him. Robert and I were at Harvard together, and were close friends, so I was happy to oblige."

"But he only lasted a few months?" Jack asked.

"Yes. Richard was a dead loss as a stockbroker."

Jack and Rhiana's research before this meeting had fleshed out the bare-bones information that Sandringham owned an investment firm. They now knew that it was a boutique firm with a list of very wealthy, very private clients, both foreign and American. They knew that Sandringham had divorced more than twenty years ago and never remarried. There were whispers that he was gay, but others they had spoken to attributed those rumors to spite and jealousy engendered by his success. Rhiana had wondered why this successful, well-connected man would ever agree to talk to them, but when Jack had said they had some questions regarding Richard Oort, the man had immediately suggested the Beekman Tower.

"Who got blamed for Richard's failure? You or Richard?" Jack asked.

"Robert knew who to blame." Was that the faintest hint of glee? Rhiana couldn't really tell. Sandringham hurried on. "Not to say that Robert hasn't been unfair at times." Sandringham sighed and took another sip of his whiskey. "Still, it must be difficult being the longed-for son, and ending up such a disappointment. Fairly or not," came the hurried addition.

"In what way?" Jack asked

"Well, Richard's been totally outstripped and eclipsed by his sisters. Amelia a surgeon, Pamela an attorney, and then there's Richard . . . a cop. After all the opportunities Robert gave the boy."

Rhiana was at a loss. The note in Grenier's office had seemed to portend something, but there wasn't anything here.

"Well, he's left the girls in the dust now," Jack said, weighting the words to give them significance. Rhiana shot him a glance, wondering where he was going with this.

Sandringham arranged his features into an expression of polite inquiry. "Oh?"

"Yeah, he's the head of Lumina Enterprises."

Rhiana shouldn't have been surprised that an investment broker would recognize the name. There was a flash of some indescribable emotion deep in Sandringham's eyes. The businessman took a long swallow of Scotch.

"Well, that's quite a lot to take in," Sandringham said slowly.

"Yeah, little bastard," Jack said softly. He leaned in across the small table. "Go on, you can say it."

The man's mouth worked for a few seconds; then he burst out, "This is unbelievable!" And the floodgates opened. "That little cocksucker threatened me ... threatened *me* as if I were some kind of common criminal. And then talked, breaking a thirty-year friendship irretrievably. I'll never forgive him."

"What happened?" Jack asked. His voice was warm and inviting, exuding comfort and inviting trust.

Sandringham lowered his voice and took a quick glance around. The only other occupied table was across the verandah. "Richard and I were lovers."

The words struck Rhiana hard. *But he was attracted to me. I know he was.* Rhiana remembered the time she had bandaged Richard's burned hands. She had watched his cock stiffen, pressing against the zipper of his trousers. She had felt his quickening breaths brushing across her hair and cheek.

She had lost the thread of the conversation. When she started listening again Sandringham was saying, ". . . a dinner party for a couple of clients. Things got a little rough. I didn't mean for it to happen, but Richard blamed me. He quit, and we haven't spoken in four years. Not until he threatened me last month. Then a few weeks ago Robert called and told me he was taking his business elsewhere. He was so cold. When I pressed him to tell me why, he said what I'd done to Richard was unforgivable, and that we would not speak on this or any other matter ever again." The man looked honestly hurt.

"Do you think Robert knows that you and Richard were intimate before this incident?" Jack asked.

Sandringham considered that. "I don't think so. He made it sound like I was some kind of rapist."

"Mr. Sandringham, what if I told you we, Rhiana and I, have the power to give you virtually anything you want? Life-changing

113

money. Power. Love, well, at least sex." Jack gave his charming smile.

"I would say I'd like some proof. I'd also say if it means doing Richard a bad turn, you don't have to give me anything at all."

"Well, we'd like to have a man like you in our camp, and we want to see you happy."

"What do you want me to do?" Sandringham asked.

"Break Richard." Sandringham smiled and nodded. Jack continued, "One more thing. We're trying to keep the pressure on Richard and the company until we can"—Jack gave a smile that was all teeth—"bring him down. Any suggestions?"

"Oh, you leave that to me. Richard's family offers a plethora of opportunities."

"Fine, we'll leave it to you. All of it."

Jack held out his hand, and Rhiana took it. She was still trying to cope with what she'd learned. They took a few steps, only to be stopped by Sandringham asking, "Who are you people?"

Jack smiled again. "The new world order."

On the elevator Rhiana watched the numbers flare to life and then die again as they dropped through the forty-two floors.

"Do you still want him?" Jack's voice was quiet.

"Yes."

"You can't change him."

"Maybe not." She paused, feeling the pressure against the soles of her boots as the elevator slowed and stopped. "But I can own him."

SEVENTEEN

Eventually they adjourned back into the living room. Grenier's belly rested on his thighs and pressed painfully against the waistband of his trousers. Once again he had overeaten. He felt so empty all the time now that his magic had been stripped away. He wiped his fingertips across his eyes, removing the betraying moisture. Overt emotionalism also seemed to be a symptom of his loss. For a moment he hated Richard, cursed the Old Ones, and thought back over the actions he'd taken in those final hours. Thought how he could have done things better. How one small change would have given him the victory.

He reached up and surreptitiously unbuttoned his pants, and gave a gusting sigh of relief as his distended belly bulged free. Grenier felt embarrassed over his lack of self-control, but it really didn't matter any longer. He no longer had to face the tyranny of the television cameras, so he could indulge himself. Sometimes it was hard to look at the image in the mirror. He had been a very handsome man. That was gone now, hidden behind a layer of lard.

On the other hand, he no longer had to mouth platitudes to the believers and launch verbal grenades at political and spiritual opponents on his nightly television show. He felt a surprising surge of relief.

And I'll never again have to kneel with blubbering politicians as they use me as a Band-Aid for their latest financial or sexual indiscretion. I'd call that a silver lining. And that thought enabled him to face Richard's entrance into the living room with a degree of equanimity.

The young man had dressed, gray slacks, a silk turtleneck beneath a beautiful Norwegian sweater. The elaborate colors of the pattern gave a bit of color to his pale face. Sam watched him with frowning concentration. The Kraut pulled a set of Turkish worry beads from her handbag. The beads were amber, and they gave small clicks as she fingered them. Grenier wondered if she was a former smoker who'd found a new hobby for her nervous hands.

Armandariz took the crutches from Richard. The judge supported Richard into the leather-upholstered recliner and carefully raised the leg support. He obviously wasn't gentle enough, for a grimace of pain flashed across that handsome face. Once he was settled, Richard looked at them all and gave a small smile.

"So, are introductions in order, or have you handled all that?" he asked.

There were murmurs of assent, but then the young FBI agent spoke up. Her tone was belligerent. "All except you. I haven't met you."

"How do you do? I'm Richard Oort," he said and inclined his head.

"I know your name. I want to know what you did to me," Sam demanded.

"I used a device, a weapon to remove your ability to ever do magic. One of the side effects is that it also restores sanity, provided the mental illness isn't due to a chemical imbalance."

"Blah, blah, blah. But what does that *mean*? I mean, really? I know that whatever you did hurt like hell, but I'm not scared anymore. Well, I'm scared, but I'm not scared of *everything* anymore, and I understand *why* I'm scared."

"Yes, it's sensible to be scared of monsters," Richard said with another smile.

The judge laid a hand briefly on his son's shoulder. Richard gave his father a startled look, and Grenier got the feeling this was not a family that indulged in gestures of physical affection. "Richard, you have three people who know nothing about the real state of the world. I think giving the full lecture would not be amiss."

Richard pressed a hand briefly to his forehead. "I don't even know where to start. Kenntnis gave you the lecture," he said, looking appealingly up at his father. "Maybe you—"

"You are the head of the Lumina."

Grenier settled himself more comfortably on the sofa and laced his hands over his belly. "And I'm here to offer a little insight into the other side," he said loudly. "We'll muddle through."

Richard closed his eyes. The silence stretched on and on. Grenier wondered what the young man was thinking, feeling. Finally, with a sigh, Richard opened his eyes and looked at them.

"Our world, our universe and this dimension, or multiverse as Kenntnis called it, is under attack by creatures from other dimensions."

He laid it out in a bald, uncompromising statement. Not surprisingly Sam and Dagmar had the look of people humoring a mental patient. Richard, empathetic, sensitive to others, and painfully insecure, read their reaction. He stuttered into hurried speech.

"There are a lot of other dimensions. Multiverses. I don't exactly remember how many, Kenntnis told me, somewhere in the twenties, I think. Anyway, there are points where they connect with our universe. There are creatures in those other multiverses, and ever since we first stood upright they've been pushing through the barriers between the universes and feeding on us."

"Feeding how?" Sam asked. "What the fuck does that mean?"

"They feed on emotional energy," Grenier said, deciding to throw Richard a lifeline. "And those of us who served them also learned to feed. It's a heady sensation. Every human has a little of it. It's why we love to look at car wrecks, why schadenfreude is such a wonderful emotion."

"Point being that the Old Ones don't like good emotions,"

Richard said, and Grenier realized the young man was trying to wrest back control. Grenier smiled inwardly. It was going to be fun playing tug-of-war for the conversation.

"Kenntnis once said that we're unique in how we experience love and joy," Richard continued. "But fear and hate, pain and suffering, those we all share alike, and sadly they are very easy to engender. These creatures stoke the flames of ethnic hatreds. They push us to kill over skin color. Most pernicious of all, they urge us to kill in the name of our gods." Passion had brought color into the sensitive face, a ring into the voice, and his pale eyes glittered.

Grenier glanced at the other listeners, wanting to judge their reactions. The sister was looking at her brother as if seeing a stranger. There was both pride and discomfort on Robert Oort's face. *Yes, you hate strong emotion, don't you, you rigid prick?*

The worry beads had fallen, forgotten, into Dagmar's lap. Angela's hands were tightly clasped, her lips parted; quick breaths lifted her breast. Sam stared. The three women who were unrelated to Richard gazed at him with varying degrees of attraction and arousal. Grenier wondered if Richard was aware of the reaction he was causing. Grenier suspected he was. He wondered how it made Richard feel.

Syd glanced at the walls of the penthouse as if expecting them to collapse in on them. "What about natural disasters? Like those tsunamis and earthquakes and stuff?" he asked.

Pamela gave the agent a sardonic look. "I think the operative word in that is 'natural.'"

"Oh, there are weather spells." Grenier enjoyed watching the Oort girl blanch briefly. "But they're the toughest magical spells to weave, so we don't try them very often. And an earthquake spell . . ." Grenier shook his head. "It would take an enormous amount of power, and if you guessed wrong you might crack the planet. Remember, we want you to *suffer*, not be annihilated."

Richard gave him a cold-eyed stare. "You might want to

remember that you're one of the sufferers now." Ice edged each perfectly enunciated word.

Grenier *had* forgotten, and for an instant he hated the young man for making him remember. He gave Richard a smile from the teeth out. "We should all also recall that magic isn't the only way they accomplish their goals. For that we've got politics."

"I always knew the Republicans were the spawn of Satan," Angela quipped.

"And your boys on the left are very good at hand wringing and shedding crocodile tears without—"

"Let's not have this reduced to political and partisan squabbling," the judge interrupted. "We have bigger problems."

"Let's get back to this eating thing," Syd said. "Why not just feed on cows heading into the slaughterhouse?"

"I think it has to do with cognition," Richard replied. "Cross said that when a species develops a cerebral cortex it attracts the Old Ones. Apparently part of the pleasure is the prey's awareness of what's happening to them. Blind animal panic isn't good enough."

"So, what do they eat when they can't get us?" Sam asked.

Richard shook his head. "I don't know. Each other, maybe." Grenier found himself on the receiving end of that blue-eyed gaze. "Do you have any insights you'd like to share with the class?" Richard asked.

Grenier stood and took up a position in the center of the room. "I know they're not all the same. I know rivalries exist. I can't guess how deep they go, or if they prey on each other." He was suddenly acutely aware of his unbuttoned pants. "My magic enabled me to use mirrors to thin the barriers between the dimensions. That's where the Old Ones and I would communicate. That's been the extent of my contact. Well, until recently."

"*Through a glass darkly,*" Richard said softly, quoting Corinthians.

"Exactly," Grenier said. The zipper on his fly began a slow, inexorable slide under the pressure from his belly. He folded his hands in front of his crotch.

"So that's why the mirrors in the trailer, and in C. Springs, and at your compound were all occluded," Angela said. "None of our forensic tests could ever tell us what had done that."

"It was the touch of the Old Ones. They're not natural to our universe, and so they have a destructive effect on our reality," Grenier said hurriedly. He hustled back to the sofa, and zipped his pants while Richard continued.

"Thousands of years ago there were actual gates between the dimensions constructed by the Old Ones, and they passed back and forth with relative ease. Then Kenntnis came—I don't exactly know when—and with the help of people like me, and this"— Richard lifted the hilt—"the gates were closed. There were still incursions, but they were more like rips or tears in the fabric of reality. Some of the Old Ones on this side of the dimensional barriers were killed, but others became so powerful that they couldn't be banished or destroyed with just the sword. I should add that that's purely conjecture on my part, but it's the only thing that makes sense."

"So, do we have a method for killing gods and myths?" Pamela asked, and it was half a question, half ironic statement.

Grenier looked at this Oort daughter with interest. Here, it seemed, was a sharp and satirical nature akin to his own. He spoke up. "It's possible that a rejection of them by humanity, together with the sword, might do the trick. But I don't think it would be easy. Some researchers think there's a god gene."

"I thought your crowd rejected science," Angela said.

"No, we *fear* science," Grenier corrected. "As the bright boys and girls keep answering the questions and dispelling the mysteries, it gets harder and harder for those of us in the pulpit to keep the sheep believing."

"So every priest, every minister—" Syd began.

"No, I don't think so," Richard said quickly. "Not all of them are cynical manipulators like him," and he nodded toward Grenier. "I've met men and women of faith who served the ideal of a loving, forgiving, generous god that had been fostered by Kenntnis, and they've done a great deal of good in the world."

Cross walked into the living room. "I believe I heard my cue." He grinned and nodded at Richard. "Is my timing impeccable, or what?"

"It's something," the young man said dryly, but he smiled.

Grenier studied the Old One curiously. It was a fractal, a splinter of the greater creature that kept dividing itself, as Judaism spawned Christianity which spawned Islam. A traitor to his own kind, Cross had thrown in his lot with Kenntnis.

Cross looked at Syd. "Consider how you've progressed as a species. You've gone from human sacrifice to animal sacrifice to ritualistic sacrifice, and if Kenntnis had succeeded you would have learned to be merciful and generous to each other because it would be the right thing to do."

"And not out of the fear of Hell or the promise of Heaven," Richard added softly.

"Of course I don't think you humans have it in you. But Kenntnis was the eternal optimist," Cross concluded.

Angela jumped in and asked Cross, "Aren't you surprised to find Grenier here?"

"Nah. He's a rat and we're the only high ground."

She wasn't giving up on enlisting allies to change Richard's mind. "Do you think it's a good idea to let him in?"

The homeless god shrugged. "Sure, why not. He might be helpful." The little coroner looked disgusted and subsided.

Richard turned to Dagmar. "As I said to you earlier, Lumina isn't just a business. The company is a front for an ancient and secret society that has fought against these creatures for millennia. Kenntnis threw all of his wealth and power behind the quest for knowledge because he believed that science and rationality would ultimately trump magic, religion, and superstition. But now Kenntnis has been effectively neutralized as a force in our world, and the gates are opening again."

Grenier cleared his throat. "And in this brave new world the

Old Ones will probably meet people's fondest expectations. Angels will fly and saucers will land, and magic will actually work."

"Not everyone who says they've been abducted by aliens is a nut. We've been taking humans for millennia."

"Why?" the judge asked.

"To breed more magic into your genetic code," Cross answered. "The more magic you have, the deeper into you we can reach. That's how we got stuck with that bitch Rhiana. She's the result of a long breeding operation—half human, half us."

"The genetic angle is why Kenntnis so heavily funded stem cell research," Richard said, directing the statement at Dagmar. "He was trying to find a way to erase those genes."

"Would that make everyone like you?" Pamela asked her brother.

"Possibly . . . maybe . . . I don't know."

"What do you mean, like you?" Sam asked belligerently. Grenier wondered if she was reacting against her attraction to Richard. "How are you any different from the rest of us?"

No, not rejected passion, Grenier decided; the young FBI agent just hated not being the most gifted, most talented, toughest person in the room. And she was still smarting under the knowledge that the gate had driven her mad.

The flush washed up into Richard's pale cheeks as he reacted to the hostility, but embarrassment was also a component of his discomfort. *Yes, little man, you are different and you hate it. You also invited it; the East Coast blue blood walking a cop's beat.* Grenier longed to say the words out loud, but Cross broke in.

"He's an 'empty one,' born without a scrap of magic."

"A magic spell per se has no effect on me. I can be hurt by the results of the spell—if you pull electricity from a wall socket the electricity can hurt me, for example—but you can't put a glamour on me, or use a spell to convince me I'm in love with somebody."

"We also can't feed on him," Cross said. "He's a cipher to us."

"The real importance of my genetic makeup is that I can use

this." Richard again lifted the hilt of the sword. "I can draw it."

"Yeah, but you removed my magic, so I ought to be able to use it now, too," Sam said. The challenge hung in the air.

Angela jumped in. "It doesn't work that way. You've had your magic negated, but you still carry the genetic code. You can't use the sword."

It was clear from the young agent's expression that she neither liked the answer nor believed it. Richard proved again he could read nuance. "If you don't believe us, you're welcome to try."

Richard tossed the hilt to Sam, who caught it with the grace and quickness of a cat seizing a bird out of the air. She studied the hilt, then laced her fingers through the curves and looked inquiringly at Richard.

"Place your free hand against the base of the hilt. Pull the hilt away as if you're drawing a sword from a scabbard," he instructed.

"I'll cut my hand."

"You won't get that far," Richard said. "Even if you could draw it you wouldn't get cut. It doesn't cut me. And don't ask me why because I don't know."

"So it is because of this . . . this thing . . . that Kenntnis has left you his entire business?" Dagmar asked while Sam swept the hilt over and over away from her hand to no result.

"Yes. I guess." The tag once again diluted the effect of a man in charge.

"*Mein Gott,*" the German repeated again.

It took Sam another few minutes of trying before she accepted the truth of Richard's statement. *So,* thought Grenier, *she's quick, coordinated, and very stubborn.* Finally, she admitted defeat and returned the hilt to Richard.

"Well, this kind of sucks," Sam said.

"On the plus side, you're not finger-licking good anymore," Cross said.

"What!?" Sam said. It emerged as an incredulous squeak.

"We can't feed on you after you've been touched. Well, when you die you can feed us. Death sort of trumps all the other emotions," Cross said. "Speaking of . . . is there anything to eat in this joint?"

Richard pointed toward the kitchen, and Cross left.

"So now you have a general idea of the state of things," Richard said. "My biggest fear is what happens to the world with Kenntnis out of it. Cross said something once that made me think that Kenntnis might be like a platonic ideal, or the rationality. And it does seem that since his capture people are having a harder and harder time keeping a grip on reality."

"So what you're saying is that people are going to start living in their own private David Lynch movies," Sam said.

Grenier entered the conversation again. "They won't be just private delusions. Before Richard sheared away my power"—he held up his stump, and was pleased when Richard flushed—"I could feel the power rushing past me like flowing water. It wasn't hard to dip in, and have the power to do almost any kind of spell. That's a big change. Before Kenntnis was bound I had to engineer the appropriate fear, pain, grief, or hate; I would feed, and then cast the spell. You're going to see a lot of strange and inexplicable things happening, and each time they happen it will weaken the fabric of our reality."

"Yes, but don't you have to learn how to do these spells?" Pamela asked. "I can't believe I just said that," she added. She pressed a hand against her forehead (it seemed to be a learned and shared gesture of the Oorts) and shook her head.

"Before the loss of Kenntnis, yes," Grenier answered. "But now I rather suspect that a supreme act of personal will will suffice."

"Monsters from the id," Angela muttered.

"So our most pressing issue is freeing Kenntnis," Richard said.

The judge entered the conversation. "I believe we had this conversation before. On Christmas Eve you said we needed a physicist to advise us since Kenntnis is trapped by this slow glass. Do we have a physicist?" The words were pointed.

The blood rushed into the young man's face, and he hung his

head. "No, sir. I'm sorry, I should have done that."

Well, damn, thought Grenier. *I wish I had known about this little family dynamic before. I could have brought Richard to his knees in no time. I applied pressure at all the wrong points.*

Of course, now that Grenier was in New Mexico and had thrown in his lot with the Lumina, he badly needed Richard to be strong and tough and decisive. Which meant he was going to have to find a way to buffer the young man from the Right Honorable Robert Oort.

Dagmar suddenly stood and walked over to Richard. "That's for another day. Right now it is more important that you have the loyalty and support of all your people." Grenier couldn't be sure, but he thought she glanced briefly at the judge.

The German continued. "Allow me to be the first of your employees to accept your condition of employment, sir," and she leaned down so Richard, from his seated position, could more easily touch her with the sword.

EIGHTEEN

RICHARD

" Think of it as a drug test," Dagmar said.

The man—I risked a surreptitious glance down at the employee list: Fred Mickelson—blinked rapidly as if processing the words. Mickelson was tall, with a sunken chest and an incongruous little kettle belly. He had been sitting in the high-backed leather chair that faced the desk, but then rose jerkily to his feet and stood, shaking his head.

"No, this is too weird."

For an instant I thought about saying this had been in the instructions Kenntnis left for me, but I was a terrible liar, and it would only make a bad situation worse. I hadn't lost that many employees with my strange request. I could afford to lose Fred. But Dagmar wasn't giving up without a fight.

"Look, I'll go first," Dagmar offered. "Just to show you it's fine."

I shifted my grip on the hilt of the sword, picked up my cane with my right hand, and pushed to my feet. After some discussion we had all agreed that the appearance of a blade out of nowhere would rattle even the most loyal and unflappable of employees. So the sword had been drawn before Fred entered the office, on the theory that coping with only one weird thing—a boss asking to touch them with a sword—would be less upsetting than dealing with the whole strange package.

Now they just have to cope with the fact that I seem to be a total nut job, I thought as I limped up to Dagmar and laid the blade of the sword on her shoulder.

Since Dagmar had already experienced the sword, she was able to bear the touch with equanimity. That had been another debate, about whether Dagmar should react as if she were in pain when we put on the little show. We decided she shouldn't.

"Better to cut the puppy's tail off all at once instead of by inches," had been Weber's opinion, while Pamela's attitude had been, *"Better to receive forgiveness than ask permission."*

However it was phrased, I was starting my tenure as head of the Lumina by lying to my people. Somehow I bet that was not in a Tony Robbins video.

I pivoted on my cane and cocked an inquiring eyebrow at Mickelson. The only thing that had made this even remotely bearable was that the pain experienced by the employees who had allowed themselves to be touched by the sword had been much less than Angela's and Weber's. Which suggested that Kenntnis had used Cross's ability to "see" magic, and deliberately hired people who had a low quotient of magical aptitude. I reminded myself to ask the homeless god if that was true the next time he wandered through.

I wish Cross had found a different paladin, too. Why did I ever go down that alley that night? If I'd just called for backup.

You couldn't, the radio didn't work.

I could have driven away.

Couldn't, the car had died.

And once I had heard Rhiana's scream of terror there was no question about whether I was going down that access alley between the buildings. But why couldn't it have been a rapist? No, it had to be monsters.

Mickelson's voice drew me back to my surroundings. "I have to do this if I'm going to keep my job?"

"Yes, I'm afraid so. But if you wish to leave you'll receive a generous severance package," I said.

"Okay. I'll do that. I've enjoyed working here, and Mr. Kenntnis had his odd quirks, but this is too strange."

I propped my cane against the side of the desk and held out my hand. "I quite understand." We shook, and Mickelson's palm was slick with sweat. I guess this was a real Hobson's choice—do something nuts or lose your job. I actually respected Mickelson. Telling me to piss up a rope had taken some guts.

"Jeannette will arrange all the financial details," Dagmar said.

Mickelson headed for the door.

In addition to money I felt I owed the man some warning. "Fred." He looked back at me while his fingers nervously explored his shirt buttons. "Look, be careful. Outside these walls things are . . ." I mentally picked up, considered, and discarded a number of words. *Crazy, dangerous, perilous, threatening.* I decided on ". . . unsettled."

The accountant nodded and left.

Dagmar pulled her Palm out of a pocket and checked the screen, then her watch. "Shall I set up the call with Kenzo?"

It took me a moment to place "Kenzo" in the bewildering array of people who now seemed to work for me. Kenzo Fujasaki, Lumina's CFO. Right. Check. Oh, no, I so didn't want to talk to him. I shook my head, set the hilt on the desk, and watched the blade vanish. I still found it unnerving, and I wondered where it went.

"Put him off for another day."

Dagmar had a mouth like a strawberry, full and soft, but now those lips compressed into a tight line. It felt like people got that expression a lot when dealing with me. "Sir, events are streaming past us. We've got bank closures in the Far East, price controls being set by the EU, borders being sealed. Every market is fluctuating wildly. We need to transfer and stabilize assets."

Uncertainty became a fluttering deep in my gut. If Lumina Enterprises collapsed financially I wouldn't have the resources to combat the Old Ones. But what I *really* needed for this fight was Kenntnis, not money.

I said as much and then added, "I've got to get him out of this slow-glass stuff if we're going to have a snowball's chance."

Dagmar's disapproval became contrition. She grabbed a handful of her hair and shoved it back. "Oh, shit, the physicist. I haven't done that. I'm sorry, sir, I keep getting distracted by some new . . ." She paused, searching for a word.

"Crisis? Catastrophe? Disaster? Cluster fuck?" I suggested.

The COO sighed. "All of the above, sir. I'll get on it now. Or at least I'll try," she said and left.

The high-backed leather chair beckoned to me. It was a lot more comfortable than the executive chair behind the desk, and the reasons weren't all physical. I sat down, sighed, and closed my eyes, but it didn't keep my mind from whirling like a pinwheel. *Breathe, relax. Breathe, relax.*

Jeannette's voice came over the intercom. "Sir, your brother-in-law is on line two."

"Did he say what he wants?"

"He says he has an investment opportunity for you."

I sighed, drummed my fingers on my knee, and considered my eldest sister's husband. Ever since Amelia had brought him home, Brent van Gelder had some get-rich-quick-scheme. None of them had ever panned out, and it had made him resentful. I resented him because it was Amelia's work as a surgeon at Mass General that kept the family afloat, and I thought he was a burden to my sister.

"Tell him I'm in a meeting and I'll call him back."

"Yes, sir."

Since the discreet announcement that I was the new CEO of Lumina Enterprises had appeared in the *Wall Street Journal*, I'd been getting calls from old college chums and high school buddies. Funny thing was I never remembered any of these people being particularly friendly to me. Then I became Bill Gates and suddenly they had a very different memory of all the good times back in the day.

My gaze fell on the morning's *New York Times*. It had been inexpertly refolded and left on the edge of the granite desk. I pulled it over, and then rubbed the tips of my fingers together, trying to remove the sticky aftermath of a jelly smear. Coffee stains had set the words to weeping. Someone had started the crossword, and given up with a scrawl of red ink across the puzzle. Probably Sam. Patience wasn't her strong suit, and she didn't look like the type who could do the *Times* crossword.

I started scanning the *Times*. Papers have always been filled with news of tragedy, but now there were so many stories there was no longer room for lighter news about actors' relationships, movie reviews, and heartwarming features about *dog saves owner*. It was a deluge of death, and the numbers were staggering. *Bombs and mortars in Varanasi, Hinduism's holiest city, kill two thousand.*

My eyes skipped away to another story and I read—

The NTSB easily determined the cause of the crash. The small commuter plane ran out of fuel. When questioned, members of the ground crew stated the plane didn't need fuel, and that it crashed because the pilots and passengers didn't believe. What they had failed to believe varied widely from person to person, but what remained a constant was the complete lack of guilt over the accident . . .

The hairs on the nape of my neck rose, and a cold line traced its way down my spine to lodge at the small of my back. This was what Grenier had been talking about. People believing crazy stuff. And not just believing; some of them might actually be able to *do* crazy stuff. As logic and rationality leached out of the world, planes might fly powered by belief alone. Unfortunately there had been no magic for the crew and passengers on *this* flight. I groped in my pocket for the snuffbox, fished out a tablet, and dry-swallowed the Xanax. I threw the paper into the waste can next to the desk.

The big copper-paneled doors swung open, and Angela entered. "No tea, painkillers, and sympathy for that one?" she asked.

I shook my head. She looked at me with concern and started toward me, hand outstretched. I dodged the impending touch by rising and limping over to the window. It wasn't that I dreaded her touch or didn't like it, but it felt dishonest to allow the contact when I wasn't sure what I wanted and whether I could reciprocate.

Down in the parking lot a woman struggled against a brisk west wind. The tail of her long coat twisted behind her. She clutched a cardboard box to her chest. Farther along the line of parked vehicles a man slammed the trunk of his Prius closed. I couldn't help but notice that there wasn't a single SUV among the employee cars.

"So, what's the tally?" Angela asked. I could feel her breath on the back of my neck.

"Out of eighty-four employees, five left," I answered.

"That's not too bad." Angela's arms went around my waist and hugged me tight. I could feel her cheek resting against my back, and her breath made a warm spot on the suit coat. The lonely isolation I had been feeling seemed suddenly too much to bear. It might not be fair, but I was going to take the comfort. I turned around and rested my chin on the top of her head. Her curls tickled, and a faint citrus scent from her conditioner wafted up.

She suddenly frowned and stepped back, and I realized the holster and butt of the pistol had dug into her breast. Angela pulled back the lapel of my coat to reveal the pistol nestled under my right armpit.

I answered the unasked question. "I told Weber to file my resignation in a round file. Don't tell," I added hurriedly and then felt stupid. This was one person I could absolutely trust.

"Like I would!" Reaching up, she brushed back that damn lock of hair that continually resisted being combed into place. She stroked her fingertips across my forehead, and I closed my eyes, enjoying their cool touch.

"You look tired," Angela said softly. "Do you want to lie down?"

I opened my eyes and looked down into her brown eyes. It was still surprising and more than a little pleasant to actually get to look *down* into a woman's face. "It's brain tired. What I really need is to give my mind a rest. Do you think I could try a swim today?"

"Sure. Just limit the time, and if it hurts in a bad way instead of a good way, quit."

The moment the elevator doors opened, I could hear splashing and sharp breaths. There was already a swimmer in the pool. A flash of resentment shook me, but I limped on through the blue-tiled archway. Maybe it was somebody I could stand to have around me. The room that housed the pool was designed to evoke a Roman bath. I watched the steam wave languidly over the top of the hot tub, and reflected that what I really wanted was some private time. A place to myself without everyone needing something, demanding something, wanting something, and it always ended up that *I* was the only person who could supply the something. I knew I was indulging in a fit of "poor me," but I was still tasting resentment as I limped to the edge of the pool.

The ripples in the water distorted the figure, and it wasn't until the swimmer approached the shallow end of the pool that I realized it was somebody I couldn't stand.

It was Sam. Ever since she had arrived she had been in my face, mocking every remark I made, wondering loudly when we were ever going to fucking *do something*, playing the kind of macho boy games that brought back all those memories of high school gym class, and my worst days on the police force.

Sam executed a neat somersault, braced her feet against the side of the pool, and pushed off again. The young agent must have caught my shadow in the water because she stopped midstroke and began treading water in a slow circle.

It gave me ample opportunity to appreciate the play of muscles beneath the skin of her arms, the sharp bones in her clavicle, the brown hair slicked against her skull. Through the slowing ripples I could see the top edge of the high French-cut one-piece swimsuit defining the slender length of her legs. She made me think of the Scottish legends of selkies.

"Come on in. The water's fine," she said.

So quick was my turn back toward the arch that the hem of my bathrobe brushed against the back of my bare heels and threatened to trip me. "I don't wish to intrude," I muttered, hoping that would suffice. I began limping away, but my progress was snail slow. The tiling around the pool felt like it had been oiled, and the metal-shod foot of the damn cane kept slipping.

I heard the water churn from a couple of hard kicks, then jerked to a halt when Sam grabbed the trailing hem of my robe. "Fuck, it's your pool."

Rage set my temples throbbing. *I could have fallen!* But then I realized I was acting like a big baby. With my temper under control I turned back to face her. She had rested her arms on the edge and was staring up at me.

"Are you always this . . ." She made a complex gesture with one hand.

"What?"

"Polite?"

"Is that a bad thing?" I asked.

"Yeah, it is when you're so fucking self-effacing that you're practically invisible. You're supposed to be in charge of this joint."

Sam suddenly grasped my bare ankle and gave a sharp yank. The metal tip of the cane chattered and squeaked as it slipped across the glass tile. I struggled to catch my balance, stepped instinctively onto my right leg, and yelped in pain. Which turned into a glissando wail as I toppled sidewise into the pool.

A house slipper floated briefly in front of me, then started to sink. And I was likely to follow it toward the bottom because the heavy terry-cloth bathrobe I was wearing was now leaden. Holding my breath, I struggled with the belt. Then Sam was there. Our hands bumped together and tangled as we both went for the belt. Suddenly her slim hand darted into my swim trunks and grabbed my penis. I was appalled, but it couldn't stop a line of silver fire running up into my belly and sending my eyes rolling back. I had been celibate for so long that outrage couldn't trump the atavistic reaction. I couldn't prevent the gasp and ended up sucking water.

I finally shed the robe and surfaced to hear Sam say, "Whoops." She gave me a predatory grin. But the smile never reached her eyes. Instead resentment looked out at me.

I pushed sopping hair out of my eyes, coughed, and managed to croak, "Are you insane?" I could feel the chlorine stinging the wound in my leg.

"Nope, I just find insecure people really boring, and I'm never reassuring. So, do you want to fuck?"

It was a boy's trick. Use the crudest term possible, remove any possibility of personal or emotional contact, and reduce the person being propositioned to an object. I hadn't been a psychology minor for nothing.

"You just can't stand it that I've seen you vulnerable, scared, and crazy, and that I made you well," I said.

We were face-to-face. I watched the self-satisfied smirk melt, replaced with blazing anger. My own anger drowned out the faint arousal I had felt. I looked down at the rounded tops of her breasts, and decided that two could play her game. Leaning forward, I pressed my mouth down hard on hers.

She didn't respond. I hadn't expected her to. Instead her arms windmilled, a bare foot caught me on the shin, and she went splashing out of reach. She sputtered, hooked her arm through the ladder, and glared.

"I thought you wanted to fuck," I said as blandly as I could manage.

"I was just fucking with you," Sam said.

"Really? It doesn't seem like it."

She grabbed the ladder and pulled herself out of the water. Every movement betrayed her annoyance. Snatching up her towel, she stalked for the elevator, her feet slapping wetly on the elaborate tiled floor.

"Sam." I tried to give my voice that snap of command that

comes so easily for Weber. I must have come close, because the young FBI agent stopped and turned back slowly. I stroked over to the side of the pool, folded my arms on the edge, and rested my chin.

"What?"

"Look, we can play mind games with each other, and keep score in blushes and outrage, or we can work together. Your choice."

She walked back and squatted down in front of me. "I want to understand you."

"I'm not that complex."

"I resent you."

"I know."

"I think I really do want to fuck you."

Well, that I hadn't expected. "We'll . . . uh, discuss it," was the best I could manage.

NINETEEN

RICHARD

An intense wet dream yanked me awake. I wouldn't have minded the damp and the sticky touch of semen if I'd actually gotten laid, but I hated to awaken with that acrid and musty smell and my thighs coated. My first gymnastics coach used to say I was like a cat because I hated to be sweaty or smell, and it wasn't a compliment. The man hated cats. He hadn't much liked me either.

The travertine tile in the bathroom was cold underfoot as I stripped off my pajamas. I ran hot water and swept the washcloth up my legs, feeling goose bumps bloom on my skin. I limped into the closet, dumped the pajamas in the hamper, and pulled out a new pair. I tried to balance on my injured leg, then decided to be a smart wimp and sit down to pull them on.

That done, I stood in the closet door, staring at the bed and trying to imagine sleep. It wasn't going to happen. Moonlight poured through the windows, making it easy to navigate around the living room. I had to be quiet. If any of them woke up they'd come and cluck at me.

I settled down on the piano stool, opened the lid, and brushed my fingers softly across the keys. It was just a feather's touch, but it drew a whisper of sound. I froze, but there was no reaction from the bedrooms. I relaxed again and tried to think about the day, but the only memory that stuck was of the swimming pool and Sam.

"*I want to fuck you.*"

And damn, I wanted to meet the request. Four years. It had been *four* years. As a teenager I had been scared to death to take recreational drugs, and I'd never been able to hold liquor worth a damn. Give me a few drinks and I'd end up in somebody's bed. Which brought me face-to-face with my greatest vice—I loved sex. If I did a burst of pop psychology on myself I'd say it was because I feel lonely and unloved so I seek intimacy, and mistake sex for love. Or maybe I just really liked sex. At least until sex became inextricably bound up with pain and guilt about my sexuality.

Life without sex won't kill you.

But I miss it.

So maybe you ought to take Sam up on her offer.

Sam's sardonic half smile seemed to hang in front of me, and I knew that even if I got into bed with her it wouldn't be sex. It would be a competition, which would only add to my anxiety. And anxiety meant impotence. I'd never be able to get it up.

I closed the lid on the Steinway, moved to the window. Heat washed through my body, and I felt sweat prickling all along my back. My breath fogged the glass, blossoming and retreating with each exhalation. I rested my forehead against the glass and relished the ache from the cold.

I shouldn't be thinking about this. We've got bigger problems than my dick—

There was the slap of bare feet on the polished floor. I jerked upright and whirled to see Grenier waddling out of the dining room. He was carrying a large mug and a plate piled high with slices of toast. Steam formed a waving pennant over the top of the mug and carried the rich smell of Mexican chocolate and cinnamon throughout the room.

"Can't sleep?" the former minister said.

"No, I'm sleepwalking. What do you think?" I immediately regretted the tone. It made me sound petulant. I folded my lips together to try to keep any other little croakers from emerging.

Seemingly unruffled, Grenier held out the plate, an implicit invitation. I was going to refuse, but my stomach gave a sharp rumble. I hadn't been able to choke down much dinner, and the butter, powdered sugar, and cinnamon drenching the bread proved irresistible. The bread was still warm in my hand as I took a slice. The first bite sent powdered sugar puffing upward to dust my upper lip. Hot and sweet burst across my tongue. It tasted wonderful.

"What's wrong?" Grenier asked.

I couldn't hold back the sharp, short bark of sardonic laughter. "What isn't."

The man settled his bulk into an armchair. "So, putting aside for the moment that alien creatures are invading the Earth from alternate dimensions, tell me what's bothering *you*."

Opposing instincts and emotions buffeted me, each struggling for primacy. Intellectually I could neither forget nor forgive what the man had done to my mother. And to me. But Grenier was the first person who had expressed an interest in just talking with me instead of harping at me.

That made me feel disloyal, and I started to run through everyone as I tried to prove to myself that there was someone else I could turn to other than the man who'd run electric current through my balls.

Grenier began to talk, and it was like he'd been reading my mind. "Really, Richard, who else have you got? Angela? She's in love with you, and you're not in love with her. If you turn to her she'll read way more into it than you want."

My traitorous mind added another reason to reject her. Hearing that you're doing great when you know you aren't is neither comforting nor helpful. Someone who is unfailingly supportive might make me feel better, but I distrusted it on principle.

"Then there's your terrifying sire. Dear God, is the man never satisfied?"

No, I answered internally.

"Ms. Reitlingen hasn't totally grasped that the P&L statements aren't your most pressing problem. And your sister . . ." He just raised his eyebrows.

Yep, Pamela and I exchanged an average of two snipes a day.

"Sam resents you because she's beholden to you. Syd worships you, which must be wearing. And you don't get to work with your best friend and mentor." Was there a knowing gleam in the hazel eyes? It was gone before I could pin it down. "Because crime is on the rise and he has little time for you." He paused to consume a slice of toast. "Which leaves you with me."

I looked hard into his round face. "I can't trust you," I said rather weakly.

"I'm not asking you to, Richard. But you can talk to me. Because you can trust me on this—there is no way I am leaving the protection of this place and you."

I returned to the piano bench, and took another bite of cinnamon toast while I tried to order my chaotic thoughts. I decided to do exactly that.

"I don't know where to start, and I don't just mean about this conversation. I mean about everything. I don't know where to put my energies. Dagmar wants me to learn about the company and run it. Angela bugs me constantly about Kenntnis. Papa reminds me that if we don't have the company we won't have the funds to do whatever it is we're going to do about Kenntnis. But I have no idea what to do about Kenntnis."

"It sounds like you're *doing* a lot, but accomplishing very little."

"Yeah, that sounds about right." I stood up and paced even though it hurt. "Everybody's got an opinion. But everybody wants me to do something different." I pressed the palm of my hand against my forehead as if that could force order on the churning mess inside my head.

"You listen. Then you go away and make the decisions. Maybe with the help of a single advisor," Grenier said.

I raised an eyebrow at him. "And would that be a role you're envisioning for yourself? Because if it is . . . don't."

Grenier smiled, and consumed another piece of toast in three big bites. "I'm many things—" he said thickly around the wad in his mouth.

"Selfish, self-centered, cruel, power hungry, greedy?" I suggested.

"But not stupid," Grenier concluded blandly.

The eighteenth-century French clock struck the quarter hour. I didn't turn around to look because I dreaded knowing the actual time. I was going to pay a heavy price for this bout of insomnia. All the tasks that would fill the coming day crashed into my head. A thundering headache was already starting. I pressed the heels of my hands hard against my temples.

"What is it that's bothering you? Really?" Grenier asked.

The words slipped out. "I'm scared." And the harsh truth of that admission left me limp.

"You weren't scared when I captured you. Frightened by the pain, but not frozen like you are now. I saw the man you're destined to become—if you'll get out of your own way."

"I had a plan. I knew what I was doing. I didn't know if it would work, but there was at least the chance." I limped over so I could look down at Grenier. "And I'm not frozen. Just the opposite. I feel like I don't even have time to breathe."

"Or think. Which means you can't plan. It's a feedback loop, and a bad one."

"I *know* that." My voice seemed to boom in the room. I quickly moderated my tone. "Thank you so much for stating the obvious."

"You need to take some time to relax. Your mind will work better."

"I can't. The world is collapsing."

"But very slowly." Grenier frowned, rolling the mug between his palms. I could tell he was puzzled and disgruntled, so I decided to push.

"And why is that?" I asked.

"I don't know. I thought the gates would open, nations would collapse, and I'd be a satrap in the new world order. But it isn't happening that way."

I was struck by that, and it helped answer a question that had been nagging at me. "Maybe that's why our government, and all the rest of the world's governments, aren't reacting," I mused. "You can ignore or explain away a little weirdness, and nobody wants to believe this is really happening."

"And by the time the weirdness becomes too big to ignore, or people realize it *is* happening, it might be too late to stop the Old Ones." Grenier drained the last of his cocoa. "I don't know what's happening at the gate, but my guess is that the Old Ones will moderate the craziness. The word will go out from thousands of pulpits that the demons appeared because Hell was trying to prevent the Lord's return. That's what I would be saying if I still had a pulpit to preach from."

"The Second Coming isn't supposed to happen in Virginia."

"Pffft." Grenier waved away the objection. "I could explain that in a second." His voice took on a deeper, more musical resonance. "America is the only sure bastion of freedom and opportunity in the world. America is the nation most loved by God."

In that moment I could totally see how Grenier had become one of the most famous and successful evangelists in America. I knew it was bullshit, but I still felt a flutter of pride at the words, because I was moved by the certainty and sincerity in Grenier's voice.

I shook my head to break the spell and asked, "So, what will happen when . . . if the government does decide to act?"

"The gate will be defended by thousands of the faithful."

I shivered even though the room wasn't cold.

TWENTY

Pamela was listening to four distinct conversations that were occurring at the dining room table.

Dagmar and her father—

"... both of the New Mexico labs are under lockdown. I can't reach anyone." Dagmar was making excuses. Pamela wanted to tell her not to bother. The judge wouldn't buy it.

"There are universities," the judge said, proving Pamela's point if only to herself. "I don't think you're devoting enough time to it."

"Okay, yes, you're right. It isn't my top priority. This company is my top priority. It has to be managed."

Because Richard sure as hell isn't doing it, Pamela thought. She glanced at her brother, seated at the head of the table, and watched him flinch and the color rise into his pale cheeks. He'd obviously overheard the exchange. Good, maybe it would get him to focus.

Weber's rough voice drew her attention. "We're the only first world country that still has the death penalty." The incongruity of that statement emerging from a policeman's mouth had her turning her attention to him.

Grenier's rounded vowels danced with amusement. "I personally like that old-time justice along with my old-time religion. An eye for an eye."

Syd and Sam were arguing with each other.

Syd said, "I think we ought to formally resign. Hell, we may be fired anyway."

Sam countered, "Hell no, we want to keep a toehold in the agency. And we can't abandon everyone."

"We make mistakes. We try not to, but it happens," Weber was saying. "I see enough crap. I don't want to deal death unless I'm damn sure we're right."

Grenier leaned across Pamela to say to Angela, "Did you hear that? Lieutenant Weber says you are incompetent." His bulging belly brushed against her arm. Pamela pulled it close in to her side.

"No he didn't," Angela replied coolly, but her hatred for the former minister blazed in her dark eyes. "He said to err is human, and since there is no God to *sort it out* we'd damn sure better not do anything irrevocable. Oh, that reminds me." She leaned across the table toward Weber. "That body . . . not a Taser. Those were sucker marks."

"Suckers don't leave burns. And I haven't heard of any cephalopods escaping from the aquarium." It was a ponderous attempt at humor from the cop, but his eyes kept darting around as if he were looking for a way out.

"That's because it was caused by magic," Angela said. It was clear this was the continuation of an ongoing argument.

Weber's lips and eyes squeezed shut. Repudiation by silence. The skin around the cop's jaw sagged, and pouches hung beneath his eyes. Weariness created the effect that his face was melting.

Pamela took a few more bites of salmon loaf with cream dill sauce, and had to praise the genius who cooked every meal for both the residents of the penthouse and the employees in their dining room. She'd never seen a company where meals were provided, but she decided she approved.

She caught movement out of the corner of her eye. Richard had stood up and was heading into the kitchen. He had his finger pressed against his temple. Angela made a move as if to follow, but sank back down in her chair when Weber shook his head. Pamela had no such compunction. She followed.

Her brother was inspecting a tray of pastries. Napoleons, eclairs, Sacher torte, cannoli; Pamela stared at the diabetes-inducing array and shook her head. Large silver carafes steamed and burbled, filling the air with the smell of fresh-brewed coffee. A basket held fifteen varieties of tea. Richard turned at the sound of her footsteps and forced a smile.

"The last rehearsal I hosted, I opened up a Sara Lee frozen cheesecake. I did tart it up with some frozen raspberries." He selected a caffeine-free peppermint tea out of the basket.

"Stomach bothering you?" Pamela asked. He nodded, and filled the cup with boiling water from one of the carafes. "It should give you a hint. You shouldn't be doing this."

"Pamela, I can't work all the time. I've got to take a break, or my head's going to explode. So just leave me alone, okay? You can go downstairs and work all you want."

"Putting aside that I think this is frivolous, your own security chief thought it was a risk."

"That was before Joseph investigated." He pulled the tea bag out of his cup, and tossed it into the trash compactor. The smell of peppermint tickled at her nose. "Bob, Lee, and Susanna are going about their lives without any overt signs of craziness. When they enter the lobby they'll be scanned for weapons, and Cross has promised to see if any of the three are armed with spells. I think we've got it covered. Oh, and thank you for your concern," her brother said, and he didn't make any effort to disguise the sarcasm.

Sam walked into the kitchen carrying her dirty plate. "Your band is here," she said.

Pamela watched Richard struggle with himself, and decide to let it go.

"Thank you," he said.

Angela came wandering in with an air so casual that it made it clear there was nothing at all casual about her arrival. She set her plate on the counter. "May we listen? I've actually never heard you play."

An expression of acute discomfort swept across her brother's face. "I'd really rather you didn't. When you have an audience it isn't a rehearsal any longer."

Dagmar entered the kitchen. "My husband is the same way," she said to the room at large. "He practices six hours a day locked away in a converted greenhouse out behind the main house."

"So your children never see either of you?" Angela said in tones of sweet inquiry.

Pamela looked at Richard with his back against the center island, and the three women surrounding him. She wanted to scream with vexation at the foolishness of her sex. Richard slipped between Angela and Dagmar, heading for the door. It looked more like flight than an exit.

The female charm bracelet followed.

As they crossed the dining room Pamela heard a *thunk* followed by the cry of vibrating strings as a cello case bumped into a wall, shaking the instrument inside.

There were three strangers in the living room. A tall, dark-haired man with a half smile and a crooked bow tie was inspecting the art. A young woman with waist-length blond hair had her violin case hugged to her chest and kept turning in circles, surveying the room with a look of childlike wonder. An older man with crew-cut gray hair and pants that rode too high on his waist was drawn to the collection of canopic jars on an inlaid table. He looked up at their entrance and said, "Could you bring some of these by the school sometime? My world history class has only seen my slides from the Cairo museum."

"Sure," Richard said. "I'll give you my secretary's number and we'll get it arranged."

"Oh, Richard, there are so many beautiful things," said the blonde in a breathy little-girl voice.

Maybe the woman couldn't help it. Maybe her voice really sounded like that, but Pamela had always suspected the baby dolls of putting on an act. Pamela also watched the interaction between her brother and the blonde, trying to judge if she was another one of his victims. Pamela had watched so many women, many of them her friends, make fools of themselves over Richard. This time it didn't seem to be the case.

The tall man with the bow tie turned to Richard. "There's art in here worthy of anything in the Uffizi."

Richard nodded his head in acknowledgment, and stammered into far too detailed an explanation. "It's not really mine. I mean, I live here, and it might ultimately be mine . . . well, at least for my lifetime, but I'm . . . we're hoping the real owner comes back . . . I'm just sort of a caretaker . . ." He stuttered to a halt.

Grenier, wandering through with his splayfooted fat man's walk, reached out and patted Richard on the cheek as he passed. "Too much information, little man." Pamela watched as Richard yanked his head away.

Weber, Syd, and her father joined them, and introductions were made. The tall art lover turned out to be Lee Titlebaum, a law professor at UNM. He fell into easy conversation with her father. Syd, Weber, and the high school history teacher, Bob Figge, found a common interest in fishing. Susanna Monroe chattered brightly with Dagmar, Sam, and Angela. Richard threaded his way between chairs and music stands, retreating to the piano. He began sorting through music.

Pamela drifted from conversation to conversation. Among the social chitchat were nuggets of disturbing information. Truancy at the high school was running at forty percent. At the law school it was, oddly, the professors who were missing. The mall where Susanna worked was an echoing cavern filled with Muzak and no customers.

The conversations began to hiccup to an end. The three string players picked up their cases and moved to their chairs. Outside the wide window, the wind whistled through the boulders and tossed fine grit against the glass.

There were sharp snaps as clasps were opened, and the hollow thrum as the violin, viola, and cello were pulled from the dark-lined interiors. Richard struck an A. There came a mewing as bows were drawn across strings, and tuning pegs adjusted. The scrape of bows on strings set a counterpoint to the wind's melancholy cry. Sliding onto the bench, Richard opened up the sheet music and then worked his hands, flexing and stretching his fingers. He closed his eyes and nodded slowly for a few seconds. Pamela wondered if he was mentally playing the first few opening bars. The mewing stopped.

"I'm heading home," Weber said. He reached up and touched his ear self-consciously. "It would be wasted on me. I've got a tin ear."

Grenier settled into a recliner and folded his hands on his belly. Sam took the love seat, and Angela sat down on the couch. By their attitudes each seemed to be claiming the entire piece of furniture. Dagmar looked from one to the other as if debating where was the safer roost.

The judge looked back from the hallway leading to the bedrooms. "I'm going to pick up some reports I was reading last night. I'll be in the office if you need me." It was a rebuke and a goad, and it had no effect on the COO.

Dagmar just looked at him impassively and said, "All right." She finally picked a seat—on the couch at the far end from Angela.

"Do you mind?" Richard asked the members of his quartet with a nod toward the ad hoc audience.

His tone made it clear what he wanted them to say, but nobody wanted to seem rude. They all nodded and said it was fine if folks listened. Richard's lips thinned to a narrow line, and Pamela took pleasure in his displeasure. She sat down on an ottoman. She should probably go and help her father. But her eyelids felt weighted, and her mind seemed too full to accept any more input. Maybe Richard was right to call for a brain break.

"Are we ready?" the law professor asked.

Pamela's eyes snapped back open just in time to see Richard nod slowly.

TWENTY-ONE

RICHARD

Six measures was all it took. Six measures and the tension in my chest uncoiled. We were playing Mendelssohn's Piano Trio no. 2, opus 66. Susanna had been asked to fill in for a touring chamber music company, and they were going to perform this piece. Since this might be her professional break, Lee agreed to sit out and critique her performance. I thought she was playing wonderfully, drawing sounds of melting sweetness from her violin.

For myself I loved the stretch and play of the muscles across the backs of my hands, the rise and fall of my foot on the pedals. I've always felt incredibly strong when I play. Especially when we get to an allegro or scherzo movement. Feeling the muscles in my forearms bunch and jump as I attacked the keys with speed and power made me feel like I was creating a vortex of sound. There was nothing but the music, the notes on the page, and matching breaths with my fellow musicians. I completely forgot the listeners.

Until my father walked back through the living room carrying a report. We were at a particularly wonderful section in the final movement. I wanted him to hear it, embrace it, realize that I hadn't just wasted the time, money, and education. You didn't have to be a professional musician for music to have value.

I threw myself into the run, trying to coax perfect sound from the piano. I looked over at my father, but he didn't look up

148

from the report, just walked into the foyer. The elevator *ding*ed as it arrived; it was in a discordant key from the trio. My fingers tangled, and suddenly I was three beats behind. I lifted my hands, counted, and jumped back in with Susanna and Bob.

We were approaching the resolution. It felt as if the passion of the music had entered my chest and gone shivering throughout my entire body. I realized it was exactly what I felt when I drew the sword, and the music swept away all thought. I was possessed by it, swept along, lost to the world.

Then the phone shrilled, harsh and metallic, cutting across the floating music, breaking my trance and bringing back the world. I try not to throw tantrums, but this time I just couldn't help it. I brought my hands crashing down on the keyboard in a jangling, dissonant chord. The strings faltered into silence. Angela darted to pick up the receiver.

"Hello? Hello?" she said, but the phone kept ringing.

"There," Sam said and pointed at a phone on the bookcase.

It was the first time I'd really noticed it, and apparently it was a different line because no other phone in the penthouse was ringing. A faint sound reached me from the bedroom side of the penthouse. Correct that, a phone was ringing and it sounded like it was in Kenntnis's . . . my bedroom. I was closest to the living room phone, so I answered, primed to bust somebody's chops because I hated to be interrupted when I was playing. Add to that it was eight o'clock at night, definitely way past business hours.

"Oort." Irritation had thrown me back into old habits, answering as if I were at APD headquarters.

"Will you accept a collect call from Dr. Edward—"

I was startled to hear an actual operator, but I'd been trained well by my parents. "No," I said quickly.

And then I heard a young man's voice in the background. "*No, wait!*"

Another voice, deeper, more gruff, with an Aussie accent, said, "That's it then, lad. That's your phone call—"

"*Back off, flatfoot!*" the younger voice shrilled.

The operator's voice, losing some of her soothing phone sex quality, asked, "Sir, do you wish me to terminate the call?"

The fact there were cops, Australian cops, involved had me intrigued, so I said, "No, it's okay, I'll accept the charges."

There were a few clicks on the line; then the boyish voice said, "Thanks. Is this Lumina Enterprises?"

"Yes. Who is this, please?"

"Eddie Tanaka, Dr. Tanaka," came the hurried addition. "I'm in Australia. I haven't got a passport, or any money, and that bastard on the freighter took my ID—"

For some reason I was finding this oddly amusing. "And now you've been arrested," I interrupted.

"Yeah, this is my one phone call, and I really need help, and—"

"Okay, I can see where *you* have a problem, but why is it *my* . . . or rather Lumina's problem?"

"Because, dickhead!" I yanked the phone away from my ear at the bellow. "I work for fucking Lumina!" The shout became a roar. "I was given this number to memorize before I left for Indonesia. I was told to call it if I was ever in real trouble! Well, I'm in real fucking trouble! Everybody at my lab was killed except me, and I had to jump ship, and it took me four days to get to Australia in a goddamn Zodiac, and I'd run out of food, and then these dumb asses arrested me—like how many Japanese American terrorists have you ever heard of?" The fury and desperation were rising again. "And then I picked you for my *one* call instead of a lawyer, and so far you've been a real fucking disappointment, so get off your dead ass and get me some help!" Tanaka was once again shouting.

There was silence, and I listened to desperate panting from the other end of the line, while my mind tried to process all that I'd heard. Only one thing was really sticking. *Everybody at my lab was killed.* Then, in an almost conversational tone, Tanaka added, "And by the way, who the hell are you?"

"I'm the head of the Lumina," I answered before I could think about it and carefully parse and pick my words.

I was suddenly distracted by someone clapping. I looked over my shoulder. It was Grenier.

Far away in Australia I heard my employee say, "Oh, shit. Um . . . whoops?"

TWENTY-TWO

"Why in the hell didn't we know about this?" Richard demanded of Dagmar as they swept through the office doors.

Pamela, trailing after them, watched her father's head snap up at the profanity and the harsh rasp of her brother's voice.

"If everyone was killed there wouldn't be anyone to report the events," Dagmar offered.

"And no one is fucking monitoring these outlying interests?" Richard countered, and he glared at Dagmar.

"Richard!" The name cracked like a whip, and the judge came out of the big chair behind the desk. His face was dark with disapproval. A momentary and errant thought disturbed Pamela's focus. She wondered why her father had always been so uptight about cursing.

Amazingly Richard rolled over the rebuke. "We've had thirty-six scientists and technicians murdered in Indonesia." The judge's disapproval dissolved as he processed this information.

"Obviously this is something we need to look at and make adjustments." Dagmar's head was erect, back stiff.

"Do ya think?" Richard said. As her father emerged from one side of the desk, Richard swung in the other side and sat down. Pamela realized it was the first time Richard hadn't approached the desk and chair with the air of a terrified dog circling a trap.

"I want the dead recovered," Richard continued.

"That might not be easy," Pamela said.

"Tough," Richard snapped. "We have relatives who've lost loved ones to violence. They'll need the comfort of having the dead returned."

Dagmar nodded. "Yes, sir."

"Next question, was this wide-scale rioting and violence, and we had the bad luck to have it roll over us, or were we the target?" Dagmar looked baffled and shook her head. "Well, find out, and while we're making that determination, let's get warnings out to every other Lumina holding. Next we need to get Dr. Tanaka papers, and get him back to the States. I want to hear his report personally."

Pamela stared at this stranger behind the desk. When had her brother become effective? Maybe his stint in the police hadn't been all bad. It seemed to have given him a spine transplant.

Their father joined the conversation. "It's hard to quickly obtain a passport."

"We're a big company. They expedite for corporations all the time," Pamela offered. "And you've got contacts, Papa . . . Congressman Waters."

Richard was flipping a fountain pen between his fingers and frowning. "Tanaka's in the hands of the police, and that's never an easy situation to resolve. I'd like to have someone with legal training handle this. Pamela, I'd like you to go to Australia."

It was couched as a request, but it was really an order. To her. Pamela damped down the coiling resentment and tried to keep her tone level as she asked, "Why me? Why not Papa?"

"Because you're right, with Papa's contacts we can get the papers arranged. We'll send you on the Lumina jet. By the time you get him back to the States we can meet you at the airport with a passport."

"There's just one small problem with this plan," Dagmar said. "Our pilot's in jail in Virginia," she said in response to the various querying looks she got.

Pamela looked back over at her brother, and saw that the sharp, commanding certainty had vanished, replaced by that lost vulnerability that always irritated her. Her mother used to get that look, too.

"He is? What happened? I didn't know. If I'd known I would have—"

"Oh for pity's sake, you can't feel guilty over something you didn't know about," Pamela said, and the words came out sharp and pointed. Richard shot her a nasty look, banishing the fragile, haunted expression.

"This must be the fellow who was flying the helicopter when we came to—" Their father broke off abruptly, and his mouth worked as if trying to expel a bite of something rotten.

"Came to rescue me," Richard said, his tone flat. "Why can't you just say it, sir?"

Well, the family melodramatics seem to be working overtime tonight, Pamela thought.

"Why was he arrested?" Dagmar asked, breaking the pattern, and bringing them back to the topic.

"Violating federal airspace. We were in the no-fly zone around D.C.," the judge answered.

"Is this going to be a hard rap to beat?" Richard asked.

Pamela shook her head. "I don't think so. Once again we've got Papa. He's a member of the federal bench."

"And *you* have the power that comes from being a very rich man," Dagmar said to Richard.

Pamela watched the weight of that statement fall onto her brother. For a moment Richard's expression became distant and faraway. Pamela wondered what he was thinking. Whatever it was, he shook it off.

"I know this isn't exactly pertinent, but why do we only have one pilot?" Pamela asked.

Richard shrugged and shook his head. He looked over to Dagmar, who said, "The plane was primarily for Mr. Kenntnis's

154

convenience. We could request to use it, but he preferred his employees flew commercial." Dagmar shrugged. "It was one of his many quirks."

"All right. Papa, you'll handle getting this gentleman . . ." Richard gave Dagmar an inquiring look.

She supplied the name. "Brook Kanadjian."

"Brook out of jail. Meantime, we'll wire money to Dr. Tanaka, and try to at least get him out of jail until Pamela can get there."

Dagmar nodded. "I'll get on it, and I want to find out why we had a breakdown of communications."

The judge cleared his throat, a dry, precise sound. "I think I can accomplish this more easily if I'm in Washington instead of the wilds of New Mexico. As Pamela pointed out, I do have contacts."

Richard suddenly lifted his head, and Pamela watched a number of emotions go washing across his face. It all happened too fast for her to get a read of what he was thinking.

"I think I ought to go with you." It was the absolute last thing she had expected out of her brother. At their father's expression Richard rushed on. "I mean, it doesn't seem like the government is responding to this . . . this invasion at all. I know what's going on, and I've got this." The hilt came out of his coat pocket and was laid in the center of the desk. "I think I need to try to work with them."

Dagmar hustled forward, rested her hands on the granite surface of the desk, and leaned in on Richard. "With all due respect, sir, that is crazy. If they learn of the sword they might take it. Why would you take such a risk?"

But Richard didn't look at her. He watched their father with an intensity that bordered on desperate.

Pamela thought Dagmar was right and said so, then added, "And they won't just take the sword. Since you're the only person who can use it, they'll take you, too."

"I believe I made just these points in Washington in December," the judge said.

"Yes, sir, you did, and they made sense—then. But things

are just getting worse and worse. Pretty soon we're not going to recognize our world, and I'm afraid if we don't mobilize now it will be too late. Nothing we do will have any effect." His gaze went around the room, resting briefly on each of them. "We need allies and we need help. We're going."

TWENTY-THREE

A phone ringing late at night always elicits gut-clenching terror. Rhiana jerked awake in her nest of Egyptian cotton sheets and fluffy down comforter. The bed was a giant Georgian with massive posts rising toward the hammered copper tile ceiling. She had them remove the high rails and the heavy blue velvet curtains. She had slept in a gossamer tent in Kenntnis's penthouse, and even though the material was vastly different it brought back memories. Memories of betrayal.

Fighting her way out of the covers, Rhiana scooted to the side of the bed and snatched her cell phone off the bedside table. As she answered she saw the time—3:40.

Shit, maybe it was her mom, or dad.

She wasn't sure why she'd called her adopted parents and given them her number. That was a different life that she was so totally done with, but she had, and she didn't really want to think too much about it.

"Hello? Hello?"

But it wasn't one of her reputed siblings. It was Doug Andresson. "Hey," he said. "I'm in a little jam. I need you to come—"

"What do you mean you're in a jam?" Rhiana combed her hair out of her face and tried to focus. "How can you be in a jam at the compound?"

"Well, actually, I'm in town. D.C." He tried to infuse the words with an insouciant little bounce.

"What? What the fuck have you done? Didn't I tell you to stay there?"

"Yeah, well, I was bored. You promised me anything I wanted, but you didn't get back to me when I called. I'm important, and you treat me like shit." He sounded angry and sulky now.

The desire to strike at him clawed at the back of her throat, but she forced herself to moderate her tone. "So, what's the problem?"

"You need to come here."

Here proved to be a hotel that straddled the boundary between official Washington, where power walked, and the decaying neighborhoods where crime preyed on the poor. Jack pushed open the pitted-glass doors. Rhiana had enlisted his help because she didn't want to meet Andresson alone again. It was starting to feel natural, even comfortable, to call the tall spiritualist when she needed help. She knew it made her vulnerable and he might take advantage, but right now she didn't care.

In the east there was a hint of gray as dawn slouched toward its arrival. Rhiana reluctantly turned her back on the sky and followed Jack into the lobby. A night manager dozed behind the desk. There wasn't a cage protecting the plump and pallid middle-aged man, but there was a prominent sign on the counter that stated NO CASH KEPT ON PREMISES.

A few stained sofas and an armchair huddled around a scarred coffee table that was littered with *People* and *Time* magazines, several years out of date. There was the smell of cheap coffee brewing and of microwave eggs being prepared for the breakfast buffet.

"Keep him asleep," Rhiana said softly to Jack.

The clerk yawned, stirred and started to open his eyes. Jack looked down at the big square-cut diamond ring on his own right hand, murmured, and the gem blazed with light. A tendril of white fire left the ring and touched the man's forehead. The clerk collapsed back into the chair, mouth open, snoring sonorously.

They moved down a hallway toward the back of the hotel. There was a faint wet-dog smell from the recently cleaned carpet. It hadn't had a notable effect. There were still stains ground into the blue Berber.

Rhiana tapped on the door, and Doug opened it a bare crack. That alone told her it was bad. "Oh, good, it's you, come in. Hey, who's he?" Suspicion sharpened the words.

Jack slammed a shoulder into the door, forcing the smaller man backward. "I'd suggest you not question the lady," Jack said. "She's your—" The words cut off abruptly; then Jack said in a suffocated tone, "Oh, shit. Oh, Jesus. Oh, God."

Rhiana rushed into the room. The cloying and yet almost metallic scent of blood filled the room. There was a man sprawled on the floor, back up against the dresser. His hands were cupped around the knife protruding from his belly. Blood stained the skin, and drops actually hung in the hairs on the backs of his fingers. Quivers ran through his body, and his eyelids were fluttering. He was alive, but only just.

Not so the naked girl in the bed. Black hair hung in thin corkscrew ringlets. Some of them were draped across her face and helped hide the protruding, bloodshot eyes. Her tongue was like a piece of purple liver thrusting from between her lips. A man's belt was wound around her throat and pulled tight. Livid bruises mottled her face and shoulders, and her breasts showed bloody bite marks.

Jack was gagging. Rhiana fell back against the door. It gave beneath her weight, and latched shut. Her thoughts seemed to be spinning, colliding, and shattering. Nothing made any sense.

"What . . . what . . . what . . ." was all she managed to say.

"I was softening her up. A little play before we got down to action. I went to get a glove, who knows what a cunt like that might be carrying, and while my back was turned she got her cell phone and called her pimp. She kept crying, and telling me to stop, that this wasn't what she did, and then this asshole"—Doug glared at the bleeding man on the floor—"let himself in. I think that fag at the front gives him a passkey so they can do a shakedown on their patrons. I'm settling with him next. Anyway, he tries to start something, but I got my knife. Then she starts to scream, and I had to shut her up." Doug shrugged as if what had occurred in this room were the most natural things imaginable. "She shouldn't have fucked with me."

Jack had pulled out a handkerchief and was wiping his mouth. He backed up to stand next to Rhiana. "Okay, what now?"

She looked into Andresson's flat black eyes, and wanted to call the police. Wanted to call Richard to come and take this man away and lock him up, so Rhiana never had to see him or deal with him again. But he was part of their plans. Their answer to getting Richard. But Andresson was awful, and he terrified her. Jack was looking at her, sensing her indecision. He took her by the upper arm and gave Doug a stiff smile.

"Excuse us just one minute." He pulled Rhiana into the hall and made sure the door was shut. "How is this guy our problem?"

"Because he is. I've been put in charge of him. He's an empty one, a person with no magic. If we . . . when we get the sword he'll use it. And I was supposed to keep track of him. Keep him safe. Keep him happy. Oh, God, if they find out . . ." She spun in a frantic circle, fingers clutching at her hair.

Jack caught her by the wrists and forced her to stand still. "Okay, we get rid of the evidence. We take him back to the compound, and you keep him supplied in hot and cold running girls, booze, anything he wants."

"What if he kills another one?"

Jack stared at her, his expression quizzical. "What do you care? If you time it right you can have a snack."

"Yes. Yes. You're right, of course. I'm not sure what I was thinking . . ."

"That you were human?" he asked.

Rhiana suddenly wanted to cry. Crossing her arms, she clutched at her elbows and thought. "We need to make this go away."

Jack nodded. "Yes, but unless you've got Harvey Keitel playing the fixer from *Pulp Fiction* I'm not sure just how we do that."

"We'll send the room away." With her forefinger she reached out and lightly touched the diamond in his ring. "Want to learn how to create a tear in reality?"

TWENTY-FOUR

RICHARD

The ferocious windstorm had the hem of my overcoat beating at my knees, and some of the gusts threatened to knock me off my precarious three-point balance. I tried to dig the tip of the cane more firmly into the concrete of the tarmac. It didn't work. The western horizon was obscured by a wall of approaching dust, and dirt was pinging against the metal skin of the Lear with enough force to actually be heard over the screaming wind. It hurt on the exposed skin of my face, so I turned my back, pulled up my collar, and hunched my shoulders.

Weber pressed his shoulder against mine and leaned down so we could hear each other. "You know if you need me you just have to call. I'd come with you now, but somebody's got to try to keep the force intact, and the city safe."

His eyes, irritated by the flying sand, were running water. I started to reach up and wipe away the trailing moisture from his cheek, but when I realized what I was doing I quickly turned it into a swooping gesture that landed my hand safely in my pocket.

We stood in silence and watched as my father vanished through the hatch into the Lear. He was trailed by Dagmar, Angela, Syd, and Sam. My security detail—Joseph, Estevan, and Rudi—were arrayed around the perimeter of the plane. At the foot of the stairs my sister stood checking a list. The paper fluttered wildly in her hand from the force of the wind. Grenier, his hand on the railing, looked up at the stairs with the disgruntled expression of a man faced with an irksome and daunting task.

"Looks like you're loading the clown car at the circus," Weber said.

"Thanks," I said. "That just fills me with confidence."

Weber cocked his head and gave me his lopsided grin. "And just how did the Bozo Brigade convince you to take them all along?"

"Well, let's see, Sam and Syd think they can help by contacting friends at the FBI, and Sam has offered to shoot people as necessary."

"That girl is just plain scary."

I nodded. "Papa needs to go so he can get Brook out of jail and arrange a passport for Tanaka." My phone was buzzing and vibrating in my pants pocket. I dug it out and looked at the screen. BRENT VAN GELDER. I put it away again. "Pamela has to fly to Australia with said passport to collect Tanaka and bring him to me, and the Lumina plane is in Virginia." I paused to catch my breath.

"Your sister must hate being your girl Friday."

"Oh, probably. Where was I? Oh yeah, Dagmar. Dagmar is still trying to teach me the business and she won't let me play hooky, and Angela is coming because . . . well . . . because . . ." I felt my face flame with embarrassment.

"Yeah, I know," said Weber. "You and your women."

"Don't start." I continued. "And Grenier refuses to be separated from me and the sword because he's convinced he'll be killed if he's not with me."

"He's probably right."

"He might actually be the most useful card I can play. He's been a Washington fixture for almost twenty years. He knows the president and a number of legislators. He can back me up."

"While admitting he's an evil sorcerer who wanted to bring the monsters into the world. Yeah, that's a real winning hand."

We both looked over at him again just in time to see Grenier shake his head, like a bull bedeviled by flies, seize the rail of the plane's stairs, and begin trudging ponderously upward toward the hatch.

"We'll just gloss over that."

"That's going to be one hell of a gloss."

Pamela suddenly darted up the stairs and tried to squeeze past the former minister, but she caught her heel on a riser and almost fell. Grenier's arms shot out, and he gathered her into an involuntary embrace. There was a moment when they looked into each other's faces. Pamela pulled back, and I watched her say something.

Lumina's new pilot appeared in the door. He was short, wide, and pugnacious. His name was Jerry Cannon, and he was a former navy pilot. He'd found commercial aviation dull, so he'd spent the last few years flying emergency supplies into the world's hellholes. I'd hired him, despite his surly attitude, because I figured he could fly us out of a fix. Jerry pointed ostentatiously at his watch and yelled over the wind, *"Hey, you may own the fucking plane, but I'm flying the goddamn thing. Let's go!"* Jerry disappeared back into the plane.

"He does know he works for *you*, right?" Weber asked. I held out my hand, palm down, and waggled it back and forth. Weber shook his head. "You've got, like, this superpower for attracting bossy assholes."

"It's a gift," I said lightly and gave him what I hoped was a confident smile.

"You used the sword on him?" Weber asked.

"No, why would I do that? He's just going to hold my life in his hands. Of course I used the sword on him."

"Hey, watch the lip, you still work for me. So, here's my orders. Make the assholes listen and get Kenntnis free."

"Yes, sir! That's the plan, but you know what happens to plans." He nodded, and my mind provided the rest of the quote. *They rarely survive contact with the enemy.* I gave myself a mental shake. "Well, Jerry's right. We should probably get the flying circus in the air. 'Bye, Damon. Take care and stay safe."

"Same goes for you, Rhode Island," the big cop replied and clapped me hard on the shoulder.

I was sure we presented an absolutely absurd picture with me limping up the stairs while Joseph walked backward behind me, eyes scanning the airport, and the other two guards held at the foot of the stairs. I hoped Damon wasn't watching this.

Once we were all inside, Pamela touched the controls that folded the steps and closed the hatch. Jerry was in the cockpit flipping switches. A soft whine rose in intensity until it was a rumbling growl. The vibration ran up through the soles of my shoes and into my bones.

Dagmar hung over the pilot's shoulder. "The radar works? It's to your satisfaction?"

"Yeah, yeah. Lady, the day I can't avoid a missile, even in a piece of shit plane like a Lear, is the day I hang it up. Now go put your ass in a seat." Jerry looked up and saw me watching. "You, too."

I gave him a mock salute and moved into the body of the plane. It seemed cramped after the Gulfstream. Ah, how quickly you got accustomed to the life of the very rich.

"What are you smiling about?" Dagmar asked.

I told her, and she smiled back at me, which intensified the laugh lines around her eyes. I realized she was probably a person who, in normal times, smiled a lot. I felt a momentary flare of guilt that I was adding to her burdens. Then I looked at it logically— *monsters/me, monsters/me.* Probably the monsters were causing more heartburn than I was.

"Yes, soon you'll be deciding which yacht you want to buy based on the draw of the keel, and which harbors you can actually enter versus having to take the helicopter into Monaco," Dagmar said.

"If I ever become that person, you have my permission, in fact, I *order* you, to shoot me," I said.

"I don't like guns. I've never shot a gun," Dagmar said.

"Okay, then have Sam do it. She'd probably welcome the chance." Dagmar laughed, nodded, and took a seat, but I pushed father back toward the tail of the plane. Pamela was leaning across the aisle arguing with Grenier.

"You violated your parole. You jumped bail. They will put you in jail."

"Your brother will protect me. And you can defend me. I'm sure you are formidable."

Pamela harrumphed and flung herself back against the seat. "This is so stupid."

I knew she meant me. I tried to explain. "Look, I think it will help having him with me. The very fact I would tolerate having him around, or that he would hook up with me, helps make our argument. We've done a lot of damage to each other." At my words Grenier lifted his right arm and inspected his stump closely; he then gave me a thin smile. "The fact we'd work together proves how serious things are."

Pamela just folded her arms and looked pointedly out the window. Grenier and I exchanged a glance. We'd actually discussed this. What I didn't mention was the added part of the conversation.

"I'm coming because you, dear boy, are going to need some respite from your terrifying sire. Not to mention all the estrogen swirling about. You'll be grateful to have me along."

I stole a glance at my father's profile. His eyes were closed, and his Bose headphones were already firmly in place. I knew he hated to fly. I wasn't sure if it was the actual flying, or the disruption of being out of his space. I knew Dagmar didn't like my father, I knew Angela didn't like my father, and now I could add Grenier to that list. If it had just been the disgraced minister I could have shrugged and thought, *consider the source*, but I liked Dagmar and I had a hunch she had a pretty good sense about people. And I cared deeply for Angela and I knew she was fiercely protective of me, which meant—I didn't like what it meant.

He's my father. But I wasn't really sure where the thought took me.

TWENTY-FIVE

Rhiana huddled against the swooping, graceful back of the Victorian fainting couch. Her bare feet were tucked up under the floor-length bathrobe, and she had an intricately crocheted afghan pulled up to her chin. It was both scratchy and greasy as wool and lanolin vied for primacy.

The heater kicked on, and the rush of air through the vent set the crystal drops on the chandelier to shivering and ringing. She was beginning to think the chandelier had been a mistake. The ceiling wasn't really high enough to support its four-foot length. Maybe she'd repaint. The rose and green wasn't working for her anymore.

Thoughts about interior decorating worked for a few brief moments to take her mind away from the hellish scene in that hotel room. Andresson was safely back at the Virginia compound, and no one seemed to know—or at least no one remarked—about his absence. Rhiana knew that women were being delivered to the dark paladin. She didn't want to know any more than that.

The darkened glass in the large oval mirror with its floral-patterned gilt frame swirled with purples and black ribbons of color. She waited for her father to speak, but the mirror returned to its nonreflective state. Suddenly viscous drops of black and purple oozed from the crystal pendants on the chandelier. Hundreds of drops pattered like a blighted rain onto the polished marble floor. Madoc's body appeared like pulled taffy. The human form stabilized, and he gave his collar a twitch.

"I haven't seen you in a while," Rhiana said, trying to keep her voice level and the tone casual.

He offered no excuse or explanation, just said abruptly, "How are you coming on securing the paladin and the sword?"

"It's coming," she replied.

"Well, it just got easier because Oort is in Washington."

Rhiana sat up. "Any idea why he's come?"

"We presume it's to sound the alarm to your kind. We'll be monitoring who he meets, and try to limit his contacts, but you should act quickly."

His exit was more conventional than his entrance. He walked out the door of her Georgetown mansion. Rhiana wondered if he'd noticed that he'd lumped her in with humanity. Two months ago it had all been how special she was, how superior she was to humans, how much they valued and treasured her.

Your kind.

TWENTY-SIX

There hadn't even been time to unpack before Richard had shoved her out of the homogenized condo. The condo had good-quality leather furniture, a flat-screen TV hung on one white wall, and pale gray carpet underfoot. The only unusual feature was a baby grand piano in the living room. The big armchair near the gas fireplace was beckoning, and she pointed out that there were only two hours left in the business day. He had overruled her, and in a particularly snotty way.

"I've got two people in jail. I know it's a huge effort, but maybe you could try."

"And what are you planning to do? Sit around and play the piano?" she'd shot back in her nastiest tone of voice.

She didn't know why finding that damn piano in the rental had irritated her so much. Maybe it was the way Dagmar petted and accommodated her brother. But Richard wouldn't fight. He just turned and walked away from her, back toward his bedroom. Which was another sore point for Pamela. Richard had a bedroom to himself while everyone else had to share. Even with five bathrooms Pamela foresaw many arguments with four women sharing the space.

Which brought her around to Angela. The little coroner had followed Richard into his bedroom, but emerged a few minutes later looking upset. Pamela would have loved to be a fly on the wall for that conversation.

Without Dagmar's gift for artless patter, and Sam and Syd's affectionate squabbling, it would have been a tense and silent ride to the various government buildings. They had dropped Angela off at the FDA, where she had an old friend from medical school. Dagmar had an acquaintance who was now an Under Secretary at Treasury. She thought she'd just try dropping in to see what she might learn. Since it was so late in the day Pamela and her father began at State, where they could at least start the paperwork for Tanaka's passport. Sam and Syd went on to FBI headquarters to beg forgiveness for Syd's sudden departure and do a little reconnaissance.

Everyone, except Sam and Syd, had rendezvoused back at the condo for dinner, which had consisted of a stack of pizzas. Grenier had managed to eat one of the extralarge pies by himself. Then, after bestowing a garlic-and-pepperoni-laden belch on them, he had demanded money from Richard. When Richard balked, Grenier pointed out that the town ran on rumors. Rumors abound in bars, and alcohol always helped to prime the pump. Like the two agents, he was also still absent.

Pamela was snuggled under the down comforter reading a travel book about Tuscany and still tasting the too greasy pizza. There was a light tap on the door. Pamela recognized the pattern. It was Richard.

Holding her place with a forefinger, she closed the book and said, "What?" She didn't make it sound welcoming.

The door opened, and Richard walked in. He was dressed casually in blue jeans, boots, and a ski parka.

"You're going out?"

He nodded. "I'd like you to come with me. It's time you see what we're up against, and accept that it's real."

The feather comforter felt suddenly even cozier. She held up *Under the Tuscan Sun*. "I'm reading. And I'd have to get dressed again," she said.

"Yes."

"This is really important?"

"Yes."

"You're not going to let this go, are you?"

"No."

Richard when he was laconic irritated her more than all the other times, but she got up and dressed.

They were escorted by Rudi and Estevan. As they stepped out into the hall, their only neighbor on the floor was also leaving. His dog, a tiny white ball of fluff, began yapping shrilly. Her owner was a tubby little man who wore three-thousand-dollar suits and pink-tinted glasses. He gave them a look, sniffed, thrust his button nose in the air, and tried to march past them, but Rudi cut him off and chivvied him up against the wall. The man's complaints were as shrill as his dog's.

"Hey, you should have sold out, man," Estevan said with a grin.

And Pamela remembered Dagmar saying something on the plane about how she had tried to buy his tiny condo for Joseph, Estevan, and Rudi to share, but the owner had refused.

Bet he's sorry now. We really are a menagerie. I wouldn't want to live next door to us.

The doorman held the door, and Joseph held open the back door of the limo. Rudi slid behind the wheel, and they pulled out into Washington's insane traffic. Even at this hour of the night the city pulsed with energy. They seemed to just be driving aimlessly, moving into suburban hell. Up ahead was a multiscreen movieplex with its surrounding growth of chain restaurants like mushrooms sprouting at the foot of a dying tree. They were soon tangled in three lanes of heavy traffic trying to leave the theater, and finally they were stopped among the cars.

Rudi suddenly ordered tersely, "Go!"

Richard grabbed her wrist, and they ducked out the back door of the limo. White streamers of exhaust filled the air as if this were a herd of steel buffalo exhaling all around them. Mingled with the reek of exhaust was the hint of brine from the ocean, and Pamela realized how much she'd missed the smell of the sea during the weeks in bone-dry New Mexico.

Richard pulled her into the backseat of a beat-up Neon. It was being driven by Sam. The light changed, and the herd rolled forward with a rumble and a growl. Brake lights flashed and flared as drivers jockeyed for position. A small opening appeared in the lane to their left, and Sam sent them rocketing through it.

The young agent drove with a mad flair. Pamela had a death grip on the panic strap above the door, and a particularly fast turn sent her careening into Richard. He hissed in pain as she fell against his injured thigh.

"Could you slow down!?" Pamela snapped at Sam. She got the expected response.

"Nope."

Just because it was expected didn't make it any less irritating.

They ended up somewhere in Baltimore, in a neighborhood that wasn't quite residential or quite urban. There were a number of three- and four-story buildings and lots of shotgun houses in between. Dumpsters, overflowing with hunks of drywall, lumber, and old appliances, lined the street. Renovation and gentrification were under way.

They pulled into the driveway of a two-story house. Sam flashed the headlights, and the garage door opened. She rolled in. The door closed, plunging them into total darkness. For an instant Pamela had a moment of irrational, throat-closing panic. Then the overhead fluorescent lights came on.

A tall, powerfully built African American man stood holding open the door into the house. He waved and beckoned. Sam hopped out and opened the back passenger door. On Richard's side. The young agent offered her hand to help him out. Forgotten, Pamela opened her door and climbed out.

Despite the cold, Sam wore only a bolero-style leather jacket over a silk shirt, a short jean skirt, and sharp-toed, high-heeled boots. She bounced up to the man in the doorway, and he enfolded her in a bear hug.

The big agent released Sam, then turned to the Oort siblings.

Richard inclined his head. "Agent Franklin."

"Good to see you again, Mr. Oort," the black man said and offered his hand. Her brother's slender hand disappeared into the man's broad one.

"Thank you for offering us this help," Richard replied.

"Oh, there's a price," Franklin said. He glanced at Pamela. She hated that measuring, suspicious look that every law enforcement person she'd ever met seemed to cultivate. "You brought an extra."

"My sister Pamela," Richard said.

"Bob Franklin." They shook hands. "Pleased to meet you, ma'am," the agent said.

"And you," Pamela responded. Now that he faced her Pamela could see the heavy bags hanging beneath his eyes. They were so pronounced it looked like he'd been punched.

"Please come in," Franklin said.

Despite the late hour there were a lot of people in the house, among them Syd. Many had that hyperaware quality that marks cops of every stripe, but there were a number of spouses and children. Franklin's wife was a good deal younger than the agent, and their three children ranged in age from two to seven. Pamela guessed it was a second marriage and a second family.

The air was rich with Cajun spices and the yeasty scent of beer. Logs crackled in the fireplace, and a few older kids were shaking an old-fashioned popcorn popper over the flames. The opening kernels sounded like small explosions, and the scent set Pamela's mouth to watering.

On the overstuffed sofa four little kids slept among the flowered throw pillows. The little round faces were red from the heat of the fire and the effort of sleeping so deeply. Nestled among the floral pattern they looked like elfin children asleep in a garden.

It would have seemed like a party but for the grim expressions

173

that formed lines around the agents' mouths and lurked like shadows in the backs of their eyes. Bowls of gumbo were shoved into their hands. Pamela accepted a beer. Richard declined.

Pamela drifted through the crowd, picking up fragments of conversation. Much of it centered around the power vacuum that was forming at the heart of the federal government. Rumor had it that the White House was divided, with some staff urging the President to address the nation, set up an international conference, take action. Another faction argued that what was occurring could not be handled by ordinary human agencies, and so a stream of religious leaders were parading through the West Wing. There was a nod at inclusiveness, but most were of the president's traditional Protestant denomination.

Wilder rumors circulated around the Pentagon that the military was planning to take control. No, the President would be imposing martial law, it wouldn't be a military coup. Congress dithered, passed resolutions, debated, tried to pass additional spending bills, hire more police, reinstate the draft, demand the president work with our European and Asian allies. In short nobody seemed to have a clue about what to do.

And Pamela realized that all these people had gathered because they thought maybe her brother would know. She circled back to Richard, and found him in a knot of agents.

". . . talk to local law enforcement," Richard was saying.

"And tell them *what*?" a woman agent asked, and her tone was sharp and brittle.

Richard's tone stayed patient and even. "To keep visible. Maintain a presence in their towns and cities. If we're AWOL it will only add to the sense of fear and chaos. We're the guardians, the bulwark against chaos," Richard concluded, and amazingly it didn't sound pompous or overly dramatic because he believed it so totally.

Maybe he didn't become a policeman just to outrage the family, Pamela thought. *But then why did he?*

"We got a report out of South Dakota that angels have been appearing in some little town, and the people have been giving them their children," said a burly young man wearing a SWAT gimme cap. "By the time a team arrived from Pierre they found the town deserted. Everybody was gone, two thousand people, just gone. Poof. Their sheriff and deputy didn't help them."

"Crime is up everywhere," another man offered. "Way past what any of us can cope with. The President needs to mobilize the National Guard."

"And I ask again," the woman broke in. "To do *what*?"

"Yeah," came a mutter from the back of the crowd. "The National Guard worked so well down in Virginia."

Richard dragged a spoon back and forth through his untouched gumbo. He had lost that certainty and fervent zeal, and had what Pamela thought of as the stricken fawn expression.

"I'm going to be meeting with senators and representatives," Richard said. "We'll find someone who'll . . . who'll . . ."

"What?" a voice demanded.

"Listen," Richard said.

"I don't want 'em to listen. I want 'em to do something."

"Okay, folks, let's go into the study," Franklin called.

All the hard-faced cop types shuffled into a room at the back of the house. Pamela was carried along with them. French doors offered a view across a small backyard crowded with a swing and slide set, a sandbox, and a big gas grill. There were a surprising number of books on the shelves, and the desk was dominated by a twenty-three-inch computer monitor. Cables snaked from the computer to the sixty-inch flat-screen television hanging on the far wall. A skinny man whose hair was rumpled like a pale brown haystack slouched in the desk chair, keyboard on his lap, fingers flying across the keys. He appeared to be playing an online game.

Franklin laid a hand on the bony shoulder of the man at the computer. "Ready, Danny?"

"Yeah, like, ages ago."

"You're sure they won't suspect?" Syd asked.

Danny made a face and pressed the palm of his hand against his chest. "Am I not the best? Seriously, I built in a trapdoor, and set up an automatic routine to imitate a hacker. They'll be chasing my little myth while we take a look at the satellite feed."

"Okay," Syd said vaguely. "I guess that makes sense."

There was the quick clatter of keys, and an image stabilized on the computer screen and the television. From her vantage Pamela couldn't see the monitor. Unfortunately she had a great view of the television. The largest topographical features—hills, a cliff face—were veiled in mist . . . or smoke, it was hard to determine which. Deep within the shifting tendrils of gray was the outline of a massive structure. But the form seemed subtly off, making it very hard for her brain to make sense of the image. Figures that defied description moved through the coiling mist.

Pamela had seen her share of special effects movie monsters, computer magic designed to terrify and disgust. Compared to what she now saw slithering through the shrouding mist, the special effects houses might have been working with hand puppets and paper cutouts. What she was seeing was *wrong* and dangerous, and she responded to it at the most basic of levels. Fear shivered deep in her gut; her breath came shallow and quick. She wanted to run, to hide, to cry, to scream.

"We're down to orbital cameras now." Franklin's voice carried through the room. "People come apart—mentally—in there. Then we tried sending in predator drones, but they all crashed."

"Technology doesn't work where there's an Old One, or that much magic," Richard said.

Around her there was a soundless reaction like the shifting of muscles on some large animal from the thirty people crammed into the room.

The image clicked away from the cliff face, and there was a flare of golden light. "There!" Richard said. He pointed. "Can you magnify that?"

More clicks, each one making the image larger, brought into focus a curving wave of glass resting in the center of a small meadow. Inside the glass there was a pale glitter like gold and diamond dust. On one side of the glass structure loomed a great gate. On the other was a black opening that hung in the air. The image on the television flickered and rolled as Danny sent commands to the satellite cameras and tried to get an angle into the opening.

"That's the best I can do," the computer tech said.

There was another shift from the crowd, and this time a murmur of distressed comments, for what they seemed to be seeing was a distant sun against a backdrop of stars.

"What the hell is that?" someone called.

"A galaxy far, far away," someone else replied. There was a smattering of hollow laughter.

Richard said something to Franklin and Syd. A man in the crowd called, "Speak up, we can't hear you."

Pamela saw the blush as Richard turned his back on the television and faced the crowd.

"I said, they don't seem to have altered the terrain around Kenntnis. And he doesn't seem to be guarded."

"Does the acres and acres of crazy-making crap count?" Sam asked blandly, and Richard's blush got even deeper.

Franklin looked over at him. "Syd says if we free this Kenntnis guy these gate things will vanish. Is that true?"

"I don't think it's quite that easy," Richard said. "But their effects will certainly be diminished. And we'll have the help of somebody who knows how to close the gates, and fight the Old Ones. He's done it before. A long time ago."

"But nobody can go in there and keep functioning," another person called from near the back of the room.

"Speaking of, could we turn that off?" a woman standing next to Pamela said as she pointed at the television. "It's making me . . ." She couldn't seem to bring herself to say it.

Apparently female machismo wasn't limited to Sam in this

crowd. Pamela said it for her. "Afraid. It makes us afraid."

Danny looked to Franklin, who looked to Richard. Her brother nodded. A few keystrokes and the screen went dark. Syd looked over at Richard. It was strange for Pamela to see people looking to her brother for guidance.

"Richard, do you suppose people like me and Sam, people who've been touched with the sword—do you think we could go in?" Syd asked.

"The sword doesn't make you brave. It just makes you sane," Richard said gently.

"And if you're sane you'll probably want to run away from the monsters," Sam added. This time there wasn't even a titter of gallows laughter from the people in the room.

Richard looked seriously up at Franklin and Syd, then swept the assembled agents with an intense blue-eyed gaze. "And while they can't feed on you after you've been touched, or use you to power their magic, they can kill you."

Franklin laid a hand on Richard's shoulder and addressed the people filling the room. "Look, the director's AWOL. We're getting orders out of Justice that are just plain nuts. I saw what this sword did for Syd."

Syd grabbed his daughter and pulled her forward. "And Sam."

For an instant the young agent hesitated, then grudgingly admitted, "Yeah, he . . . it fixed me."

"Well, I'm going to do it," Franklin resumed. "Anybody else want to join me?" He looked around. There were confirming nods from everyone.

Richard had the hilt of the sword in his hand. The room went very quiet. People watched him with varying degrees of skepticism, fear, and dread. He drew the sword, and skepticism vanished. Pamela leaned back against the wall and felt her shoulder blades grate against a framed plaque. Each time the sword was drawn now the musical overtones became deeper, stronger, and more resonant.

Pamela had now gone past tired to total exhaustion. Not

because it was after eleven at night but because of fear. What she had seen sapped her, and turned her worldview to chaos. She wanted to get this over with, go back to the condo and hide under the comforter. But somebody had to do it. It had to be said.

"Richard," she called sharply. He looked over at her. "What about the children?"

TWENTY-SEVEN

RICHARD

The water in the swimming pool was bathtub warm. Pretty soon my strokes had slowed, and I was taking a breath every two strokes instead of every four. Only the pain as my wound pulled and tugged kept me awake.

The hilt hung on a lanyard around my neck, and it felt like it was trying to drag me to the bottom. *Man falls asleep in swimming pool. Drowns. Film at eleven.*

And the sword would be the thing that tipped the balance. I tried not to read significance into the thought.

Back home I would have left it rolled up in a towel. But not here. Here it was never leaving me.

Pamela had fallen asleep in the car on the drive back from Franklin's. Even her terror over Sam's breakneck driving style hadn't been able to keep her awake. One particularly fast turn sent her falling against me. I had clasped an arm around her shoulders to steady her, and had the disorienting sense of protectiveness. Who knows, maybe some day we'd actually like each other.

Whoa, let's not go too far here.

I kicked harder. The sound of the churning water was both muffled and hollow in the echoing, tile-lined room. We'd gotten back to the condo at 1:00 A.M., but my sleep had been disturbed by the memory of crying children. The adults had experienced the sword, so they knew how much it would hurt, but most hadn't been discouraged. Only one woman had refused, saying she didn't want to deny her child his dreams and imagination. She had taken her son and left.

Her argument had actually shaken me. Maybe kids did need pretend games and imaginary friends to develop normally. What if the sword took that away? I didn't understand this weapon, and the man . . . creature who could have enlightened me was well out of reach. Which left me relying on my own judgment, and my choices so often sucked. Fortunately, Franklin was made of sterner stuff. He shrugged off the woman's objections as dumb. *"Hell, I can still imagine. In fact I can imagine a whole hell of a lot. More than I'd like."*

I had warned that he might not feel that way when his children were crying in pain. But again Franklin had brushed if off. *"It can't be any worse than a vaccination for school, and this is more important than a damn shot for whooping cough."*

So, in addition to reassuring me, the conversation had also provided me with a way to describe what happened when I used the sword. *Being inoculated.* It beat every other phrase people had come up with. When Cross called it "the touch" it sounded sleazy. When Pamela called it "submitting to the sword" it sounded like an S&M sex act. Dagmar had suggested "the dubbing," but that was even worse. "Inoculated" worked.

I tucked, somersaulted, caught the side of the pool with my feet, and pushed off again. Estevan's shadow fell across the water. What a life—rich as hell, and I had to be guarded around the clock. Boy, that's living. The deep end seemed a long, long way away. The muscles across my shoulders and down my triceps shivered with effort. It was time to admit defeat. I sidestroked over to the ladder, pulled off my goggles, and climbed out.

Estevan held out a towel. I dried off. Next he held my robe. It felt so odd to have people waiting on me. I muttered a thank you, and we left the pool and gym area and headed for the elevators.

It was inevitable. It was karma. It was kismet. We met Shih Tzu Man and his dog on the elevator. He was clutching a long pooper-scooper, and he treated us to his usual glare. The little dog seemed to be calming down about us. She just sniffed our ankles. Though Estevan looked like he wanted to drop-kick the little thing. The dog looked up at him. He looked down at her, and she reverted to form. She backed up against her owner's legs and started yapping. Naturally that was when my cell phone started to buzz and vibrate. I pulled it out.

"Oort."

"This is Senator Aldo's office."

"What?"

"Aldo, Senator Aldo."

Holy shit! Aldo. The senator from Nebraska held no official leadership position, but his influence went wide and deep. He was one of those figures the American people, whether Democrat, Republican, Independent, or Apathetic, seemed to embrace. Members of his own party deferred to him, the loyal opposition feared him, and the president heeded him. He sat on the Intelligence Committee and Foreign Relations, and he chaired the Armed Services Committee. It meant he'd most likely been briefed about conditions at the gate. The fact that he was calling me was significant.

"The senator would like to see you tomorrow at eleven A.M. in his office. Can you be there?"

"Yes. I'll be there."

Both Grenier and my father told me that Senator Aldo had the same office that John Kennedy had occupied back in the 1950s. It was appropriate. Both Kennedy and Aldo had been military men. Both were Liberals. Both entered Congress in their early thirties. Where they differed was in ambition and background. Aldo had chosen to stay in Congress rather than run for president, and he had not come from wealth. He had grown up on a farm, and watched a way of life vanish under pressure from corporate farming. In his autobiography he'd written that the experience had killed his father and shattered the family. All of it combined to make him a fierce defender of the common man.

Grenier had also told me that Aldo valued courage and independence, so I arrived solo. Well, solo was a relative term—Joseph, Rudi, and Estevan waited with the limo in one of the underground parking garages. I'd met a lot of politicians over the years, dated their daughters, seduced a few of them, and even slept with a couple of their sons. Politicians, simply by virtue of being politicians, held no mystery or awe for me, but I still wished my father had come along. The judge's calm gravitas would have been so much more effective than I could ever be.

I was reflecting on all of this as I walked down the hall. The three-beat rhythm of my footfalls and the awkward swing of the cane added to my nervousness. The hilt had been mounted on top of the cane so it wouldn't cause any problem when I went through security. We knew it registered as inert, but it would have seemed too strange to have had it in my pocket. It did overbalance the cane, however, and made it hard to control. The fact that my palm was sweat-slick with nerves didn't help either.

At the far end of the hall a group of tourists clustered around a portrait. As a cop I had been trained in situational awareness. I never entered a room without checking out every person in it, and I always got seated where I could watch people entering and leaving—even if I had to use a mirror to do it. Which meant I noticed the gaggle of tourists. I noticed the swing of long black hair, and the light glittering off the line of earrings running from the tips of her ears to the lobes. She had also been much on my mind during the intervening weeks since our last meeting in that dell in Virginia. *Rhiana.* I wasn't hallucinating; she was actually here.

I tightened my grip on the hilt and stopped, waiting for whatever might be thrown at me. But she didn't do anything. The tour was moving again. As they disappeared around a corner, she glanced back at me from beneath the brim of her fur hat. I made a hobbling run down the hall and spun around the corner. The tourists were still moving, the sound of shuffling feet and winter coughs loud in the enclosed space. They were all large, pallid, and older. A beautiful girl in a sable coat was not among them. I remembered when Grenier had vanished into a crack in a wall in a church in Colorado Springs. Rhiana had her own way of escaping.

As I retraced my steps I tried to comfort myself that there was more than one senator on this floor. They wouldn't know I'd been to see Aldo . . . I stopped myself. Of course they would know. There were appointment calendars and sign-in sheets, and—I glanced down at the white tag pasted to my label—and badges issued.

Secrecy was never going to work for us. If anything, we needed more transparency, more light shined on what was actually happening to our world. I pushed open the door into the senator's outer office. I was going to have to warn him that meeting with me might endanger his life. Yeah, that was going to go over well.

The staff didn't make me wait. Moments later I was in Aldo's personal office. I was surprised when Aldo left the power position behind the desk and indicated a pair of deeply upholstered chairs clustered around a low coffee table. We sat down, and for a long moment we just looked at each other. Fortunately, quiet had never bothered me. I've never felt the need to rush into conversation, and it gave me the time to study the man. Even in repose Aldo was an imposing figure. Six foot four, with broad, thick shoulders, and a neck as wide as his ears. Despite his age he hadn't run much to fat. I glanced over at the Heisman Trophy on the bookcase, and the framed Silver Star that hung above it. Suddenly I felt very intimidated by this man. Why on earth would he listen to me?

Aldo leaned back in his chair, fingers steepled before his face. "So, the message made this sound like the fate of the nation was hanging in the balance, and you were our only hope." The talking heads on the news channels described him as blunt rather than charming. They weren't kidding.

I felt my face flame with embarrassment, and my knee began jiggling nervously. I didn't think that would impress the senator, so I laid my hand on it, trying to hold it still. "Well, I wouldn't . . . I don't know who phrased it quite . . . well, it's half true."

"Which half?"

"Oh, come on, sir. You didn't actually think I'd say the second half, did you?"

A smile split the craggy angles of his face. "You'd be surprised. Politics is an egomaniac's game."

"First, I'm not a politician. Second . . . you are."

A rumbling chuckle shook the barrel chest. "Touché. Fortunately for you I know your father. Six years ago Judge Oort and I joined forces on an amicus brief in a gay adoption case coming before the Supreme Court, and worked together to oppose presidential signing statements. I respect your father, and somehow I don't think his son would be a liar."

"I'm not, sir," I said.

"So what is it you want to tell me?" Aldo asked.

I caught the piercing gleam in his brown eyes, and suddenly I knew what to do. "I don't need to tell you anything, sir. You're on the Intelligence Committee. You've seen the satellite images. You know this goes way beyond a foiled plot to detonate a nuke. This is much, much worse."

He leaned slowly back in his chair. "Those are classified. One call and I could put you in a world of hurt."

"And I can say I never saw those damn images. Remember, I was there when the gate first opened."

"A gate. Why do you call it that?"

"Because it's an opening through which an invading army is entering, and the government isn't doing squat. What's happening in Virginia and Jerusalem and India requires a unified and international response." I couldn't sit still. I jumped up and started pacing. "It may be there's a military solution to what's happening, but whatever action we take, it needs to be coordinated and guided from the highest levels. This isn't something the governor, the state police, or the National Guard can handle. America is the last superpower. The President has to act. I need to get in to see him. You're the man who can make that happen."

Aldo lowered his hands and began beating out a rhythm on the arms of the chair, while his big, square-jawed head swiveled slowly, assessing the pictures on the wall. I followed his gaze. Most of them were photos of the senator with five different presidents.

After a long moment he looked back at me. "Initially the FBI supported your position, but they've backed off that, and now they're in agreement with the NSA and Langley."

"And what might the NSA and Langley be saying?" I asked.

Aldo's lips never parted when he smiled. The corners of his mouth just stretched, making his cheeks more prominent. "That's classified."

Frustration can have an actual taste. I clenched my hands and gritted my teeth, trying to hold back the profanity.

"Yeah, it makes you crazy, doesn't it?" the senator said softly. "Look, I can tell you this much. Lobbing a bomb into an area where guns, radios, cameras, and so forth don't work wouldn't be all that effective."

"Meaning they tried it," I said, and I sat back down.

Aldo just smiled again. "But of course a place where weapons don't operate would have some really interesting applications for a government that understood and controlled that technology."

This time I couldn't keep control. The words burst out, hot and intemperate. "It's not technology! It can't be controlled. And any moron who tries is going to end up dead or worse."

"There's a worse?"

"Oh, yeah. And these things that are pouring through the gates are going to prove that to us."

Suddenly Aldo leaned forward. He was so tall that he came almost completely across the coffee table. His face was inches

186

from mine. I could smell the breath mint he'd chewed. "And why should I believe you over all these other people and agencies?"

It was something I've had to learn; it was not my nature to get in people's faces. But I was a cop, and if there was one thing we knew it was how to push back. I leaned forward, and was surprised when Aldo retreated. I pursued the advantage, saying, "Because I've come here at no small personal risk to offer my help. I could have stayed in New Mexico, and been safe for a little while longer. But sooner or later it will be everywhere. It will cover the world. *Unless we do something.*"

Aldo leaned back in his chair and regarded me for a long, long time. "What do you do, son?"

The question surprised me, and I answered instinctively. "I'm a policeman."

"I thought you were the head of Lumina Enterprises."

"I'm that, too, but . . ." I pulled out my badge case, opened it, and studied the badge. The light from the ceiling fixture gleamed on the gold shield. The hilt, perched precariously atop the cane, leaned heavily against my knee. and for one strange, distorting moment the shield seemed to expand until it filled my sight, blotting out the room.

I was jerked back to the moment when a hand fell heavily onto my shoulder. Aldo was looming over me, holding a glass of water.

"Here."

"Thank you." I took a sip. Clearly lack of sleep was catching up with me.

"Well, you're not telling me everything. Not by a long way," the senator said. He paused. The silence was excruciating. Then he suddenly added, "But that can wait until we sit down with the President."

I nearly spilled the water in my haste to set aside the glass and stand. "You'll do it? You'll get me in?"

"Can you tell us why people are losing their minds?"

"Yes."

"Can you tell us what these things are?"

"Yes."

"Can you tell us how to fight them?"

"Yes."

I hoped my bravura performance was enough to hide the fact that my final answer was a lie.

"You'll be ready to go at any time?" Aldo asked as he moved back to his desk.

"Day or night."

"I'll be in touch."

It was dismissal. I hesitated at the door, then looked back.

"Sir." He looked up from the papers he was reading. "By helping me you're putting yourself at risk, too. Be careful, okay?"

"Always am."

Yeah, but you don't know that one of them was in the hall outside your office. That they can walk through walls. That they can use magic against you because I wasn't able to inoculate you. Because that really would have been a bridge too far.

I let myself out and went limping through the outer office. It was humming with activity. I noted that the senator's staff tended to be young and passionate. At one desk a couple of staffers were reviewing legislation. At a corner table a trio of young women shook letters out of a mailbag.

As I passed the receptionist's desk, she looked up and gave me a white-toothed smile. Her perfectly coiffed and sprayed hair didn't move.

"Have a blessed day," she chirped.

I got into the hall, leaned against the wall, and realized we were surrounded.

TWENTY-EIGHT

From the bitter cold of a Washington, D.C., January to the sultry heat of an Australian January, and Pamela hadn't packed a thing appropriate for a southern hemisphere summer. On her way to the Air Raid City Lodge, the taxi passed a mall in downtown Darwin, and she had the driver stop. She ran into a department store and bought jeans, a T-shirt, and sandals. "I'll wear them," she told the salesgirl, and had them put her wool slacks, cashmere sweater, and pumps into the bag.

During the seemingly endless flight, she'd spent time on what passed for research in the modern age—she'd Googled Darwin, Australia, and read all the tourist information sites. They had all agreed that Darwin had the youngest population of any city in Australia. Her brief foray into the mall had provided anecdotal proof of that—it was filled with lots and lots of young people.

Of course, most malls were filled with young people. The sway of the taxi was like the rocking of a hammock. *Or maybe we have a visceral memory of floating in the womb, or being rocked in a cradle.* She realized she was maundering in her own head, and she gave herself a physical shake. Once in the lobby of the lodge she called up to Dr. Tanaka's room.

"Hello?" It was a surprisingly young voice, and he sounded hesitant and suspicious.

"Hi, this is Pamela Oort, Lumina sent me. Are you ready to go?"

"Oh, shit, yeah." And the connection was broken even as she was opening her mouth to tell the scientist what she looked like.

She took up a position where she could watch for a Japanese American entering the lobby. The room was buzzing with activity—people booking tours, and a party of young Germans, all wearing backpacks, checking in at the front desk.

Moments later an incredibly tall, incredibly thin Asian man dressed in jeans, a white tee, and tennis shoes hurried into the lobby. Pamela stood up, but he looked right past her. Instead he zeroed in on an older, heavyset woman. He said something, and she shook her head. Frowning, he moved on to the next closest woman. For some kind of physics genius he seemed pretty damn clueless, Pamela thought. After the fourth such encounter Pamela took pity on the other guests and walked up to him.

"Dr. Tanaka?" she asked.

"Yeah."

"I'm Pamela Oort."

"Oh, okay. Huh, I didn't think you'd look like . . . well, like you do."

"And just how do I look?" The moment the unwary words emerged Pamela wished she hadn't uttered them.

"Kind of pretty." She drew herself up and gave him the patented Oort disdainful glare right down the nose. He seemed unfazed and in fact continued to dig deeper. "You don't expect that from a corporate drone."

"Are you trying to be rude?"

"Oh." His mouth worked as if he were chewing on something. "So, that came across as rude rather than as a compliment?"

Pamela looked him directly in the eye, but he wasn't being sarcastic. It still didn't incline her to be charitable. "Well, duh," she said and was pleased when he blushed. "Do you have anything in your room?" He shook his head. "Do we owe anything on the room?" He again shook his head. "So, we're ready then." Turning on her heel, she headed for the door. Tanaka took two long strides like a wading stork and fell into step with her.

"Actually, I'd like to get something to eat before we leave. I was using the computer in the business center and I kind of forgot to eat."

The reminder set her stomach to growling. There was a small galley on the Gulfstream, but the choices were limited to cold cuts and bread for sandwiches. A hot meal and a martini sounded lovely.

As they walked toward the door he added, "Actually I used up a lot of the money you sent me buying computer time." He glowered at the front desk and added, "It's just bullshit. It's so cheap, but these hotels just stick it to you."

"Your work must have been very important," Pamela said.

"Oh, shit, this wasn't work. I can't do my work without an accelerator. No, my raid group was entering a dungeon, and it took a lot longer than I thought it would." This time she didn't have to explain her expression to him. He looked momentarily guilty, then sulky, and finally devastated. "I just wanted to feel like things were normal again," he said in a tone barely above a whisper.

Pamela laid a hand briefly on his upper arm. "I know. I understand."

As they stepped into the tropical heat and Pamela waved for a taxi, she reflected on how terrifying that statement actually was— that an online computer game felt more normal than the world they presently inhabited.

They found a restaurant right on the beach. Pamela watched the waves rush forward and then retreat with a hiss and a chuckle, like mischievous children begging the grown-ups to chase them. Running in pursuit of the white foam were tiny, long-legged birds pecking at the wet sand.

Pamela leaned back in the fan-backed wicker chair and took another sip of her green appletini. Her lobster thermidor had been wonderful and very rich. Eddie Tanaka was still masticating his way through a giant plate of fried seafood and french fries. He had downed five refills of Coke thus far. She could only conclude that he burned off the calories with the caffeine high. She had finished first because Eddie had been punctuating bites with tales of his escape from Indonesia.

"I was really careful not to speak English. I mean, I'd watched them burn down the American and the British embassies, and I speak some Japanese so I could fake people out, but man, it was scary. I got down to the docks and managed to get on this old freighter. I got lucky—one of Talafani's crew had landed in jail, and he didn't want to brave the city when things were going nuts. I was there. I'm tall, and I didn't seem nuts." He stuffed a breaded jumbo shrimp into his mouth, and Pamela watched his throat work as he swallowed the massive bite. A Coke chaser and he was back talking.

"You know how people are always talking about the romance of working a tramp steamer, exotic ports of call, sloe-eyed women in the exotic ports—well, it's a crock. They ought to ban kids reading Hemingway. Anyway, Captain Talafani worked us like slaves, and I was awful seasick, but he expected me to keep working anyway." The outrage rang in his voice. "I'm never eating curry again. We had a lot of curry, and it just turns your vomit yellow and it's like eating it again only worse.

"Even though this was a really big ship . . ." He spread his arms out like a fisherman displaying a prize catch. "There were only fourteen of us on board—automation's really changed things—and none of them would talk to me." He considered and then added, "They didn't talk to each other either, but I didn't totally get how much they were channeling Greta Garbo until one guy punched me in the stomach. That made me sick all over again, and I was blowing chunks—"

Pamela interrupted a new rendition of exactly what he'd eaten and how it looked when it came back up. "The police said you came ashore in a lifeboat. Why did you leave the ship?"

"'Cause Talafani was steaming right back to Libya, and I sure as hell didn't want to be in another Islamic country after what had happened." For an instant his gaze seemed lost, and distant, and frightened. He quickly ate an oyster.

"I really sucked up to the captain. He liked this gross, really sweet tea with condensed milk in it, and I kept bringing it up to the bridge for him. I finally got a look at the charts, and realized this chunk of coral represented the Sylph. That was the ship's name. Anyway, I saw we were close to Australia, so I stole food out of the galley, filled some empty bourbon bottles with water, and hid them in the lifeboat. I waited for the first moonless night, and then lowered the lifeboat, and dove into the water after it. I had to swim like hell to catch up with it. It got caught in the ship's wake."

"You dove off the side of a commercial freighter?"

Eddie shrugged. "I grew up in San Diego, practically in the water. And I was a competitive diver in high school and college. It was no worse than a platform dive." He mopped up more ketchup with several french fries and gobbled them down. A few more massive bites and the last of the breaded fish was also gone. He drained his glass, burped, and sighed.

"All set?" Pamela asked.

He nodded. "You're taking me back to California, right?"

"Actually no, my brother needs to talk to you first."

"He can come to California." He sounded pugnacious, and Pamela decided it wasn't the right moment to argue with him. Then he added in a little boy's voice, "I want to go home, and see my parents."

For the first time she realized how terribly young he was, and she saw the fear that he'd been holding at bay.

The visit to Britches, Washington's premier old-line men's clothier, had been necessitated because Grenier could barely zip his slacks closed over his burgeoning paunch. As he had told Richard, he needed a new wardrobe before he was arrested for indecent exposure. The young man had taken a look at the pale skin and graying chest hair revealed by the gaping buttons and quickly agreed.

Grenier had really stressed the outing because there were things he needed to report, and he didn't want that gray presence of the judge interfering with Richard's natural cunning. Aside from the ever-present guards they were alone, which suited Grenier just fine. He hated the judge's constant hovering over Richard. It had stopped seeming protective, and had started to feel more like a doctor making sure a mental patient didn't do something dangerous or foolish. Grenier had only been with Lumina for six days, but he couldn't find the young man who had defied him, challenged him, and played him for a fool. Instead Richard had retreated to hesitant childhood.

While these thoughts ran through his head, Grenier was issuing orders to a young salesman. "I want a gray suit with a small pinstripe of lavender. I want a blue suit with a pinstripe of yellow and brown. And I want the buttonholes enlarged. I have to work one-handed. Also a selection of slacks and shirts, and a black sports coat. Go." He waved the young man away. "Oh, and shoes, wing tips in black and brown, size ten—"

"And who's going to tie them?" Richard asked. He had his back to Grenier and was sifting through a stack of cashmere sweaters displayed on a polished cherrywood table.

Grenier flushed and couldn't control the glance down at his stump. The rush of fury, regret, and grief left him breathless. He regained control and said smoothly, "An excellent point. Loafers, then, and let's try a C width." He joined Richard and said in an undertone, "Even my feet are getting fat. I didn't know that could happen."

"You could try eating less."

"Leave me a few of my pleasures. You've taken so much from me." Their gazes locked, and Richard looked away out the front window. Grenier watched Richard stiffen. "What?"

Richard indicated a car driving slowly past with a jerk of his chin. It was a BMW convertible. The driver's long black hair floated around her, and though her eyes and much of her face were hidden behind large dark glasses and a muffler, it was clear she was gazing at the store.

"My, my," Grenier said.

The car passed the store and suddenly accelerated away.

"So, you said your barhopping had yielded results?" Richard asked.

"You're not going to deal with that?" Grenier asked and pointed at the rapidly dwindling car.

"What would you suggest? Run down the street with the sword drawn? Shoot her in the head? And she's careful never to give me a chance to get close to her."

"So this isn't the first time you've seen her." Richard shook his head. "Why haven't you mentioned it?"

"Because everyone would start clucking."

Grenier chuckled. "Good point." He hurried into speech after seeing Richard's impatience. "Ah yes, what I've learned. The Cardinal of Washington, D.C., has sent for a team of experts from the Vatican. No details on what kind of experts, but I think it can only mean one thing. They're going to try an exorcism."

Richard gave a short bark of laughter. "Whoa, wow, I bet the Old Ones are scared now."

"I think the Old Ones will let it . . . work," and Grenier bracketed the words with quote marks in the air with his one hand. "Miracles will occur, stigmata will bleed, the Madonna will cry, maybe even the face of Jesus will appear in some interesting foodstuff. The Catholic faithful will be ecstatic. But in the evangelical churches the preachers will be thundering from their pulpits that this is the Antichrist, and that the Catholics, by worshiping a false god, are preventing the real Jesus from returning."

"Oh, the Catholics hate the Protestants and the Protestants hate the Catholics, and the Hindus hate the Moslems and everybody hates the Jews." Richard softly sang the old Tom Lehrer song.

"Exactly. Also, word about the sword is leaking out. People are talking, at least in the bureaucracy. If we verify its existence I think you'll have takers just like you did with those FBI agents."

"Career bureaucrats may not set policy, but they actually run the government," Richard mused. "We need a mechanism for meeting with them. I can't just go walking in and out of agencies whacking people with a sword."

"If Aldo succeeds and you manage to see the President, he may mandate it," Grenier said.

The young salesman returned. "Sir," he said diffidently to Grenier, "I have a selection of clothing for you to try."

"Thank you, I'll be right there," Grenier said. He waved the man away. "There's one more thing we need to consider—media." Grenier watched as Richard's nostrils narrowed with disdain. He threw back his head and laughed. "God, you old blue-blood families and your elitist attitudes. It's the twenty-first century, baby," and he reached out and patted Richard on the cheek. He was surprised when Richard didn't jerk away as he had every other time Grenier tried for physical contact.

Richard sighed. "I know you're right. You've got the experience. Are you willing to take it on?"

Grenier struggled to hide his surprise. "You're actually going to give me some responsibility?"

"Yes."

"Power?"

"Limited."

"Okay. Money is no object, so let's have some very slick and very scary commercials made, and air them nationally. Interviews, articles, blogs, Web sites, podcasts, chat rooms . . ."

Richard's phone rang. "Oort."

Grenier watched as all the color drained from the young man's face, and his eyes seemed suddenly dark and sunken. Richard hung up the phone and looked up at Grenier.

"Aldo's been killed."

* * *

The vibration from the engines seemed to have permanently embedded itself in her bones. Pamela sighed and leaned her head against the plane's window. At least the seats in the company jet were wide and very comfortable. They even went flat so you could sleep. But that constant thrum! She shook her head and picked back up the Bose headphones. They helped with the engine noise and the Eddie noise. The young scientist snored like a log stripper.

There had been a bit of a kerfuffle when they stopped to refuel at an airfield in eastern California. Eddie had tried to get off, saying he needed to stretch his legs, but Pamela had caught the furtive look toward the small building and the cars in the parking lot, and said no. It hadn't escalated because Pamela had the very good idea to have Jerry stand in the door of the plane and openly wear his pistol. Apparently Tanaka's high IQ allowed him to add two and two.

Pamela looked out the window again. They were flying over the great flat empty of the Midwest. Much of it was snow covered, and Pamela wondered what the people in those small towns and farms thought, or even knew, about what was happening. It was a part of the country that grew wheat, made cheese, and sent kids into the army and Republicans to Congress.

Eddie awoke with a snort and a mumble. He gave her a bleary-eyed look across the aisle. "Hungry. Gonna make a sandwich. Want one?"

She shook her head, and turned back on the music she'd been listening to, and watched the clouds they were now flying over. Occasionally wisps of cloud swirled up, smokelike, to caress the wings of the plane.

Eddie returned from the galley with a true Dagwood sandwich, piled high with turkey, pastrami, and liverwurst. He settled back into his seat; his jaw seemed to crack in half as he took a bite. He glanced out the window, let out a whimper, and lettuce and lunch meat rained into his lap.

Pamela unsnapped her seat belt and rushed over to him. "What? Are you all right?"

He pointed wordlessly. His hand was shaking. Pamela looked out the window at another plane that was rising through the clouds like a breaching silver whale.

There were winged *creatures* beneath the wings and belly of the plane. Holding it up. Slowly one of the massive heads turned and *looked* at them.

Pamela jerked down the shade over the window, as if that could somehow protect them. Then a sudden banking of the Gulfstream sent her falling against Eddie. He caught her, and she didn't try to pull free. Instead she wrapped her arms around him, too, taking comfort in his human touch.

TWENTY-NINE

"Would the two of you care to explain why I had to arrange the murder of a United States senator?" Madoc said as he continued in rapt contemplation of the delicate Japanese painting of cranes in a snowy landscape.

They were in the Freer and Sackler Galleries at the Smithsonian Institution. Despite Madoc's mild, almost plaintive tone, Rhiana took a step back and to the side so she was standing partly behind Jack. Neither of them dared to answer.

"I thought you were getting the sword and neutralizing the paladin. Not letting the paladin nearly reach the President. So, when do we get the sword?" Madoc asked.

"Why does it matter so much?" Jack asked. "You've told us the sword alone can't close a gate. So what if Oort gets to the President, or the Joint Chiefs, or the Chamber of Commerce for that matter. They throw more troopies at you, you kill them or make them nuts, and hey, it's all-you-can-eat night."

"Because, you fool, *we* have a paladin. If we also have the sword we can kill competitors." Jack flinched. "Now go, and get this done." Madoc sat down on a bench and stared at the paintings again.

Neither of them spoke until they were walking down the Mall toward the gleaming white spire of the Washington Monument.

"So, what's with the art connoisseur? The past three times I've met with him, it's been in art galleries or museums," Jack said. The sound of his voice sent a trio of crows flapping up into the sky like animated apostrophes. "Or is he just planning which ones he's going to steal after the great monster conquest?"

"They don't get creativity. Music's alien to them, too. They don't even like to hear it." The dried winter grass crunched beneath the soles of her boots. There was a brisk wind whipping the hem of her sable coat around her ankles. It smelled of impending snow.

"Huh. I wonder what that means."

"That they're alien," Rhiana said shortly.

Once again silence stretched between them; then Jack said, "So, it sounds like it's not all Universal Monster Brotherhood." He tried to keep it light, but the worry crept in. "I thought I was safe because I was on your team, only now I find out there's an NFL and an AFL. Did I pick the wrong team?"

"I don't know, Jack, you want to try getting traded?"

Her long hair, caught by the wind, snaked across her mouth and eyes. She clawed it back and held it in a mock ponytail as she said, "You need to call Sandringham. He's got to get this done."

"He will," Jack said. "He's a smart, methodical guy. He's not going to rush this and blow it. He knows these people. For years. He'll play it right."

"But we need to rush. If the others learn we have a paladin and we're after the sword, they're going to gang up on us. We need the sword to protect us," Rhiana said, and it gave her a perverse pleasure to watch Jack's expression go from worried to outright sick.

"Great, I'm in a fucking shark cage."

"Yeah, well, I'm in it, too! I'm the one who said I could get him."

Jack stopped walking, stepped in front of her, and put his hands on her shoulders; they were warm and heavy. "Rhiana."

But she didn't see Jack or hear his voice. Instead she heard and saw Richard. He had said her name. And then he held out his hand to her and said, *And I choose you.*

If only that had been true.

Emboldened by her silence, Jack slipped an arm around her shoulders. "Hey, at least it won't be so lonely with two in the cage," and she felt his lips against her forehead. She yanked away from him.

"Don't! Just don't. I don't want you."

Rudi had picked them up at the private airstrip in Maryland, and Pamela was surprised to find Richard had ridden out with him. Eddie and Richard's first meeting had been chaotic because the young scientist was trying to explain what he'd seen in Indonesia and what had happened during the flight, and terror was making him nearly incoherent.

Richard had laid a hand on Eddie's shoulder and given it a hard squeeze. "You've been incredibly brave and very smart to get away." Then Richard surprised her by adding, "But maybe we should let Pamela explain. She's very good with words."

Pamela had recounted what she had learned from Eddie about the events at the lab, but when she got to a description of what she'd seen beneath the wings of the other airplane, she was having trouble keeping her voice level and her hands from shaking.

"It saw me, Richard. It looked right at me. It will know me if it sees me again. It wants to hurt me."

And Richard put his arm around her shoulders and gave her a tight hug. "I won't let it," he'd said, and she was surprised when she felt gratitude welling up like a warm bubble into her chest, and even more surprised when she realized she believed him and felt safer.

Before they left the plane, Richard unlimbered the sword and made his request. Pamela had expected Eddie to refuse, but he had been fascinated by the sword blade that appeared out of nowhere. He was muttering about "pocket universes" even as the blade touched his shoulder. It hadn't hurt him as much as it had others, which supported Richard's theories that a grounding in math, science, and music seemed to reduce a person's quotient of magic. Which was contrary to conventional wisdom—creativity was supposed to be magical.

During the ride to the condo Richard gave Eddie a crash course on the world according to Lumina, and Pamela turned on her phone and checked her messages. She had three from Amelia. Only the final one told Pamela what was on her older sister's mind.

"Hey, Pammie, I know you're with Richard and I know he's really busy, but could you please get him to call Brent back? My husband's about ready to kill our brother, and I'm in the middle, which is not a good place to be. Thanks. Love ya."

Pamela looked over at her brother, but Richard was deep into the explanation and she hesitated to interrupt. Then when they reached the condo Angela took one look at their wan faces and ordered everyone into the kitchen, saying, "As my *abuela* always said, when people are stressed, scared, and tired you feed them."

Their father held Richard back. The judge had his glasses perched on his nose, and he was frowning down at a piece of paper. "I have a list of legislators we need to visit. Not one of them is as powerful as Aldo, but perhaps a coalition can be formed."

Richard had stepped away. "Not now."

"This needs to be—"

"I said, *not now.*" And Richard walked away.

Pamela's stomach became a small aching ball when she watched her father's face twist with pure rage. The judge stormed away, and Pamela dithered between running after him or joining the others in the kitchen. *Richard shouldn't have been rude,* she thought as she tried to catch her breath. *But Papa keeps bemoaning the fact that Richard is so biddable.* There had been plenty of times when he snapped at Richard for not taking control of his life, making decisions and living with his choices.

But the one time Richard did, the big choice when he became a policeman, Papa was furious.

Pamela didn't like that thought. She put it aside and decided to wait to talk to her father. She entered the kitchen; Angela handed her a wooden spoon and set her to sautéing meat. Joseph stood at another burner toasting fresh garlic to go on the bread. The blade of a knife clacked against the wood cutting board like a rhythm-impaired flamenco dancer as Dagmar chopped the ingredients for an enormous salad. Angela was dropping lasagna noodles into a pot of boiling water, and Sam was grating cheese.

For a moment Pamela considered the biological or societal pressures that had a lawyer, a doctor, an FBI agent, and the COO of a major international company attending to the traditional female role of cooking while most of the men sat at the table and talked. But perhaps that was more a testament to the actual superiority of the female sex. Men talked and posed and blustered, but women got the job done—they kept bodies and souls together.

Pamela looked back over her shoulder to where Richard sat at the head of the table with the young scientist, Eddie Tanaka, on his left, and Grenier on Richard's right, idly spinning a wineglass by its stem. Syd was farther down the table, topping off his glass from a bottle of Chianti. The bottle headed back up the table. As usual Richard wasn't drinking, satisfying himself with a glass of cranberry juice.

Eddie had his chair pulled around until he was actually sitting at the corner of the table rather than on the side so he could be closer to Richard. Pamela had noticed that as they moved from plane to car, and car to condo, and around the condo, Tanaka had walked directly next to Richard, his arm often brushing against Richard's shoulder. Pamela wondered how Richard liked having a duckling.

But right now Tanaka's focus was on the screen of a laptop. He had his elbows on the table and his chin cupped in his hands, watching satellite images from the gate. Pamela respected, and resented, his ability to look at the pictures with interest rather than terror.

"Rhiana called it slow glass," Richard offered as Eddie continued to watch and didn't respond.

Angela's hands jerked and she tore a noodle, and Pamela realized that even hearing the girl's name infuriated the older woman.

"She must not be very bright. That term was used in a really great science fiction story, 'Light of Other Days' by Bob Shaw, but the technical term,"—Eddie leaned back in his chair and gestured at the computer—"is a Bose-Einstein condensate. But this doesn't look like a condensate." Eddie suddenly jerked his head around to look at where Joseph spun the handle on the Mouli, grating Parmesan cheese over the garlic-and-butter-drenched bread. "Oh, gross," Eddie said. "Cheese on garlic bread is gross."

There was an almost audible sound as everyone tried to shift gears mentally. Joseph looked down at the skinny young scientist.

"So, don't eat any. We all like it with cheese."

Eddie got a funny look on his face, and his lips moved as if he were repeating something to himself. "I'm sorry," he said formally to Joseph. "That was rude of me."

Richard took control. "So, if it's not a condensate, what is it?"

"I think it's a spin glass," Eddie said.

"And what's that when it's at home?" Syd asked.

"It's a way to slow or even freeze light so you can study its properties," Eddie answered.

"Why the fuck would you want to do that?" Sam asked as she washed her hands.

"Because it's really cool, but here's an explanation even you might get," Eddie said. "It's got economic applications. It's a way to build a quantum computer that would be screamingly fast. Whoever succeeds gets really, really rich."

"But how does this trap Kenntnis?" Dagmar asked before Sam could blow.

"And these things are real?" Syd's question tripped over the COO's.

Eddie started with Syd's question. "Yeah. They've been created in the laboratory. Cornell, Wieman, and Ketterle won the Nobel back in 2001. But they don't withstand contact with the real world, so this thing"—he gestured at the computer screen—"shouldn't exist. Of course, who the hell knows what's real anymore. And it certainly can't trap a person." He laid a pencil against the screen. "It looks to be only a few centimeters wide."

Richard cleared his throat, a nervous little sound, and he looked from Eddie to Bob to Syd to Sam to Dagmar, then cast his eyes upward. "Well, actually I don't think . . . in fact, I'm pretty sure that Kenntnis isn't human."

Dagmar sank into a chair. "Oh, dear, I was coping so well, and now you add this."

"We're talking about my employer. The man I worked for for seven years?" Joseph asked.

"'Fraid so," Richard said.

"Rhiana said . . ." Richard closed his eyes trying to recall. "Slow glass traps light, and she said that's all Kenntnis was—just light."

Eddie leaned into the computer screen again, narrowing his eyes. A few clicks of the mouse enlarged the image.

Eddie leaned back in his chair. "Okay, let's assume for a minute that I'm not crazy and something that you thought was a person was actually just a stream of photons. And you wanted to trap it. The experiments have shown that you can store light's information in the form of an atomic 'spin wave.' Atoms spin like tops, so they sort of act like little bar magnets. So, what you do is introduce the light signal—a probe laser, but in our case it's this guy, Kenntnis—into the glass. At the same time you use another laser, a pump or control laser, to create electromagnetically induced transparency. Then the light interacts with the atoms, which changes the atoms' spin states coherently, and that creates a joint atom-photon system, and that's called a polariton."

"Help," Dagmar said, and the word was a plaintive squeak.

"I guess another part of being such a big genius is you can't put anything in simple English," Sam remarked to the room, indulging in a little payback.

Eddie looked up at the young agent. "Yeah, I guess you'd need it simple."

Sam leaned down and held up two fingers. "That's *two*. One

more and I'm gonna punch you real hard in the stomach." Eddie looked alarmed, Sam looked satisfied, and Richard looked pissed.

"Stop it. I don't have time for this kind of childish bullshit."

"Hey," Sam squawked. "That's one to you."

"I mean it." Pamela had never heard that tone in her brother's voice before, and she realized she didn't want to hear it directed at her. "Go on," he ordered Eddie.

"Okay, well, what that means is that it weighs down the massless photons and continues to slow down the pulse's speed. You keep adding mass and eventually the light pulse stops moving, and the information that the pulse carried is stored in the atomic spin wave. It can be released again as a light pulse, and it's virtually identical to the frozen pulse." Then the young scientist realized that everyone was staring at him in varying degrees of desperate concentration. "You're taking this seriously?" he asked feebly.

Richard turned until he faced the young scientist full on. "Yes. We really are."

"But this isn't real," Eddie protested feebly.

Grenier spoke up for the first time. "You said yourself, son, you don't know what's real anymore. Your scientific principles still apply, but they're being affected, warped, by the magic."

"Magic isn't real," Eddie said. The frown and tightly compressed lips showed the level of his denial.

"It is. And getting more real by the minute," Grenier countered. His voice was thick with amused enjoyment.

"That's enough for him right now." Richard stood up. "Dr. Tanaka, you're tired, you need to process what I told you about the Lumina and the multiverses, and you need to come up with a plan to break Kenntnis free. How did you put it? Release the pulse. But right now I've got other things, mundane but pressing, that I have to do."

Eddie looked up at Angela. "You won't let me sleep through dinner?"

She laughed. "We'll ring the dinner bell real loud."

"I'd like to study that sword thing," Eddie mumbled as he headed out of the kitchen. "But if it won't stay in phase unless he's holding it, how do . . ."

Distance reduced the words to a baritone hum, and then they were gone with the shutting of a bedroom door.

THIRTY

RICHARD

It was like feeling eyes or tasting a change in the air. *Someone was in the bedroom with me.* I opened my eyes to the barest slit. Fortunately there was enough city glare leaking around the folds of the drapes to make out shapes. A shadow within the shadows hovered at the side of the bed. My stomach gave a lurch, and suddenly my decision to keep my guards outside the condo seemed beyond stupid. These were people who could travel across the continent using a tear in a wall.

I dropped a hand off the side of the mattress, and my fingers touched the textured edge of the pistol's grip hidden beneath the bed. Once I had the gun firmly in hand, I shot my right hand up and grabbed the material at the person's throat, dragging him down toward me. At the same time, I brought up the pistol and jammed the barrel deep in under the intruder's short ribs.

There was came a *woof* as the air was driven out of his lungs and a strangled squeak of fear. My eyes had adjusted to the gloom, and I found myself face-to-face with Eddie Tanaka. The young scientist's breath, blowing across my face, was unpleasantly sour. The small amount of lasagna I had managed to choke down was threatening to make a return.

"What do you want? What are you doing in here?" I demanded,

and Eddie recoiled. I realized the words had emerged in a harsh, tense whisper.

"I had a question." The words emerged as a croak because I had the material twisted tight against his larynx.

I checked the clock and tried to process that. "You came into my bedroom at three in the morning to *ask me a question*?"

"Yeah."

"It couldn't wait until morning?"

"I couldn't sleep," came the disingenuous answer.

"Well, *I* could."

Not that it had been easy. Watching the red sauce bubbling had taken me back to the house on Quincy, and Aldo's death had left me feeling like this entire excursion had been a waste of time and fucking dangerous as well. I truly didn't have a clue about what to do next. And added to all this there was Rhiana. I had spotted her BMW ineptly following our limo as we returned from the airport. Since it was no secret where we were going I just let her follow, but it was scary and confusing. When I had three seconds to myself I needed to analyze her behavior and try to figure it out.

Tanaka frowned. "Oh, yeah. Didn't think about that. Do . . . do you think you could take the gun out of my side? And then answer my question."

I sighed and released him, and set the Starfire back under the bed. "Okay."

"You always keep a gun with you?" Tanaka asked.

"That was the question?"

"Uh. No. But do you always keep a gun with you?"

I was suddenly wavering between screaming annoyance and laughter. I thought back on my psychology classes in college. *Asperger's. It had to be Asperger's syndrome.*

"Yes."

"Why?"

"Because people keep trying to kill me."

Tanaka's eyes widened. "Wow. Really?"

"Yes, really. Can we get to the question?" I prodded.

The scientist sat down on the mattress. His hip was pressed against my thigh. Fortunately it wasn't my right leg. "I've never seen anybody die before . . . before . . . Indonesia," the young man said. "When my grandma was dying I wouldn't go in the hospital room until it was all over. And I get the shakes just thinking about . . . what happened."

"Dr. Tanaka, forgive me, but it's late and I'm tired. Is that question at least on approach? Will it be arriving soon?"

"Oh, yeah, sorry. And could you call me Eddie? I get real uncomfortable when people call me doctor." I nodded. "Anyway, they said you used to be a policeman. So, have you ever killed anybody?"

"Yes." It was such a small word to encompass so much, but I didn't amplify.

"Is it hard to do?" Eddie asked. "I mean, would the way I feel about seeing people die affect . . . I mean, keep me from—"

"Killing someone?" I broke in.

"Yeah. Did it bother you? When you killed them?" Eddie asked.

I stood on the edge of a sea of complex emotions—grief, guilt, pride, excitement. I was afraid I'd drown if I went in. "Yes. Look, Eddie, if you don't have to kill people, I don't think you should."

"But I want them to pay! For what they did . . . to everybody!"

I laid a hand over the young scientist's and felt Eddie's fingers close convulsively over mine. "You figure out how to free Kenntnis. That's a far better thing to do for the memory of your friends," I said.

Eddie stood, and his hand slipped free. My hand felt suddenly very cold. "Thanks." He got almost to the door before he slewed around like a gawky foal and added, "Oh, yeah, I'm sorry I woke you up." Eddie slipped out of the room.

I pummeled a pillow, trying to get some lift in the feathers. Great, now I was wide awake, and I had to go back up the hill to Congress today. I tried to think about what I had to do, had to say, but disjointed thoughts and memories kept flashing like brief bursts of lightning through my mind. I saw the blood pumping from a throat wound when I'd shot the perp who nearly killed my partner. The bone chips flying when I'd killed Snyder. There was another thought buried deep. I dug it up and looked at it. I wanted to find the men who'd brutalized me, and let a bullet peel back skin and muscle and listen to them scream. But of course I knew where one of them lived. Drew Sandringham was a quick flight up the coast in New York City.

My fantasies shattered when faced with the tangible reality of killing a man I'd known for most of my life. Maybe I wasn't really a killer. Which should have made me feel good, but instead I felt depressed, as if I didn't have the grit to do a hard job.

All these thoughts of death had me thinking about morgues, which made me think about Angela. We had been dating back in Albuquerque, trying to see if we could build a relationship. We hadn't been alone since I'd swept us all off to Washington. She'd suggested a date night, and I'd put her off. Honestly, I'd even felt resentful. She shouldn't have come; she should have stayed in New Mexico and done her job. Weber needed her. A conversation we'd had about the dead scientists from the Santa Fe Institute came floating to mind. Like a puzzle piece, it snapped into place with the killings in Indonesia.

I came out of bed and made a limping run into the living room. Laptops, their lids gleaming silver, lay on various surfaces like tiles in a giant's Mahjongg set. I found one open and still running. I logged onto VICAP and typed in *scientists* and *murders*.

The list of incidents scrolled by for a long time. And that was just crimes in the United States.

THIRTY-ONE

"What's been accomplished?"

Grenier looked up from his book at the sound of Richard's voice approaching down the hallway of the condo.

What emerged into the living room looked more like a flying wedge moving down the field during an Australian rules football game. Richard, walking quickly, was pulling on gloves. Dagmar strode along at his side. Angela, with her short legs, was almost trotting to keep up, and she kept offering Richard a fedora. Tanaka, towering over everyone, looked like a wading stork. Behind him were the judge and Pamela, and bringing up the rear were Rudi and Estevan.

"I've blanketed our scientific facilities with security," Dagmar said.

"And alerted local law enforcement?" Richard asked.

"Alerted and paid off as necessary depending on the part of the world," Dagmar replied.

"Is it enough? Depending on how badly they've been affected by the gates, the guards might turn on our people. And they're functionally mercenaries. We bought them. Someone else could buy them." Richard ran a hand through his hair. "Do we need to get our people out?"

"We could charter planes and hire pilots, but where do we take them? And if we remove them from the companies and facilities, we're going to see a profound drop in productivity and income."

"Dagmar, scientists are being targeted and killed. I've got to protect my people. I can't worry about money right now. And we've got to get the warning out to universities and laboratories everywhere."

"We're working on that."

"Work faster."

Richard finally took the hat from Angela, but he just held it by the brim and kept turning it in his hands. The physicist saw his moment and pushed Angela aside.

"Richard, I think I have a plausible answer to your question."

"Which question was that?" Richard looked up from checking his inside breast pocket. "I ask so many people so many questions every day that I end up not remembering anything I said to anybody." He lifted out a checkbook, looked satisfied, and put it back in the pocket.

"About why the craziness and . . . magic"—Tanaka stuttered over the word, and Grenier smiled to himself—"hasn't spread faster and gone more deep."

"And why is that?"

"Okay, so our universe is a universe of laws and probability. Take an action, you get a reaction and an expected result. And we can reproduce those results time after time after time," Tanaka said.

"The basic scientific method," Richard said. They were moving again, the people breaking into discrete streams as they flowed around the furniture. "And by laws you mean like gravity?"

"And relativity, and the first and second laws of thermodynamics, and conservation of energy, yeah, that kind of thing. Of course, down at the quantum level there is an element of chaos in our universe."

Richard's expression was both dismayed and frustrated. "I don't have time for this."

"Yeah, right, okay, so let's ignore that for now."

"Yes, let's."

"Anyway, I put together what you told me about how magic violates natural law, and how every magical act tears a hole in the fabric of our reality. Then I talked to Mr. Grenier." Tanaka nodded to him, and Grenier nodded back. "About how he did magic, and it became pretty clear that the same spell won't get the same result every time. It might use electricity, but how it manifests can be totally different. So it seems that magic is random and essentially chaotic. Magic is the result of a supreme act of personal will, which makes it antithetical to our multiverse of probability and order."

"But isn't magic normal and natural in the other universes?" Richard asked.

"Yes, they have their own laws, however weird they might be, but they're alien to ours, so our multiverse is pushing back, resisting and to some degree neutralizing the effect of the invaders."

"So you're saying it's a stalemate."

"No, I don't think we're going to be that lucky. I mean, I'm flying blind here, but I ran some calculations and it seems that the continued pressure from these other multiverses bulging into our multiverse will begin to break down our reality. The more magic, the more erosion to our physical laws. The more erosion, the more magic. Eventually . . . well, I don't know. Do we just get torn apart and subsumed into these other multiverses? Or do we become a place of functional chaos that's indigestible to the other multiverses, and we mess them up, too?"

"That strikes me as the very definition of a Pyrrhic victory,"

"So we have to close the gates," Pamela spoke up, and for an instant the cool facade pulled back and Grenier saw her fear, but Richard reacted to the sharp, hectoring tone.

"Yes, thank you. I have grasped that."

"What happens to the creatures who've come through these gates after we close them?" Dagmar hurriedly asked.

Richard didn't sugarcoat it. "They're here." The German blanched, and Richard gave a short laugh. "What? You were hoping they would shrivel up and die if they got stranded?"

"I could hope."

"Nice thought, but wrong. Remember, some of the ones who came through thousands of years ago are still here."

"So what do we do about them?" Tanaka asked.

"Same thing our distant ancestors did. Hunt them down and kill them," Richard answered.

The scientist was shaking his head. "We haven't got any ancient ancestors. What we've got is *you*. *You're* gonna have to hunt them down and kill them." Richard seemed to shrink as if the words had weight.

"And that's why he needs allies," said the judge. "You're due on the Hill in fifteen minutes. "I do hope you've prepared what you're going to say. You can't skate through this on charm and a smile. I would have gone over your statement if you'd finished it last night."

The long veiling lashes were quickly lowered, but not before Grenier saw the flash of pure fury in Richard's eyes.

Yes, yes! Do it. Say it!

But the moment passed, and Richard seemed to become smaller yet as he said, "I should have, sir, but I was making notes at five A.M., I didn't want to wake you."

Grenier sighed and threw aside the book, stood, and gripped Robert Oort's shoulder.

"What?"

"You are such an ass." Pamela's inhalation was almost a moan. "My life depends on your son. So I'd appreciate it if you'd cut it . . . the fuck . . . *out*."

"What are you talking about? It? What does *it* mean?" Robert demanded.

"Cutting him down, demeaning him, undermining—"

"How dare you, sir!" the judge bellowed and shrugged off Grenier's hand.

"Stop it! Both of you!" Richard yelled. "Stop talking about me as if I'm not here. That's pretty damn demeaning, too." He turned to Rudi. "Is the car at the door?"

"Yes, sir."

"Then let's go."

They left, and Robert Oort stepped in close to Grenier. He was tense with fury. "I know the game you're playing. He is *my* son."

"Then fucking act like his father," Grenier shot back.

The judge spun and walked away. Pamela glared at Grenier. "He's trying to help Richard."

"Really? From where I'm standing it looks like he's working for the other side."

"Oh, fuck you," Pamela said, and she also walked away.

"You know, right now I almost like you," Angela said, and she patted him on the arm.

THIRTY-TWO

RICHARD

"We've got to stop meeting this way." The rolling baritone turned the words into a pronouncement.

I looked up from the report I was reading. Grenier, his bulk swathed in a red-and-black-striped bathrobe, stood in the kitchen door.

"You look like a circus tent," I said and pushed away my cup of cold tea. The light reflected colors off the oily slick on the surface.

"My, my, feeling pissy tonight, are we?" He waddled in and began pulling out the ingredients for cinnamon toast and hot chocolate. "So, how did it go? Promises of support? Are you off to the White House in the morning?"

"The only sound other than my voice was the rip of paper as I tore out the checks I'd written."

"You should have used the stick, not the carrot," the former minister grunted. "'I'll throw my not inconsiderable millions behind your opponent in the next race.'"

"Somehow I don't think we've got two years." I watched my knuckles whiten as I closed my hands into fists. "They are such weasels and cowards."

"What did you expect? They're politicians."

"Aldo was a statesman." The bittersweet scent of chocolate began to fill the room.

"One of the last. And now he's dead, and I'm sure many others have received discreetly worded warnings. It's—"

"What you would have done," I said before Grenier could get it out.

"Exactly." He pulled the pan of steaming cocoa off the stove and filled two cups.

I cupped my hands around the warm ceramic sides of the mug, and realized the condo had gotten very cold. I found myself looking at the reflective surfaces of the stainless steel appliances.

"What?" Grenier asked.

I took a sip of cocoa, then stood and drew the sword. I quickly touched every reflective surface in the room.

"Ah, yes, that was probably wise," Grenier said. I sat back down, and we drank in silence. The toaster gave a loud, annoyed-sounding *ding*. Grenier moved to the counter and began scraping butter across the bread. "You know your father is going to blame you for the failure to garner any support."

"Thank you, really what I needed to hear in the dark hours of the night."

"Yeah, your father is the stuff nightmares are made of."

"Don't. I really don't want to go there."

"Actually you do. You got mad at him today. I'd go so far as to say furious. You should have followed through."

I squirmed under the penetrating hazel gaze, and hated myself for the wash of heat through my body, and feeling like a vise was closing around my head as the anger came sweeping back. "He knows my pattern," I said levelly.

"Thus ensuring you will repeat it. You're so cowed from constant criticism that you can barely function when you're around him. My advice is get your father the hell out of here, and start using your not inconsiderable gifts—charm, charisma, and that wry little sense of humor that breaks out at unexpected times. You're also cunning and conniving, and I bet you could play dirty if you needed to. So stop censoring yourself, watching every word, and weighing every action. Oh, and among your gifts . . . your handsome face. So use it."

Beneath my usual writhing desire to elude the praise, the germ of an idea began to coalesce. I grabbed for it, then pulled back mentally, trying to coax it into focus.

"Papa says—"

"I don't care what Papa says." Grenier abandoned the toast and moved in on me. "He distrusts beauty. I'm betting he blames her beauty for drawing him to your mother, and they didn't suit at all, so he rejects the thing that attracted him."

"You *really* don't want to go there after what you did to my mother."

Something in my eyes sent him skittering in retreat back to the counter. He cleared his throat. "Yes, well, then let's focus on Daddy. Stop being so damn scared that he won't approve. He's never going to approve. He doesn't like you. He never will. Give it up."

Occasionally in life you hear something that you just sense is true. It happened in that moment, and it hurt more than any blow or any wound I'd ever received. I pushed away the devastating conclusion, and grasped for the memory of what had happened in Grenier's office when Papa had come to rescue me. He hadn't actually said he loved me, but he said the answer to my question was yes. What I'd written was *I hope someday you'll love me, too.* Saying yes was the same. Wasn't it?

No. It wasn't.

Grenier hadn't been a pastor for almost thirty years for nothing. He saw the hit, and he surprised me by adding softly, "I'm sorry."

I waved it away. "Doesn't everybody feel misunderstood by their parents?"

"I think my point was a little stronger than that."

"Please. Just drop it." He nodded, and finished thickly powdering the toast with confectioner's sugar and cinnamon. He returned to the table with the plate, and I took a piece. Butter oozed onto my fingers. "If the monsters don't get me, heart disease will," I said.

We then ate in silence for a few minutes. It felt oddly companionable sitting at the table with him after what he had said.

"Rhiana was loitering outside the Capitol today," I said after I finished off my second slice.

Grenier set down his fourth piece of toast. "And she did what?"

"Nothing. Just watched me." I took a sip of cocoa. A skin had formed over the top and tried to affix itself to my upper lip. "You know, she phoned me. To warn me that someone was going to try to kill me."

"Hmm. And from this you glean . . . what?"

"Bear with me for a minute. There was this girl in high school who really liked me. Somehow everywhere I went, she'd turn up. She took up fencing. She started swimming."

"Did you go out with her?"

"Eventually."

"Did you nail her?"

I gave an exasperated sigh. "I don't know what that has to do with anything, but yes. Anyway, I think Rhiana's doing the same thing, because when you get right down to it, she really is just a kid. I also think she's finding that life in Monsterville isn't as wonderful as she expected, and . . ." I coughed as I breathed in powdered sugar. "Bottom line, the crush endures."

"And you're going to use that to try to lure her back from the dark side of the Force."

"I'm thinking about it."

"You'd be stuck with her. It'd be like bedding a cobra. And you're going to annoy a lot of other women. Probably a few men, too."

Annoyed, I waved him down. "She comes back. She frees Kenntnis. I don't see a downside."

"Just to you."

"So you're not in favor of this?"

"I didn't say that. I just want you to go into this with your eyes open."

"Believe me, they're wide open."

"How are you going to ditch the watchdogs?"

"Enlist one in my desperate need to get laid." I pushed back my chair, picked up the report, and headed for the door.

"That probably won't require a lot of acting," Grenier said, and I felt my ears turning red.

I picked Estevan. He was the youngest. He was also the horniest and the most romantic. I found him in the room he shared with Joseph, Rudi, and Syd. Everyone else was either on duty or out of the condo. It was Estevan's sleep period, and he was stripped down to his boxers and starting to lift the covers on the twin bed.

"Hey, *Esse*," I said, and then I stayed in Spanish. "Sorry to bug you when you're about to go to sleep, but"—I looked around, and even opened the door, took a look into the hall, then shut it before continuing—"I really need a favor."

"What you need?"

"I met this girl. Up at the Capitol. I can't really bring her back here. Talk about trying to fuck in your parents' house . . ."

"Oh, shit, man, yeah, I can see that."

"Anyway, I want to meet her, but turning up with a bunch of guards would sort of wreck the moment."

"Yeah, no shit."

"So, I was thinking . . . hoping that the next time you're assigned to me you could just . . . sort of . . . look the other way."

He was frowning a little and slowly shaking his head. "I don't know. If you got killed and I was supposed to be guarding you . . . Oh, man, Joseph would have my ass."

I let my shoulders slump, and I began to turn away. "Yeah, it's cool, it wasn't fair of me to even ask. I just thought you'd understand more than the others. We're younger than . . ." I let my voice trail away sadly.

"This girl. She's special?"

"Very special." And that, I reflected, was certainly not a lie. "I'll be careful, I promise. Look, I'm a cop, I know how to look out for myself."

"Yeah, I guess that's true."

"Please, Estevan. You're the only person I can trust with this." And I had him.

I waited until I was back in my room. I turned on the television, and then pulled out my cell phone and hit speed dial for her number. She answered on the fourth ring.

"This is Richard."

THIRTY-THREE

"*A*mericans *never take anything on faith. We question. We challenge. We think.*"

The music was stirring and patriotic. The images were of American triumphs—Henry Ford and his assembly line, the Wright Brothers at Kitty Hawk, American GIs being embraced in France in 1944, the flag going up at Iwo Jima, and finally a montage of space shots culminating with the first step onto the moon. The narration was supplied by Grenier. His voice was rich and comforting, and it echoed with pride. The final image was the notation THIS MESSAGE WAS PAID FOR BY LUMINA ENTERPRISES. The whole thing made Pamela squirm.

"Little manipulative, isn't it?" Pamela asked.

Grenier dropped a hand onto her shoulder. "That's what advertising does, my dear. This is our setup, our mood piece," he said. "We'll start getting a lot more pointed and specific in subsequent ads. Danny has done an incredible job with the Web site, and has literally hundreds of links to scientific and rational links."

"You mean like debunkers?" Pamela asked.

"Yes."

"I see a problem." Grenier cocked an inquiring eyebrow at her. Pamela had always wanted to be able to do that. Richard could. She had never mastered it. She thought it would have worked well in front of juries to cast doubt on a prosecutor. "According to you the magic is going to start being real. That means the debunkers are going to start having a hard time debunking," she said.

Grenier stroked a palm across his beard. "An interesting point," the former evangelist said. "We may need to—"

At that moment Sam came striding into the living room. Angela was with her, and the coroner's face was tight with tension.

Pamela jumped up from the sofa. Panic was hammering in her throat. She realized she hadn't experienced a moment without fear since she'd seen that monumental figure beneath that plane.

"What's wrong?"

Angela opened her mouth, but Sam grabbed her hard by the wrist. "Emergency girl shopping," the FBI agent said. Her expression was flat and hard, giving away nothing.

Grenier pushed to his feet with a grunt. "Sam, if you're ever playing poker you probably don't want to bring Angela along. Judging from the strength of her reaction this probably has to do with Richard, and since I take a very personal interest in Richard—"

"Oh, shut up. Don't be such a windbag," Pamela said. She stepped up to face Sam. "Tell me what is going on."

Sam shrugged, then said, "Richard's off the reservation."

"What does that mean?"

Angela broke in. "That he's slipped away from his security. He's somewhere in Maryland, and he doesn't have any protection."

"And you know this how?" Grenier asked, but Pamela saw a strange expression flash like summer lightning deep in his eyes.

"Because I put a tracer in the foot of his cane, and one in his money clip. The schedule said he was having drinks with Congressman Wilson at the Mayflower, but GPS puts him on the coast in Maryland," Sam answered. "Estevan was supposed to be with him, and I was trying to handle this without Joseph finding out, but now it's going to be this big deal and Estevan will probably get fired. I was just going to kill him," Sam concluded.

"Perhaps Richard has his reasons, and since he is the head of

Lumina you should stay out of his plans," Grenier said.

Pamela rounded on him. "You know about this. What is he doing?"

Grenier's lips worked for a moment; then he said, "Meeting Rhiana."

Angela's hand went to her throat, Sam let out an expletive, and Pamela found herself saying, "You bastard, you're behind this. You've sold us out." She pressed a hand against her forehead. "Joseph and Rudi are off with my father and Dagmar. Oh, God, what do we do?"

"You've got me," Sam said. "I'm just as badass as any of the boys. Let's go." And Pamela joined Sam and Angela as they headed for the front door.

"Wait! Don't!" Grenier called, but they ignored him. Pamela saw him waddling to the phone as the door shut behind them.

They were in the hall when Sam suddenly froze. She unlocked the door and rushed back into the condo as Grenier was punching buttons on the phone. Sam crossed the room in two strides, yanked the receiver out of his hand, and slammed it back in the cradle.

"Oh, no, you don't. You don't get to warn your buddies," she said.

"I'm warning *Richard* because you're going to fuck this up. He's trying to *turn* her!"

"Yeah, right," Sam said, and Pamela was startled to see her take the former minster in an armlock and handcuff him to the leg of a heavy table.

THIRTY-FOUR

RICHARD

I made it a point to apologize for the venue. The Riverside Inn wasn't elegant, but I explained that we could lose ourselves in the crowds who flocked to the restaurant in search of the famous Chesapeake blue crabs. Rhiana had sounded breathless when she said that was fine. She also assured me she would come alone. I thought that was nice, but I still had both my guns and the sword, and another reason for the Riverside—I could get lost in the crowds if I had to run for it.

Despite my warning that the restaurant had all the ambiance of a bus station, Rhiana turned up in a clinging, floor-length silk dress that left one shoulder bare. The color was a peacock's tail; blues, greens, and lavenders shimmered through the folds. Yes, I had been right. This was prom night, and I was the dream date.

I looked around at the graying wood plank walls, the photographs of crusty old sea captains, lighthouses, and fishing boats, and the scarred wooden tables covered by long sheets of newspaper stock. Napkins and crab mallets were thrust into small buckets, and plastic bibs were available. Conversations and the pounding of wooden mallets attacking the shells of the crabs roared through the room. The smell of drawn butter and citrus hung in the air. I was going to have to do something to recover my status as dreamboat.

We were seated at a corner table where I could watch both the

226

front door and the kitchen entrance, and there was a window close by. I had parked my car right under that avenue of escape.

I brought my attention back to Rhiana as she reached up and pushed her long black hair behind her ears. I watched the play of muscles beneath her smooth skin, and how the movement set her silver earrings sweeping across the tops of her shoulders. The metal had been pulled and twisted like spiderwebs, and trapped within them were scattered jewels, amethysts, emeralds, pearls, and sapphires. I hoped I wasn't going to join them, caught in her net. No, I was the one angling. I had gotten her this far. I just had to hook her.

I continued staring at her, struck again by her incredible beauty and lost in the scent of her floral perfume. She suddenly gave a smile that was both shy and young, and wise and mysterious. Apparently—fortunately—my hesitation and calculation had been read as mesmerized. But I needed to say something. Never had so much been riding on a seduction, and never had I been more clueless.

You're good at this, an inner voice berated. *You've talked how many people into bed over the years?*

But I couldn't come across like a third-rate Lothario. Rhiana was young, but she wasn't stupid. Sincere. I had to be—feel—sincere. Did I feel sincere? I sincerely thought she was beautiful. I sincerely thought she was dangerous. And I sincerely thought she was the key to freeing Kenntnis, and getting this monkey off my back. I decided I sincerely wanted this to work.

I sucked in a deep breath and said, "Thank you for your call, for trying to warn me. It came a little late, but I appreciate the impulse that generated it. It was kind of you." And I reached out and very lightly brushed the top of her hand where it rested on the table.

A slow blush rose into her cheeks. "I . . . I shouldn't have done it." She got control over her voice. "I got in a lot of trouble."

"Your . . . father," I said. She nodded, and I saw the shadow of fear and pain in her eyes. I gripped her hand. "He hurt you?"

She gave a tense little nod. I allowed anger to show, and it wasn't totally an act. "You gave up . . . so much—"

"What? What did I give up?" She tried to sound bellicose, but there was sadness beneath the anger.

"A different life. Relationships you might have had." This was dangerous territory, so I said it very cautiously.

"There was only one I wanted."

I hung my head, but made sure I could still watch her from beneath my lashes. "I know. It was my problem. I was worried about your age, and other things . . ."

"And now?" she demanded.

"We're in a different world."

She took a sip of her piña colada. I gulped down a mouthful of my Hendrick's gin martini. If this worked we'd end up in bed together. Alcohol had always been part of my seductions. Maybe it would work again, and overcome my fear.

"I'm eighteen now," Rhiana said suddenly.

"I'm glad, but it really doesn't matter any longer."

"Why not?"

I leaned back and gestured at her. "Well, look at you. You're . . ." I deliberately hesitated.

She leaned toward me, expression intent. "What?"

"Beautiful. Sophisticated. Powerful."

Her cheeks were bright with color and the green eyes shining. She really was so young, and I really was such a cad. I pushed away the thought and concentrated on what I had to do.

"Fathers are . . . difficult. I'd get in trouble if mine knew I was here . . . with you . . . now. He would say I was a fool." An ember of anger began to burn beneath my breastbone. My entire life I'd done what he wanted except for one time. Couldn't he trust me to take what he'd taught me and do the right thing? My breath caught, and I returned to the moment. "That you couldn't be trusted. That you'll hurt me," I finished.

"I won't hurt you." She reached out and gently touched my

cheek, allowing her fingers to linger against my skin. She smelled of jasmine and girl.

And then artifice became reality, at least so far as my body was concerned. Bodies hate denial, and I had been denying the physical for a long, long time. Desire sent heat flaring through me, and I suddenly felt light-headed. I was glad I had my napkin in my lap.

Her face was very close. It was the next logical move. I kissed her. Her lips were warm, soft, and pliant, but she was so inexperienced, and doubt once again shook me. Then I remembered what I'd seen in Virginia and my resolve returned. I caught her full lower lip gently between my teeth, then allowed my tongue to enter her mouth. She tasted of pineapple and coconut and ice cream, but there was also an underlying harsh oily taste. I noted that it began to fade and she tasted more like a girl the longer we embraced.

She's not human. She's not human, came a nervous little voice.

Not totally *human,* I corrected and soothed. We broke the kiss when our waitress came over. The beads in her beautiful cornrowed hair clashed like tiny cymbals. She gave us an indulgent, knowing smile.

"You all ready to order?"

Rhiana leaned against my shoulder. "I don't know how to eat these things."

"I'll show you. They're actually kind of fun, in addition to being delicious. And they're a great way to work out your aggressions." I ordered for us, and got refills on our cocktails.

After another fortifying sip I said, "Rhiana, forgive me if this is out of line, but you seem . . . sad."

I knew I was pushing things fast, but it was going to be damn hard to keep arranging to play hooky so I could go on dates with the enemy. I needed to seal the deal tonight.

She rolled her glass between her palms, and hid behind the curtain of her hair. "Sometimes I'm lonely." She set aside the glass and began to shred a roll. "I grew up in this world. I'm comfortable here. The only people I see are Jack and An—" She broke off abruptly and took a big drink of her piña colada.

"Jack?" I inquired as casually as I could manage.

"Rendell. I'm teaching him magic." I filed the name away. "They've been trying for years, centuries, to get someone like me, but once I did what they wanted—" She just stopped and stared unseeing into space.

I rifled through what she had said and left unsaid, and took the risk. "Because you're comfortable here, they relegated you back here. Made you human again, at least in their minds," I quickly added at her look of confusion. Rhiana nodded. "But if they think of you as human you're not safe." She turned stricken fawn eyes on me. "I'm sorry, I don't mean to frighten or hurt you."

"It's okay. I put myself here."

Suddenly I saw the strain and the fear and her loneliness and her youth. I put my arm around her shoulders and rocked her gently and murmured into her hair, "Then let me bring you home." She sagged against me, all resistance gone.

Movement at the front door caught my attention. Three women were entering. Pamela, Angela, and Sam.

The expletive burst from between my lips. Rhiana lifted her head, stiffened, and drew away.

THIRTY-FIVE

Pamela had never seen the much talked-about Rhiana. Cross hated her and said she couldn't be trusted. Angela hated her, but Pamela thought that had more to do with Richard than Rhiana. All the men said she was beautiful first, and then decried her betrayal second. Now that she was actually looking at the woman—girl—Pamela concluded that beautiful didn't begin to describe it. Here was a worthy match for Richard, and Pamela thought she could hate Rhiana, too.

Richard had come out of his chair and was wending his way through the tables toward them. Pamela had never seen such an expression on her brother's face, and she suddenly didn't feel so confident in the rightness of their rescue. Rhiana also stood up, giving them the full effect of her dress.

"Crap, if you wanted a hooker why didn't you say so? We could have brought one to the condo and saved you a lot of trouble," Sam said in her piercing way.

Richard grabbed the FBI agent's wrist so hard that Sam's hand went white.

"*Shut up!*" And it was a tone Pamela had never heard out of her brother.

"Richard, we were worried—" Angela began.

He flung away Sam's hand and leaned in on Angela. "I am so

sick of all of you handling me and fussing over me. Leave me the fuck alone!" His voice was a low harsh whisper.

Suddenly a woman screamed, and Richard's head whipped around. Rhiana had begun to dissolve, her body pulling apart like strings of red and purple taffy, but before her face vanished Pamela saw where tears had run her makeup.

The windows in the restaurant all blew in. Shards of glass stung Pamela's cheeks, and she felt one large splinter lodge itself in her back. She screamed at the sudden, stabbing pain. People were screaming, ducking under tables. There was a cry of terror from the kitchen, and the sound of an explosion. Cooks and servers came running through the swinging doors leading to the kitchen. Flames came boiling after them. Panic was spreading through the room. Richard pulled the hilt off the end of the cane, and drew the sword.

"Listen!" The basso overtones together with his shout brought everyone's attention to him. "The windows are out. Those closest to a window, go out that way. Those of you near the front, line up and use the front doors. There is *plenty* of time. Stay calm. Help them," he ordered Sam.

Angela also began guiding people, and Pamela took an elderly woman's arm and helped her out the door. She could feel blood trickling down her back and soaking into the material of her sweater.

Within moments the restaurant was cleared; the flames were taking hold, dancing like red and orange fans in the empty window frames. In the distance Pamela heard approaching sirens. The briny scent of the sea was overlaid with the wet heavy smell of impending snow, and the stench of burning plastic and wood.

"I'm sorry," Angela was saying to Richard. "We were worried, so I talked to Sam and—"

"I put a tracer in your cane, and I'm *not* sorry. So go fuck yourself," Sam said. Her tone was pushing for a fight. Richard almost joined the battle, but then Angela said, "We just wanted to protect you."

Richard abandoned Sam and turned back to Angela. "I am not weak. I am not helpless. I am not your damn child! I didn't do this on a whim or out of caprice. I had a plan, but thanks to your jealousy and interference it's been ruined and the situation is now a whole hell of a lot worse. She'll never believe I didn't betray her, and arrange this so she could be humiliated. She's a fucking kid, but a kid with terrifying powers, and you've, you've . . ." He gave a strangled, inarticulate sound and pushed Angela away.

He walked away, then whirled and kept walking backward as he said, "I want you to go back to New Mexico. There never was a reason for you to come here other than to chase me. Well, it's over. Just leave me the hell alone."

And he turned and almost ran toward a nondescript parked car. The three women watched in silence as he drove away.

"What a fucking prick," Sam said, but it sounded defensive.

Pamela realized Angela was crying softly. She put her arm around the smaller woman. "He didn't mean it. He's angry. He'll cool down, and realize he was out of line."

Angela stepped back, and wiped her cheeks with the backs of her hands. "Things only hurt this much when they're true. I'll get myself home. You guys go on," and she walked away.

"Take the car," Sam ordered. "I'll keep an eye on Angela and get her home."

Rhiana walked the darkness until she felt the pull of the gate and then allowed herself to re-form. Not too close to the gate. Truth be told, it disturbed her, too.

Rhiana scrubbed at her cheeks, feeling the sticky wetness of her tears. The naked boles of the trees marched away from her and stretched bare limbs toward the white sky. The smell of snow was stronger here. Growing up in California she had never seen snow. Once her adopted parents had taken the family to Knott's Berry Farm just before Christmas, drawn by the lure of man-made snow.

It had felt like ice, as if someone had dumped a truckload of sno-cones on the ground. Kids had tried to innertube and sled on the hill, but it had felt like a fake and a cheat, like so much of her life.

Had he planned this? Had he done this to hurt and humiliate her? He was going to pay. She would find a way.

But his lips had been warm and soft, the kiss deep and passionate. He couldn't have faked that.

But that woman had said that awful thing about her. Rhiana looked down at the dress she had picked with such care, and she suddenly reached down and tore away most of the trailing skirt. It was trashy, not elegant. She'd made a fool of herself.

She remembered the one time Drew Sandringham had come to her house for a meeting. The way his upper lip had lifted, and his nostrils narrowed, and she realized the house was tasteless and gaudy and she had made those choices.

Her thoughts jumped away from that memory and became impaled on another. Richard had gone to Angela. Straight to Angela. He had talked only to Angela. What if they had planned this together? He must have told her where he would be. How else could they have found them?

She coughed out a sob, and walked on through the Virginia forest.

A lump of darkness caught her eyes. Something lay on the fallen leaves and pine needles.

"Hey," Rhiana called, and her voice sounded dull and flat in the darkness. There was no movement or reaction.

She approached cautiously. It was a young woman dressed in student chic—blue jeans, oversized pea coat, boots. Once, in another lifetime, Rhiana had dressed that way. A small section of the girl's scalp was bare and bloody. The hank of long hair lay tangled around a branch as if the tree were playing cat's cradle. Rhiana's head twinged in sympathy. The girl had been caught, and slowed by the grip on her hair. It was a measure of her desperation that she had pulled so hard she'd let her hair be ripped out. Or maybe Doug had done it just for the fun of it. And then the knife had been applied to her gasping throat. In the cold the blood had coagulated into a viscous pool. Rhiana remembered when this one had been snatched off the campus of UNLV.

Another of Doug's toys. Only now he'd taken to breaking them.

It was 3:00 A.M. when Sam entered the room she shared with Pamela and Dagmar. Sam reported that Angela had checked into a hotel. That had ended any hope of sleep, and when Pamela finally emerged from her room she found the psychodrama continued. Joseph had tried to fire Estevan. Richard had intervened and overridden the security chief's decision, which left Joseph fuming. Estevan was sulking. Sam glared at Richard over breakfast while he ignored her. Dagmar tried to keep up an artless patter of conversation.

And the judge capped the morning by lecturing Richard about how lack of planning was always a recipe for disaster. Richard had listened in silence, then stood and said, "It was planned, and it would have worked if they hadn't interfered."

"But in fact it *didn't* work, and you endangered yourself in this foolish act of bravado. I don't know if this is a function of being a policeman, but acting like some kind of movie hero is not the way to succeed."

"Thank you, sir. Dagmar, don't we have reports to review?" Richard said, and they left.

Now it was past one o'clock; Pamela was hungry and frustrated because they seemed to have wasted the entire morning. The judge's meetings at Justice had proved to be a fruitless three hours. Three of the four people they wanted to see weren't in, and it seemed to take an inordinate amount of time to ascertain that they weren't in. The person who did keep the appointment was distracted to the point of incoherence. She kept checking her watch, answering the phone even though it hadn't rung, getting up to look out the window. Finally Robert admitted defeat, and they went in search of lunch.

They selected the Tabard Inn, one of Washington's more elegant eateries. As they approached the front doors, a man stepped out of a parked taxicab and approached them. It was Drew Sandringham, and Pamela greeted him with pleasure. She hadn't seen him since her mother's funeral.

"Drew." She gave him a hug. "What are you doing in Washington?" she asked. "Where are you staying? We should have dinner."

But the glance, smile, and hug he spared for her were fleeting. All of his focus was on her father. She looked over at the judge, and dread settled coldly across her shoulders. She had never seen her father look so forbidding and so furious.

"How dare you approach me," Robert said. His tone was low and intense.

Pamela stared at him in confusion. "Papa?" She was ignored.

"Hear me out, Robert. After thirty years of friendship you owe me that at least," Drew said.

What the hell? she thought as she watched her father struggle with himself.

"You have five minutes."

"I won't need that long." Drew took a long steadying breath. "Look, I won't deny that what happened, happened. It was undoubtedly a bad call, showing poor judgment on my part. But Richard isn't the innocent in all this. Whatever he's told you—"

"He's told me nothing. Ever. And I have not asked. I learned about . . . the incident . . . from another source."

"Then you probably don't know that Richard and I were lovers long before that night. He came to my bed within three weeks of starting to work for me." Drew rushed on. "And I wasn't the first. There had been a young man, an actor, but he'd left for California. I was the replacement."

Oh my God, now so much makes sense. But I know he was sleeping with my friend Gail. And there was Margo, but he did spend so much time with Paul that summer. Her whirling thoughts bumped against each other in a chaotic game of point/counterpoint.

"So, he was the aggressor. Seduced you, did he? Or did he force himself upon you?" The judge's words were as cold and sharp as glass.

Drew looked wryly amused. "Oh, Robert, you've always been oblivious. I'm surprised you managed to father three children. People like me, we recognize each other. I've known from the time he was ten that Richard liked boys. When you asked me to give him a job I was delighted. I knew I'd end up fucking that tight little ass."

Pamela was shocked by the crudity. It was completely unlike Drew. A dull brick red blotched her father's pale cheeks, and Pamela realized that it had been calculated. A shot aimed with perfect accuracy to cause the maximum amount of hurt. This was not a man attempting to make peace with an old friend. Something far darker was at work here.

"I don't believe you," the judge said, but the words sounded weak.

"Alannis knew. I assumed that was why she . . ." Sandringham executed a knowing gesture with no more than a turn of the wrist.

My God, he's implying that Richard caused Mama's suicide. Papa will never buy that. He knows how Richard adored her.

But all the color had drained from Robert's thin cheeks. Her father whirled and rushed away. His strides were long and so fast that he was almost running. Pamela dithered, unable to decide whether to follow or confront Drew. Sandringham's satisfied smile made the decision.

"Why?" she demanded.

Sandringham didn't pretend not to understand. "Payback."

"You'd shatter their relationship for spite?"

"And what relationship is that, Pamela? There's never been love there. Just fear and the need to be loved on one side, and disapproval on the other."

"Then why in front of me?" Pamela cried.

Drew shrugged. "It just worked out that way."

And Pamela realized that the man she'd thought of as an uncle, and a far more acceptable one than her real uncle, hadn't given a tinker's damn for her, or Amelia, or their mother. It had always been about Robert and later Richard. Sickened, she turned away, but her father had vanished. She knew where he would go, and feared what he would do. Which meant she had to reach the condo first.

THIRTY-SIX

RICHARD

Dagmar spread another set of reports across the coffee table in front of me. The numbers seemed to get tinier and tinier the longer I stared at them. Meaningless ant tracks across a white desert. I hadn't really wanted to work. I'd just wanted to get away from my father.

My mind kept straying back to the events of last night. What could I have done differently? Maybe told Angela my plan, and involved her in the decision. But I'd assumed she'd be jealous. Which was pretty arrogant. She wasn't an idiot. She would have seen what I was doing. But if it meant I had to be with Rhiana permanently, I couldn't see Angela agreeing to that... ever. I should have suspected Sam. I should have checked for bugs and tracers. God damn it, I was in charge; she shouldn't have been spying on me.

I kept seeing Angela's hurt expression. And Rhiana's hurt expression. I looked around the room, seeking a respite from my guilt and fury. Eddie was sprawled on a love seat set at right angles to the long sofa. The faint rumble of a bass line leaked around the edges of the young scientist's headphones, and his head bobbed in time to the beat. A laptop rested on his chest, and he was typing furiously. I got a glimpse of the screen. More numbers.

"We're spending eighty-seven thousand dollars a day," Dagmar said.

That got my attention. "Did you just say *a day*?"

But before she could answer, the front door flew open, and Pamela hobbled rapidly through it. Her face was blotched red and white, partly from the cold, but I knew from the set of her mouth that she was in distress. The anger I had been nursing faded into alarm, and I hurried to meet her.

"What's wrong?" I took her arm and helped her into a chair.

"Slipped on the ice," she said. She grimaced and leaned down to rub at a rapidly swelling ankle.

I dropped onto one knee, slipped off her shoe, and gently palpated the ankle. After years in gymnastics I had a good feel for injuries. This one wasn't bad. I looked up and said as much, and was dismayed when her gray eyes filled with tears. In all the years of our childhood I had never seen Pamela cry. The only time I'd even heard her weep was when she called to tell me about Mama's death.

"Richard, Papa is coming. He's . . . he's . . ." She stammered to a halt and looked around the room. "Drew talked to him." The words came out in a whisper.

Nerves fluttered deep in my gut, but Kenntnis had fixed all this. "He knows," I soothed.

The incredulous look I got in response told me that somehow the situation had changed. The front door opened. I could see Rudi's broad back where he stood guard in the hall. Then every other bit of my surroundings disappeared and all I could see was the expression on my father's face. I stood up so I could face what was coming on my feet instead of on my knees. Pamela clutched my hand, and I could feel myself choking on fear.

"Out. All of you. Everyone who is in the condominium, out!" my father commanded.

Dagmar stood, and moved very deliberately to my side. "Would you like to continue with our meeting, sir?" she asked.

"No. Go." My lips felt numb and I could barely force out the words.

Dagmar went to the love seat and gave Eddie a shake. He lifted one earpiece of the headphones. She gave a terse gesture. He swung his legs off the love seat and sat up. They headed toward the bedrooms.

"No," came the snapped command from the judge. "Outside. You, too, Pamela."

My sister surprised me. "No. I'm staying."

Eddie clutched his computer like a child hugging a favorite toy and scuttled for the front door. Dagmar went to awaken Syd and Estevan, who were sleeping. The seconds stretched endlessly. It was all taking so long. I couldn't stand it.

"Sir—"

"Be quiet! I will deal with you presently and privately!"

The front door closed behind Syd's slippered heels. I scanned the chiseled planes of my father's face, and saw no softness, no love, nothing but anger and disgust

Without preamble he asked me, "Are you a homosexual?"

For one wild moment I considered lying. I'd been lying to him my entire life. Why not continue?

"Papa, he's always had girlfriends," Pamela said, trying to break through the heart-stopping tension. I was touched by the unexpected defense.

"He'll answer for himself," Robert grated and spun back on me. "Do you sleep with men?" The words were enunciated so sharply they seemed to cut.

"I . . ." I coughed to clear the obstruction in my throat, and suddenly I was just so sick of it. Of him. "Yes. Yes, I do."

My father made a disgusted noise. "This is what your mother was alluding to in her note. She tried to bargain with God for your worthless soul! You caused her death!" Pamela gasped, and I took a step back because of what I saw in my father's face.

I knew I was codependent to the point of absurdity, but if there was one thing being a cop had taught me it was how to assign blame. Anger began to lick at the edges of the shame and fear.

"No, sir. You don't get to lay that off on me! Grenier's people played on Mama's love for me, and her weakness and neuroses, with fears of hellfire and eternal damnation. If you want to bust somebody's chops you go bust Mark's!"

My father's deep blue eyes looked me up and down. Bitterness, disappointment, and anger were all there. "To get *you*." The word dripped disgust. "Alannis risked her health and emotional stability. Because she wanted a son."

I wasn't prepared for the explosion of rage that seemed to scorch behind my eyes. Where was the gut-shivering fear and guilt? Caution was also missing. It seemed like some other person was saying, "Not the way I heard it. Uncle David said *you* were the one who forced the third pregnancy. Over her doctor's objections. And when she started drinking and using the pills, instead of helping her, you hid her away in institutions! She was always terrified you'd send her back. So when you're looking for reasons for her suicide, maybe you ought to look in a fucking mirror!" Pamela made an inarticulate sound.

The blow came so quickly and was so unexpected that I actually didn't register it until the pain exploded across my cheek. The force of the backhand slap drove my cheek against my teeth and I tasted blood. Pamela gave a cry that turned into a sob.

And my courage crumbled. He had never before struck me, and I realized I was about to lose another parent. I raised my hand, a pleading gesture. There had to be a way to fix this. Apologize enough. Twist myself into a new shape. Become what he wanted.

"Papa, I'm sorry. I shouldn't have said that. Please, I'll—"

But he turned away. "Come, Pamela, we're leaving. We shall go to your sister's."

And the world started spinning backward when Pamela said, "No, Papa. I'm staying with Richard." She got out of the chair, took hold of my arm, and clutched it tightly to her side.

"I see. Well, when you come to your senses, you may join us."

As I watched my father's retreating back, I explored the vast hollow that seemed to have opened in my heart.

"Papa."

"You will not address me. We are finished." The bedroom door closed behind him.

A shiver ran down my arms and into my legs. I turned and headed blindly for my room. Pamela hung at my side like a lamprey.

"It'll be all right. He'll think about this and calm down, and be back. If he can trust that you'll never do . . . it . . . again."

I paused, my hand on the door to my bedroom. "I'm bisexual, Pam. I can't make that promise. And why should I have to? I've spent my life twisting myself to fit his image of what I should be. Well, I'm done." I drew in a shuddering breath. "Just tell me when he's gone."

I shut the door on her worry and desperation. I pressed the heels of my hands hard against my eyes, and my back found the wood of the door. I slid down it until I hit the floor. Suddenly the adrenaline was gone from my system, leaving behind only nausea. I didn't quite reach the toilet before I hurled.

THIRTY-SEVEN

The fair head was bent over papers as he sat at the desk. Richard looked up, irritated by the intrusion, and Grenier realized in his agitation he hadn't knocked.

"Pardon me, that was rude. I'm sorry, but Richard, I *must* speak with you."

He paused, and Richard growled, "Fine. Speak."

"They're manipulating you. This didn't happen by accident. They're trying to force you into an emotional reaction that will play right into their hands. Think, you minored in psychology. Don't be a fool. They're isolating you, and—"

Richard leaned back in the chair far enough to cause the springs to squeak, and laced his fingers behind his head. "You think I don't know that?" His voice was filled with amusement.

"Well, I . . ."

The smile flickered briefly, like a glimpse of sun through clouds, and the young man said, "Richard's been abandoned by his daddy, so he's going to rush off and find a replacement. Kenntnis is the logical choice, so of course Richard is going to go in and get captured by the bad guys. Does that pretty much sum it up?"

All Grenier could manage was a slow nod.

"Actually we're going home."

"What about alerting the government?"

"I did my best. I prodded the dinosaur as best I could. No, I think Eddie and his kind are the better bet for us. Lumina has scientists all over the world. We're gathering them up, and they'll figure out a way to free Kenntnis. *Then* we'll be back."

Grenier was suddenly aware of how badly his back hurt and how weak his knees had gone. He dropped into a chair. "I'm so relieved. And . . ." His mind searched for a less pejorative word than he'd been going to use. "And impressed."

Again the smile appeared. "You could have said it."

"What?"

"What you were really going to say—amazed. Now get out of here, and start packing."

Pamela pressed her cell phone tighter to her ear, tossed the sweater into her suitcase, and sank down on the bed as her sister said, "He took everything. Paul's college fund, my retirement, his retirement. He took out a second mortgage on the house." Panic had turned Amelia's voice into a shrill flute.

"What did Brent do with the money?" Pamela asked.

"There was this business deal, the United Emirates Fund. We ran it by Drew." Pamela's stomach gave a roll at the sound of the name. "And he said it looked good, so I agreed to the first payment, but there were more, so many more, and Brent didn't tell me about them. He just took all our money!" The words became an anguished cry. "Oh, Pam, we're losing the house!"

"How did Brent even find out about this deal?" Pamela asked.

"He met this man at the racquet club. They had lunch together, and the man invited him in. You know how Brent is, he likes to feel important."

"What about Papa? Is he still there?" Pamela asked.

"Yes, but what can he do? He doesn't have the money to pay off the loan, and we can't even go home with him because his house is gone, too. Burned down." Tears thickened Amelia's words. "Papa forbid me to call Richard, but I have to. We've got no place else to turn."

"Well, call him."

"I was hoping you'd talk to him first. Brent's been calling and calling him, and Richard's never called him back. I didn't know if Richard was mad at me, or . . ." Amelia's voice trailed away.

"No, no, he's not angry," Pamela said quickly. "He's just had so much . . . he's been so busy . . . don't worry, we're going to fix this."

Pamela snapped shut the phone, and went in search of her brother. She found him in his bedroom. He was also packing one-handed while he talked on his iPhone.

"Yes, Kenzo, I understand. If you think that's more secure, then let's do it—"

"I've got to talk to you," Pamela said. He waved her down, and she added in a much sharper tone, "*Now!*"

"Let me call you back," Richard said. "No, no, go ahead and get started, we'll just talk in more depth later." He turned to Pamela. "What?"

"Amelia just called me. Brent's managed to lose everything— house, savings, everything—in some business deal."

Now it was Richard's turn to sink down on the bed. He ran a hand through his hair. "Oh, crap, that must be what Brent kept calling about."

"Yeah, it would have been helpful if you'd taken the damn call. So now you can call Kenzo back, and arrange to have him pay off what they owe and fix this." Richard was frowning at the far wall. "Are you listening? Did you hear anything I just said?"

"Yeah, okay, we'll take care of the money, but I'm wondering if it goes deeper than that. Do you have any details?"

"Just that it was called the United Emirates Fund."

Richard moved to the door of the bedroom and called down the hall, "Dagmar, check out something for me."

She stuck her head out of her room. "What?"

"The United Emirates Fund. And find out how they got a line on my brother-in-law, Brent van Gelder."

"Right-ho."

"And make it fast," Richard added. He took out his phone and punched in a number. "Jerry, file a new flight plan. We're not leaving right away, and we may have to add a stop in Boston." He ended the call and reacted to her look. "What?"

"Papa's there."

"I know."

"If you have to go to the house, I'll come with you."

"I'd like that."

THIRTY-EIGHT

RICHARD

Even just four years as a cop had made me suspicious and paranoid. I couldn't imagine what I would have been like if I'd put in my twenty. Dagmar got back to me, and it was just what I'd expected. Drew had been behind it all. He'd covered his tracks pretty well, but I had the resources of Lumina behind me. Between Dagmar and Kenzo they had the threads untangled in four hours.

War had been declared on me and mine, and Drew had been one of the soldiers for the other side. I'd deal with him soon enough, but right now I needed to protect my family.

As the big limo rolled quietly down the Boston street, I had the sword drawn just in case. Pamela sat next to me. Joseph drove while Rudi rode shotgun. The blade of the sword was deep matte black with just the hint of lights deep in the darkness. There wasn't a net of swirling light in the air around the blade. That reassured me; when magic or Old Ones were present the lights came out. I sheathed the sword and put the hilt in the holster at the small of my back. What I was going to say to my sister and brother-in-law was crazy enough—I didn't need to be waving around a sword while I said it.

Trees overhung the street, and every available curb was taken up with parked cars. The long line of redbrick row houses were all dark except for a few porch lights spilling their light down the steps leading up to high stoops.

"I don't know why they didn't get a house with a yard after Paul was born. Get out of the center of the city," Pamela said in that exasperated tone siblings reserve for the perceived foolishness of each other.

"Because this one's close to the hospital," I answered.

I'd phoned the hospital to make sure Amelia hadn't been called in for an emergency surgery. She hadn't. Dr. van Gelder was at home.

"That's it," Pamela said pointing.

Joseph braked, and we climbed out. The cold, damp air carried the scent of brine off the bay, rotting leaves, car exhaust, and wood smoke. I'd grown up with these East Coast smells, and now I found myself longing for the bite of winter-dry air, turquoise skies, and the smell of burning piñon.

Just a few more hours. The Gulfstream was parked at Logan International. Since Syd and Sam had opted to stay in Washington, I had plenty of room for my family.

"Just shark around," Pamela added. "We shouldn't be long."

"No, ma'am, I'll double-park. I don't want to be around the block if you need me."

"Joseph's right," I said. "Come on. It's eleven o'clock at night. There's not going to be a lot of traffic."

Side by side we climbed the steps up to the front door. The brass knocker held an elaborate swirl of initials, *V* and *G* overlaid on an *O*. Pamela hesitated with her hand on the knocker.

"How do you think Papa is going to react?"

"Badly."

"Are you . . . scared?"

I analyzed that. What I felt was the churn of bile in the pit of my stomach. I was having a hard time figuring out what emotion was fueling the burn. "Nooo," I said slowly. "I feel anxious because I don't like fighting. But I'll fight if I have to. So knock."

The hammering of the knocker against the brass plate seemed

to echo down the street. I heard footsteps approaching.

"Who is it?" My sister Amelia's voice, soft and gentle. She had always been the turtledove trying to broker peace between Pamela and me.

"Richard."

"And Pamela."

The door was flung open, and Amelia grabbed me in a tight hug. If she'd looked tired and old in December at our mother's funeral, she looked like a gray ghost now. She was still dressed in her Professional Woman Uniform of knee-length skirt, sensible pumps, sweater, and a gold chain at her throat. "You could have just called. You didn't have to come. But oh, I'm so glad to see you. Come in, come in."

We stepped into the entry hall that ran straight through to the back of the house. To the right a set of stairs hugged the wall, with an Oriental runner splashing color down the middle of the steps. The left wall was punctuated with doorways—living room, dining room, kitchen—and overhead the crystal teardrops in the small chandelier flickered with rainbow colors. From the living room there was the flicker of light from a television, and I heard the *Tonight Show* music. I swallowed hard. It had always seemed like Amelia had telepathy.

"Papa's gone to bed," she said quickly.

"Who was it?" I heard Brent call.

And then he emerged from the living room, tying the belt of his bathrobe, one foot scuffing for a fleece-lined leather slipper. He was sporting several days of beard growth, and dark pouches hung beneath his eyes. I'd been a cop for enough years that I'd seen every variety of despair and depression. Brent was sporting them all. His face hardened when he saw me.

"So, you couldn't return my calls when it would have made a difference. Why'd you turn up? Just to gloat?"

"First, I'm sorry I didn't call. Second, you were deliberately targeted and led on so you'd lose your money, but third, it wouldn't have happened, Brent, if you weren't such a damn moron."

"I don't have to listen—"

"Shut up." My sisters jumped, Brent took a step backward, and I felt perversely pleased since he's six inches taller than I am. "Actually, you do if I'm going to bail you out. You've been living off my sister for eleven years, always looking for the big score. Well, butch up, get a job, and start acting like a man—but you're going to have to do it in New Mexico."

Brent just kept opening and closing his mouth. Amelia was frowning. "What do you mean we were targeted?"

"I'll explain it all on the flight," I said.

"Flight? We're not going anywhere—" Amelia began, while at the same time Brent said, "New Mexico? Why the hell would we go to New Mexico? It's the middle of fucking nowhere. We might as well be on the moon."

"You may end up glad that it's remote. This mess you got into made me realize that you're in danger, and next time it might not be as benign as just bankrupting you. I need you where I can keep an eye on you, and keep you safe." Brent was looking sulky again. Probably because I used the word "mess."

"Richard, this is ridiculous," Amelia said. "I have a job here. Paul's in school, we have a house—"

"Actually, you don't, unless I pay off the mortgages. This is not a negotiation. This is me rescuing you, or at least doing a preemptive rescue. They'll use you against me, and it might work. I don't know if I could let them hurt or kill my family, so I just can't risk it."

"Kill us? What are you talking about?" The fear in Amelia's voice had the words emerging in a strangled croak. "And who are *they*?"

"I really don't have time to explain all of this—"

Pamela laid a hand on my arm. "I'll do it." She put an arm around Amelia's waist. "Meli, the world has changed. You really aren't safe, and only Richard can keep you safe. Why don't you go in the kitchen and start some water for tea. I'll be there in just a minute." She gave our older sister a push toward the kitchen door. Brent followed her, but, of course, he always had.

Pamela turned to me. "We need to enlist Papa if we're going to have any hope of convincing them."

I knew she was right, but I felt that clutch of fear that, when I looked back, seemed to be the primary emotion associated with my father. Just as suddenly it was gone and I *wanted* to talk to him.

The narrow staircase seemed claustrophobic. I trailed my hand along the wall beneath the ascending framed family photo gallery, and began marshaling my thoughts. I didn't exactly know what I was going to say, but I had the shape of it. Perhaps I wasn't as confident as I thought, because my knock was a breath of sound.

"Yes?"

He didn't sound like he'd been asleep. Maybe he'd been up here all the time listening to us, but then I remembered that he had always awakened instantly. You could roll him out of bed at 4:00 A.M. and he'd give you a perfect sound bite. It was the one trait I shared with him.

I didn't answer him; I just walked into the guest bedroom. He sat up and switched on the bedside lamp. I noted that the ceramic base was painted with flowers, and the carved Chinese rug on the floor had a floral pattern. Amelia's two china patterns were also floral, and the bedspreads and even the sheets in all the bedrooms. But she lived in a row house with no yard. It's crazy how your mind will flit away when you're faced with something you don't want to do.

"What is this, sir?" My father's voice was icy.

I wanted to match his cool, but I found anger blazing through my body, so intense it made me light-headed.

"You're going to go downstairs and tell Amelia that she has to move her family to New Mexico," I ordered. "Because she'll do exactly what you tell her to."

"I will not have you influencing my grandson."

"And I won't let *you* get him killed." That shocked him, and for

252

an instant his features sagged. "Don't act like an ignorant cracker. You wrote the brief on gay adoption when Alabama tried to strip parental rights and remove the kids. Paul is in no danger from me, and you know that. We're being torn apart, and Drew was behind it. He lured Brent into this disastrous deal, and . . . well, you know what he did to us. He's working for the Old Ones. But since subtlety failed, they may try more direct measures. My family isn't safe. They'll use them against me, and like I told Amelia, I don't think . . . no, I know I don't have the strength to resist them if they threaten my family. So they're coming back with me so I can keep an eye on them."

The covers were thrown back so violently that they looked like a tsunami wave breaking across the footboard. Papa swung his legs out of bed and headed for the closet. "Very well, you've made your case." He pulled his suitcase out of the closet. "But I'll be watching—"

"Actually, sir, you might notice that I didn't include you."

He froze, and his back stiffened. Slowly, slowly he turned to face me. "I don't understand."

"I'm done with you," I heard myself saying. It wasn't what I'd expected, but it felt right. I could have left it at that, but all the years of pent up anxiety and anger clamored to be expressed. "For years I've tried to figure out what you wanted from me. I did everything to please you, including giving up everything I wanted. But then I got hurt, and I realized I couldn't live afraid anymore. You're the last thing I'm afraid of, so it's got to end. You never have loved me, so I'm not giving up all that much."

"That's not true. I'm not . . . demonstrative, I show my love in other ways, by trying to teach you your duty—"

"No, you tried to make me into you. You're a complete narcissist. What you wanted was to look in my face and be looking in a mirror. All this crap about service and duty. Yeah, you meant it, but it was my duty to serve you by being a reflection of you."

I couldn't read anything in the spare planes of that face. I started for the door. I put my hand on the knob, hesitated, then turned back to face him one last time. "Oh, by the way, I didn't quit the police force when you ordered me to. I told Weber to shit-can my letter of resignation." I opened my coat and displayed the pistol. "See, I'm still me. Not you."

Paul's room was at the far end of the hall. A night-light cast a soft glow, and on the ceiling stick-on stars glowed in the faint light. *Star Wars* posters hung on the walls, and the floor was littered with toys. I caught my heel on a toy truck, and struggled to keep my balance. The little boy, sprawled in the bed, didn't stir. One bare foot thrust from beneath the covers, and Paul was muttering. He was in the throes of a dream, and it looked to be fun because he was smiling.

I gently touched my nephew's shoulder. "Paul, Paul, wake up."

The gummed lashes pulled slowly apart. Sleep was congealed in the corners of his eyes. "Uncle Richard . . ." It was both a question and a statement.

"Paul, you have to get dressed now."

The boy looked to the window and frowned. "Is it snowing? Is that why it's so dark?"

"No, it's still night, but we have to go." I threw back the down comforter and helped the child to his feet.

"Where are we going?" Paul mumbled around a yawn. He pulled open a drawer and pulled out underwear.

"You're coming to New Mexico."

"There are cowboys and Indians there, aren't there?" I helped him tug a sweater over his head, flattening the tousled hair.

"Yes."

"Will I get to see them?"

"Uh-huh."

"Oh, good."

"Do you have a suitcase?" I asked.

"Uh-huh. On the shelf in the closet."

I grabbed the chair from the desk, stood on it, and unearthed the case. "Let's pack some of your toys. Just your favorites, 'cause we can't take all of them right now." The lower lip protruded and trembled. "Everything's going to be sent to you, and if anything gets lost I'll buy you new ones," I promised.

"Really?"

"Honest," and I crossed my heart.

"Okay." Paul dumped the armful of toys into the open suitcase. A few switches were tripped by the rough handling, and lights blinked and there were halfhearted hiccups of sound from the abused toys. "Okay, I'm ready. Let's go," Paul said.

I zipped shut the case, hefted it, and followed Paul into the hall. There were sounds of drawers closing from the master bedroom. Obviously my father had done his job, but Brent's mutters of complaint were like a piece of heavy equipment growling nearby. Paul and I went downstairs, and found Pamela in the dining room, loading an antique silver tea set into a suitcase.

"I don't want movers packing or handling Great-Grandmother's tea service," she said. I nodded.

"Can I have some milk?" Paul asked.

Pamela gave him a hug. "Sure, kiddo, you need help?"

He gave her an offended look. "I'm eight."

"Right, go ahead." She waved him off, then looked at me. "Everything . . . okay?"

"Yeah. Yeah," I said and then with greater force and more certainty added, "It is. There's just one more thing to do."

It was 3:00 A.M., and the steady drone of the engines had put most of my crew to sleep. I was too tense to sleep. Pamela and Eddie's story about the creatures supporting the plane had me on edge, so I had the sword drawn and I kept pacing through the fuselage.

Paul was stretched out across two seats with a blanket tucked around him. Amelia and Brent sat directly behind him. Her head was on his shoulder, and his head was thrown back against the window. I don't know how she could sleep, because he was snoring like a chain saw. When you added in Eddie's snores it was a nasal symphony.

Dagmar, a seasoned traveler, had inserted earplugs. Rudi and Joseph had been soldiers and could sleep anywhere. Grenier was in the galley making a sandwich.

Estevan and Pamela were playing cards, but her face looked drawn, the muscles in her neck looked like corded steel, and she kept staring out the window at the blackness beyond. I reached out and yanked down the shade.

"You've been looking out that window for three solid hours. Stop it."

"But what if they're out there?"

"And you watching obsessively is going to help . . . exactly . . . how?" Her lips tightened into a thin line. "We've got a former navy pilot on the controls. I'm keeping the sword drawn. We're going to be okay."

Grenier came waddling back down the aisle, dropped into one of the commodious leather seats with a grunt, took a bite of his sandwich, and then brushed bread crumbs off the mound of his belly. "The sword does seem to confuse them," he offered.

My iPhone rang. I checked the number and felt a smile curving my lips. I had a feeling it was a really ugly one. "I think you deserve to hear this," I said to my sister, and I hit the speaker icon.

"What the hell have you done?" It was Drew, and he sounded furious and frightened.

"Hi, Drew, so good of you to call."

"I've got an—"

"A call on your note. Yes, I know. I bought your building, and all the outstanding paper. All you have to do is pay off your loan . . . Oh, but wait, your company is experiencing some cash flow problems, isn't it? I wonder why?"

"Why?" came Sandringham's question. I knew what he meant, but I decided to draw out the torture. I was beginning to understand why cats played with mice.

"Why the financial problems, or why as a more general question to the universe? You blew it, Drew." I couldn't maintain the light, bantering tone. "You threw in with my enemies, and you overpromised on what you could deliver. They're not going to be happy with you, and I'm *really* not happy with you. You should have taken into account that I control one of the great fortunes of the world before you decided to screw with me and mine. And just so you know, right now my only interest is in using that money to fuck you. I've wrecked your company and I'm throwing you out in the street. Sort of a nice symmetry, don't you think? It's what you did to me. At least I won't put you in the hospital. Your new friends will take care of that. 'Bye, Drew, have fun being broke and hunted."

"Wait, Ri—"

I cut the connection and put the phone back in my pocket. Pamela was staring at me in shock.

"Richard, who are you?" she asked.

"The man he was destined to be," Grenier said.

Hateful? I thought. I excused myself and retreated to the aft of the plane, where Kenntnis had a private office. Closing the door behind me, I sat down behind the desk and tried to analyze what I was feeling. Proud. Nervous that I was feeling proud. Guilty because maybe I shouldn't feel proud.

I stared at the empty chair across the desk. In November Kenntnis had sat where I was now sitting and I had occupied the other chair. Kenntnis had discovered that Rhiana was not completely human, and I'd been called into the discussion of what to do with her. It had become a debate between Kenntnis and me about our roles. I had told him I had to be in charge. Little had I known how prophetic that would be. I had decreed that Rhiana wouldn't be harmed. Because of that decision on my part, Kenntnis was gone, and I was well and truly in charge.

And proud.

THIRTY-NINE

RICHARD

Vertebrae popped as I stretched my arms up over my head, and I realized I felt at peace, like I had come home. That surprised me. My first year in New Mexico I had found it brown, dusty, and ugly. I thought the Hispanics were making fun of me with their lilting accents, just putting it on for the gringo. The mañana attitude drove me crazy with my uptight, rush, rush, rush East Coast style. My intention was to work a few years with APD and then look for a job someplace civilized. But years had gone by and I hadn't sent out the résumés, and that afternoon in Washington, as I had tried to figure out where to go and what to do, I imagined I smelled the sharp pungent bite of roasting Hatch green chilies, and the spice and evergreen aroma of burning piñon crackling in kiva fireplaces.

I turned my back to the window and sat on the windowsill and critically examined the office. There was room in the far corner for my piano. I'd have Jeannette arrange for movers. Actually, I'd have her clear everything out of my apartment; I was never going back there.

I was just settling into the chair behind the desk when Cross slouched in. He was stuffing the final enormous bite of a cheese Danish into his mouth. "Well, you finally look like you belong here. You should have dumped Daddy a long time ago," he mumbled around the wad of dough.

"First, I was the dumpee, not the dumper, and secondly, we don't talk about this. Ever. Got it?"

He gave me a mock salute. I leaned over and depressed the intercom. "Jeannette, a couple of things. Figure out what time and day it is in Tokyo. I need to talk to Fujasaki, and please close up my apartment. Bring the books, music, and piano here, and you can store everything else."

"Yes, sir. Ms. Reitlingen is here. Should I send her in?"

"Yes, please."

I pointed at the opening door. "See how Dagmar asks if she can be admitted. Why don't you do that? Why do you just walk in?"

Cross shrugged. "I'm a god. And Kenntnis let me."

"You can use the second reason to keep doing it," I said.

"*Was ist loss?*" Dagmar said. Then shook her head. "Sorry, I've been talking with Peter. What's—"

"I've got a question."

"Let's see if I've got an answer," my COO said. "I'm bright, my dear, but amazing as it might be, I don't know everything. *Nearly—*"

"Cut the burble." She gave me an impish smile and subsided. "Why did a building this size only house eighty-four people?"

"Give the boy a gold star," Cross said. "I've been wondering when you'd notice. Kenntnis left it up to me to decide if and when you were ready for the real tour. When you didn't fall for the daddy trick, I figured you just might be bright enough to see past the obvious, and tough, smart, and brave enough to survive, at least for a little while. So now you get all the secret schnaba."

"Does that include a decoder ring and a secret handshake?" I asked.

"You got a fucking sword, what more do you want?"

So with Cross in the lead we began a tour of the Lumina building. On the fifth floor someone was typing on a computer keyboard, a sound like rain pattering on plastic. The heater kicked on, the rush of air overrunning the sound of the typing.

"This building is a fortress," Cross said. "A place for us to ride out bad times. It wouldn't be comfortable, and you can forget about privacy, but we can house three thousand people in this building." The heater shut off, and the sound of the lone typist returned.

"Where do they sleep?" Dagmar asked.

"Air mattresses," Cross answered.

I shook my head. "No, bunk beds. We might be able to house more people that way. If it comes to that. I'm still hopeful that Eddie and the other scientists are going to find a way to free Kenntnis," I said while Dagmar scribbled in her Palm.

"The rest of the floors are pretty much the same, so we can skip them," Cross said and led us back to the elevators. When we reached the lobby, Joseph was waiting. He nodded a greeting.

"Show Richard the security setup," Cross ordered.

The chief of security crossed to the circular reception desk, murmured an apology to Paulette, and reached down by her right leg. "Sorry, not getting fresh," Joseph said.

"Oh, please, get fresh," Paulette replied. She had a lilting French accent. The long lashes brushed the tops of her high cheekbones, and the tip of her tongue lightly touched her lower lip.

Joseph grinned at me. "Does that count as sexual harassment?"

"Do you want me to stop her?" I asked.

"Hell, no," Joseph said, and we all shared a laugh.

There was a loud click followed by the quiet hum of motors, and heavy steel panels came rolling up out of the floors and sealed the windows. Within seconds the lobby was plunged into darkness. Halogen spots in the ceiling switched on.

"These can be keyed from a number of locations in the building," Joseph said. "Your office, my office, the penthouse, and on the third floor."

Cross piped up. "You know how we're tucked in among the boulders. Well, anyplace we don't have big rocks to protect us, steel and concrete barricades have come up to keep any mad bombers away."

"Every window is sealed?" I asked.

"Yes," Joseph said. "But there are pumps and scrubbers to pull in outside air."

"And what happens if someone cuts the power? It's going to get pretty dark and hot or cold, depending," I said. The thought of being sealed in here, away from the touch and sight of the sun, had my claustrophobia jumping.

"The roof, the south wall, and the west wall are covered with solar panels. We also have battery storage for night and during cloudy weather as well as diesel generators," Joseph concluded.

"So we should go down there now," Cross said.

Back in the elevator Cross touched the button for the swimming pool. One level below the garage. The elevator doors opened, and the light from the halogen spots danced on the gently swaying surface of the pool.

"Not just a swimming pool . . . water storage. There used to be big cisterns down here," Cross said. "But Kenntnis knew you liked to swim, so he had this built. He figured we could store the water this way."

I was stunned and oddly warmed by the thought that Kenntnis had put such effort into my comfort. "When did this get built? I've only known you people for three months."

"Right after Thanksgiving. It only took a couple of weeks. Enough money and you can get anything done."

Dagmar walked to the edge of the pool, leaned down, and trailed her fingers in the water. She stood up and shook the droplets of water off her fingers. "I have to ask, if this is meant to be a water source, aren't the chemicals going to be a problem?"

"The water purification system is in the next room."

"How do we replenish the water if the city's water system goes down?" I asked.

"We'll get to that. Let's finish the building first," Cross said.

He led us through the room holding the purification system. The next room housed the backup generators. Cross pointed at another door. "That room has stockpiles of diesel, gasoline, and replacement solar panels. Do you want to see it?"

"I better. Let's make sure they're actually there."

"Taking that definition of assumption a little too much to heart, aren't you?" Cross asked.

"No," I said.

The room did indeed contain the promised fuel and panels. We traipsed back past the pool, and through a door at the opposite end. The rooms held vast stockpiles of food.

"Okay, now the cafeteria and industrial kitchen make sense," I mused.

"Okay, next level."

Cross fished a key out of the front of his sweatshirt, inserted it in the lock in the elevator, and sent us down another floor. "Kenntnis didn't want any kids wandering in here." He looped the chain and key over my head. "Here, it's yours now."

We stepped out into an armory. The collection of weapons ranged from TOW missiles and M-16s and grenades to spears and bows and arrows and swords. The accompanying ammunition, both low and high tech, was also present.

"*Mein Gott,*" Dagmar whispered.

The room to the left was a training gym stocked with weights, aerobic machines, and the accouterments necessary for gymnastics. Fencing masks and padded vests hung on one wall. On the other side of the armory there was an indoor laser shooting range.

"So we don't waste ammo," I murmured as I picked up the pistol and sighted down the barrel. "Damn, he thought of everything. Is that it?"

"Nope. Now we go outside."

We rode the elevator up to the lobby, and Cross led us out the back door. We walked past his packing-box shelter, squatting like a wart against the clean steel and glass lines of the building. Boulders and concrete retaining walls were only a few feet away. Cross turned and looked like he was walking directly toward the rocks, and then he disappeared. When I got close enough I spotted the narrow opening between boulders. The passageway extended about six hundred feet, and the rocks towered ten feet above my head.

Suddenly the terrain opened up into a narrow box canyon. Buffalo grass, brown now from winter's grip, crackled under the soles of my shoes. At the far end of the canyon was a small grove of cottonwood trees: five aspens swayed softly in the wind. With their smooth white bark the aspens were like slender dancers swaying among the hoary gray of the cottonwoods. The trees signaled the presence of water.

We walked the length of the canyon. The rock walls to either side had deep overhangs, and I saw score marks that indicated the rocks had been cut away to make a deeper cleft. Livestock sheds were tucked in underneath on one side, and a huge stack of hay was protected by the rock on the other. In one area there was a riding arena complete with a few jumps.

I started counting my steps, and my best guess was that we had walked almost a mile before we passed out of the bright sunlight into the barred shadows of the winter-bare limbs of the trees. I heard the tinkle of water falling into water. I hurried forward and found an artesian spring in the center of the grove. Water, silver bright, welled up from a cairn of rocks and spilled into a large metal cistern. There was a capped pipe in the bottom.

Bending down, I cupped a hand beneath the water, and gasped as the intense cold stung my palm. I braved a sip and felt a sharp pain behind my eyes from the chill. It tasted sharp and wonderful.

"We pop off the cap and replenish the swimming pool," Cross said.

"Is there enough water here for crops?" Dagmar asked. She looked around the canyon. "Not that we could grow much here."

"Not crops, just livestock, and that includes the human variety," Cross said. He showed his teeth in a smile. "Just joking."

I made a slow 360-degree turn, evaluating the canyon. "Dagmar, I think I know why, aside from your obvious brilliance, you're Lumina's COO."

"Oh? And why is that?"

"You were a dressage rider. Dressage arose out of mounted warfare." I pointed at the shed row. "I'm betting these are here for horses. You probably ought to buy us some."

"Horses," Dagmar murmured as if the word were alien.

"Look, if things get real nuts, gasoline is going to get scarce," Cross said. "And a car won't work when there's powerful magic or a powerful Old One around. We'll only be able to keep one running—the one *he's* riding in." Cross pointed at me. "And that's only if he's got the sword drawn. Let's just hedge our bets, okay? Any more questions?" Cross asked, and I realized that blue-gray shadows were creeping across the grass. Beyond the rock walls of the canyon the sun was almost down.

"Yeah, one. Where do we park the planes and how do we keep them flying?" I asked.

"We own a big hunk of mesa to the north. The runways are dirt 'cause we didn't want to raise too many flags by starting a big permitting fight. And there are cisterns of jet fuel buried on the property."

We returned to the office and watched while New Mexico treated us to one of its spectacular sunsets. The rounded cones of the Three Sisters, extinct volcanoes, looked like the backs of broaching blue whales silhouetted against a riot of gold, crimson, purple, and blue. Well, at least the two humans stared in silent appreciation. Cross ate through a jar of mixed nuts that he found in the bar. Pamela walked in.

"Hey, she didn't get announced," Cross said in a tone that was both triumphant and accusing.

My sister gave him a puzzled, irritated look. "What?"

I waved it away. "Never mind. Hey, guess what, I'm Bruce Wayne." This time I got the look. "Batman," I amplified.

"Nah," Cross said. "You're that wimpy Peter Parker."

"Who?" Pamela asked.

"Spider-Man," Cross and I said in chorus.

She rolled her eyes. "Dinner is almost ready." Cross jumped up and tossed the empty jar into the trash with a long throw like a basketball player giving a "score" pump with his arm. "Oh, I invited Weber," she added casually.

I stopped midstep and looked at her erect back. *Well, that was interesting.* I tried to picture them as a couple. I tried not to be depressed. I told myself I was just trying to protect her.

"He's married. Separated, but they haven't gotten a divorce," I said.

"Good God, Richard, must you try to make everything into a romance?" she said. "He called, wanting to see you. He said he tried you on your cell, but you didn't answer."

I pulled out my cell phone and found his message as we rode up to the penthouse. "Guess there was no reception in the canyon," I said lamely, but I felt absurdly pleased.

Eddie was slumped on the sofa with his laptop and headphones. We walked past him and into the kitchen, where Grenier was inspecting a bottle of wine. "Ah, good, someone to open this. I think a Malbec with pork loin." Dagmar went to help him.

Amazing aromas were issuing from beneath the silver tops of the chafing dishes. I hadn't realized I was starving until that moment. And then Weber came in. I moved forward with my hand out, but he ignored the handshake, grabbed me in a rough hug, and then pounded me on the back.

"So, you couldn't set 'em straight?" he said.

"Nope. Looks like it's back to us, but I've got some ideas."

Eddie wandered in. "Is it dinner yet?"

Grenier was handing out glasses of wine. I was feeling expansive. I took one. Weber and Eddie were introduced. Weber took a sip of his wine, then looked around with a questioning expression.

"Where's Angela?"

The buzz of conversation died. Pamela answered, "She came home. Three days before we did."

"Then why didn't she call me?" Weber asked.

I dropped my eyes. "We . . ." I coughed and continued. "We had a little . . . disagreement."

"Okay, but that doesn't explain why she wouldn't call me," Weber said. "And she hasn't been in the office. I know because I watched an autopsy yesterday. Jeff was still handling things."

I set down the wineglass, and was startled when the stem snapped. Wine flowed across the granite countertop and began to drip onto the floor. Pulling out my phone, I dialed her home number. It rang and voice mail picked up.

"Angela, it's Richard. Are you there?" Silence. Next I tried her mobile. It went to voice mail on the first ring. "Her cell's been turned off."

We all just looked at each other.

And deep inside me a murmur of fear and guilt became a shout. *I sent her away. I sent her away, I sent her away. And I didn't arrange to protect her.*

FORTY

RICHARD

"We better hope she's *not* in there," Syd said.

We were back at Bob Franklin's house. This time the warm smell of roasting turkey and garlic mashed potatoes had replaced the smoky bite of gumbo, and this time there were no spouses and kids. Just agents. The only additions were Grenier and Damon. There was no way Weber would have stayed behind. Grenier hadn't wanted to come, but I'd threatened him. *I wonder if he still likes the man I've become,* I thought.

My gut told me they had taken Angela to Grenier's compound, so I wanted him here to give us advice about entering the place. Danny had been running through satellite images to try to turn my hunch into a certainty.

"They've set up a perimeter of marines called in from Quantico. Nobody gets in," Franklin amplified.

I shook my head. "Not true. There's one group they're sure as hell going to let in. There's a team arriving from the Vatican. They're going to perform an exorcism."

Grenier paused with his fork halfway to his mouth. "Are you seriously suggesting that we put on dog collars and traipse out in fancy dress to confront monsters and rescue the damsel?" His tone held a sneer. I guessed I hadn't been forgiven.

"Hey, those dress thingies can hide a boatload of guns,"

Sam broke in with delight.

She was the only woman present, and she stood out like a lily in the middle of a redwood forest. All the agents were *big*. The only other woman in the house was Franklin's wife, Michelle, who had set out the food and disappeared. She didn't seem real happy to have us back. I couldn't blame her.

"Uh, Sam, I think this is going to have to be a stag party," Weber said.

"And remember, guns won't work," Franklin reminded her.

Sam's mouth opened and closed a few times before she finally said, "Well, crap."

Cross mopped up gravy and cranberry sauce with a crescent roll, and then stuffed the entire dripping mess into his mouth. He mumbled around the doughy glob, "Well, that might not be strictly true. They might work if the sword was nearby and drawn."

"Now we're talking," Sam said. "Hey, I could dress up like a nun."

One of the younger agents, I couldn't remember his name, leered and said, "Oooo, Sammy as a naughty nun. Will you rap me with your ruler, Sister?"

"Jay, I'm gonna kick your nuts up through—"

It was entertaining, but we had too much to do. "Sam," I said warningly while I committed Jay's name to memory. Amazingly the young agent subsided. I looked back to Cross. "Okay, that's promising. Look, it's going to be awkward, and I'm going to feel like a *Highlander* reject—"

"Too short," Sam broke in. I gave her an exasperated look. She held up her hands. "Okay, jeez, oh man, sorry, go ahead."

"Are you normally this manic?"

"I want to kick some monster butt."

"Are you done now?" She pressed her lips into a tight line and made the zipping motion. "As I was saying, I think I need to keep the sword drawn all the time now. So how do I do it?"

"Can't," Cross said. He craned his head and looked down his nose at the untouched plate of food resting on my knee. I'd never seen a starving vulture, but I had a real sense it would have looked just like that.

I knew I wasn't going to be able to eat. I was projecting businesslike competence, but my gut felt like I'd eaten acid and ground glass. I handed over my plate to the homeless god and said, "You can't tell me that Charlemagne or Arthur or other paladins in ancient times didn't wear the sword openly."

"Yeah, but the blade wasn't there." Cross encompassed them all in a wide grin. "It's actually kind of funny. All those incredibly gaudy scabbards you see in museums, they were just for show. Something to draw the eye so people would be less likely to notice there was nothing actually *in* them."

"So if I'm not holding the hilt, the blade's not there?"

"Yep."

"Well, that's a terrible design." I pulled the pill case out of my pocket and dry-swallowed a Xanax and a Pepcid.

"You can take it up with the designer if we ever manage to bust him loose."

And that's when a new thought entered and I found myself thinking more about Kenntnis in his crystal tomb than Angela and what might be happening to her.

I forced myself back to the conversation to hear Cross ask, ". . . question, if you have to go in there, do you want me along on this little party?"

I pressed a hand against my forehead and considered the options. A big one occurred to me right away, but it wasn't a scenario I liked, so I hesitated for a few more seconds. Finally I smoothed back my hair and said, "Yes, I want you along because if anything happens to me—if I get killed—you need to grab the sword and run for it. With your powers you can find someone to replace me. Find another paladin."

Cross said, "I don't want to be trying to do magic in there. First, if I'm close enough to you to take the handoff, that means I'm close enough for the sword to affect me, and it's going to fuck up my magic. And second, my brethren *way* outclass me. I get into a magical pissing contest with them, and I'm gonna get squashed. Oh, and one more thing; let's say you're swashing and buckling with the sword in one hand and a gun in the other, and you come up against an Old One. Even if they've gone physical, you've got no idea what part of them is vulnerable to a bullet."

I waved a hand in front of his face. "Hello. I use the sword. It kills your kind, remember? What it won't kill is humans, and there are humans in that compound, and I damn well know guns work on people."

"Got it," Danny, the computer geek, sang out.

There was a general shuffling as we all gathered where we could see the screen of his laptop computer.

"This is surveillance tape from the Hyatt Regency at Reagan National. There's Angela." He pointed, and a fist seemed to clench in the center of my chest. Angela looked so very tiny in her ankle-length coat. "The doorman calls over a taxi. And there." He froze the tape and pointed again. "That's where it happened."

A car had pulled up next to the taxi as Angela was climbing in the backseat. I recognized the car—it was a BMW convertible, but this time the top was closed. It was hard to see the man who jumped out of the Beemer through the windows of the taxi, but I recognized that whip-thin body as he yanked open the taxi door and pulled Angela out. *Doug Andresson. My counterpart.* I could almost feel his fists connecting with my face again. I forced myself to watch as he shoved Angela violently into the backseat of the car, and the car raced away. Someone was driving that car. I couldn't see her, but I knew with certainty it had been Rhiana. This was where mercy had taken me.

"The dark paladin, Doug Andresson." Grenier said.

"That's the perp who attacked you back in November. Cut you, too," Weber added.

Grenier gave me a significant look. "You still want to take the sword anywhere near the gate? Knowing they've got him?"

"We can't go in without the sword, and they've taken Angela to the compound—"

Weber was shaking his head. "Whoa, there. There's nothing on this video"—he hooked a thumb at the computer screen—"to support that. Have you got anything beyond a gut-level hunch?"

"Where else would they keep Andresson?" I asked.

"Oh, I don't know—a hotel? Someone's house?" I was suddenly the junior officer being gently flayed by his superior. "We know there are humans who are working for these pukes," and I watched Weber's eyes slid toward Grenier. "One of them might be holding him."

Support came from an unexpected source. "No, they would keep him at the compound," Grenier said. "They'll want him close to hand. I did."

Syd shivered. "That place ain't good for humans. It's gotta be worse now. I don't see how he could take it."

"Because he's our very own version of a monster wrapped up in human skin," Grenier said. "He's the coldest psychopath I've ever met."

"And he has Angela, so we're going in. We don't have a choice," I said.

"Of course we have a choice. We could *not* go in," Grenier said. "There are going to be casualties. Angela just had the bad luck to be the first. You feel guilty because you couldn't return her love and you sent her away, so you're acting—"

When you're emotionally raw you don't handle getting whipsawed real well. From support to betrayal, and it felt like something had exploded behind my eyes. I found myself spinning around, and my hand closing around Grenier's throat. The rolls of flesh gave under my fingers. I didn't know how I did it, he outweighed me by a hundred pounds, but I drove him back across the room and slammed him up against the wall. Anger had my breath coming so short and shallow that I couldn't manage to say a word.

"Not an option, I take it?" Grenier rasped, his voice stretched and tight from the pressure of my hand against his larynx.

FORTY-ONE

It took a while for Jack to respond to her knock. When he opened the door he was rubbing his eyes, his hair was tousled, and he wore only pajama bottoms and his feet were bare. Rhiana looked at the face of her diamond-encrusted watch and realized it was 2:00 A.M. Sleep, like hunger for traditionally human food, pricked her only after days spent on this side of the gate. Even in human form she sipped and supped from the chaotic, roiling emotions of the crowds she passed on the street, and the person trapped in the smashed car at the scene of an auto accident, or a married couple fighting in a restaurant. There was a reason her father called Earth a buffet.

"Jesus, Rhiana, what's wrong?" Jack asked.

"Nothing. I forget about time and night and rest."

"Nice for you. You want to come in? What's up?" His words were still thickened by sleep.

Rhiana followed him into the room. It was a nice room. Georgian inspired with a king-sized four-poster bed. The sheet and comforter were twisted and rumpled. A sofa and a couple of chairs clustered around a gas fireplace. There was a desk in an alcove. An open laptop sat on top, sending slow flashes of color across the wall as the screen saver roiled. It had seemed strange to her that Jack lived in the Hay-Adams Hotel across the street

272

from the White House. Now it made sense. He was a man and a bachelor. Why not have maid service, room service, health club, pool? Especially when you didn't have to pay for it.

"What do you need?" Jack asked as he pulled on a bathrobe.

"If I did something that got Richard to come back it would be a good thing, right?"

He scratched absently at his chest, his finger probing at the mat of brown hair. "Well, yeah. What did you have in mind?"

"Oh, I already did it."

"Okay." He waited.

Rhiana clasped and unclasped her hands. She walked to the window and looked out at the White House. "I got Doug to help me."

"Okay," Jack said again, only more slowly, and she heard the distaste frosting the edges of the word.

"I gave him Angela," Rhiana finished in a rush. She didn't have to explain who Angela was. They had all obsessively studied the people around Richard, looking for any opening that could be exploited.

"Jesus!" Jack ran his hand through his hair. "You're for sure going to have to kill him now. He'll never forgive you."

"He won't necessarily know I did it. It might just—"

"He'd be an idiot if he didn't. Jesus, Rhiana." Once again his hands went to his hair, frantically combing and tugging. He paced a small circle. "We're trying to take over a world, and you're acting like it's high school." Guilt and embarrassment fueled her fury, and she felt the bonds encompassing her human body threatening to shred. "We had a plan—" Jack continued, and she cut him off.

"And your big plan didn't work! You and Sandringham with all your psychological crap about daddy transference. Richard didn't go after Kenntnis. He went home. *I'm* the one who got him back."

"Okay, fine. You're a genius. You got him back. So why come bother me at two in the morning?" He moved to the minibar, turned the key, and pulled out a miniature of bourbon. Screwing off the cap, he drained it in two swallows.

"I thought you should be kept informed. You are my assistant," and the words sounded ludicrous even to her.

"Bullshit." He turned back to face her. "It's because you're scared and feeling guilty, and you want me to tell you it's all going to be okay, and your fantasy crush won't care that you gave his lady to a fucking *psychopath*!"

Rhiana groped in her pocket and pulled out a penny. "She was *not* his lady." She set the coin to spinning and sparking in her hand. "And you will never, ever speak to me like that again." The flare of copper fire danced across the wallpaper as Rhiana murmured the spell. Jack's back stiffened in surprise and fear. Rhiana reached out a hand, fingers curled like talons. The spiritualist gasped, and a hand flew to his throat. She pulled him toward her. His cheeks were a dull brick red. She released him, and he fell heavily onto his knees. His fingers clutched convulsively at the nap of the carpet.

Rhiana walked toward the door. She didn't quite reach it before Jack said, "There's one thing you ought to remember, princess." His voice was hoarse and he could barely speak above a whisper. "You really should be nice to the people you meet on the way up, because you're going to meet them on the way down."

FORTY-TWO

RICHARD

I couldn't sleep. We'd checked into the Mayflower, and the suite was filled with the guttural snores of men sleeping heavily. Joseph was taking this third watch, and he nodded to me but didn't speak when I walked in carrying my laptop. I settled onto a sofa and logged on to the APD computer to review Andresson's rap sheet. The list of assaults on women soon had my gut burning.

People had accepted my position that we had to go in, but I could sense the support was soft. If I couldn't produce hard evidence Angela was in the compound, I needed another reason. The reason was obvious. Kenntnis was there. We needed him. We could try to free him. Or if that was a bridge too far, we could do some reconnaissance. But for that to make sense I needed someone who understood how Kenntnis had been trapped.

Rather than wake up people in New Mexico, I logged on to the secure and encrypted Lumina server to see who might be awake. I wasn't surprised to find Eddie online, and he was the person I needed.

Hi. What are you doing? I sent.

Playing WoW. I'm fighting a balrog.

Want to face some real monsters?

No!

275

Want to take a close look at spin glass? Seconds ticked by. *Are you there?*

I'm here. You're going in?

Have to.

They have her?

Yes.

I liked her.

Don't make it past tense.

Sorry. Is it okay I'm scared?

I'm scared.

There was another long moment with the cursor just blinking at me; then a single word appeared.

Okay.

Pamela arrived with Eddie.

"Are you going to let us in?" Her tone was waspish. I hurriedly stepped aside and let them enter the suite.

"What are you . . . why are you . . . huh?" It was not my most articulate moment.

She suddenly looked vulnerable. "I want to help. I looked at Andresson's rap sheet. He . . . he . . ." She temporized. "Hurts women. When you go in after Angela, I'm going, too."

My head had started shaking halfway through. "No."

"Yes." She grabbed me by the upper arm and pulled me away from Eddie. "Angela is going to be terrified and traumatized. She will be more comfortable with a woman. Believe me, I know. I've already discussed this with Sam. We're going with you."

The whole thing about Sam and Pamela colluding went right past me. *Believe me, I know,* that's what had my attention. "What do you mean by that?"

She didn't pretend not to understand. "My friend Julie, you remember, you dated her. It happened while we were in law school. She told me, and I went with her to the hospital and to the police. Trust me, you want a woman along."

"We're going in as priests."

"You can't tell me some private pulling guard duty will know the intricacies of the rite of exorcism. For all they know, the nuns are there to hand you holy water and wipe your sweating brows while you contend with demons."

It actually made sense, and I remembered the rape victims I'd dealt with. Even the sound of men's voices had many of them cringing. "Okay."

She gave me a push toward Eddie. "Go talk to Eddie. I'll arrange for our costumes."

"Hey, would you be in charge of getting the cassocks, too?"

She nodded. Eddie was standing by the desk perusing the room service menu. I realized I was hungry, too, and we ordered sandwiches. We settled onto the couch, and I prepared for another crash course in physics.

"Okay, so, you know we're going into the compound. Kenntnis is trapped there, and I figured as long as we're there we may as well try to bust him out. So how do we break this spin glass?"

The gawky young scientist leaned down, untied his tennis shoes, and pulled them off. He rubbed his stockinged feet on the carpet, hissed as he sucked in a breath through his teeth, pinched the bridge of his nose, plucked at his collar, cracked his knuckles. I wanted to throttle him.

"In a lab we'd turn back on the pump laser, and that would start the probe laser . . . uh, that'd be Kenntnis . . . moving again. But it looks like they used light from that star that we saw through the opening as the pump laser, and I don't have a clue how to turn back on a laser that's powered by a fucking *star*."

"That glass looks to be only five or six inches wide," I said. "What if we just pushed it over and busted it?"

Grenier waddled in and checked abruptly at the sight of Eddie. I ignored him.

Eddie shook his head. "You don't want to do that because you run the risk of disrupting the light pulse. Remember, whatever this guy was, his knowledge, mind, everything is stored on an atomic spin wave. If you just break the glass, the information that is Kenntnis might end up scrambled. Also, the longer it's . . . uh, he's stored, the more he degrades. He's functionally frozen, but the atoms still move slightly, and that alters the stored information."

"So we need to get this done and get it done soon."

"And right. Right would be also good," Eddie added.

"So when you turn on this pump laser, what is it about that laser that will make Kenntnis move?"

"The light from the laser."

"And how much light does it take?"

"Normally, not much. But nothing about this is normal."

I took the sword hilt out of the holster at the small of my back. "There's always a swirl of light around the blade whenever I've drawn it where magic or a tear in reality is present. The more the magic or the bigger the tear, the brighter the light."

"I'm guessing with that gate it will turn into a torch," Grenier interrupted.

"Exactly." I turned back to Eddie. "So, could we focus the light from the sword onto the spin glass?"

"The pump laser is tuned to the frequency of the probe laser. It's not like frying an ant with a magnifying glass," Eddie said.

"Kenntnis made the sword. I think it's actually maybe a part of him. It might be tuned to him," I said.

Taking his lower lip between thumb and forefinger, Eddie pulled at it. "Maybe we could use mirrors and lenses to focus and intensify the light," he mumbled. The torment of his lip was interfering with his diction. "It might work. And it will also tell us a lot if it doesn't. It'll help me figure this thing out."

"That was my thinking. We'll try for a double rescue, but we'll be happy if we end up with intel and one rescue."

Grenier cleared his throat and took a step toward us. "What?" I asked, and I didn't care that it wasn't friendly.

"*Now* this plan actually has some merit. So let me offer my help."

"You're a fat man with one hand," I said, not caring that I was rude.

Alarm pulsed across his face. "Oh, I'm not going with you. I'm not going anywhere *near* them. And there's nothing you could do that would make me go with you, but there's an alternative to going in the front door."

"What?"

"There's a tunnel. It runs from my basement wine cellar to a quarter mile past the fence. The exit is screened by trees."

For a moment the rest of the sentence didn't register. I remembered that basement. I remembered the toe of Andresson's cowboy boot connecting with my balls, and his fist crunching against my face. *He took Angela. He has Angela.*

Eddie asking a question brought me back. "Why would you have something like that?"

"For a very smart man, you're singularly stupid," Grenier said.

"Hey!" The word emerged as a strangled squawk.

I waved down Eddie's outrage as Grenier placed a finger at the side of his mouth and cast his gaze up toward the ceiling.

"Let me think—I was a traitor to humanity, in league with monsters from other dimensions. Of course I had a bolt hole."

Now it was my turn to feel a growing outrage. "And you didn't tell me earlier. *Why?*"

He shrugged. "I was hoping you would look at the situation, see it was hopeless, and give it up. But if you have a chance to free Kenntnis . . . now it makes sense to go in."

"Angela wasn't worth it, but this Kenntnis guy is?" Eddie said.

"Yes."

And Grenier's eyes were on me because he knew, on some level, I'd made the same calculation.

FORTY-THREE

The limo, towing a small U-Haul trailer, rolled down the two-lane blacktop, headed deeper into the Virginia countryside. On either side leafless trees seemed to claw at the flat gray sky. Pamela, wedged against the left side of the car, could just see one of the Vatican flags fluttering on the hood. She and Sam were pressed thigh to thigh, and Pamela realized that what she felt digging into her leg was one of Sam's guns that had been strapped beneath her nun's habit.

Despite the February cold, sweat was prickling on her scalp beneath the heavy cloth of the wimple. Pamela tried to put it down to eleven people in a car designed to comfortably carry eight, but she knew it was a lie. This was nerves, and nothing else.

Joseph was driving; Rudi was up front with him along with another FBI volunteer, a wiry skinny man named Jay Haskell.

The men all wore the Catholic dress well. Her brother's face above the black of the cassock and the white collar looked like the chiseled features of a Della Robbia angel. Rudi and Estevan both looked at ease. Pamela suspected years spent as altar boys. Franklin and Joseph seemed clothed in dignity. Syd, Weber, Jay, and Eddie seemed the most uncomfortable. She glanced over at Sam. The agent was stunningly beautiful, as the wimple formed a frame for the oval face, setting off her dark eyes and the slashing line of her eyebrows.

A large, heavy cream parchment folder embossed with the presidential seal and adorned with gold seals and fluttering ribbons rested on Richard's lap. He had his hands folded on top, and the family gold signet ring glinted on his right hand. They had burned more jet fuel to bring it from New Mexico. Dagmar had explained that Kenntnis had received a Presidential Medal of Freedom back in the Reagan administration, and the portfolio looked impressive. They had then fancied it up with more seals and ribbons. They also had forged letters from the pope and the Cardinal of D.C.

Rudi had voiced strong opposition to using the documents. He had been a marine, and felt any soldier would want orders from his immediate superior officer, not a bunch of shit from civilians, especially wop civilians. Richard had overruled him.

"It's going to be one more ring in the circus I'm going to be ringmastering."

Pamela wondered what he had in mind.

A few miles farther on a soldier, dressed in mountain camouflage, stepped out from between the trees, and held up a hand, palm out. They rolled to a stop. The soldier approached cautiously. He was a baby-faced private with a heavy machine gun slung across his body. The weapon looked outsized against the bony and knobby wrists of a boy just flirting with manhood. Joseph had the window rolled down by the time the young marine had reached the side of the car. The soldier reacted to the sight of the collar. Tension flowed out of his shoulders, and he shifted the gun to the side and behind him.

"Where's the officer in charge, son?" Joseph asked.

The boy pointed southwest. "A mile further on, Father."

"Radio him and tell him the team from Rome has arrived."

It could have been a hundred miles. It seemed like hours passed before they reached the final line of defense against the gate. Here a barricade had been constructed across the road. Humvees were pulled onto the shoulder on either side of the road.

The silhouettes of the trees seemed subtly wrong. Pamela peered closely and wondered what she was seeing.

Syd leaned across his daughter to say, "Camouflaged artillery piece, and there's a couple of tanks in there, too."

Joseph pulled forward until the limousine had its grille nudged against the red-and-white-painted board that formed the levered gate. Rudi rolled down the window and handed the pile of documents to the lieutenant in command, a handsome black man whose high, chiseled cheekbones hinted at Native American in the mix. He looked through the papers, and Pamela felt her stomach clench as he began to frown.

Richard threw open the door, jumped out of the car, and assaulted the marine with a barrage of rapid-fire Italian complete with expansive, swooping gestures and much pointing at his watch. Pamela knew they had to do something. This was taking too long. The lieutenant would call someone higher in the chain of command, and they'd all be arrested.

Suddenly Weber got out of the car, leaving the door open, and pulled the young officer aside. He said in a low voice, "Kind of crazy they'd send us a guy with no English, but also kind of typical. Can't you help us out here?"

There was a low, unidentifiable sound, growing in intensity. Pamela glanced around looking for the source, but couldn't locate it.

Richard let fly another rippling batch of Italian. A thunderous frown lay across his brow. Weber pretended to listen, nodded, made a placating, patting-the-air gesture muttering, "*Si, si.*" The cop turned back to the officer. "Look, son, the sooner we get in there, the sooner this thing ends."

The drone and whirr grew louder, and suddenly a new factor literally flew into the equation. The sunlight was blotted out, throwing them all into deep shadow, and they were deafened by the whir and clatter of wings. Everyone, soldiers and fake priests alike, ducked and looked up. The sky was choked with thousands of birds of every variety. Geese, sparrows, ducks, crows, all fleeing northward as if carried on a hurricane wind. Feathers drifted down, and then dead birds began dropping all around them. One smacked onto Richard's shoulder and slid down his chest, leaving a red smear against the black material of his cassock. He gave a cry of disgust.

Joseph's hands clutched convulsively on the steering wheel. It was hard to see through the front windshield, but what Pamela saw was alarming. She jumped out and joined Richard. He was looking beyond the clouds of birds at a sky gone purple and black. Shapes writhed within the sullen clouds. The lieutenant produced a small sound between a gasp and a whimper. Pamela wanted to scream, but her throat and mouth had gone too dry. Richard gripped the marine by the shoulder and broke character, saying in English, "Get your men out of here, Lieutenant! Get them out *now*!"

The marine was terrified, but managed to stammer out, "Our orders are to hold here"

"If you do you'll either die or go mad. You can't do anything more. We might be able to."

"You can't go into that," the lieutenant said as dead and dying birds continued to rain down around them.

Richard's face had gone bone white down to the lips. "Can and must. Please, Lieutenant. Will you let us pass?"

"You're fucking crazy! Fine. Do whatever you want." The marine ran away up the road, bawling into his radio, "Fall back! Fall back!"

The soldiers were shaking, flinging down their guns, dropping to the ground crying. Discipline eroded into blind panic. Richard drew the sword. The overtones were massive, and the swirling light around the blade illuminated the ground all around him. The panic abated, the troops began to listen, and an orderly retreat began.

Diesel engines growled and rumbled to life, and trucks and Humvees began to pull away.

"What are we waiting for?" Pamela asked.

"For them to get clear," came the tense response.

"Well, they sure as fuck know we're here now," said Weber as the overtones from the sword continued to press against their eardrums.

It sounded like distant thunder or pounding rain against the glass. Rhiana ran into the living room to see hundreds of birds flinging themselves against the windows. They smashed against the glass, shattering fragile wings and breaking their necks. She shrieked, disturbed by the wanton destruction, and then screamed again when the glass broke and the birds poured in. She flung her arms over her head, trying to ward off the assault. Feathers drifted down around her. When she finally raised her head there were birds perched on the mantel, on the backs of the chairs and sofas, on lamps, and clinging to the chandelier.

She held out her hand, and a large crow hopped onto it. The skin of its feet felt almost scaly, and the claws pricked her skin. Its head cocked back and forth, a movement both sinuous and mechanical. The hard black eyes glittered as she got the message. Humans were on the edge of the compound. The weapon was with them. The paladin was with them. There was an edge of fear and alarm in the query that was more felt than understood—*is Prometheus secure?* There was an imperative. *You will come.*

A flick of the wrist sent the crow exploding into the air. She had been rough, and its claws left bloody scratches on the back of her hand. Rhiana circled the room, clasping and unclasping her hands. He knew. What if Angela was still alive? Dead would be worse. She should never . . . She needed to make sure he never found Angela.

He attention was caught by the couch. It was smeared with white and gray bird dung. Rhiana had a sudden vision of herself as a wrinkled old hag, surrounded by familiars in a house that reeked of animal droppings, and alone, utterly alone. Her human body shredded as she ran for a mirror.

He mustn't find her. He mustn't ever know what I did.

Eddie was blathering. ". . . they didn't attack us. For it to be *The Birds* the birds would have had to attack us. This is like the anti-*Birds* because they were all dying instead of attacking us—"

"Eddie," came the soft admonishment from Richard. He laid a hand on Eddie's knee. "Calm down. Focus."

"Shit. Sorry."

"Where's Cross?" Sam asked.

"I don't know," Richard answered. "He'll be there when we need him." Richard drew the tips of his fingers slowly up the side of the blade. The net of light caressed his hand. When he pulled his hand back, the light flowed after it like pulled taffy. Pamela found it disturbing. Eddie was staring at it hungrily.

Weber shifted. "You know that or are you just hoping?"

A faint smile touched her brother's lips. "I don't know, Damon. I only know I can't do this alone." Pamela noticed how thin Richard's face had become. "So I have to have a little faith."

Rudi lifted the topo map and peered through the windshield. "Turn off here."

Joseph spun the wheel. They left the road and went jouncing across the shoulder and into the cover of the woods. Branches snapped as the car rolled through the trees, and scraped across the top of the trailer with a rending shriek.

"That's a great sound. Chalk on blackboard," Franklin said.

"Wow, if that's how chalk on a blackboard sounds, then I'm really glad blackboards were something that belonged to the Dark Ages," Eddie said.

Syd laid a hand over his heart and pretended to wilt. "Oh, that hurt."

"We're not old, Syd," Joseph said. "We're seasoned."

"Actually, I think you're old," Eddie said, and Sam wrapped her arms around her waist and started laughing.

It spread like a yawn, and suddenly everyone in the car was

whooping with laughter born of panic. Pamela wiped her streaming eyes, looked around at the red faces, and realized that for the first time in her life she belonged. A lump formed in her throat, and suddenly the tears were from emotion. She sniffed and hoped no one would notice. But Richard was looking at her. He stretched out his right hand. She reached out and clasped it.

Suddenly they broke through into a small clearing. Joseph glanced over at the topo map and took his foot off the gas. They rolled to a stop, and Joseph turned off the engine. It pinged as it cooled. The tops of the pines whipped back and forth as the wind roared through them. For a long moment no one moved; then Richard opened the door, and they all exploded into action.

Piling out of the car, they stripped off their cassocks and habits. Sam and Pamela helped each other with the pins that held on the wimples. "Man, it would suck to be a nun," Sam said, and she ripped away the material and shook her hair loose.

Rudi and Estevan walked in circles, kicking at the fallen leaves and needles as they searched for the hatch. Eddie opened the top of his shoulder pouch, reached in, and pulled out a velvet-wrapped package. He untied it and threw back the material to reveal mirrors and lenses.

Weber helped Richard shrug into a tight-fitting leather jacket so Richard wouldn't have to release his grip on the sword. Next the cop buckled the belt of a pair of cycling chaps around Richard's narrow waist, and then knelt in front of him to thread the zippers on the legs. Pamela watched and had a sudden memory of the color plate in their grandfather's copy of *Men of Iron* showing Miles being dressed for battle.

Rudi and Estevan pulled up a metal hatch. Dirt, needles, and leaves cascaded off the gray metal. Joseph came down the ramp of the trailer trundling a large red-and-silver motorcycle.

Pamela circled the bike. "I've never really known you, have I?" The smile she got back was rueful, and Richard shook his head. "Well, we'll fix that once we've finished," she said briskly, and blinked hard again. It had to be nerves that had her so emotional. Fortunately Eddie drew attention away from her.

"I thought it took two hands to ride a motorcycle," Eddie said.

"Not this one," Richard answered. "Gilera Ferro 850 automatic. One hand to steer. The other hand to use the sword."

Bob Franklin had a quiver full of arrows slung over his back and was stringing a large bow. Weber lit cigarettes, puffed, and handed them to everybody.

"Don't puff, just keep them lightly between your lips. We don't want them to burn away before we reach the house."

"And we're lighting them here because . . . ?" Jay asked.

"Because fire won't burn near the gate," Richard said. "At some point they will seem to go out."

"And we're gonna be climbing ladders, and maybe fighting bad guys. These cigarettes are gonna be a handful of tobacco," Jay said.

Weber looked disgusted. "Doesn't anybody fucking smoke anymore? When they stop burning, you're going to tuck them behind your ear." Weber demonstrated with an unlit cigarette.

Joseph handed out nightsticks. Jay and Syd transferred metal canteens from a box into backpacks. There was a greasy residue around some of the caps, and Pamela coughed as the throat-biting smell of gasoline hit the back of her nose.

Richard thrust a helmet at Eddie and swung onto the bike.

"Where's your helmet?" Weber yelled as Richard gunned the engine.

"I need my peripheral vision," Richard yelled back. "Eddie, if I give you a gun, can you manage not to shoot me? I don't need you to actually hit anything, just keep people's heads down."

"I'd only have one arm to hang on with." Eddie's voice quavered like a fifteen-year-old's.

"Never mind."

Pamela watched the resolve harden the young scientist's chin. The look he gave her brother was pure hero worship. "No, that's cool. I can do it."

Weber handed him a pistol, grip first. "When you're on the bike, keep your arm straight out to the side and pull the trigger. Don't try for anything fancy, just aim toward any people or . . . other things you might see. Here, try it once so you see how much pressure you actually need."

Eddie strained, the trigger snapped back, the gun roared, his arm jerked up, and the pistol flew out of his hand and landed in the winter-withered grass. The smell of gunpowder brought back memories of Fourth of July parties and fireworks on the beach near their house in Newport, and suddenly Pamela wanted to cry; for her lost mother and absent father, and a world that made sense.

"This isn't a good idea," Weber said to Richard. "You should have gotten the sidecar so I could have ridden shotgun."

"I'm going to be weaving through trees to get to Kenntnis. That's why it had to be a bike, not a car, and the passenger has to be Eddie. He's the only one who can inspect the glass," Richard said.

"No, no, I can do it. It just took me by surprise," Eddie said.

Richard nodded. "Let him try again."

Weber retrieved the pistol. Eddie took it, closed one eye, and aimed at a tree across the clearing. This time he didn't lose his grip on the gun. Wood splinters exploded out of the tree trunk.

"I *aimed* for that tree," Eddie said loudly and looked around at everyone.

Sam patted him on the shoulder. "You're a real natural."

"We need to start humping," Syd called from where he stood at the tunnel entrance.

Weber checked the face on an old-fashioned spring-wound watch. "It's about two miles, and then we need to clear any bad guys out of the house and set up. That's going to take at least forty minutes."

"I'll start moving in twenty," Richard said.

"See you at the compound."

"I'll be there."

Pamela joined the group gathered around the hatch. She looked back at her brother, and suddenly it hit her—this might be the last time she ever saw him. She ran back and gave him a fierce hug.

"When we get back, teach me to shoot." she said.

"I thought you hated guns."

"Teach me."

He nodded. "Come *on*," Weber yelled. She ran to join them.

The chemiluminescent light sticks worked surprising well. They were bright enough that Pamela could see the shadows of the men in front and behind her bobbing and swaying on the tunnel walls. Sam was disgusted at the march order, which had her and Pamela sandwiched between Weber and Franklin and Rudi in the front and Syd, Jay, and Estevan bringing up the rear. When Sam squawked, Weber had pointed out that Franklin had a compound bow, he had a hunting knife, and they were stronger than Sam. Pamela didn't mind being in the middle.

When they'd first entered the tunnel, there had been the buzz of whispered conversation, but that had died away. Now only an occasional cough or the scrape of shoe leather on grit marked their passage. Pamela tried to identify the men by the sounds of their breathing. Syd had a habit of pulling air through his teeth, a sort of tuneless hum. Estevan was a quick, sharp panting. Pamela wondered how much air was actually reaching the young man's lungs.

She had been told to expect it, but as they moved toward the compound the thin wisps of smoke stopped rising from the lit cigarettes. She tightened her ponytail and tucked the cigarette behind her ear. Pamela normally hated the smell of cigarette smoke, but now she missed it because nerves had somebody's bowels in an uproar.

The stink of flatulence mingled with the loamy smell of moist earth. Another fart erupted somewhere back in the line. It was a series of squeaking pops like someone walking on bubble wrap. Her reason to come along now seemed thin, and her determination dropped with each passing minute. She wondered how Richard was doing, and envied him the open air. She wished she could have ridden the bike with him. But it had to be Eddie, and the logical place for Angela to be held was in the house, and her reason for coming was Angela.

FORTY-FOUR

RICHARD

Eddie climbed awkwardly onto the backseat of the bike and wrapped his arms around my waist. It felt like a hug by a Kodiak.

"Not . . . quite so . . . tight," I managed to squeeze out.

"Sorry, sorry. I've only been on a bike once before. My dad hated these things, and forbid any of us to ever ride one. But my half-uncle Chet came through San Diego when I was thirteen. He was on his way to Mexico, and my dad was at a conference at JPL so he got to stay, and he took me for a ride. He had this big old Harley."

I was having to concentrate on the uneven ground as I guided the bike back toward the road. Eddie kept going.

"The problem was that he didn't mention that the exhaust pipes run the length of the bike, and man, they get really, really hot. That's why I was so careful when I got on this bike, because after the ride I just slid off the bike 'cause I was, like, scared and tired and feeling really guilty, and I was wearing shorts, and I rested my calf against the exhaust pipe and got a third-degree burn on my leg. It was so gross, it smelled like roasting pork at a luau. Anyway, my mom was so scared that Dad would find out that Uncle Chet had been at the house, and that I'd ridden on a motorcycle, that she didn't take me to a doctor. That's why I've got this scar. Solarcaine and Neosporin don't do much on a third-degree burn."

The artless, never-ending blather had my neck tensing. Now

I was almost wishing I'd worn a helmet. It would have kept out the verbal diarrhea. We reached the road, and I opened it up. The trees flashed by like a gray film unwinding. My ears began to burn from the cold.

We went into a curve, and Eddie stayed stiff as a board and bolt upright. I had to fight to keep the bike from falling. Eddie started yelling in my ear. I got us through the curve, and half-turned my head to shout, "When we take the turns you've got to lean into them. Go with the bike so you don't throw us off balance. Remember, I only have one hand to steer."

And I looked down at my left hand balanced on the handlebars with the blade of the sword pointed straight forward. The swirling lights around the blade were bright enough to throw a spear of white light into the sullen red gloom here beneath the clouds. I wondered how much darker it was going to get, and if the sword could keep pace.

Another curve was coming. Eddie tightened his grip on my waist and placed his head on my shoulder. This time he stayed in sync with my body, and it worked perfectly. The bike leaned over and came back up smoothly. Eddie gobbled a little as the pavement rose up toward us, but I couldn't control the whoop of delight.

"That's the way to do it. Good job," and I threw back my head and laughed.

"Who are you, and when did you steal my uptight boss?" Eddie yelled into my ear.

I didn't answer, because I saw the stone gatehouse up ahead. Twisted metal gates lay to either side of the road, torn down by the FBI when they raided the compound. I gunned the engine, and the bike leaped forward. I had a brief glimpse of a man's face poking out the door of the gatehouse before we flashed past, but there didn't seem to be any organized security. A crowd of people were streaming down the road toward the gates as if they'd been summoned, but they seemed confused, just a milling mob.

"Eddie! Be ready to use that gun,"

I should have spoken sooner, because a man darted out of the crowd and flung himself at the bike, as if hoping to bring it down with the momentum of his body. I swung the sword and took the attacker in the solar plexus with the flat of the blade. Even over the rumble and roar of the engine I could hear the man's screams as the magic was stripped out of him.

"I'm going to lean way forward. Use my back to steady your arm, and start shooting," I instructed Eddie.

I dropped until my chin was almost on the handlebars. One bump in the road took me by surprise, and they hit my chin, and I bit my tongue. The warm coppery taste of blood filled my mouth. I felt Eddie's elbow gouging into my right shoulder blade, and then the roar of the pistol so near to my ear deafened me. We were getting so close, and no one was reacting. Eddie fired another shot. Again there was nothing. Then on the third shot finally a reaction. A woman in the crowd threw up her arms and fell backward.

The crowd lost cohesion like a ball of yarn unspooling. Only two people remained in the road, a man and a woman. The man reached out as if preparing to grab the handlebars. I abruptly straightened and swung the sword. This time I didn't have a chance to turn it and use the flat of the blade. The dark metal peeled back the dirty sweater and the flesh beneath. He looked down, reacted in surprise, then slapped his palms down on the cut as if trying to hold in the blood. I reversed my swing and brought the blade down on the top of the woman's head. She collapsed.

"Are they still following?" I yelled back over my shoulder.

I felt Eddie half-turn. "Yeah, they're trying, but we're leaving them in the dust." To my gunfire-deafened ears his words sounded distant and muffled.

"Are you all right?" I asked next, because Eddie had just shot someone, and that is never easy to handle. I glanced at the blood on the blade. It was rippling under the wind created by our speed.

He was quiet for a few moments and then yelled, "They cut up my friends. They had it coming. So yeah. Yeah, I'm fine." The logic didn't exactly track, but if it kept him calm and functioning I was all for it.

Then the strange red/orange light was blotted out by something huge overhead. We both looked up, and Eddie screamed.

I had the impression of darkness and thousands of tiny eyes. But I wasn't sure what I'd actually seen because there was a wavering all around the creature that made it hard to focus. It seemed to be flat and large and black, as if a stingray the size of a basketball court had taken to the air. I thrust the sword point up toward the sky, hoping maybe that would hold it at bay. It felt pathetic, and I felt stupid for even trying it.

A high-pitched keening began. It seemed to resonate in my bones. I took us off the road, but the creature stayed with us and the keening became even more piercing.

It's tracking us. Marking where we are. Summoning others.

It was a guess, but it felt right, and I hated that it felt right. I was thinking frantically. I had to touch that thing, kill it before any more monsters arrived. My mind seemed to be chattering as it flipped from thought to thought, and then I remembered sitting on the window seat of my bedroom in Newport reading *The Lord of the Rings*.

I had to let go of the handlebar, but we stayed upright as I sheathed the sword. The engine coughed, the bike shook as the smooth flow of gas stopped, and then the engine died. We rolled a few more feet, and then I threw down the kickstand.

"What are you doing?" Eddie was almost sobbing.

"Run!" And I gave him a hard shove.

Eddie practically fell off the bike. I grabbed his arm and started running toward an opening in the trees. There was a small meadow just beyond it. The seared grass brushed like blades against the leather of my chaps. The shadow hung over us. Eddie was in bunny mode, and he didn't respond to my tugging at his arm, trying to stop him. I didn't have a choice, I kicked his feet out from under him. The young man face-planted in the dirt and dead grass, and I threw myself down on top of him.

"Come on, come on down, you bastard. Squat on us!"

"No! No! I don't want it to come down! Are you fucking nuts!" Eddie was crying.

I really wished I had time to explain, but the creature was spiraling closer. I waited, and tried to appear shattered and terrified and hopeless. It didn't require much acting. I had my right hand resting against the base of the hilt. The air was filled with a hot metallic scent. I risked a glance. It was close.

I waited a few more seconds, then leaped to my feet while at the same time drawing the sword. I took three running steps and launched myself into the air, arm and blade extended. I pushed it so hard that I felt my shoulder catch and twinge.

The blade was frothing light like the biggest Roman candle ever made. The foible connected. There was a jar that shook my arm and slammed into my side, and then the resistance was gone, and the blade sank deep into the shadow. There was the thunder of sound like a sonic boom directly overhead, and the thing was gone.

I failed to stick the landing. I staggered and fell onto my back. I gripped the hilt so tightly that my fingers cramped, but I didn't drop the sword. The light from the blade shot into the air. The clouds burned away, and normal sunlight poured through the hole in the clouds. For an instant I just lay there trying to catch my breath and taking joy in the touch of sun.

Then I bounded back onto my feet, grabbed Eddie by the collar, and hauled him up. We ran back to the bike and climbed on.

"Start. Please start," I crooned. The engine roared back to life. We were still in the game.

FORTY-FIVE

Doug sprawled on a glider on the front porch of the big stone house. His hand rummaged in a box of Honey Nut Cheerios while he frowned off toward the gate. He looked up at the sound of Rhiana's footfalls, stuffed a big handful of cereal into his mouth, and gave her a black frown while he masticated. Four raw and deep gashes ran from the corner of his left eye to the corner of his mouth.

"Where's my food? I can't fuckin' cook anything. I told them I wanted a surf and turf. I thought somebody would be back by now."

Rhiana forgot he was crazy, forgot he was dangerous, forgot her magic couldn't affect him. She grabbed him by the front of his stained T-shirt and hauled him up out of the glider. The sour smell of an unwashed male body washed over her.

"Where is she? Where's Angela? We've got to get her out of here." The smile was chilling. "Well, she's going to be a little sloppy to carry."

Panic closed off Rhiana's lungs. She wheezed, and then gagged on the harsh taint that filled the air. "What did you do?"

He was starting to look like a sulky two-year-old. "You told me I could do anything I wanted."

"Oh, God, how badly did you hurt her?"

"Well, pretty bad since she's dead." He offered up his face for inspection. "Bitch clawed me. *And* got me in the nuts. I don't mind a little fight, makes me hot, but *nobody* gets to hurt me. I made her sorry."

The moan bubbled out as if propelled by the spasm that clenched at her stomach. Rhiana released him and folded her arms over her aching belly. "We've got to get her out of here before he gets here. Before he sees. He can't know. He can't find out. Oh, God, what am I going to do? He's at the front gate." The hysteria rang in her ears.

"He. The fag. He's coming here?" Andresson stepped forward eagerly.

"No, no, you have to help me."

"Fuck that. I want that sword."

"You listen to *me*," Rhiana shouted shrilly.

"No. They told me I don't have to. You've done your thing. Now it's *my* turn. I'm more important than you." He started back into the house.

Rhiana ran after him and closed her hand on his shoulder. He winced as her nails dug through the material of his shirt and into his skin. "Who told you that? Who said that?"

The smile was pure poison. "Your dad."

He broke free and continued into the house. Rhiana ran after him. "He didn't. You're lying."

The narrow shoulder rose and fell in a dismissive shrug. "Think what you want."

They were down the hall and into the master bedroom. Grenier's taste had run to the Baroque. There was a huge four-poster bed with heavily carved dark wood, and thick chocolate brown velvet curtains. A matching armoire and mirrored dresser stood on opposite walls. The dresser mirror was occluded from the touch of the Old Ones. As soon as they were through the door a girl began whimpering, small animal sounds of pure terror.

Andresson went to the dresser and got a large .357 Magnum. He checked the ammo and headed back for the door. "Oh, and don't worry about your little boyfriend seeing anything, or knowing that you gave her to me. I'll stop him *way* before he gets to the house."

"No!" Rhiana yelled. "You've got to help me get her out of here."

"You're the one who wanted her here. You deal with it. She's in the tub," he said indifferently and left.

"Please, lady. Help me."

Rhiana glanced over at the bed. The girl was naked and tied spread-eagle to the posts. Sweat-matted and tangled red hair lay across the pillow like a flame. Her small breasts were bruised, and in places teeth marks were edged in blood. Her thighs were smeared with blood and sperm. The room smelled of pee, and there was a dark stain on the sheets beneath her.

Rhiana ignored her, and moved hesitantly to the door that led into the opulent bathroom. The smells in the room, sperm, blood, sweat, booze, and sewage, caught in the back of her throat like claws.

The horror in the bathtub set her stomach to heaving. That and sheer panic over what Richard would do. The physical confines of her body seemed to blow apart as she fled wildly from the world.

Her last conscious thought was, *I'll tell him I didn't know.*

The tunnel ended at a cinder-block wall. Moisture had wept across the concrete, leaving Rorschach patterns in the gray matrix. A metal ladder was bolted into the blocks. They formed a milling herd at the base of the ladder. Weber put a hand and a foot on the ladder, only to be stopped by Jay saying, "No offense, Pops, but how about sending someone younger and more agile?"

"How about I bust your face?" Sam suggested sweetly.

"Sam," Syd said. "Save the 'tude for the bad guys."

Pamela watched the waffled soles of Jay's hiking boots disappearing into the darkness. The ladder shook under the man's weight. She didn't like climbing, ever since that fall out of the apple tree in the backyard that broke her arm, and this ladder looked rickety.

Sam shrugged. "Okay, I'm cool with letting Jay be a monster magnet."

Pamela noticed that the rattle of the iron ladder against the concrete lost its rhythm for an instant at Sam's words.

Pamela glanced around the circle of faces. Estevan's eyes had a ring of white all around the iris, and his pupils were wide. She stepped over to him and gave his hand a squeeze. The skin of his palm was clammy with sweat.

There was the sound of grunting from over their heads. Jay's voice drifted down. "It's not opening. Hope it's not locked."

"Shouldn't be," Joseph called up. "Grenier said it wasn't, but that it hasn't been opened in a long time."

"You need some more muscle?" Weber called up.

"Not enough room," Jay's voice floated down.

"Probably enough room for me," said Sam, and she went eeling up the ladder.

There were more sounds of effort, then a loud *clang* as the trapdoor flew up. Light poured through the opening, and Jay scrabbled for purchase. The unexpected lack of resistance had taken him by surprise, and he lost his footing. Sam clutched at him, caught him by the shirt, but she couldn't hold him. He came half sliding, half falling down the ladder. His ankle buckled as he landed wrong. A string of profanity erupted. Franklin jumped past him and climbed rapidly up the ladder.

One by one they made their way out of the tunnel. As Pamela climbed, her mind kept stupidly repeating, *once out of the well our heroes . . .* , *once out of the well our heroes . . .* But she could never figure out what the heroes did, and then she was through the trapdoor and standing in the basement.

Franklin leaned against a tall wine rack. He had an arrow nocked, the bowstring pulled, but not quite to the ready, but they heard nothing and saw no one. There were six rows of eight-foot-tall wine racks, but most of the racks were empty.

The stairs from the basement brought them into a walk-in pantry. There was very little left on the shelves. A bag of sugar had toppled and torn, making the tile floor both gritty and sticky. Pamela suddenly realized that sweat was beading beneath her bangs, and it wasn't just from nerves. Now that they were no longer below ground, it was incredibly warm for February in Virginia.

Pamela hung back while the law enforcement types used their training to check the kitchen. After a few seconds they waved her in. The stink from rotting food left lying on dirty plates was stomach churning. A few fat flies buzzed lazily over the moldy scraps. Overlaying the cloying sweet stench of decay was a throat-burning chemical odor. Mold, like soft green velvet, draped itself over the food scraps on the plates.

"Weird," Estevan whispered. "Who's ever heard of flies in the winter?"

They moved on, using door frames for cover and leapfrogging each other. Pamela could see their discomfort at holding nightsticks and knives instead of guns. The dining room was empty. There were faded places on the walls where art had once hung. The seeded glass doors of the buffet hung open, and one creaked as the hot biting wind found its twisting way into this interior room. There was no sound beyond the monotonous *creak, creak, creak* and the sigh of the wind.

"I gotta pee," Estevan said, and his whisper seemed horribly loud.

"Tie a knot in it," Rudi advised.

Apparently they had been louder than they realized, because suddenly a girl began screaming. "*Help! Help! Please, somebody, help me!*" Sobs punctuated the words.

Weber took off running down the hall, away from the public rooms, back toward what Grenier had said was his private living quarters. Weber was only a half second faster than the rest of them.

"Cops! Always playing the hero," Pamela muttered as she ran after them.

The screams emanated from behind the heavily carved door. By the time Pamela got there, Jay and Rudi were pulling security in the hall, and the other men and Sam were inside the room. Pamela stepped over the threshold. There was a girl tied spread-eagle to the heavily carved wood pillars of his four-poster bed. The room was awash with the sour smell of unwashed bodies, the cloying scent of sperm, and the sharp reek of spilled liquor.

Pamela noted the blood smearing the girl's thighs, and the fact she was a true redhead. She would have been pretty had her face not been splotched with bruises and puffy from crying. Mucus smeared her upper lip. Her face and body carried a layer of baby fat. Pamela guessed her age at fourteen or fifteen.

Weber cut at the ropes securing her wrists. Judging from the swollen red skin around the cords, and her puffy purple fingers, she had been there for a long time. Sam was muttering a running string of curses. Pamela pulled off her jacket and laid it over the girl, shielding her from the men. Sam looked startled and then chagrined.

"Hush. Hush. You're going to be all right now. What's your name, honey?" Pamela kept her voice low and soft, the tone you used to soothe a frightened horse. The girl's sobs died to whimpers as Pamela put her arms around her.

"Jessie."

"Jessie, is there another woman here? Older than you."

"The black woman," the girl said, and her voice shook. "She fought him. He hurt her. Bad. She screamed and screamed. For a long time." Pamela tightened her grip as the shivering became massive shudders that threatened to pull the girl out of her arms.

"Do you know where she is?" Weber said, and the girl shrank away with a cry. Sam pushed past him and repeated the question.

"In . . . in the bathroom."

"Angie! Angie!" Weber yelled and ran through the bathroom door. Then there was silence—for a long, long time.

Everyone moved to the bathroom except Pamela, who kept holding Jessie. There was a cry of disgust from Estevan. He burst back into the bedroom. Joseph had his arm around the young man, who was crying and gagging.

Dread closed in on her. "What?" Pamela whispered.

"Angela's dead," Joseph said. "You don't want to know more than that."

The other members of the team returned to the bedroom. Weber's skin was gray, and the effort not to weep gouged lines in his forehead and around his eyes.

Franklin took charge. "We need to get Jessie out of here."

"She can't go alone, and we can't spare anyone to take her," Jay argued.

"No, we can spare someone. We probably *shouldn't*, but we can," came the agent's response.

Joseph stepped into the huddle. "Send Estevan. He's just a kid, and he's terrified."

"What about Angela?" Weber asked thickly.

"We save the living," Syd said to him softly. "You know that. If we can, once Richard gets here, we'll take Angela home, too, but right now Jessie's got to be our first priority."

It was quickly arranged. At the kitchen they separated. Estevan, supporting the girl in the circle of an arm, headed off toward the stairs to the basement. The rest of them went down the hall and through the door that separated the private living quarters from the public rooms. In the living room, there were more dirty dishes piled on end tables and the coffee table. Stuffing exploded like dandelion fluff through the ripped and stained blue velvet upholstery on the couches and chairs. The white carpet looked like an experimental painting. Pamela had a feeling that some of the stains were blood, but she didn't want to ask.

She also didn't want to ask Sam what she had seen in that bathroom. She didn't want to know what had been done to Angela. But the not knowing and wondering pricked at her mind, trying to drive her to ask. She pushed the impulse aside.

The backpacks were unlimbered, and they pulled out the

gasoline-filled canteens, and began dousing the furniture cushions and the carpet.

"Why haven't we met anyone?" Joseph asked the room.

"I think everyone's off planning a reception for us on the main road or at the dell," Weber said. "I think those birds were carrying a message. Kenntnis said the things around us could be used against us."

Jay spun, looking at the walls as if expecting them to collapse on top of him. "If it's a trap, shouldn't we be getting out of here?"

"And how do we tell Richard we're bookin' out on him?" Sam asked.

Syd spoke up. "No, we gotta stick."

Joseph and Rudi exchanged glances. Rudi nodded, and Joseph said, "We're not leaving."

Jay looked to Franklin, who shook his head. For a long moment Jay struggled with himself. The syncopated ticks from old-fashioned spring-wound watches seemed deafening in the silence.

"Well, we better get these cushions against the walls," Jay said. Sam gave him an approving smile and slapped him hard on the shoulder.

They hurried about, propping the split cushions against the wood walls. Next they splashed gasoline across them, and finally the cigarettes were carefully tucked into the rents in the cushions. Pamela noticed that the cigarettes were no longer burning. She wondered what it was about fire, light, and Old Ones.

"Now what?" Jay asked.

Weber checked his watch. "We wait another five minutes, and then some of us hold down the fort, and the rest of us go toward the gate and raise some hell so Eddie can get a look at this glass thingie."

FORTY-SIX

RICHARD

There was a ragged sound to the bike's engine that I didn't like, but I could understand. The air was horribly dry, and tainted with stinks that bit at the back of my throat and had my eyes watering.

We were moving so fast that both tires left the ground as we crested a small hill. Eddie gasped and giggled, but for me the euphoria was gone. Only the skeletons of dead trees and one final hill separated the gate from us. We were two guys on a motorbike, and arrayed against us were monsters—

I caught movement out of the corner of my eye. *And people*, I added as I spotted the two men hiding in the trees.

One jumped out directly in front of us. I had a split second to decide what to do. It was too close quarters to use the sword, I didn't have time to dodge him, and if I hit him straight on the bike would go down, and then his buddy would have us.

I wrenched the handlebars hard to the left and hit the brake. The front tire locked, and I felt the muscles in my shoulders and neck spasm as I braced against the hard jerk. I then let the back tire fishtail, spinning us 180 degrees. Eddie's scream was a high-pitched whistle of terror directly into my ear. The back of the bike slammed into the man and knocked him flat. The second man started running toward us as I fought for control of the bike.

We were wobbling, but I gunned the engine anyway, and drove straight at him.

At the last minute I pulled to the right and stabbed hard and fast, catching the man in the chest. There was a moment of breath-stopping terror when our momentum sent us hurtling past while the blade was caught in his ribs. I almost lost my grip, but the sword wrenched loose before the hilt slipped out of my sweat-slicked hand. It still pulled the hell out of my fingers where they twined through the hilt.

As we clawed our way up the final hill, I realized that other than that sentry creature, we hadn't met anything but humans. I glanced down the length of the glittering blade. *The Old Ones fear it. The barest touch and they die.* Kenntnis's voice rumbled in memory.

They were afraid to come too close. They were letting humans face me and get hurt. *Die,* my innate honesty forced me to acknowledge. There was a sharp pain at the hinge of my jaw as I gritted my teeth. I wanted something to die other than my own kind. I wanted to kill the creatures that had brought us to this.

We crested the final hill, and suddenly my thoughts about killing monsters seemed like a bully's bravado. A hot, life-sucking wind swirled in the dell, kicking up errant dust devils that filled the air with a choking grit. It stung the exposed skin on my face and hands. The gate filled the entire cliff face. Mist, like steam from quiescent geysers, trailed from the various glass sculptures that dotted the ground in front of it. Kenntnis's glass tomb was centered among the other sculptures.

"Holy crap," Eddie said, and he was looking off to the side of the gate where another, much smaller opening in the gray stones showed space and that burning star. "Why isn't our atmosphere getting sucked away?"

And now I had another gut-burning problem. If Rhiana's magic failed, it was most definitely game over. I had to close at least that opening between the multiverses.

But between me and that tear in reality were humans. And

others. They were just disturbing shapes that my mind failed to grasp, but they were utterly terrifying. I felt the rim of Eddie's helmet digging into my shoulder as the young scientist pressed closer to me. I wished I had somebody to hide behind.

The desire to turn the bike and flee back the way we had come was so strong that my arms were shivering. There had to be somebody else who could deal with this shit. But Pamela and Weber and Angela were here.

I had to be here, too.

FORTY-SEVEN

There had been a sharp but short argument about everybody staying at the house as Richard had instructed, or some of them going out to meet Richard and help him get back to the house. Weber and the "help Richard" cadre had won. So they left Jay and Bob at the house to hold the retreat. As best Pamela could follow the discussion, it seemed they thought the bow gave Bob the best chance to keep the crazies at bay.

Weber had been to Grenier's compound before, so he led the way. A policeman's nightstick swung in his hand. Rudi, big and powerful and armed with a nightstick and a knife, brought up the rear. Syd had a nightstick and a knife, Sam had a knife in each hand, and Joseph had brass knuckles armoring each hand. They had Pamela tucked in the middle again. She realized they thought she was helpless and useless, and she suddenly resented it. Pamela stole another glance at Sam, looking like a pirate, and decided if she ever got out of here she was going to have somebody teach her how to fight.

A strong, hot, harsh wind was blowing against them. Pamela assumed it was flowing through the gate. *I'm breathing the air of an alien universe,* she thought.

It was hard going, and Pamela wondered how Richard was going to stay upright on the bike. A dark red sand that glittered with mica flakes pushed across the ground like the final eddy of a wave flinging itself high up the beach. But unlike the wave, the sand never retreated. It insinuated itself between the ground and the soles of their boots, making them slip and stumble, and worked its way around the laces until their socks were thick with sweat and grit.

"Okay, don't go near the sculptures," Weber said. "Rhiana came out of one of them, so they may be entryways."

"And don't walk under anything," Syd said, and he shuddered.

"Basically, don't expect the world to remain normal," Weber concluded.

"What the fuck does that mean?" Pamela asked, and felt suddenly both daring and guilty at the profanity.

"Whatever you can imagine probably won't be strange enough," Weber said.

"Greeaaat," breathed Rudi.

Weber's head jerked up, and then Pamela heard it, too. It was faint and distant like the buzz of a solitary bee. It was the sound of an engine approaching. They picked up the pace, and soon broke free of the dying trees.

There were a number of people in the clearing. They were dirty, skinny, and wandering about in confusion. Pamela studied the faces of the advancing people. They held every possible vile, frightened, mournful, and violent emotion. And Pamela realized she had seen them before in the carved grotesques adorning the columns of European cathedrals and etched in the walls of Mayan temples. What attention the mob could bring to bear seemed focused on the rapidly approaching motorcycle.

Blood sacrifice, crusade, jihad, pogrom. This is where it leads. Why didn't we realize that before it was too late?

And then she lifted her eyes to what lay beyond. The gate, and the *things* that hid in the smoke, mist, fog?—it defied her ability to describe. Pamela's legs lost all strength, and she collapsed under the sheer weight of terror and wrongness. Syd grabbed her under the arm and yanked her back up. His fingers digging into the soft skin of her armpit sent a flare of pain through her body.

The motorcycle was heading down into the dell. Even from here Pamela could see the flare of the sword. It was so bright it threw light onto the roiling mists, and they seemed to recoil from its light. The filthy, blank-faced attackers began moving toward Richard.

"I'm gonna try to get around these guys so I can help out Richard," Rudi said.

"Good idea, let's do it," Sam panted.

And before Weber could respond they went running off to the left, circling around the mob.

Rudi ran between the curving glass mausoleum that entombed Kenntnis and the gate to an alien sun. Sam was right on his heels. Suddenly Rudi's back arched. The skin on his hands and face reddened and split, and oozed blood and fluid. Sam gave a cry of horror and panic and threw herself backward. She lost her balance and fell hard on her tailbone.

The material of Rudi's shirt and pants darkened as they soaked up blood from his rupturing flesh. He writhed like a jerked puppet, and his screams echoed across the dell. Joseph started to rush to him only to be tackled by Syd and Weber. Tears were spilling down Pamela's cheeks. They evaporated in the terrible heat.

Rudi collapsed onto the sand. His face was a ruin. Blood and mucus oozed from his sockets where his eyes had exploded. Weber was cursing. Joseph was crying. Syd was gagging, and Sam was making a keening cry like a hurt rabbit.

Pamela jerked her gaze away from the horror and saw that the mob was converging on Richard. She picked up the nightstick that had dropped from Weber's nerveless fingers and yelled, "They're going to try to take down Richard. If that happens we're *all* dead!" and she went running after the people converging on her brother.

She heard the other's footfalls behind her. She reached the edge of the crowd. For an instant she hesitated, and then she swung the nightstick. It connected with the back of a man's head and dropped him in his tracks. Pamela didn't have time to feel guilty. They had noticed her. She swung again.

FORTY-EIGHT

RICHARD

I was shouting *no, no, no* as I watched Rudi fall to the ground, and I couldn't understand why they were out here. They were supposed to wait for me at the house, free Angela and *wait at the house*. If they'd done what I said Rudi wouldn't . . . wouldn't . . .

Then I heard Eddie's voice, surprisingly calm, saying, "Get us out of here. I've learned enough, and I don't know how to counter it. The pump laser is still operating. Given this set of parameters I have no clue what to do. I've got to thi—"

The word cut off, Eddie was suddenly making choking sounds, and we were both being dragged off the back of the bike. Or rather Eddie was being dragged, and he was maintaining his death grip on my waist, which meant I was coming with him whether I wanted to or not.

I didn't have a lot of options, and the only good one meant I hurt Eddie. I offered up a mental apology, and slammed the end of the hilt against Eddie's hands. I felt fragile bones shatter, and his hand sprang open.

"*You fuck! You bastard!*" Eddie screamed, a long wail of despair as he was yanked off the back of the bike.

I had a brief glimpse of Weber, Joseph, and Pamela attacking a milling group of people while Syd pulled Sam to her feet, but I couldn't help them yet. I had to get Eddie. I planted my left foot, and spun the bike in a fast turn, and nearly laid it down as the tires slipped in the slick red sand. My arm shook with strain as I struggled to control the bike. I finally had it upright, and then I narrowed my focus to the core of my body, tightened the muscles in my back and stomach, and found the balance point. I took my right hand off the handlebars and awkwardly pulled the pistol out of the shoulder rig. I dropped the heel of my left hand onto the handlebars to steady the bike against the recoil that was to come, lifted my right hand, braced my body even more strongly, and pulled the trigger. I had figured I'd miss by a mile, but maybe spook Eddie's attacker. Instead the bullet took the man full in the face. Blood, brains, and shattered pieces of skull formed a halo before the body collapsed. For an instant Snyder's ruined face flashed in front of me.

A woman was running toward Eddie. He lay on his back, chest heaving, mouth opening and closing like a landed fish, hands pressed against his chest. The bike wobbled, threatening to tip. I tried to stuff the pistol into a jacket pocket, but the butt overbalanced it, and it fell away. I felt incredibly naked, but I pushed aside the dithering thoughts that had me wanting to stop and recover the gun, and took back control of the bike. I roared up between Eddie and the woman and used the sword to cut her down.

"Get up! Get on! Hurry!" Adrenaline seemed to be popping and fizzing along every nerve.

But Eddie just lay there. I put down my foot, leaned way over, grabbed the scientist by the belt buckle, and yanked him up.

"Behind . . ." Eddie croaked.

For an instant I was befuddled by what seemed to be a non sequitur. Then I glanced into the side mirror. "Oh, shit!" I reversed my grip and stabbed straight backward. The man folded around the blade and grabbed it with both hands. I yanked it free. I thought I saw fingers dropping toward the ground. Eddie flailed, struggled, and finally got his leg over the bike.

I headed for our companions. Out of the corner of my eye I

saw a man walking deliberately down into the dell. His right arm was at his side, and a gun hung negligently from his fingers. I recognized the narrow, acne-scarred face. Doug Andresson. My counterpart. The man who had taken Angela. Four raw scratches ran down his face. It looked like Angela had paid him back.

My mind spun like a frightened, maddened top. *He'll get close enough . . . into the effect of the sword, and shoot me. And I don't have a gun. I'm dead.*

I remembered how the sword had swallowed up the effects of spells that had been thrown at me. *Maybe it would do the same with a bullet?* came the pathetic little thought.

You idiot. This isn't Star Wars. The sword negates magic because magic is alien to our world. There's nothing more natural than a goddamn bullet.

Andresson was close enough now that I could see the smirk of satisfaction. I was so focused on Andresson that I didn't notice the man huddled on the ground. He leaped up and threw himself against the front tire of the bike. It was too sudden, the sand was too deep, and I was too tired. The bike, me, the man, and Eddie all went down in a welter of flailing arms and spinning tires. Gymnastics had taught me how to fall and how to avoid falling. As the bike was going down, I swung my leg over the handlebars and jumped. I had only one thought, *don't drop the sword, don't drop the sword.* But trying to hit and roll with a five-foot-long blade is not a lot of fun, and I wrenched my shoulder badly as I landed.

I staggered to my feet just in time to see Andresson pull the trigger. I recognized the gun now. It was a .357 Magnum, a real penis pistol. A gun for men who liked to prove they were macho. It was stupid to try to outrun a bullet, but I threw myself off to the left in the faint hope that I could. The hammer hit the shell, the cylinder spun, but the gun didn't fire.

And an image of my pistol, barrel torn open like a blossoming flower, flashed across my mind. Back in another lifetime I had fired my pistol at the monsters attacking Rhiana. It hadn't been

313

good for the pistol, and there was *way* more magic flowing here. A desperate plan began to coalesce. My timing would have to be perfect, and the results would be fatal if I failed, but it was all I had. I began to back away from Andresson, but not too fast, and with not too much agility. The wounded bird leading a predator away from the nest.

As I'd hoped, Andresson squeezed the trigger again. A look of frustration crossed his face when the gun again failed to fire. He charged at me. I showed him my heels, and ran like the proverbial bunny. I was beginning to get a feel about how much distance I needed to keep between his gun and my sword. When I'd reached it I abruptly stopped and spun back to face Andresson as the hammer fell for a third time. I was gasping. Each breath seared my throat and lungs. I had been lucky so far. I couldn't keep this game up any longer. I just hoped that three unfired bullets would be enough.

I couldn't know with any certainty how close was close enough, but I would have to make my move before Andresson came into the field effect of the sword. My eyes flicked between Andresson's face and each of the footsteps that brought him ever closer to me. He was swaggering now, and he said conversationally, "Thanks for sharing your little sweetie. A little old, but soft and warm where it counted." I didn't answer. I was staring intently at each step he took, measuring the distance, trying not to react too soon. "You just can't keep any girl happy, can you? Oh, wait a minute, that's 'cause you're a fag."

I judged it to be the right moment. I took three running steps and threw myself in a long slide toward Andresson's feet.

"What the fuck!?" I heard him yell, and then came the sound I'd been waiting for, hoping for, and on which I'd bet my life.

I heard the roar of three jammed cartridges exploding in the cylinder of the Magnum, and Andresson's shrill screams of agony. Fragments of hot metal seared the exposed skin on the back of my neck, followed by the warm patter of blood. I rolled back onto my feet. Andresson's face was bleeding from a myriad of small cuts, and his right hand looked like something from the butcher's block, with fragments of white bone glinting through the blood.

Andresson cradled his mangled hand. The black eyes that stared out at me through a mask of blood were those of a maddened animal. The hate and ferocity were so great that I took a step backward. That show of weakness was all it took. Andresson flung himself on me. We went over backward, and I hit the ground hard. I clung desperately to the sword, but my hand was slick with sweat and the hilt slipped through my fingers. The basso hum of the weapon was gone, and I felt cold and lost. Andresson was pressing his knees into my chest, and I felt my ribs creaking under the pressure. His good hand closed around my throat. Fortunately it was slippery with blood, and he only had the one hand, but red spots were dancing at the corners of my vision. I punched him hard in the face, but his grip didn't lessen. It felt like I was fighting a berserker.

I reached down and gripped the ruined hand and exerted all my strength in a bone-crushing squeeze. The bones really did crush. They shifted and slid and ground against each other. It was grotesque, Andresson howled in pain, and the pressure on my throat eased. I rolled sideways, and exalted because he was now beneath me. It didn't last. He bucked like a desperate horse and threw me off. We were exchanging wild punches. Some of mine connected. Some of his hit. He was hurt, but I was exhausted from the strain of keeping the bike upright across that harsh countryside. And I was hampered by my own doubts and insecurities. I had always sucked at hand-to-hand combat.

He ended up behind me, and was bending me backward over his knee. I was frantically trying to relax the muscles, bend and flex, but I knew that eventually he'd break my back.

And then Eddie came hobbling up, swinging the pouch that held the lenses. He slammed it into the side of Andresson's head, and the man fell to the side. I rolled away, and groaned as the muscles and tendons in my back went into a spasm. I was facing the gate, and what I saw made my gut clench in terror.

The Old Ones were moving. With the power of the sword shuttered, they were moving in on the puny invaders.

I managed to get to my feet and crabbed toward the hilt. Eddie was sobbing and beating Andresson around the head and shoulders. I could hear the lenses shattering.

"You bastards! You fuckers! You monsters! You shits! You killed them!"

Then I saw the knife in Andresson's hand. It hurt like blazes, but I lunged the last few feet for the hilt, drew the sword, and drove the point through Andresson's back just as the blade of his knife cut open Eddie's sweater and shirt and left a long gash in his belly.

"Oh, crap! Oh shit, that *hurt!*" Eddie wailed and clasped his hands against his stomach.

I pulled the sword out of Andresson. He wasn't dead, but he soon would be. The red sand was sucking thirstily at the blood that poured down his chest and back. I glanced toward the gate. The fogs and mists had drawn close again. The things were retreating, and the comforting thrum of the sword and the nimbus of light were back in place.

I grabbed Eddie's arm. "Let's go!"

And we started hobbling across the dell toward our companions, who were rushing to meet us, knocking aside the people with blows from nightsticks and knives. I was amazed to see my sister laying about with a nightstick like a Pinkerton beating striking steelworkers.

Suddenly Eddie collapsed and nearly pulled me down with him. "My leg," he moaned, and then I saw the long, deep gash that looked like it went to the bone. Adrenaline and rage had kept him going; now both were gone. I debated defending our position and waiting for the cavalry, but then I saw an enormous piece of granite breaking free of the cliff face. It bobbed in the air like a child's balloon, and floated toward my friends and sister. If it hit, the cavalry was going to be a smear on the sand.

I yanked Eddie onto my shoulder in a fireman's carry and started running toward them. I didn't have an actual plan, just the hope that the sword could stop the tons of rock heading toward them.

A cloud of dust, choking and impenetrable, swept over us, carried on a blazing hot wind. The grains of sand burned where they struck bare skin, and it felt like it was trying to push me back. I'd never reach them in time, and they hadn't seen the death coming their way. They were all way too focused on me. I tried yelling a warning, but my throat and mouth were Sahara dry, and when I parted my lips I felt the skin tear and I tasted blood. Eddie seemed to be getting heavier by the second.

And then Cross was there. Coalescing out of the flying sand. Or maybe out of the mist, or . . . or . . . or . . . His abrupt arrival gave me a chill despite the scorching heat. Oily coils of color swirled around his body; he was well away from me, on the gate side of the mob. As I watched he threw back his head, his neck swelled, and inhuman screeching cries echoed against the cliffs—it might be language, but it couldn't be interpreted by a human mind. I had heard these sounds once before—when he had challenged his doppelganger in my apartment back in Albuquerque. He was answered by the monsters at the gate.

Cross's body seemed to swell and shrink in time to some alien rhythm, and then the granite slab raced through the air toward the homeless god. He waved it past, and I watched in jaw-dropping amazement as he let it fall on the crowd of people turning to attack my people.

Eddie and I reached our little outpost of sanity. Weber and Joseph lifted the scientist off my shoulder, and instead of relief it started to hurt worse. To my amazement Pamela threw her arms around me and hugged me tight.

"What the hell are you doing out here?" I tried to keep the annoyance out of my voice, but wasn't sure I'd succeeded.

Sam's pugnacious tone made it clear I hadn't. "Helping you."

I couldn't control it; my eyes flicked to where Rudi's body lay on the sand. Sam seemed to fold in on herself.

"It wasn't my fault," she said.

I ignored her and said, "I told you to wait at the house. Did you find Angela?"

Pamela's face told me everything even before Weber spoke. "She's dead." Gentle in tone, but blunt and factual. It was how we were trained to deliver news of violent death to a victim's family.

My head swam for an instant. "How?" There was no quaver or anguish in my voice. I wondered how long I could maintain control.

"Let's just say it wasn't easy. You don't need details."

"Thanks for sharing your little sweetie." I wished I could kill him again. I wished I could kill him slower. I wished none of it had been necessary. That I had protected her and kept her safe. I looked at each of them in turn—Pamela, Weber, Sam, Syd, and Joseph. I wasn't going to fail them.

Suddenly Cross came barreling into the center of us like a cue ball making the first break. He looked thin, gray, and haggard.

"Okay, kiddies," he said. "Party's over. I've shot my wad, and they've still got many wads in reserve. We've got to get out of here." He turned to me and gripped my shoulder with a veined and ropy hand. "You've got to fuck 'em up and give us time to retreat."

I looked to Weber and Joseph. "Is everything in place?"

Weber nodded. "Yeah. I still don't understand this plan."

"You need to read more Kipling. Now get going."

"I'm not leaving you out here alone," Weber demurred.

"I can concentrate better on what I have to do if I don't have to worry about anybody else. Now *go!*" I suddenly grabbed Weber's arm tightly. "Don't leave her behind."

He knew who I meant. "Not a chance."

Pamela surprised me again by giving me another hug. I watched as they all started back toward the house. Their prog ress was painfully slow as Syd and Joseph supported Eddie between them. They disappeared among the bare trees.

"What are you gonna do?" Cross asked. "The sword alone can't cut it."

I didn't answer him immediately. "I need you to get Rudi's body. We're not leaving him here."

His head was bobbing like a dash toy. "Okay, but how are you—"

"Kenntnis used *music* to shield Rhiana from the Old Ones." And I had a sudden vivid memory of how the strings of my piano had vibrated softly whenever Kenntnis entered the room.

He was nodding again, but this time in agreement. "Yeah, yeah, might work. Music is pure mathematics. Supports your entire universe. Just let me get Rudi and get clear before you start. How you gonna make music out here?" I touched my throat. "Oh. Well, don't get stage fright."

I forced a smile, and felt my lips tear again. It felt like pulling apart the pages of a rain-soaked book that had been left to dry. "I don't really care if they like it."

I gave him a push toward Rudi's body. How much time had passed since Pamela, Weber, and the others had started for the house? How much more time would they need?

The Old One opened his mouth, and a roaring like waves through a cavern emerged. There was also the glow of sullen red from the back of his throat. Every muscle tensed, and then Cross shot away, running easily across the sand. The sand blew up around him in twisting tendrils. Perhaps it was only a trick of the light and the eddies of grit, or perhaps his body was dissolving into flesh-colored streamers that stretched behind him. The tendrils of light sparkled as he passed through the laser. They enfolded Rudi, and then they were both gone.

My turn.

And I didn't have a clue what to sing. The place in my head where every piece of music I'd ever memorized was stored was an echoing void. Maybe if I picked a composer I'd remember something. Bach? Perfect mathematics, but mostly religious music. Uh-uh, no way. Mozart? Nothing but love songs or religious text. No. Schubert? Too light.

I found myself thinking about how my piano and the Celtic

harp in Kenntnis's penthouse had always sung to him. A crooning whisper of sound as if something had breathed on the strings. It was always the same sequence of notes. Suddenly I was grateful to have perfect pitch, and an ability to hear a tune once and remember it.

The air burned as it entered my lungs and stretched my rib cage to capacity. I had a terrible feeling that my voice would emerge as a thin thread, but then I realized that the shivering that had always run along my muscles and affected my diaphragm when I sang wasn't happening. I sang the notes as a vocalist carried on a column of air.

The power and resonance of the opening note made me take a step back as if I could retreat from myself. The sword, which had always hummed with escalating musical overtones, picked up the sound, amplified it, and carried it into the highest and lowest registers beyond the ability of the human ear to hear. The air shivered with the power of the music. And there was a flare of light from inside the spin glass.

Even from this distance I could see the confusion and consternation at the gates. The monsters rolled back like the ragged edges of a thunderstorm scudding away before a powerful wind. All my rage and hatred got channeled into the singing. The Old Ones withdrew until they were close to the gate, but they didn't retreat past the threshold. Apparently the sword and the song could hold them at bay, but not repel them totally.

My lungs felt abraded by the air I was forced to breathe. My throat was growing raw, and my tongue seemed stiff and swollen. It was probably too early, but I couldn't stay in this place, facing these things, any longer. It would be enough. We'd get away. I cast a final look to the glass that held Kenntnis. The diamond and gold motes suspended in the glass were still flaring. I amended the thought. *All except two.*

The thought of Angela caused my voice to break. I just stopped singing, turned, and started running toward the house with every bit of strength that remained to me. I risked a glance back and saw a pack of humans in pursuit. The Old Ones followed, but not too close and not too fast. The power and danger of the sword were keeping them at bay. I stumbled on the rough ground and almost fell. My right hand did touch the ground, but I managed to steady myself and push back up. I kept running.

A stitch began digging its way up my side. It felt like a knife turning slowly, cutting the ribs and closing down my lungs. I threw back my head and gulped in air. The house drew closer. The front door stood open, and Franklin knelt to one side, waiting. He had an arrow nocked and the string pulled back to his ear. *They were supposed to get to the basement and into the tunnel!* But I had to admit I was relieved to see him.

I could hear the rasping breaths of my hunters. My cunning plan had been to slow down so they would be relatively close when I entered the house. Exhaustion had made it less a choice and more of a necessity. And now they were very close indeed. I imagined I could feel their breaths on the back of my neck. My thighs ached and shivered as I took the stone steps two at a time. A hand scraped at the back of my jacket. There was a hiss past my ear, and the sound of impact. I looked back. The woman in the lead was down with an arrow in her shoulder. I gave a convulsive leap, and then I was into the living room. Bob Franklin was ahead of me, already running down the hall toward the kitchen.

And the cigarettes that had lain dormant under the blanket of magic suddenly flared to life as the sword and I entered the room. The burning ash hit the gasoline-soaked cushions, and they went up with a roar of flame and a blast of heat that singed the back of my neck.

Behind me people screamed as the flames jumped to their clothes and hair. I ran harder, feeling the heat washing across my back, and the passage that had suggested this mad plan came back to mind.

"But the buck lived."
"How?"
"Because he came first. Running for his life."
"It is to pull the very whiskers of death."

FORTY-NINE

A couple of the pursuers followed them into the tunnel, but now they had Richard and the sword, so Jay and Sam just shot them. Pamela tried to think about who they might have been. Did they have families who missed them and worried about them? But the truth was that if she'd had a gun she would have shot them herself. When did a person get used to death and the dealing in death?

Richard had wanted to carry Angela's body, but Weber had gripped it jealously. It had been Sam who rudely pointed out the obvious—that Richard had to carry the sword, and he was too small to carry Angela one-handed.

The tunnel seemed endless, but ultimately they reached the hatch, and found the car and trailer and Estevan and Jessie waiting. Syd and Franklin had unhitched the trailer; they didn't need it anymore, and the car could go faster and was more maneuverable without it. Joseph took Estevan aside and told him about Rudi. Pamela turned away from the sight of the burly young Hispanic wiping his eyes with the backs of his hands.

Jessie was huddled in the backseat of the limo. Richard knelt in the open doorway talking with her. Pamela moved to where she could hear. He had switched the sword to his right hand, and his left was resting on the door frame to steady him. His hand and wrist were crusted with dried blood. Pamela didn't want to look, but had a hard time looking away.

"You'll testify to what he did to you, and what he did to Angela?" he was saying. The girl just stared at him. He made no attempt to touch her. In fact he leaned back a bit farther from her, and added, "He's dead, Jessie. He can't ever hurt you again. You're safe now."

"Then why do I have to say anything?" she asked.

"Because we're coming back to Washington with a body." Richard briefly closed his eyes. "Two bodies, and the police will get involved. You have to make them understand that we did what we had to do."

Jessie looked dubious. "I know you said that guy is dead, but what about that girl? She was part of this, too, and she's still out there. What if she comes after me because I talked?"

"Girl?" Richard asked, but Pamela could see from his expression that he already knew.

"I don't remember too much. Black hair. Lots of earrings. I asked her to help me and she just looked straight through me." Jessie's lip began to tremble, and Pamela saw the shudders running through her body. Richard held back from her, but cast Pamela a look. She knew what her brother wanted. Pamela stepped around him, gave the girl a quick hug, and felt her relax.

Jessie took a deep breath and continued. "She was telling him about how she wanted . . . her," Jessie's eyes shifted to Angela's body, wrapped in a sheet, and still held in Weber's arms. "We're not gonna ride with that in the car, are we?" she asked in an abrupt change of direction.

Richard's voice was gentle but firm. "We have to. We have to take her back to her family. Just like we're going to take you back to your family."

For a long moment the girl's brown eyes were locked with Richard's; then she slowly nodded. Richard signaled Joseph, who took his place behind the wheel. Everyone started piling into the car. Sam surprised Pamela by insisting that Jessie sit next to the door with Sam beside her, away from any male touch.

Pamela grabbed Richard and held him back. "You need to wash your hand. Hands."

The blood drained from his face as he gazed down at the stains. He looked like he was about to vomit. "There were so many of them. I've lost count," he said softly.

Pamela pulled out a large bottle of water from the trunk. Richard ripped up a cassock and used it to scrub at the blood. When he finished his hands were still red, but from the force with which he had washed.

Finally they were all in the limo, and went rocking and jouncing back onto the blacktop. Joseph floored it, and the bare trees became a gray blur. Weber continued to hold Angela's body wrapped in the sheet. In places blood had darkened the cotton. Pamela breathed through her mouth—the body had started to smell.

"That girl," Jessie said in a whisper as if afraid Rhiana would hear her. "She looked in the bathroom and then she sort of . . . melted. How can somebody melt?"

"Because she's not human," Richard said, and it sent a chill through Pamela. Not because of Rhiana, but because of what she saw in her brother's face.

The bodies had been taken to the morgue. Pamela wondered when they had gone from being Angela and Rudi to *the bodies*. She felt guilty that they had, and resolved to keep using their names. At the morgue six degrees of separation set in. It turned out the ME in D.C. knew Angela from conferences, so when he called the police he wasn't as suspicious as he might otherwise have been.

As for the police, the phalanx of FBI agents surrounding her brother, and the badge he flashed, worked wonders. Pamela's presence as attorney had been unnecessary. From suspicious hostility the mood had quickly softened to amazed admiration that they had been to Virginia and returned, and there was soon a discussion over the breakdown of civil society in the tri-state area of the Potomac.

Pamela had always despised cops, but she saw the weariness and the worry that laid dark circles around their eyes, and grayed their skin, and she grudgingly had to admit that maybe the police were the first defense of a civilization, and that some, maybe many, of them took that oath "to serve and protect" seriously. She wanted to say so to Weber, but he had disappeared as soon as they reached the morgue.

Jessie had been questioned at the hospital, and the female cops were gentle and understanding. They took swabs from the bites on her breasts, and vaginal swabs. Richard was confident that they would find matches once the DNA tests were run.

In the car, as they drove back to the Mayflower, he had said, "Nobody makes the jump from B and E's and assaults to felony rape and murder in one jump. There'll be other women he hurt."

"Jessie told the cops that you told her that Andresson was dead," Pamela said. "They're going to want to know how you know, and that might come back to haunt us."

Richard shrugged. "They haven't got a body. They're sure as hell not going to go into the compound to look for one. As far as they know we ran a hostage rescue operation where we lost one and saved one." His voice was dead level and even, but Pamela could see what it cost him to keep the clinical tone.

She laid her hand over his. He turned it to grip her hand hard, and the sleeve pulled up on the leather jacket. The cuff of his shirt was stained with blood. They stared at it for a long moment.

"We'll get back to the hotel, and shower, and burn these clothes," Pamela said.

"Getting rid of the evidence," Richard said with grim humor.

"No, I just can't stand the touch of that place, and my clothes reek with it."

"Some things never wash out," Richard said, and then gave her his profile as he stared out the window at the passing city.

* * *

Weber was waiting in the sitting room of the suite. The muscles in his jaw bunched and flexed as he gazed down into Richard's face.

"Okay, this has gotta be said. This shouldn't have happened. Points that you tried to get her. Points that you killed that motherfucker, but *this should never have happened!*" A universe of rage and anger simmered in Weber's words.

"Yes, you're right," came her brother's simple reply.

"You should never have sent her off alone."

"I know."

"*You* got Angela killed!"

"Yes."

"Goddamn it! Fight with me!" The words were a roar, and Pamela retreated. Richard and Weber were only inches apart, but Richard didn't move. Slim, erect, unflinching, he faced the older, larger man.

"Why? There's nothing you can do to me that would make me hurt any worse. I suspect it's the same for you. But if it'll make you feel any better, take your best shot. You get one for free."

Weber's hand closed into a fist. Pamela was fascinated with the way his knuckles looked like pale walnuts, and how the veins stood out like pale blue snakes. She hadn't expected it, and she squeaked when Weber took the swing and hit Richard hard on the jaw. Richard staggered sideways, caught himself on the back of a sofa, and managed to stay upright.

Her brother touched his jaw gingerly, worked it a bit. "Okay." He started toward one of the bedrooms, only to be halted when Weber said, "Maybe it's time for somebody else to be in charge."

"Don't be stupid," Richard said. "I'm the only—"

Weber let out a roar and charged. And Richard met him with murder in his blue eyes. Just as Weber was about to grab Richard in a bear hug, her brother stepped lightly aside and delivered a kick to the side of the big cop's knee. The roar became a yell of pain, and Weber fell sideways against a chair. It seemed to topple in slow motion. Richard moved in and punched Weber in the ribs. After that any sense of order disappeared. It was a kaleidoscope of windmilling arms, fists, feet, knees. The torchère lamp went over with a crash.

"Stop! Stop! Stop!" Pamela realized she was the one yelling.

The commotion brought Joseph and Estevan. Estevan displayed the barely suppressed glee of the very young enjoying the excitement of catastrophe. Joseph looked disapproving, but resigned. Pamela rushed to him.

"Do something!"

"Let 'em have it out," the security chief said.

Pamela let out a sound like an outraged cat. Her gaze fell on the enormous bouquet of flowers that the hotel management had sent up to welcome the CEO of Lumina Enterprises. Running over, she pulled out the flowers. It sloshed most satisfactorily when she picked up the vase.

She ran over to the grunting, fighting males and threw the water over both of them. They broke apart spluttering and cursing.

"Now *stop* it! Do something useful! That's what Angela would say." The fight leached out of both of them. "And that we all need something to eat," Richard added softly. Pamela couldn't tell if the water on his face was from the vase or from tears. She decided it didn't matter.

Weber leaned down with a grunt and rubbed at his knee. "You got a kick like a mule." He held out his hand to Richard. Her brother didn't take it.

"Not yet. It's too soon. Don't forgive me yet. Forgive me when I've earned it." They all watched as Richard walked to the bedroom and closed the door.

Weber suddenly frowned and looked over at Pamela. "What the fuck do you think that meant?"

"I have no idea," she said. "But it sounded ominous."

FIFTY

RICHARD

The GPS system in my phone had taken me right to the house in Van Nuys. After the cold and sleet of Washington, the seventy-plus-degree weather in Southern California felt like a caress. I had the windows rolled down, and the scent of star jasmine was carried on a soft wind.

That hadn't been the case overnight. A harsh Santa Ana wind had come roaring out of the east, vibrating the windows in the hotel and hissing through the pine trees that dotted the grounds of the Beverly Hills Hotel. I had taken one of the private cabanas and phoned room service for breakfast. The staff knew the CEO of Lumina Enterprises was in residence—I'd gotten great service.

The winds had ripped this neighborhood as well. Palm fronds lay scattered across the road and postage-stamp front yards. They looked like wings torn from the bodies of gigantic insects.

The Lumina jet had touched down in L.A. at 2:00 A.M. I had checked into the hotel for a few hours of sleep, a shower, a shave, and a meal, and then I'd had a car delivered. Now I was here, and Rhiana was only a few hundred feet away.

Finding her hadn't been that hard. My badge had enabled me to run the plates on her BMW convertible. To my surprise the car wasn't stolen. Rhiana had bought and registered it, which gave me the address of her Georgetown house. I had searched it last night, and I hadn't even had to pick the lock; I'd just climbed through the broken windows. Inside I'd picked my way through the welter of dead birds. I'd used the sword on every mirror and the chandelier. The teardrop crystals just hadn't looked right to me.

Others had entered the house before me. Dangling cables showed me where a television had once stood; there were racks of CDs, but no player; and in the upstairs bedroom, which had been decorated like a scene out of the Arabian Nights, the tall jewelry case stood with its drawers hanging out like tongues. The thieves had missed one earring. The emerald lay sparkling, as green as Rhiana's eyes, in the back of a drawer.

I'd been trained on how to make a search, so I went through the drawers, checked in the toilet tank, in the freezer, and in the canisters. I found sweaters and underwear and flour and sugar, and frozen food—most of it Ben & Jerry's ice cream. I didn't know what I was looking for. Something to give me some idea where Rhiana might have gone. If she'd fled this multiverse I was screwed, and I couldn't bear the idea that she'd get away with it.

But then on the bedside table I'd spotted a leather-bound scrapbook. I had sat down on the bed to look through it. As the mattress sank beneath me, the sheets released the smell of Rhiana's perfume. There was a time when even the memory of her scent affected me. Not last night. I remembered only the wounds on Angela's body.

The scrapbook was on the seat next to me. I parked the car a half block from the house and flipped it open. It contained photos of Rhiana, and press clippings from a small local Van Nuys newspaper as well as the *Los Angeles Times*. When I saw that, I knew where to find her.

It had been easy. I had her last name. I knew the city. The family was in the phone book. No detective work required. I had run my theory past Grenier while Brook prepped the plane. Grenier concurred with my analysis, which, of course, made him a genius.

"Of course she's going to run home. She's a kid. Think about it, if you'd done something terrible, wouldn't you want to run home to Mommy and have her kiss it and make it all better? Tell you everything will be all right?"

He had then fallen suddenly very silent as he realized that he had manipulated my mother into committing suicide. But I let it go; he had given me what I needed.

I closed the scrapbook, checked again to make sure I had the sword, got out of the car, and walked down the street toward the house. The sword killed magical . . . alien creatures. Rhiana was only half human. Whatever happened, it was going to be profound.

The house was a small, boxy affair with white stucco stained from years of winter rains. Four hoary old palm trees swayed above the house. As I watched, another frond sailed down and landed with a crash on the roof. There were no cars in the oil-stained driveway. I reminded myself that that didn't mean anything. Rhiana didn't need a car.

As I approached the front door, a chorus of barking welled up from the backyard. I could discern three distinct voices—a deep throaty *woof*, a high-pitched hysterical yapping, and the bell-like bay of a basset hound. Well, the element of surprise was definitely gone. I stepped to the side of the peephole, drew the sword, and knocked.

She just answered. Probably because she was home. Probably because she felt safe. Emotions flickered across her face like slides in an old-style carousel—joy, fear, relief, surprise, confusion, terror, and it ended on guilt. I didn't let it sway me. I forced her back into the house and shut the door behind me. She was staring at the sword. I cursed myself. I should have just used it. Touched her the instant the door opened, done the deed and gotten it over with. I guess her guilt had swayed me.

"Are you . . . are you . . . are you?" She sounded like a lawn mower engine trying to catch.

"Why shouldn't I?" Now that I was inside I got a sense of the clutter. Piles of newspaper stood by the torn sofa. There was a giant fifty-two-inch TV on one wall. The picture had to be blurry in a room this small. There was the smell of toast and bacon grease and pet urine. There were large stains on the cheap green carpet.

She almost ran toward a wall. I bounded after her, thinking she was trying to escape, but she stopped and pointed at the frame hanging on the wall. On the floor beneath were the shards of a mirror. "Look, see, I broke them all. I'm done with them. They used me. They tricked me. I can help you."

"Too little, and way, way too late." I didn't recognize my own voice. It sounded faraway and very cold.

"I didn't mean for that to happen. I didn't think he'd . . ." She stopped and tried again. She shouldn't have. "She was just always there! Getting between us!"

"There was no *us*, Rhiana. And you killed her."

"No. No. Doug killed her. He was a killer. He killed this other girl. He killed lots of girls—"

"And *you* gave Angela to him." Rage had a taste, like iron filings on the back of the tongue. It was becoming hard to breathe. I took a step toward her and lifted the sword.

She wrapped her arms protectively around herself and sank down on the floor. "No, Richard, please don't." The words echoed the whimpering of the dogs pressed up against the sliding glass patio doors. "Please don't. Please don't take my magic away. It's all I've got. It made me special."

And I realized she didn't truly understand what was about to happen. I was suddenly back in the office on the Gulfstream V listening to Kenntnis saying, *"My guess is it would be similar to a lobotomy."*

And I remembered my response. *"I'll be on Rhiana's side. I won't harm her . . . or allow anyone else to."*

Things change, I thought.

You're breaking your word.

Things change.

She seemed unaware of my turmoil. She looked up at me.

332

Those amazing green eyes were filled with tears. They spilled over and ran down her face.

"You can't have it both ways," I said. "You can't reject the Old Ones and still keep your magic. It ends here."

I laid the sword on her shoulder.

And then I called 911 because it was the worst reaction I'd ever seen and I thought she might die. During that call the phone beeped, indicating another call. I took it after providing the address to the dispatcher. It was Joseph, and he sounded like a man who'd just run a marathon.

"Richard! Sir. It's Kenntnis. He's back. He's here, but—"

"Tell him I can't talk right now." I had run into the kitchen for a butter knife to place between Rhiana's teeth.

"Sir—" Joseph began, but I hung up. And then I turned off my phone because I didn't want to hear from Kenntnis about how I'd *done the right thing*. I knew that, but I wasn't sure I recognized or liked the person who had done the right thing.

Four minutes later the ambulance arrived. It was forty minutes until the last seizure shook her body. Her mother was called away from the school where she worked in the cafeteria. Her father was just up the Ventura Freeway overseeing the loading of his rig with cantaloupes bound for market. In the chaos that was traffic in Los Angeles, he arrived only a few minutes after his wife.

I waited in the visitors' lounge. I wanted to leave, but I had to face her parents. I briefly wondered if Cross had sensed Rhiana's half-death and reported it to Kenntnis. Kenntnis would understand why I needed time and space to deal with what I'd done. I couldn't shake the memory of the blank-eyed creature that lay in the hospital bed and plucked mindlessly at the sheet. I had only been allowed to look through the window in the door. It had been more than enough. But Kenntnis was back. It was the right thing to do. For all of us, but most of all for Angela.

I heard them coming when I heard the neurologist, who'd met us in the emergency room, saying, "It appears to have been a stroke."

They turned the corner, and I saw them for the first time. They might not have been related by blood to Rhiana, but there was no doubt they were her parents. Tears coursed down Lottie Davinovitch's round face. In her haste to reach the hospital she was still wearing a hairnet and apron. Todd Davinovitch was a big man with a linebacker's shoulders and neck, and the big belly bestowed by middle age. He had his arm around his wife. Behind his beard his face was set in a rictus of grief.

"But she was only eighteen," Todd said. Unshed tears roughened his voice.

"It doesn't matter the age if there's a flaw in the brain," the doctor said gently.

"If I'd just been there," Rachel said. "She seemed so upset. I should have called in sick—"

"Even if you'd been there, there was nothing you could have done." The doctor indicated me. "We're just lucky this gentleman found her, or she might have died."

I wondered if my guilt showed on my face. I stood up. "I'm Richard Oort," I said. "Rhiana was working on a project for my company."

"Physics?" Todd asked.

"Yes, my company specializes in high-tech projects. I was out here on business, and she'd told me she was coming home to see you. We met for an early breakfast, but she seemed disoriented and confused, so I stopped by your house to check on her." The lies flowed so easily. "The front door was open. I knocked, but nobody answered, so finally I went inside. I found her and called 911."

It was the hardest thing I'd ever done to stand there and accept their fervent thanks. Each word of gratitude struck like a blow. When they finally fell silent I said, "Since Rhiana was an employee, she's fully covered under our health plan. All the bills will be paid by Lumina."

I saw the wave of relief go across Lottie's face, followed by immediate guilt that she had even been thinking about financial matters at a time like this.

"I'm very sorry, Mr. Davinovitch. Mrs. Davinovitch. If there's anything you need, don't hesitate to call." And I gave them my Lumina business card.

"He just was just suddenly *here*," Joseph said as we left the underground parking lot and headed for the elevators.

We were starting the conversation for the third time since he'd picked me up at the airport. I understood his need for constant repetition; despite everything Joseph had seen and experienced in Virginia, it was clear he'd never really believed that Kenntnis wasn't human.

"It scared the crap out of Paulette. I was upstairs, and when I got down to the lobby I could see right away that Mr. Kenntnis wasn't right." He shot me an anguished look. "He's smaller and his eyes are weird and he won't talk to me, but you'll see."

The elevator deposited us at the penthouse, and I stepped out into a wash of dissonant sound. It sounded like a maddened piano tuner was torturing the strings of the piano and a monster was clawing the strings of the Celtic harp.

The living room was very full of people, all watching Kenntnis. Cross sat on the arm of the sofa eating chocolate cake. His expression was the most interesting. Grief and calculation was how I read it, and it made me nervous. Sorrow and devastation sagged the contours of Dagmar's face. Grenier, Weber, and Pamela looked confused. Eddie was completely fascinated.

I reluctantly turned my attention to the founder of Lumina Enterprises. In the past, whenever Kenntnis would enter a room where there was a musical instrument, the instrument would react. Almost like it was singing a greeting, and it was always melodic and beautiful. This cacophony told me more clearly than anything that Kenntnis indeed wasn't *right*.

Kenntnis was pacing up and down in front of the bookcases, trailing his fingers across the spines of the books. The man I'd met last year was a spectacular figure—six foot six, and massive.

At first glance he appeared to be African American, but as you studied his features you realized they were an amalgamation of every human racial type. He was Everyman. And not human. Hints from our conversations led me to believe he was hundreds of thousands if not millions of years old.

I stepped in front of him, trying to halt the pacing. The not human became very clear when I looked into his eyes. Before, they had been dark pools that would occasionally flare with silver lights that were reminiscent of the nimbus that surrounded the sword. Now, they were filled with whirling lights both silver and gold. He was physically smaller, and the body seemed more like a hand puppet being imperfectly manipulated. It was a different emptiness than what had faced me in California, but the result was the same. The essence was gone.

Kenntnis frowned and stepped around me. I darted in front again. This time he froze, looking confused. "Sir," I said gently. He shook his head, and the dissonance from the instruments grew louder.

"Maybe he'll recover," Dagmar said.

"I don't think so," Eddie said. He turned away from the glares from Joseph and Dagmar and looked at me. "The information on a light particle degrades the longer it's held in spin glass. I think that's what happened. He lost part of himself—whatever himself was . . . is. It's certainly fascinating proof of the theory. Shame I can't write a paper. But everybody would think I was nuts."

"If he's so degraded, then how did he get back here?" Pamela asked.

"Keep in mind that I've never met an alien light creature before," the physicist said. "This is my guess. I think he was frozen at the exact moment he was preparing to escape. That decision was set, at a quantum level. So when he was suddenly freed, the last conscious action was completed. He ran and ended up here."

Weber shook his head. "Okay, I didn't get that at all."

"Doesn't matter," I said. "What's clear is that he's not going to be any help to us."

"So what do we do?" Dagmar asked.

"Well, let's start by checking out the gate. I'd always assumed that when Kenntnis was freed the gates would close. Let's see."

"You got it," Eddie said, and he lunged for his laptop.

I pressed my hand against my forehead; the noise from the instruments was maddening. "Joseph, could you please take Mr. Kenntnis to the conference room? I can't take this noise any longer."

And I realized I'd said the wrong thing. Joseph bridled. "This is Mr. Kenntnis's home."

Cross stood up. "Nope, it's not. He gave it to the kid here. And he's not Mr. Kenntnis anymore. Face it, he's a 'tard."

There it was, stark and cold. Fortunately Eddie provided a distraction before I descended into gibbering panic.

"Got it," he sang out.

We all gathered around the laptop. From the corner of my eye I saw Joseph gently taking Kenntnis by the arm and leading him toward the elevator.

The satellite feed from the compound showed that the opening to the distant sun was closed. The boiling clouds had been replaced with a normal-looking blue sky. And the gate itself was gone. Where Kenntnis's tomb had stood, there were just shards of glass glittering on the red sand.

"Well, yay us," Weber said.

People began to grin. Pamela laid a hand on my shoulder and gave it a hard squeeze. But I was watching Cross, and he still looked grim.

"What?" I asked the homeless god.

"Yeah, it's good news, but who knows how many of us came through? They're going to have to be hunted down. And they're all going to be working just as hard as they can to tear open the membranes between the universes," Cross said. "So, what are you gonna do, paladin?"

Everybody looked at me, and I realized that even though I'd freed Kenntnis, we still had big problems, and I was still in charge.

It was a situation I'd never foreseen or planned for. I played for time.

"I need some rest. I really haven't slept in a couple of days. What say we regroup later."

There were nods, and people began to scatter. I touched Weber's shoulder as he was starting for the door.

"I took care of Rhiana," I said.

"Is that why Kenntnis came back?" he asked.

"Yes."

"Did you kill her?" he asked, and his face was very hard.

"Worse."

Weber nodded, satisfied, and I watched him and Dagmar disappear into the elevator. Grenier headed toward the kitchen, Eddie was lost in his computer. Pamela suddenly put her arm around my waist and gave me a hug.

"What was that for?" I asked.

"You looked like you needed it."

"Just tired," I temporized.

She stepped back and looked at me. "You did the right thing. You gave Angela justice."

"No, I gave her vengeance. Don't be mistaken about what I did."

"And now you're feeling guilty," Pamela said.

I considered that, then slowly shook my head. "No, not guilty. Puzzled, uneasy. I don't exactly know who I am anymore."

"And you have to figure out what to do about Lumina," she said.

"If I figure out the answer to the first question, the second will follow." And I walked away.

I wandered through the building. I even dove into the pool and swam one lap, but anyplace in the Lumina building was too fraught. I got out, dried, dressed, and thought about going back to my apartment, but it had never really been a home. Just a place I slept and ate.

There really wasn't a question about where I'd go—I went back to headquarters. I refused a driver. I'd always wanted to try out the dark gray Lamborghini Murciélago in the underground lot. This was my chance. I accepted that Estevan would follow me—my life was constrained by security now—but I could at least be alone in a car and inside my own head.

And what a car it was. The thunder from the powerful engine could be felt through my body, and the stick moved smoothly through the gears as I raced down Montgomery toward the freeway. Estevan was good; he stayed with me. I realized that Joseph needed to hire someone to replace Rudi. That made me remember Rudi, and how he died, and my eyes burned.

My fault, my fault, my fault.

No, not my fault. I told them to wait for me at the house. Get Angela and wait for me. But we hadn't gotten Angela because she was dead. *My fault, my fault, my fault.*

There are going to be casualties. Grenier's words came back to me as I crested the ramp onto I-25 heading south.

But not my people. I should have kept my people safe. And then I thought about the people I'd cut down at the compound. They were casualties, too, and somewhere people were going to weep for them. As for me, the tears were gone. My eyes burned and ached, but the opportunity for grief was once again past. *Maybe grief was a luxury that you engaged in when you had time?* In that case I was never going to have the opportunity. I had a feeling a shrink wouldn't approve.

Weber had reported that absenteeism was bad, and he wasn't kidding. APD headquarters was a ghost town. But Lucile and Dolores, bless them, were at their places in dispatch. Weber wasn't in his office. I was glad. I really didn't want to talk to anybody.

Since I was on medical leave, the metal surface of my desk was empty except for a single piece of paper, a notification that I was due at the range to requalify. Perfect.

I didn't feel like driving to the west mesa and the outdoor range. I settled for the private indoor range that had a deal with APD.

Back to the Lamborghini. Estevan gave me a "what the fuck?" look, but I didn't respond. We drove back uptown.

When I reached the range, I just had to flash my badge at the hard-bitten woman with too-bright, dyed-red hair who sat behind the counter. She had a pistol on each hip, a package of Nicorette gum on the counter in front of her, and an open can of Red Bull. I hoped I hadn't just seen Sam in thirty years. The woman waved me back to the range.

I hung a target and sent it whirring to the far end of the range, slid in a clip, and settled the earmuffs over my ears. I raised the gun, took aim, and started shooting. I emptied the clip and brought the target back. There was a reasonably close grouping (mostly) in the center of the silhouette's body mass.

I hung a new target, reloaded my clip, and went again. This time I didn't just bang away. I paused before each shot.

Kenntnis was functionally gone. *Bang.* Who knew how long the shattered creature would clothe itself in a people-suit? *Bang.* I was still the head of Lumina. *Bang.* I was still the paladin. *Bang.* The gates were closed. *Bang.* There were still Old Ones, or rather *more* Old Ones. *Bang.* They would try to reopen the gates, or at least tear holes in our universe. *Bang.* I had people who knew the truth, supported me, and had been inoculated. *Bang.* How could I use them effectively, in ways that would counter the Old Ones? *Bang.*

I slowly lowered the gun onto the divider in front of me. *I was the paladin. I was the head of Lumina. I had people. How could I best use them?*

It really was all up to me.

CODA

It was surprisingly heavy, and while the exterior was smooth, the turns that cradled his fingers were rough enough to help the hand keep its grip.

Make more of these? How the fuck am I going to make more of these? I don't know what this is. I don't care if we hired ten thousand scientists. They're not going to know what it is either. I just wanted to study it. I can't reproduce it. He's smoking crack.

But it'd be kinda cool. He said anybody Eddie knew. Guys he'd met at conferences, people he played World of Warcraft with. Professors. People he'd gone to school with.

Hello. I am authorized to offer you a job with Lumina Enterprises at triple your last salary. We will relocate you and even buy you a house. Why, you ask? Because you are being recruited to study an ancient, alien artifact. Your job, should you choose to accept it, is to make more of these artifacts that will be used to protect the world. Who will carry it, you ask? Oh, don't worry about that. Those people are being located and recruited even as we speak. You just focus on your job.

How cool would that be?

There was a soft throat clearing from behind him.

"Eddie, the sword stays with me."

* * *

Travel around the world rescuing eggheads, and attacking Old Ones? He was forty-three years old, for crap's sake. He'd left the army when he was twenty-five.

Richard did say they were also going to recruit and train. Weber thought he'd rather do that, and not take part in the run-around-the-world part of the plan. Sam wanted to shoot things. Fine, let her go. He'd shot enough things.

But Cross was going to be looking for more paladins. And the other monsters weren't going to like that. They'd try to kill those people, just like they were going to try to kill Richard. And suddenly Weber remembered a little boy whom he and Richard had rescued out of one of those dimensions. With so many monsters in the world, there were going to be a lot more kids disappearing, and he just wasn't going to let that happen.

Suddenly he felt better. This was no different than the work he'd been doing. The perps were tougher and the stakes higher, but it was still about preserving and protecting . . . just on a global scale.

"Did I mention, you're going to be in charge?"

Looked like he and the FBI Scoobies needed to get in a huddle.

They were going to be spending more money than the GDP of many small countries. When Dagmar had pointed that out, he'd said, "Make more money." She almost got mad, except he spun around the notepad and showed her his ideas. If Kenzo hadn't signed off she would have thought he was crazy. Now they were going to undertake the largest privately funded space project ever.

Then he ended it with the news that Peter and the kids were on their way.

"Don't get a divorce yet."

* * *

Track them, was the order. After all, Grenier was the best person to spot Old One activity because he'd helped organize and abet their incursions for years.

"And then what?"

"We shut them down."

Simple, matter-of-fact.

Apparently a response team was being organized to then deal with these hot spots. Grenier pointed out that he'd need a staff to sift through news reports and rumors and stories to find the places where reality was being torn apart.

Already in the works. The fourth floor was his. Grenier could hire his own researchers, and it would be up to him to teach them what to look for. Once he'd established his team he would be allowed to live in the Lumina building.

Grenier was on board with the plan.

"Welcome back to the human side of the equation," Richard said.

"What am I doing?" Pamela asked.

"I'm going to teach you how to shoot."

"Why?"

"Because we're not going to just watch any longer. We're going to fight. And there's nobody I'd rather have covering my back than you."

ACKNOWLEDGEMENTS

I want to thank my amazing writers group, Critical Mass, who every month helps me to become a better writer. So, thanks to Daniel Abraham, Terry England, Emily Mah, George R. R. Martin, Victor Milan, Walter Jon Williams, Steve Stirling, Ian Tregillis, and Sage Walker.

ABOUT THE AUTHOR

Melinda Snodgrass has written multiple novels and screenplays, and worked extensively in Hollywood. She is best known for her work on *Star Trek: The Next Generation*— her episode 'Measure of a Man' was nominated for the Writer's Guild Award in Outstanding Writing in a Drama Series. She has also worked on numerous other shows, including *The Profilers*, *Sliders* and *Seaquest DSV*. She coedits the Wild Cards series with George R.R. Martin, and has recently turned in her Wild Cards screenplay to Universal Pictures, for which she would also be Executive Producer. Melinda is the author of The Edge series, and the forthcoming Imperials series for Titan Books. She lives in Santa Fe, New Mexico.

THE EDGE OF REASON

MELINDA SNODGRASS

A contemporary fantasy series that explores the tensions between science and rationality, religion and superstition.

Richard Oort is a cop. He's also the last Paladin: a reluctant hero, fated to defend the world against demonic forces that threaten to plunge us into another Dark Age.
Richard is on patrol one night when he leaps to the defense of a terrified young woman fleeing something impossible: beings that can only be described as monsters. Beings that can only have been created by magic. But in saving the beautiful Rhianna, he gets drawn into the machinations of a mysterious billionaire who just might be Prometheus and Lucifer. And who claims to be waging a millennia-old war on the side of reason and light, defending humanity from others of his kind who want nothing more than to see us destroy ourselves with superstition, religion, darkness, fear.
But when Richard discovers he's a Paladin — product of a genetic fluke that enables him to wield Lucifer's sword — he becomes a central figure in the battle between Light and Darkness. But is he strong enough to bear the burden?

PRAISE FOR *THE EDGE OF REASON*

"If H.P. Lovecraft and H. L. Mencken had ever collaborated, they might have come up with something like The Edge of Reason. This one will delight thinkers—and outrage true believers—of all stripes." **George R. R. Martin**

"[A] gritty narrative of a war between light and dark... Balanc[es] a harsh critique of organized religion with touches of humor and a good-hearted priest who grounds his faith in the Golden Rule..." **Publishers Weekly**

"Peopled with a richly drawn cast of characters... the story is a big, complex and ambitious tale that rarely rests and demands the reader's full attention. Thee ideas are provocative, strongly so... Readers looking for a thoughtful, action-packed and fascinating story, this one is for you. Strongly recommended." **SF Revu**

"Interesting religious arguments aside Snodgrass crafted a tightly paced supernatural thriller that manages to stay interesting and thrilling from beginning to end."
King of the Nerds

'I really enjoyed this book. It's thought-provoking and certainly memorable, with an intriguing concept and a cast of characters begging for further exploration. I'd love to see more of this world." **Green Man Review**

TITANBOOKS.COM